Chasing Thieves

by J.F.R. Coates

This is a work of fiction. Any names or characters, businesses or places, events or incidents, are fictitious and the products of the author's imagination. Any resemblance to actual persons, living or dead, or actual events is purely coincidental.

CHASING THIEVES

Published by Fenris Publishing
Flagstaff, Arizona
https://www.fenrispublishing.com

ISBN: 978-1-62475-267-4
Printed in the United States, United Kingdom, or Australia
First trade paperback edition: January 2026

Cover art by Sleepymuu
Edited by C.L. Methvin

Chapter One

Lucca silently padded through the dark corridors of the Esfyr's Wold chapterhouse. Rumours and intrigue swirled as thick as shadows, the shouts of disgruntled mages still filled the lion's mind as though they were freshly uttered. Classes had been cancelled without explanation, and now Lucca found himself on a crucial mission set by the chaptermaster himself, an invisibility spell wrapped around his shoulders like a cloak.

The lion held his target in mind. The chapterhouse had a habit of twisting the corridors around the unwary, guiding them towards unwanted destinations. Mages liked to keep their secrets, even from the pupils in their school. This included Lucca, who was in his second year as a mage's initiate. Many mysteries of the chapterhouse were still elusive to him, none greater than the upheaval that had rocked the entire guild since dawn had broken.

Security gems buzzed through those corridors with him. The large, floating purple crystals crackled with ominous magical potential, vibrating with increased intensity as Lucca approached. No invisibility charm was strong enough to fool them, but they recognised his presence as a student and left the lion alone to his prowling.

Lucca wanted answers. Security had increased and many of the masters were frantic with worry. With the importance of his task in mind, the lion stopped outside a nondescript oak door at the end of a dark corridor. Light flickered through the cracks around the door.

This was where he could fulfil his task and get the answers his insatiable mind craved. What could bring the wrath of Archmage Mafren down upon the chapterhouse and set the guild masters into a frenzy of arguments and debate? And why was the badger beyond the door not a part of that chaos?

He would get no answers by dawdling outside. Lucca's invisible hand pushed open Master Roe's door. He quietly peered inside the study. The aged badger was sat at his desk, and though it faced the door, the master did not look up from his work. A single candle lit the room. The candle had long run out of wick and wax, yet it still happily burned on the table as though nothing was amiss.

Master Roe mumbled beneath his breath as his quill scratched across a blank sheet of parchment. "Protection... burden... siren... cripple." Four runes shone bright orange on the parchment, before fading to a deep, rich crimson. The badger admired his handiwork for a moment, before shaking his head. "No, that won't work. What if he has an annulment charm? Stupid idea." He waved a hand over the parchment and erased the runes into a puff of orange vapour.

Lucca chose his moment to slip in through the open door, still maintaining his invisibility charm. The door creaked as it opened, but it was the beam of light that fell on the badger's parchment. that caused Master Roe to put down his quill at last. The badger massaged his writing hand and sighed.

"Intrude if you must, Lucca, but make your appearance brief," the badger growled.

The lion dismissed his invisibility and pouted. "How did you know it was me, Master Roe?"

The badger wrinkled his nose. "There are few students or masters here who would wear Winterpaw scent musk on a late night stroll through the academy," he said brusquely. He placed down his quill and stretched out the fingers on his right hand. "I take it Master Juff sent you?"

Lucca smoothed down a wrinkle on his green and gold robes, indicative of all second-year initiates. The lion thought he looked quite resplendent in the green and gold affair, and he was almost dreading his graduation to his third year. They wore a horrible wine-red robe with silver trim. They would clash horribly with his eyes, not to mention his short, alchemically-dyed emerald mane.

The lion flashed a smile at Master Roe. "I chose the wrong moment to take a quick visit to the restrooms and bumped into the taskmaster. He asked I deliver a message. 'Where is Master Roe and how goes the charm?', he asked me to say." He paused for dramatic effect. A mischievous smirk spread across his face. "That's the abridged version, at least. It would be unbecoming of me to repeat it word-for-word."

The badger hissed in frustration and clicked his tongue. "How well do you think it's going, Initiate?" he said with another low growl. "It's nearly midnight and I'm at the same place I started at breakfast." He rubbed the palm of his right hand with his left thumb.

"I'd probably place it somewhere between disaster and catastrophe," the lion replied with a grin, gesturing to the overflowing waste bin beside the desk.

Master Roe sighed and rose from his desk. The badger was diminutive compared to the lion, but he pushed aside the student as he hobbled towards the nearest bookshelf that ran around the headache-inducing six walls of the square room.

Above the bookshelf, the wall was covered with thousands of small pigeonholes, each housing at least four scrolls of parchment. The holes ran as high as the ceiling, and perhaps further. Lucca's eyes always watered a little when he looked too high in Master Roe's study.

The badger pulled a hefty tome out from the bookcase. "I mean, come on. A thief-catching charm? It would be easier to forge gold from sand," he said grumpily. He slammed the tome down on the desk and turned to scold Lucca, but the lion was gone. "Door, Lucca! You forgot the door!"

Master Roe wearily trudged towards the open door and peered out into the corridor. He pushed the door closed after making sure the lion was no longer there, only to turn and jump in surprise as Lucca leaned nonchalantly on the lectern.

"Thief charms, Master? Is that what they have you working on?" Lucca said, a cheeky grin spreading across his face as his hands rubbed together. "You have made some great progress."

Master Roe sighed and placed his head in his hand. "First grade transparency magic, Lucca. Ought I be impressed?"

"That's entirely up to you, Master Roe," Lucca said, shrugging. "Sometimes you can have a lot of fun with the basics, especially when they help in avoiding other upset masters all too keen to unload their problems on a poor, innocent student like me."

Master Roe marched back to the lectern, shooing Lucca away from the spare quills and parchment. "I won't deny you that, but there's nothing fun or basic about advanced inscription, so I'll ask you to keep your hands where they can't interfere with my work."

Lucca stepped back, hands raised. "Well yes, Master. That would be implicated in the word 'advanced'," the lion replied. "But the basics give you the power to hide, charm, and irritate, so who am I to complain?"

Master Roe raised one striped brow. "The archmage wants to do much more than irritate this thief, Lucca."

Lucca put his hands behind his back and puffed out his chest. "Speaking of which, you haven't said how honest you want me to be to the taskmaster," he said, glancing down to the blank parchments with a smirk. "Shall I tell him the great Guild Inscription Master struggles fruitlessly into the night?"

Master Roe placed a hand on Lucca's chest and pushed the student back. "Don't you dare," he said sharply. "If you must provide an update, you can tell Master Juff that it will be done when it's done. It is no simple task that Mafren has given us. Juff and Alber have only made it more impossible with the constant demands for updates. If I didn't work this late, I'd have been too busy with their meetings and reports to actually get any work done."

Lucca's ears flicked up in curiosity. If ever he was going to get answers, then this was his opportunity. "What can you tell me about this task, Master Roe? I know there's a thief and it's got the guild trying not to burn itself to the ground, but I think I'm still missing some pieces of the puzzle."

"You know Master Alber won't appreciate me telling you, Lucca," Master Roe said. He gestured to a chair in front of his desk that had not been present a few moments earlier. "So sit down and let me tell you all I know. You've heard of the relic thief, of course?"

The lion's ears pricked at the name. He perched on the edge of his seat as he nodded eagerly. "Of course! Who hasn't? The enigmatic relic thief, scourge of even the most secure vaults. So elusive, no one even knows what species he is, let alone his name," Lucca gushed.

"All he leaves are these infuriating things," Master Roe said, sifting through a few sheets of parchment and tossing one across to the lion.

Lucca looked down at a small note written in an elegant style.

'Missed me! Your Favourite Relic Thief ♡ '

The lion couldn't help but smile. A calling card. As if the story of the relic thief could get any more storybook and, dare he think it, romantic.

Master Roe hobbled towards the comfortable armchair in one of the many corners of his office and steepled his hands together. He held his hand out to take the note back, flicking it onto the table again. "They're calling him an honourable thief."

Lucca leaned forward a little further, almost falling from his chair. "They?"

Master Roe waved his hand dismissively. "Guildmasters. Investigators. Reporters. The usual lot."

"I see, Master," Lucca said, though he still felt quite nonplussed by the badger's explanation.

"Honour doesn't mean much when he's stealing all our relics. He might not kill or harm the person he steals from, but he harms our reputation," the badger said with a low growl. He leaned back in his chair and ran his hands over the bridge of his muzzle. "And now, if you'll believe it, the cod-choking archmage has demanded that we develop a ward to place upon relics to stop thieves such as this relic thief from stealing them."

Lucca blinked. "A thief ward."

"That's the long and the short of it, yes," Master Roe said with a weary sigh.

"No offence Master, but that's not how things work."

"I know that, Lucca," the badger said, shaking his head. "Thieves are always a step ahead of us. If we use a burden curse, they use a moonlift charm. If we have a sentry ward, they have an invisibility potion. We turn our corridors into a labyrinth, they use string. So, as though it's simply one issue, we've been tasked with creating this mystical thief ward that stops everything."

"But we've known about the relic thief for years. What's got the archmage so desperate to catch him now?" Lucca asked. He picked up a quill and twirled it between his fingers. Purple sparks floated from the nib, twinkling in the air briefly before fading like fiery embers in the night.

The badger grimaced. "He stole the diamond phylactery as it was being transferred from our chapterhouse to Cofferknell."

Lucca almost dropped the quill. "The phylactery of guild-founder Neur Auphaven?"

"The very same." The badger threw his head back and closed his eyes. "The archmage is desperate because if the Mages' Guild can't protect its own relics, then why should we be trusted to courier and guard those from the other guilds? Our reputation is at stake here."

The lion furrowed his brow. He tapped the quill against the blank parchment on the mahogany desk. A few errant sparks scattered from the nib. "And so, Archmage Mafren wants you to construct a thief ward to capture the relic thief and prove to the other guilds that we can be trusted?"

"That is the gist of it, yes," Roe said, stifling a yawn behind his hand.

Lucca stared at the blank parchment, then towards the impossible shelves of books around the study. One of them needed to have the answer they sought. Few musteliads in Lutrea had access to a library with so many rare and esoteric tomes as the badger. "Master, might I perhaps try something?"

"Just so long as whatever you do is reversible," the badger replied wearily. He didn't even look at the lion.

Lucca grinned toothily as he eagerly raised the quill. He recalled the different runes he had learned during his studies, pondering some of the more interesting combinations he had concocted. He quickly scribed three basic runes, before muttering a simple incantation spell.

A book dislodged from the shelf and smashed into Lucca's face. The lion didn't have a moment to react before a second followed, and then a third. Heavy spines of hard covers clipped against his cheeks and his chest and his arms, no matter how much he tried to fend off the violent repositories of knowledge.

"Master! Help!" the lion yelped.

"What have you done?" Master Roe groaned, tired irritation evident in his voice as he rubbed his temples with weary hands.

The lion held his hands over his head for protection. Another book thwacked against his shoulder. A dozen others lurked menacingly. "I don't know! How does it stop?"

"Hold on," Master Roe grumbled. He hauled himself up to his feet and dragged away the used parchment. He held out his hands. *"Haud delecti lucis."*

The books clattered to the floor, inert once more. Lucca cautiously peered out behind his fingers. Master Roe glared at him.

"I told you there's fun to be had in the basics," the lion said weakly.

Master Roe snatched the quill from Lucca's limp hand. "Advanced inscription parchment amplifies the basics, Initiate Lucca. And it amplifies any error," the badger growled. He scratched his chin. "What were you even trying to accomplish?"

"I thought that would help absorb knowledge from books. Some of them might have the answers to your predicament," Lucca replied bashfully. "They were a bit more aggressive than I thought."

The badger sighed and shook his head. "Or were you hoping to shortcut your studies? You used the wrong rune for that." He tapped the quill against the discarded parchment, sending up another shower of purple sparks. "This is the rune for attraction. Physical attraction. You became a magnet for the knowledge. For the books. We should be thankful you didn't try anything destructive if you're still making those errors."

"No worries, Master Roe. You heard me. I bewitch, charm, and irritate. Destruction isn't my thing," Lucca said. He managed a grin, though his ears pinned back as he read over his work again. The mistake was so obvious now.

The badger tossed the quill onto his desk, safely away from the dangers of Lucca's hand. The old master shook his head, hands on his hips as he looked around the mess the student had made. "You can tidy this all up. Without magic."

Lucca resisted the temptation to grumble. He kept his head low as he started to pick up the scattered tomes. Other, less generous masters would have inflicted harsher punishments for such an error.

The lion returned the books to the impossible bookshelf, though identifying the correct locations proved a challenge, with no obvious system of organisation. Instead, a gap appeared to materialise whenever he picked up a book where none had been before. He quickly learned to show haste as he returned the tomes. The bookshelves were hungry for their knowledge, and books quickly ripped themselves from Lucca's hand, tearing away more than a few strands of fur.

The whole time, Master Roe grumbled and growled to himself, the words too soft even for the lion's strong ears to detect them.

Then, just as Lucca was preparing to finish his work, the badger froze. An almost predatory grin spread across his muzzle as his wide, bright eyes slowly turned to the student.

"Uh, Master?" Lucca asked warily, letting the last book return to the bookshelf. "I don't know if I like that look."

"You're right. You're absolutely right," the badger whispered.

Lucca blinked, but didn't bother saying anything. He was sure the badger would continue his train of thought once it finished arriving in the station.

"I've been a fool," Master Roe muttered. He rummaged through the bookshelves and pulled down a book Lucca was sure he had just put back in a wholly different location. The heavy tome even had a couple of tawny strands of fur stuck to the cover, which the badger nonchalantly brushed away. "I've been looking at this from the wrong angle. We all have. We don't want to repel the thief. We want to attract him."

"I'm still not quite following you, Master," Lucca admitted. He ran his hand through his short mane. "Isn't the whole point of this thief ward to stop thieves from stealing our shinies?"

Master Roe waved off Lucca's words as he flicked through the tome. "Yes, but also no. If I'm right, then this won't work on everyone. But we don't want everyone. Yet. The archmage just wants the relic thief, and then hopefully this clamour for a thief ward will die down. We don't want a spell that targets the relics to protect them. We want to target the thief," the badger said. He tapped his hand on a page in the tome, but it was all written in a language incomprehensible to Lucca's eyes.

The badger retrieved his quill and erased Lucca's earlier botched charm. He scratched two simple runes onto the parchment and grinned up at the lion, then cleared his throat.

"*Diligo scopus Lucca*," the badger chanted. Rays of purple light beamed out from the parchment to surround Lucca. When it ceased, the lion was still surrounded by a soft pink glow.

Lucca's heart fluttered as a warm shiver passed through his

body. A sickly sensation rose in his stomach. He hugged his arms around his belly. "What spell is that?"

Roe waved his hand to hush Lucca. "*Amor dato relilatro.*"

The pink light faded.

Lucca shuddered as the spell dissipated. "Are you going to explain yourself now, or not at all, Master Roe?"

The badger grinned. "I shouldn't tell you too much, Lucca. It could do more harm than good if you know all the details, I'm afraid. Let's just say that you somehow stumbled on the right answer. Simple charms in the right hands can do so much more than previously realised."

"Or the wrong hands," Lucca retorted. He hugged his arms around his torso protectively. A strange sensation had settled in his gut.

"Absolutely," Master Roe agreed. He took hold of Lucca and guided the lion to the comfortable armchair in the corner, sitting the student down in it. "Thanks to you, I've come up with this wonderful plan to catch the relic thief. What I have cast is a love charm. A very powerful one at that."

Lucca raised his brow. "A love charm? I don't know how that can be the answer to our problem, Master. I didn't think they were even legal."

"They exist in a certain moral murkiness, yes," Master Roe admitted. The victorious smirk never left his muzzle. "But you have to see how this can only be a success."

Lucca's mind worked slowly. He knew the obvious answer, but it made no sense to him. Love charms were forbidden for the obvious issues around consent. He still felt like he was missing some crucial puzzle pieces for this great game the guild masters were playing. Now it felt like Master Roe had given him some pieces for an entirely different puzzle.

"So... your plan involves me... a love charm... and the relic thief?" Lucca asked slowly. "That's not going to work, surely? I didn't realise you had such a bizarre sense of humour."

The badger sighed. "No Lucca, I'm not joking. You're smart enough to work all of this out, and I'd have thought you of all students would see this as a brilliant plan. The best plan we have, at least."

Lucca opened his mouth for a moment, realised how ridiculous he must look, and hastily closed it again. He shut his eyes and nodded. He had to agree with his master. There was a seed of logic in the plan. Didn't mean he had to like it though.

"Now, you know the guild won't approve of this plan," Master Roe continued. He slowly paced around the office, gesturing with his hands as he thought things through. "Love charms are, shall we say, frowned upon. Sometimes, though, the end justifies the means. We need to take down this relic thief, and this is the only way it can be done in an expedient manner."

Lucca thought he knew where the badger was going with this. He grimaced, but he also felt his chest puff out with a little pride. "I'm the only one you can trust with this task, then?"

Roe chuckled, instantly deflating Lucca's chest. "It's not a question of trust, Initiate. There are many I could loop into this charm. I could go myself, even." The badger paused and steepled his fingers together. "I feel like you will provide the most enthusiastic act."

Lucca wrinkled his muzzle. "I don't know if I like where your mind goes, Master Roe," he said with a shudder. The bitter taste in his mouth returned as he thought about what the badger asked of him. He leaned forward in his chair, thinking of any way he could avoid this poisoned responsibility. "But there's one teeny tiny flaw in your plan, isn't there? You want me to track down this elusive thief, who no one has ever been able to find. Then you'd like me to seduce him. And I'd like to re-emphasise the use of the word 'him'."

The pair stared at each other, eye to eye. Lucca bared his teeth for added emphasis, but his master remained silent.

"You don't see any... compatibility issues?" Lucca tapped his hands together and entwined his fingers.

Master Roe tilted his head. "You speak as though we know this thief is a 'he'."

Lucca blinked. "I thought we knew that?" he stammered. He grabbed hold of the tip of his tail. "Don't we? Every story says the relic thief is male."

"None can be verified," Master Roe said. The badger's fingers tapped together. "Though I do suspect the thief might be. Some male musk was detected on the courier two weeks ago."

"Which leads us back to our compatibility issues," Lucca protested. His heart pounded. He wasn't sure his ruse was working.

The badger winked.

Lucca shuddered. He hated it when his master did that. It rarely ended well for him.

"You act like that's going to be such a challenge, Lucca. Every mage and their familiar are perfectly aware of your preferences, so there's no need to look so shocked."

Lucca took a dramatic step backwards and held his hands up innocently to his chest. "What stories you tell, Master Roe. Pray, where did you learn this one?"

Master Roe rolled his eyes. The badger held up one finger. "Well there was that excursion to the Winterpaw tribe for the runes lecture."

"I remember it vividly. Learned a lot about runes then."

"Studying more than just the runes, weren't you, Lucca?" Master Roe said with a sly smile. "From what I recall, you spent most of your time admiring the tribesmen."

"So were the other students."

Master Roe sighed. "The other young males there were

staring at the tribes*women*, Lucca. Quite the difference."

"So? They were a noble and handsome race of people. Fine specimens all around. I don't see what you're trying to imply here," Lucca said, still trying gamely to keep up the ruse he knew his master wasn't buying.

"They weren't wearing clothes, Lucca. You were quite blissfully aware of this fact too."

"Their liberties exceeded mine. That's hardly my fault now, is it? I was merely observing a curious lifestyle that's most unlike any on Lutrea or Da'Manyr."

Master Roe hid a grin behind a hand as Lucca failed to do the same.

"If you ask me to, Master, then I'll strip off now to emulate the noble master runesmiths of Winterpaw and scribe whichever rune you like, if you doubt how much I learned. I don't know why the nudity is necessary, but they were adamant, so who am I to disrespect their culture?"

Master Roe shielded his eyes. "Please, spare me from that, Initiate. I have already seen enough of your runecrafting for one night, and I have no desire to see you naked."

Lucca grinned. The tip of his tongue emerged from between his lips. At the very least he was distracting the badger and having fun with it, even if he wasn't convincing his master to call off the plan. "Any other accusations you'd like to lay at my paws, Master?"

"Where do I begin? Faye Rhiana. You rather firmly rejected her invitation for the Riverside Debutante, am I right in saying?"

The lion pretended to gag. "Faye? She's a herbologist. Such a dirty craft."

"You can't talk. You're minoring in alchemy. And just look at your hair," the badger said, gesturing to Lucca's green, spiked mane.

"I've explained that before, Master. It was an accident which I have never been able to truly get over," Lucca said, almost managing to succeed in sounding hurt. He ran a hand vainly through his short mane. "I'd appreciate it if you didn't try to constantly remind me of my past failures."

"I heard you only claimed it was an accident so you wouldn't have to pay for the reagents," Master Roe said with a chuckle.

Lucca shrugged. "I guess that's another way of putting it. Prefer my version to be honest. Both have their merits though."

"You certainly don't seem too eager to remedy the situation," Master Roe pointed out. "But be that as it may, young Faye still almost bested you for the achievement award last year."

"Emphasis on 'almost', Master. I could never respect such an underachiever," Lucca said, but his smile faltered slightly. "Besides, she just asked me because I'm exotic and strange. A felian in Lutrea, how exciting!"

Master Roe stared the lion down. "I won't hear any of that, Initiate Lucca. You know the other students respect you for who you are, and whatever background you may have does not come into it. And nor does this preference that you seem frightfully eager to avoid speaking of."

Lucca threw up his hands, knowing the game was up. The old badger had seen right through him. "Alright, I suppose you've got me, Master. Maybe I do take a fancy to men, but I thought Lutrea was meant to be more civilised than thinking it's a thing to be ashamed of."

Master Roe shook his head. "Nothing to be ashamed of, no. I'm sure you'll find it's forbidden in some hidden guild code, but it would be easier to find what isn't forbidden in one of those."

"Master, please. You know as well as I do that all the old druids had the best sort of parties. I mean, they could turn into animals. Shapeshifting. All that malarkey. You know that if you give a guy an inch over his physical form and he'll take a yard."

Master Roe raised a brow. "Yes, but moving on..."

"I mean that literally," Lucca said, chancing a wink towards his master.

"May the gods have mercy on your fourth-year masters," the badger said, rubbing his hands over his muzzle. "But for now, it is your preferences that will make this ruse all the more convincing."

Lucca grimaced in resignation as he watched the badger move across the office, towards a locked cabinet squeezed between a couple of bookshelves. "This is all well and good, Master. But there is still one other obstacle, is there not? I may take a fancy to him, but what if he doesn't take a fancy to me? Like, naturally? Without the love spell? Won't he know he's been charmed?"

Master Roe held up one hand. "I have considered that. Rumour swirls that the relic thief takes a fancy to men. He certainly seems to have more male targets than female," the badger explained, before that devious grin came back to his muzzle. "Besides, the charm will deal with any preference issues he may have. No matter who usually takes his fancy, he will find you irresistible."

"Which leads to my final problem," Lucca said, trying his hardest to suppress the uncomfortable shiver that threatened to pass down his spine. "Finding him. How do I do that?"

Master Roe swiped his hand over the padlock that kept the cabinet sealed tight. The lock phased out of existence. "That's why we need a lure. Come here and see."

As the lion cautiously approached, Master Roe flung open the doors to the cabinet. That was the last thing Lucca saw as the inside of the cabinet shone with a burning luminosity.

"Warn me next time, Master," Lucca cried, shielding his eyes from the intense glow.

"Quit your complaining," Master Roe retorted. "This is just a security measure. It will be fine in a moment."

As though attuned to the badger's words, the glow diminished and faded to nothing. The contents of the cabinet were revealed.

"Whoa," Lucca gasped, his eyes glossy with intrigue and his jaw hung agape.

"Not the response I hoped for, but for some reason the one I always get whenever I show this to students," the badger mused.

Lucca squeaked in excitement. "May I point out that this is the guild's relic vault?"

Master Roe was busy fishing around through the cabinet, which was larger on the inside than it had any right to be. The badger had already been swallowed up to the waist. "You could, but you'd be wrong," he replied, his voice muffled as it seemed to emanate out from behind the bookshelves. "This is just the inscription relic... vault, if you must call it that."

The lion crept forward to get a better look inside the vault. He hopped from paw to paw, his hands wringing as he stared with child-like wonder. He had an incredible urge to touch something shiny, and there were plenty of those inside the vault.

"I was thinking of something fairly standard at first, but because I'm feeling so confident... no, get back," Master Roe said, slapping away Lucca's outstretched hand as the badger backed out of the cabinet. He held a heavy book to his chest.

"Ow," Lucca whined, pulling his hand back quickly.

Master Roe pushed the cabinet doors closed. The padlock instantly materialised and heavy chains locked the cabinet again. The badger took the book over to his desk and placed it down carefully. "I was thinking of something a bit more tempting for our notorious thief."

The badger kept his hands on top of the gilded tome, keeping the many pages hidden away beneath the ornate cover. Lucca frowned and peered down at it. The book was fancy, but he couldn't see why it would be a tempting target for someone like the relic thief.

Master Roe sighed, seemingly disappointed his student hadn't immediately recognised the tome. "This book is a concise registry of every guild master and student. Everyone who has ever called themselves a part of the Mages' Guild is in here, with their portrait and own unique seal. It's really quite valuable."

Lucca looked perplexed. "So what, this is some type of all-powerful year book?"

Master Roe glared at his student. "If you must insist on using such layman's terms..."

"Which I do, Master," Lucca said, beaming. "But please, enlighten me. Why would the relic thief want this?"

The badger grumbled. "Well, unlike your simple yearbook, this text features the signature and seal of every guild master. For a master scribe or conman like the relic thief, that sort of information is incredibly valuable as it would allow them to scribe any decree written by anyone in this book and project it as an absolute truth."

Lucca twitched his nose. "Wouldn't they suspect a trap with something so important? Surely if a guild master wanted this moved, they'd just... I dunno... astral project it to the destination?"

The badger barked out in laughter. "Astral project it? Thinking outside the box, I like that, Initiate. But no. Any attempt to move this tome with magical means will fail. Any illusion cast on it to duplicate the text will result in every guild master being notified, if anyone were foolish enough to try."

"Was just throwing thoughts out there," Lucca grumbled. "The real thing has to be moved then. How do we tip off this relic thief?"

"Think about it for a moment, Lucca. This relic thief has been able to predict our travel routes and intercept our couriers with alarming regularity. How do you think he can do this?"

Lucca pondered it for a moment. "He's either a master of divination, or he has a source high up in the guild," the lion mused.

"Or a good old-fashioned eavesdropper," Master Roe added with a nod and a smile. "It doesn't make sense, but I thought we'll not only tempt him with a great prize, but we'll test his skill to know of our relic transfers."

"Go on..." Lucca said uncertainly.

Master Roe leaned forward and slid the gilded tome across the desk towards Lucca. "You're going to courier this for me."

Lucca's hands trembled as he picked up the tome. "Will you be teaching me some defensive magic to protect my fragile self from the thief? Maybe some offensive magic?"

Master Roe shook his head. "Not at all. You won't need any of that."

Lucca raised his brow and took a step back from his master. "Well how do you expect me to catch this thief if I'm lying dead in a ditch somewhere?" he asked, clutching the tome tight in his hands. "I'm liking this plan less and less, Master. And I'll be honest, I had a nasty prickling down my tail to start with."

Master Roe looked taken aback. "Do you remember nothing of what I've told you of this thief? He's a noble rogue, not some backstreet murderer. And even so, I'm sure that your repertoire would be more than enough."

Lucca flicked his tail and stared at the book. "I could count the number of offensive spells I know on one hand," Lucca said bashfully. His ears flicked and his tail curled between his legs. "And I'd have four fingers to spare."

"Really, Initiate?" Master Roe asked in surprise. "I thought Master Cull had been effusive in his praises of your talents."

Lucca shook his head. He pinned his ears back and grimaced. "That would be Master Wavebreaker. Master Cull has been quite exasperated at my lack of progress."

Master Roe frowned. He half turned away from Lucca and took a step away from his desk. He furrowed his brow in thought. "Be that as it may, I don't think it changes anything. I am sure your illusions will make Wavebreaker proud," the badger said after a short silence. "It should all be irrelevant anyway, as I will arrange for some battlemages to follow half a day behind you."

"Won't he be suspecting a trap?" Lucca asked. He couldn't suppress the feeling he might be walking into a trap of his own. Not one for the relic thief.

"Of course he will," Master Roe said, doing nothing to reduce Lucca's worries. The badger's eyes sparkled. "But he won't be expecting *this* trap. When the charm activates you will be in no danger and have plenty of time."

Lucca raised his brow. "Plenty of time? Before what, exactly?"

"You're going to spend the night with someone who will be deeply and utterly infatuated with you," Master Roe said. Another of those infernal winks. "No one will begrudge you the chance to take advantage of that situation."

"Come off it, Master. I'm not that kind of guy. He'd have to buy me dinner first," the lion said. He tried to stop the nausea welling up anew within his gut. The mere thought of abusing the love charm in such a way sent ripples of revulsion through him. He managed to mask that and flash a passable attempt at a nervous smile. "I'll stall him. Don't worry."

"Very well, Lucca," the badger said. He pulled a pocket watch from his robes. "You'd better get back to your dormitory now. You'll need your strength for tomorrow."

"Tomorrow?" the lion yelped. He clutched the gilded tome to his chest.

"Well, I suppose it's today now," the badger said, glancing to the window. "I said I wanted to test this thief, so let's give him a mark only he would dare attempt. No one knows of this transfer but us, and he has only a night's start. He'll have to work hard for this one. I'll send a few d-mails and deal with all the red tape tonight so that everything is prepared for you to leave early tomorrow morning."

"Oh goody." Lucca turned his back on his master as he started to make his way across the badger's office.

"In all honesty, I think it's best that you're far from here by the time Chapter Master Alber wakes and finds out what I've planned. If there's one thing he hates more than inaction, it's someone taking initiative and acting before he can claim it was his idea. Probably why he gets on so well with the archmage," Master Roe said. He wrinkled his muzzle and shook his hands. Then he rolled his eyes and sighed. "The next time I see you, the relic thief will have been captured, and you'll be the hero to bring him in."

Lucca shuddered at the thought, which he tried to disguise as a shiver. He paused for a moment at the door to look back to his master. A pained smile was forced onto his muzzle. "I can only hope you're right about this, Master."

Exhaling slowly, Lucca cast a new invisibility charm around himself and stepped out into the corridor. He remembered to close the door behind him.

There was much to distract Lucca's mind as he made his way back to his dormitory, but he didn't allow himself to become so unfocused that he lost his way in the ever-changing corridors. He would have to delay most of his ruminating until he was in his bed. The few thoughts that did break through his focus were mostly to do with the relic thief. Of course he knew all about the rogue. Everyone did, but Lucca was particularly enamoured by the narrow and daring escapades the mysterious thief pulled off without fail, or so the likely embellished news reports claimed. It was the sort of romanticised life he could see himself doing if he wasn't so good at his studies.

The young lion reappeared in his dormitory; a small, square room with the most basic of commodities. A shelf ran across one wall, an armoire and a desk on the opposite one, and a second door that led to his private bathroom. He levitated the tome to one of the few clear spaces on his desk, where it landed with a soft thump.

Lucca took a moment to secure the dodgy latch on his window, before he collapsed onto his bed and ran his hands over his muzzle. His heart and mind warred with each other as he considered Master Roe's plan one more time. The plan was a bad one. Almost every voice that clamoured for attention within Lucca's mind warned him against the idea. But there was one small voice that whispered seductively. The voice came from his heart, or perhaps a little lower.

What if?

Chapter Two

The windows slammed open with a rude crash, waking Lucca in an instant and letting out all the warm air like a punctured balloon. The lion immediately regretted his usual habit of sleeping in the Winterpaw fashion. He clutched at his sides in a futile attempt to keep some warmth in his naked body, but the chill air stole it away.

"*Ka'heirbek*!" Lucca swore, thoughtfully borrowing from the Winterpaw tongue for the occasion. He thrashed clumsily at the bedsheets, thrusting an arm out from beneath to gesture wildly in the direction of the cold air. The window rattled against the frame as the lion's sleepy attempts to secure the broken latch with his magic failed.

He cautiously peeked his head out from beneath the thick blankets. The sun had yet to grace the sky with its presence. Lucca growled in distaste. There were still several hours of sleep left to catch up on, especially after his late night in Master Roe's office.

The lion closed his eyes again and tried to return to his dream. He had forgotten all the details about it, but for a lingering sense that it had been a pleasant one. Before he could doze off again, a sudden whirring sound filled the room. The lion's ears twitched as he tried to triangulate and identify the sound.

After a few seconds, he realised it would be easier to open his eyes.

A small green gem zipped around the room, occasionally giving out a bright flash of emerald light. A short-range messenger gem, simple to program to carry short messages over close range. They were often used by couriers, or by masters too lazy to go to the kitchens to pick up their own dinner.

Lucca gazed at the shiny gem with sleepy eyes. His feline instincts made him track the dazzling speck of emerald through the air, but he was still too tired to make a worthwhile attempt at catching it. His hands swatted limply at the empty air before the gem stopped moving just out of reach.

"Recipient for message: Lucca. This is your early morning wakeup call, as authorised by Guild Inscription Master Roe. Recipient Lucca must make his way to the central garth immediately."

Lucca frowned at the small gem, trying to determine some form of sense from the words. He quickly gave up. "What?"

"Recipient for message: Lucca. This is your..."

"Yes, I know that part already," Lucca said. He sat up and rubbed his eyes. "What time is it?"

The gem floated on the spot for a moment. "Early."

Lucca groaned, figuring the gem would be of no further use. He lazily waved his arm at some undergarments draped over the armoire. The clothing heeded the call of their master and flung themselves haphazardly all over the bed. Early morning spells were never reliable at the best of times. Luckily, he wasn't trying to cut his mane.

"Alright, I'm moving," the lion growled at the gem, which had continued to whir and flash. He scuffled awkwardly as he tried to get his clothes on without leaving the warm embrace of his bed. "Where am I going?"

"The garth," the gem answered proudly.

"The what? We don't have a garth."

The gem was silent for a moment as though it was stuck in thought. Then it zipped outside. Lucca's instincts overtook his rational mind as he jumped after the gem, almost falling out the window before he came back to his senses. He squinted outside. The gem had spiralled down to the guild courtyard, which was coated in a grey sludge that had probably been snow when it had fallen.

"Looking good, Lucca!"

The lion redirected his gaze from the gem as he noticed the musteliad standing just beside it for the first time. The otter, one of the regular guild couriers, raised her hand and gave the half-naked lion a thumbs up.

As Lucca struggled to find something to say, his eyes were caught by Esfyr's Wold beyond the most distant buildings of the guild chapterhouse. Slowly the memory of the previous evening's task bubbled to his conscious mind.

There wasn't too much Lucca could see from his fourth-story dormitory window. He could certainly see the shorter oaks that bordered the wold, though before long the trees became too tall to see beyond. The nearby village was completely swallowed from view. In the absence of the stars and moon, everything he could see was lit by the lights of the chapterhouse windows and the rustic torches Kyde must have lit. Everything was wrapped in a thick layer of fog.

The lion felt a sharp, cold stab of wind as it cut through his fur. He fastened his arms to his naked chest and rubbed briskly. His teeth rattled as he shivered.

"Cold up there, Lucca?" the courier called out. "Don't have anything warmer to wear? As much as I'm enjoying the view, I don't want you to freeze."

Lucca retreated into his dormitory. He held his hand out, summoning the first robe he could see to his body. He quickly slipped it on over his head, before returning to the window. The thin robe didn't do much to prevent the cold wind from chilling his body, but it did more than just his fur alone.

"Here to see me off, are you Kyde?" he called out down to the otter.

"That's my job, yes. But I'm not about to serenade you, so get your tail down here before I freeze mine off. This weather is absolutely criminal," the otter snapped.

"I'll be down there soon," Lucca replied. He stepped back into the dormitory and quickly glanced around his room. He had thought he would have had a little more time to prepare, so he hadn't even thought about packing before going to sleep. The old badger had apparently been very serious with his threats of an early start. Other than the gilded yearbook, he also plucked up a leather-bound book from beside his bed, and he secured them both in his travel satchel. He doubted whether he would have the chance to keep up with his alchemy studies, but the textbook would at least keep up the pretence.

Though Lucca couldn't have anticipated such vile weather, he needed no second excuse to wear his warmest furs. He opened his wardrobe and grinned at the Winterpaw robes that had taken up the prized place amongst his many clothes.

They were all marvels of the Winterpaw leatherworking, and they had been given to him as a gift from a particular Winterpaw hunter. Lucca had 'spoken his mind' at the right place and time, and it had resulted in both Lucca and the young hunter learning a few interesting discoveries about themselves. The hunter had tanned and crafted the leathers just for the lion, and he had presented them bashfully on the final day of the excursion. The Winterpaw runes of vitality and kinship were inscribed on leather bands around the cuffs, along with a third rune. Lucca's ears still burned when he thought of the day that he had finally translated it from one of Master Roe's most obscure tomes. He had never uttered the translation to another, especially not his runes master.

In the warmer climate of Lutrea there hadn't been many opportunities to wear the thick fur-lined leathers. He wasn't going to pass off this chance. Plus it would make him look quite fabulous for the relic thief.

Before long, Lucca was straightening the leathers in front of a mirror, adjusting the small bone ornaments to his liking. He grinned at the mirror, and his reflection grinned back. His spiked green mane was certainly his most distinctive feature, clipped short in a deliberate attempt to prevent the shaggy growth of hair that would overwhelm his features. He wasn't opposed to the idea of a mane; he just hadn't worked out how to make one work for him yet.

"Got to look good for your first date," he said, managing to bring out a confident smile. A flicker of doubt passed across his bright amber eyes. The thief would be bewitched. The relic thief wouldn't give a damn what he looked like, though Lucca still wanted to believe that the rogue would like him for what he was, love charm or no love charm.

Realising he was wasting time and making Kyde wait in the cold, Lucca picked up his satchel and slung it over his shoulder. He made sure it still contained the almighty yearbook before he doused the lights in his dormitory. When all was ready, he made his way out into the darkened corridors of the academy.

By the time Lucca reached the courtyard a few minutes later, the weather had taken a turn for the worse. There was noticeable drizzle in the air now, and the wind was blowing even stronger than before. The lion trudged towards the courier, who was wrapped up tightly in a waterproof cloak.

"Where the hell is the garth, Kyde?" Lucca asked, having to raise his voice over the wind.

The otter smacked a hand to her forehead and chuckled. "Don't blame me, Lucca. It's tricky technology to get working properly. I was telling it to say courtyard."

Lucca laughed as well. "What is a garth anyway?"

The otter shrugged. "No idea. But that's all it insisted on calling the courtyard. Must need an update."

"So what exactly are you doing here?" Lucca asked. He knew it was pointless trying to get more sense out of the inane meanings of the gem. Kyde was right. They managed simple messages well enough, but sometimes they spat out archaic and inane nonsense. No one quite seemed sure why that was.

"I've been asked to give you some advice, as well as the gear you'll need on your journey," the otter said. Sure enough, she did have a rather large and heavy-looking pack on the ground next to her paws. Lucca hoped he wouldn't have to carry it all. "Normally I'd complain that you'd be so keen to do my job for me, but right now all I'm thinking of is the hot chocolate I'll have in five minutes, while you're out on the road in this."

"Ooh, any chance of one of those before I head out?" Lucca asked, licking his lips.

Kyde shook her head. "Not a chance, kitty-boy. That's for us trained couriers," she said, patting a hand on the lion's shoulder. "Now, you're to deliver this... whatever it is, to the merchant guild hall in Emberfade. That's about eighty miles by the main road. An easy job were the weather more agreeable."

"Is the weather ever agreeable at this time of year?" Lucca sighed, forlornly mourning the loss of the hot chocolate. He squinted and looked up the road, which quickly vanished into the fog.

Kyde snorted with laughter. "You've got to ask the Fisherman *really* nicely for that. Now, I don't know what it is you're carrying. This mission is of unusual security, but we've sent a d-mail to the Emberfade branch to know to expect you. Given your lack of training, should take you the better part of a week to get there, so long as you don't dawdle."

"A week? What's my mode of conveyance?"

The otter blinked. "Your what?"

"How am I getting there that fast?"

"Oh... why didn't you say so then? Head out through the north gate. Then, after about a mile, take the east fork. From there just stay on the road and follow the signs. A few villages along the way, but nothing too complicated."

The lion nodded. "That's great, but how am I getting there? Like a mount or whatever?"

Kyde frowned. "Then why didn't you say that in the first place, felian? Seriously, your kind need to stop fancy-talking so much. Others may not take it as lightly as me."

"Sorry, Ky. Habit," Lucca said, shrugging.

The otter glared for a few moments before continuing. "You're using your own two paws. You could use the exercise, and it's not just because you smart-mouthed me."

The lion's eyes widened. For one of the first times in his life, he found himself speechless.

"Commissioner's orders, Lucca. Something about security, I think."

Lucca found his voice again. "Security? Whose security? The mount's?" he blustered. He ran a hand through his mane. "I've got to trek all by my lonesome, through the mud and the rain, and you think all of that will take just seven days? What's the old codger playing at?"

Kyde shook her head. "I don't know, Lucca. Truth be told, I know very little about this. None of the couriers do. Whatever you and Master Roe have arranged, we know nothing about it."

Lucca rubbed his hands over his muzzle and groaned. "Alright then. No mount." At least he wouldn't risk outpacing the relic thief. He nudged the massive pack with a paw. "Please tell me that is somehow not all mine. You've still got some of yours in there to take out, right?"

Kyde shook her head. "First, this is for you." She fished out a small blue gem from her pocket and handed it to the lion. A black wire was wrapped around the iridescent stone.

With her hands free, the otter crouched down next to the pack and pulled it up to her chest in both arms. She staggered backwards as she rose, her tail flicking out in instinctual counterbalance. Her biceps were noticeably strained against the weight of the pack. Hugging it close to her chest, she shambled blindly towards the lion, the pack extending above her head. "Then this is the rest of it."

The lion took a step back. "Ugh, really?" he growled. He doubted he'd be able to lift the thing, let alone carry it for some eighty miles.

"Uh-huh," Kyde replied, her voice muffled by the pack.

The lion sighed and muttered a quick incantation beneath his breath. He extended his arm in Kyde's direction and snapped his fingers.

The otter immediately loosened her grip on the pack and stepped back in alarm. The heavy pack slowly floated down to the ground, as though in slow motion, before coming to rest horizontally a couple of inches above the wet mud. She stared at it for a few moments, then closed her eyes and grimaced.

"You know, there are times when I really hate you guild types. Do you know how much easier my job could be with a feather charm from time to time?" she grumbled.

Lucca swished his hand towards himself in a beckoning motion. The pack heeded his call and slowly drifted towards him. It bumped into his leg and lingered around his ankles as it waited for him to move.

"Hey, there have to be some benefits to all of this," he said with a shrug.

Kyde scoffed. "Some benefits? Seems to me that your life is nothing but benefits."

"It just reminds me of how lucky I am to be here, and not slaving away in some jade mine like most felians in Da'Manyr," Lucca muttered darkly. He shivered and tucked his tail in close to his legs.

"I'm sorry, I didn't mean to..." Kyde said, but Lucca held up a hand and smiled weakly.

"It's alright. I haven't been back there in over ten years," the felian said with a shrug. "I'm not like them. I'm... what did Master Aria call me the other day? Ah, yes. Civilised."

"Why don't we see more felians here?" Kyde asked quietly. She lowered her head, not quite meeting Lucca's eye. "Not even a tiger or anything?"

"Not all of my kind can do this magic thing, Ky," Lucca replied with a shake of his head. "And definitely not tigers. They've got the magical ability of a grain of sand."

The otter raised an eyebrow. Lucca knew it was a concept that was difficult to accept on the peninsula. Many musteliads, the prevalent species across the Lutrean peninsula, whether humble or noble, had the potential within them to learn the craft of magic. For a lot of them, it was simply an aptitude; a choice of developing the ability or not. Not a lucky genetic fluke like it had been with Lucca.

"So that's why you came across the sea to study? Because others can't?"

Lucca flashed a nervous smile. “I’m one in a million, and you know it,” he replied.

Kyde chuckled. “Alright, chosen one. In the pack is seven days of rations, any supplies we foresaw an amateur courier may need, a handful of scalls from Master Roe in case you need to purchase some emergency supplies, and some collapsible lodgings.”

“You mean a tent?”

“Right,” Kyde said with a nod. “You shouldn’t have any problem assembling it with your magic fingers.”

There was a brief pause.

“What the hell is a ‘collapsible lodgings’, Kyde? Seriously, you accuse me of fancy-talking.”

Kyde smiled weakly. “Just courier talk. You wouldn’t understand,” she muttered. Her rounded ears pinned back.

“And what’s this?” Lucca asked, smirking as he lifted his hand to show off the blue gem. “A blue sparklestone with a prodding wire?”

“It’s a tracking stone. Should fit in over your ear,” Kyde replied. She opened her mouth and paused, before batting her forehead with her webbed fingers. “You knew exactly what it was, didn’t you?”

The tip of Lucca’s tongue pressed between his sharp teeth as he grinned. He said nothing.

Kyde hugged her waterproof coat closer to her body. “Ok, kitty, get yourself moving before I consider murder for delaying my hot chocolate.”

Lucca fiddled around with the gem to secure it against his ear. He then waved his hand at the backpack, which lifted itself off the ground and hovered loyally by the lion’s side. “Don’t need to tell me twice, Ky,” Lucca said, giving a quick two-fingered salute to the otter before heading off on a steady pace down the torch-lit, dirt road.

The otter raised her hand in a quick wave. "Good luck Lucca, take care."

The lion waved back over his shoulder, and soon not even the torchlight could reveal him through the fog.

Chapter Three

The morning was dark and gloomy.

Because of course it was.

Lucca grumbled and growled to himself as he walked, wrapping his leathers close to him in a futile attempt to keep warm in the wind. He spent a good portion of the first few hours of travel staring up at the sky, almost missing the fork he had to turn at in the process. He kept hoping for the sun to come out of hiding, but all it did was bleed red dye between the clouds. It was very pretty, but not exactly helpful at the moment.

The fog had partially lifted, though the thick grey clouds still covered the sky and threatened more than just the light drizzle that had been damping Lucca's fur. Torchlight had become a distant luxury to more civilised parts, leaving the disgruntled felian to trudge in an eerie half-darkness.

To add to his annoyance, the tracking stone proved a constant irritation, buzzing incessantly in his ear. The sound grew so intolerable that he didn't make it to midday before he ripped it from his head and stuffed it into a spare pocket in his satchel.

A few times Lucca thought he was being watched. He was sure he could see eyes peering at him from the darkened trees that lined either side of the road like a never-ending hallway. Not wanting to offend any possible admirers, the lion waved heartily to the shadows between the trees. They didn't wave back, but that wasn't the point. He was just trying to be friendly, and to ease his worries that the darkness was anything malicious. The company of the shadows was nice, even if they didn't wave back.

Lucca started humming. Apart from the weather, everything seemed pretty simple. So long as he tried to forget about the missed hot chocolate, ignored the wind and the drizzle, and didn't think about the clawing sense of loneliness, he could even find himself in a good mood about everything. All he had to do was walk to Emberfade and deliver the almighty yearbook. Four days of solitude in the wilderness. Easy. Almost like his own little adventure. He had always wanted one of those. He would have preferred it to be a little less... wet.

The lion stopped suddenly. The levitating pack bumped into his leg, just as surprised about the sudden pause as the felian was.

"You're forgetting something, aren't you?" the lion exclaimed. He smacked his head with a hand as he remembered the *other* part of his task. The more important part. "Relic thief!"

"What about him?" a voice asked brightly from just behind the felian.

The fur on Lucca's back stood on end. He quickly whipped around, hands raised, to face... nothing. He blinked in confusion.

"That's right, now look down, felian."

Lucca instinctively complied. At his paws was a two-foot-tall, bipedal blue dragon, standing proudly with his hands clasped behind his back. His horns and claws were all vivid red. A lap-dragon. Lucca had heard of them before, but he'd never actually had a chance to see one. This one was as adorable as he had imagined a diminutive dragon to be, but he suppressed the immediate urge to squeal in delight. Instead he raised an eyebrow.

"How long have you been following me?" he asked warily. Lap-dragons were rarely by themselves, as they were frequently dependent on their owners to function. This far out in the wilderness there was little to keep a lap-dragon alive without assistance. They were technically nothing more than magical constructs, designed to look like real dragons. Only much, *much*, smaller.

"Not long," the lap-dragon replied eagerly. He looked pensive for a moment, displaying a hand and counting on his dull crimson talons. His small wings fluttered. "An hour... maybe three... or two. Half an hour. How long ago since you passed that, yannow, tree thing? Back there?" The dragon pointed back down the road. He looked very serious.

Though he was still on guard, Lucca's senses indicated they were completely alone for now, although that didn't discount the possibility of the hidden owner spying on him through the lap-dragon. There was every possibility that the lap-dragon was a trap designed to lure him in with overwhelming cuteness. If that were the case, then Lucca couldn't allow the invisible owner to know he was onto them.

Putting aside his worries, he allowed himself a smile at the adorable antics of the diminutive creature. "Oh, the tree? With the bark and the leaves? Back there?"

The lap-dragon's eyes lit up. "That's the one! You waved, so I figured I'd hang with you for a bit," he said brightly. He then shook his head. "You don't talk much."

Lucca ran his hand through his short mane. "I didn't know anyone was following me. If you wanted to talk so much, why didn't you say anything?"

The small creature gasped and held a hand to his chest. "I don't talk to strangers!" he squeaked, looking utterly appalled at the mere thought of doing such a thing. Then he beamed widely. "But then you spoke to me and now we're not strangers."

Lucca kneeled down to the dragon's level and looked into his luminous blue eyes. "Do you have a name?"

The little dragon croaked. Lucca almost fell over backwards.

"Think you could spell that?" Lucca asked nervously, unsure if that had been the lap-dragon's name or not.

"Probably not. It doesn't translate too well into this language, but I think it has, um..." The lap-dragon paused and drew a few circles in the air with a talon. "A quadruple L."

"Like, four Ls in a row?" the lion asked in disbelief. He shook his head. "I'm not going to get my tongue around that. What do musteliads call you?"

The lap-dragon tilted his head back in thought. "Oh, runt, scamp, imp. That sort of thing," he said slowly. His eyes suddenly lit up. "One person calls me Palmer. He's a musteliad."

"Is he an otter?" Lucca asked, knowing they were the most common species on the peninsula.

The dragon shrugged his small wings. "I've seen him swim a few times."

"That's good enough for me then. Palmer it is," the lion said with a smile. He rose from his haunches and returned to slowly walking down the road. With a snap of his fingers, the pack began loyally tailing behind him.

As he walked, Lucca could hear the soft sounds of the lap-dragon's pawsteps in the wet mud. Not that Lucca minded.

Besides the pack, the little dragon was the only company he could expect to have before he reached Emberfade.

After just a few minutes though, the pawsteps ceased. To his surprise, Lucca suddenly felt a wave of loneliness wash over him. The lap-dragon had only been there for a few minutes, but already the lion had appreciated the sound of someone else walking by his side.

Lucca looked back, hoping to catch some sight of the lap-dragon disappearing into the trees again. Instead, he saw Palmer right behind him still, seated excitedly on the levitating pack of supplies. Lucca chuckled to himself. He would have appreciated a free ride himself.

The lion turned back to focus on the road. His brow was furrowed in thought as he tried to recall everything he had learned about lap-dragons. He knew they were magical constructs, designed mainly for guilds and laboratories. They were capable of storing knowledge with incredible precision, and also had access to the telepathic communication networks that true dragons utilised. They were not creatures that wandered the wilderness alone.

If the lap-dragon were a danger or otherwise preparing a trap, then Lucca knew he needed to try to prise information out of the magic construct quickly. He chewed on his lip thoughtfully as he wondered what the best approach may be, before settling on the simplest. The lap-dragon appeared willing to speak freely.

"Palmer?" Lucca asked, breaking the companionable silence that had fallen between them. "Why are you out here in the woods?"

Palmer looked puzzled for a moment. Then he raised his hand. "I could well ask you the same question, felian."

The lion rolled his eyes and sighed. "I'm on an errand. Now your turn."

"I'm out researching. It can get a little drab on my own," the lap-dragon replied. He shifted himself slightly so that his haunches flopped over the side of the pack. "Nice to have someone to talk to."

"What are you researching?" Lucca asked. His ears perked up. His hunch had been right. The lap-dragon seemed all too eager to talk and share information that might be best hidden.

The dragon shook his head. "Nope. Your turn to answer first."

Lucca raised his brow. He was beginning to see the rules of this new game they had apparently started to play. "Alright. What do you want me to answer?"

"Relic thief. You mentioned him. Why?"

Lucca sucked in his breath. He wasn't sure how much he wanted to tell the lap-dragon. Lap-dragons could be in constant communication with their owners, and he didn't want to tip off Palmer's owner of his mission. He bit his lip as he thought of the best way to answer. "I have something he may want," the lion said slowly.

The dragon's eyes brightened again, shining so much it lit up the drizzling rain around him. "Ooh, like a... chha... fzzzt. Your turn to ask."

Lucca wasn't sure if he should be concerned for the lap-dragon. It had sounded like Palmer was choking on something, but he didn't appear to be suffering at all. In fact, he was beaming brightly up at the lion.

"Alright. What are you researching?" Lucca asked warily, keeping one eye on the lap-dragon behind him, just in case he started acting oddly again.

Palmer grinned widely. "You could say I'm scouting. Eyes and ears. A spy," he said, showing off every one of his needle-like teeth.

"You going to explain what you mean by that?"

The dragon shook his head vigorously. "Not unless you give me the password," he said in a sing-song manner.

"Well if you're not going to explain yourself, then I'm not going to tell you anything else about what I'm doing," Lucca said, folding his arms across his chest. He hoped to tease more information out of the lap-dragon without having to work out the password.

Palmer was not so easily swayed. "I already know everything about what you're doing."

Lucca suddenly through the wide grin looked quite sinister. He turned away in alarm. "I highly doubt that," he muttered. He nervously chanced a quick glance back. "I barely understand what I'm doing."

The lap-dragon smiled again. A nice smile, this time. "Can we go any faster? I want to be at Emberfade before the week's over," Palmer said, leaning forward on the pack. "Couriers usually walk faster than you."

Lucca felt a shiver run down his tail. He stared at the lap-dragon.

Palmer shrugged his shoulders. "I told you I knew everything," he said, quite casually.

The lion shook his head and faced forward again. The lap-dragon knew what direction he was travelling. There wasn't much on this road before it reached Emberfade. Nothing but small villages of little consequence. Palmer had just taken an educated guess on his final destination. That was all. Even so, Lucca still felt another shiver of unease trickle down his spine. He would have to be on his guard with what he said around the lap-dragon.

Palmer had been right about one thing though. He was walking too slowly. He picked up his pace and pulled his Winterpaw cloak a little tighter around his chest.

"Felian. You're leaving me behind," came the lap-dragon's voice, a few moments later.

Lucca glanced back. The pack was still languidly hovering along at the same slow pace. He whistled to his supplies. The pack, as though it had suddenly noticed how far behind its master it was, darted forward to return to the lion's heel.

"The name's Silven, by the way," the lion said, plucking a name from his favourite adventure story. He glanced down to the pack and lap-dragon by his side. If Palmer already knew so much, then at least he could keep his name hidden.

The lap-dragon rocked back and forth on the pack, digging his heels into the leather bag. "Is it?" he said brightly. He grinned widely and showed off his teeth once more. "We're going to have so much fun together."

The sun showed its face during mid-afternoon, if only briefly. It brightened up the forest significantly, dazzling Lucca's eyes with spectacles of green light reflecting off the dew-laden leaves. For a short while the fog and clouds were burned away, and the day was utterly transformed.

Before Lucca had a chance to enjoy the light and dry off, the clouds returned. The light was gone, and with it, so was the resplendent beauty of the forest. Everything returned to gloomy shadows, leaving just the memories lingering in Lucca's mind. The lion's smile remained though, in the hope that the weather was finally starting to improve.

The thunder came first: a low, ominous rumble from the west. Lucca wasn't too concerned. So long as the storm stayed to the west and didn't come too close, then he wouldn't need to worry about it.

Lightning arced across the sky.

A deafening peal of thunder followed moments later.

Palmer squeaked and tried to bury himself in the pack. He succeeded only in squeezing his head between the straps, with the rest of his body exposed.

Lucca's fur stood on end, giving a frazzled look. "Static. Just static. Not scared," he said, trying to convince himself more than Palmer. He tried to smooth his fur down as he looked around. It was about time to set up camp anyway.

"Not under the trees, felian Silven," Palmer warned, lifting his head back out of the pack.

"There's nothing but trees here," Lucca retorted, sweeping his arm around.

Palmer looked thoughtful. His eyes lit up. "Doot! Follow me." He leaped from the back of the pack. The diminutive creature veered off to the right and careened off the road.

The lion was caught unawares. He struggled to run after Palmer as they crashed through the undergrowth, pack bouncing just behind him. He stumbled a few times on upturned roots and mossy stones. Everything was sodden already, leaving every step a slippery gamble. His tail lashed out behind him as he fought to keep his balance.

Rain started to fall. Not like the drizzle that had been falling all day, but actual rain that felt like it was hurled to the ground by a malevolent god with a personal vendetta against the lower elements. Lucca felt like he was being pummelled by small stones that tore through the canopy.

Minutes later, the lap-dragon stopped so suddenly that Lucca almost tripped over him before he was able to arrest his run. In front of them was a small cave, notched modestly in the side of a medium-sized cliff face that had assembled itself seemingly from nowhere.

Lucca could see nothing as he stepped into the cave. He held a hand to his satchel, feeling the outline of the tracking gem in the front pocket. If he got delayed in the cave, then at least the battlemages would know where he was.

Palmer followed just behind the lion, one dainty hand resting atop the floating luggage. The pack dropped to the ground with a gentle thud as Lucca stopped.

"Let there be light," Lucca said, snapping his fingers at the pitch black. A gentle, white glow emanated from Lucca's outstretched hand, illuminating the darkness around him.

The lion froze. The cave was not empty.

Large crates were piled up towards the back of the cave. Just a few feet from where Lucca was standing was a bedroll, a small lantern, and several containers of food. Three wine flasks were propped up against the crates.

Palmer hurried past the lion, completely unperturbed by the belongings scattered through the cave. The lap-dragon pottered around, peering into the crates inquisitively.

"I don't think we should stay here," Lucca said uncertainly. At his request, the pack lifted back up off the ground as the lion turned around to look outside. The rain had formed a curtain of water pouring down over the cave's entrance.

"You worry too much, felian Silven," Palmer said. He plucked a small, blue mat from inside one of the crates, which he lay down on the ground.

"You've been here before, haven't you?" Lucca asked.

The lap-dragon curled up on the mat and looked up at the lion. He nodded. "Many times. Now, if you don't mind, I need some sleep. It's been a long day."

Lucca tried to put aside his worries. Whoever used this cave would surely be alright with sharing it for one night. He rested the pack down on the ground and sat beside it, leaning his back against the cave wall. He rummaged through his supplies to find the rations Kyde had provided for him. He found a delectable meal – for an otter.

Partitioned into seven separate containers, one for each expected day on the road, was a colourful array of fruit and nuts, with a side of lemon couscous and tuna. Though the lion grumbled a little, he was too hungry not to eat anything, and he soon devoured one of the meals. He did quite enjoy the tinned fish, though it had been a challenge to claw his way into the tin – Kyde had neglected to provide him with a tin opener.

By the time Lucca had finished his meal, Palmer was already asleep. The lap-dragon twitched a little in his sleep, with his little wings draped over his body like a blanket.

Lucca sighed. "Just you and me now, pack," he whispered to his bag of supplies. The lion shifted slightly, and his movement caused the pack to promptly flop on its side, almost as though it, too, had fallen asleep. "Tchh. Typical."

There was nothing else left for the lion to do but join his companions in sleep. Lucca glanced across at the bedroll. It would be a damn sight more comfortable than the rocky ground, so he figured he may as well take advantage of it while he could.

The lion slipped out of his leathers and set them out neatly to one side, hoping they would dry a little overnight. Left in just his underwear, he felt the bite of the cold air cut into him. If anything, it felt colder than it had in the morning. He quickly pulled a thick blanket out from the pack and wrapped it around him, before flopping down on the bedroll.

Lucca pulled his small satchel containing the almighty yearbook closer to him. He rested his hand protectively on top of it, feeling the protrusion from the tracking stone safely tucked inside as well. With a flick of his other wrist, he extinguished the light inside the cave.

The sound of drumming rain and the occasional muffled peal of thunder sent him to sleep with surprising ease.

Chapter Four

The morning was clear and cool. The clouds of the previous day had been replaced by a crisp, pale blue sky with a weak and watery sun that failed to provide any heat to the air. The grass and trees were covered in a fine layer of damp frost.

Lucca had woken early. Lingering memories from his dream soon faded from his mind, tickling his ears as they fled into the morning air. The lion had enjoyed a quick breakfast of fruit and nuts – Palmer had refused to share, and the lap-dragon didn't appear hungry at all – before setting out to Emberfade again. The lap-dragon led the way back to the main road before returning to his usual position resting atop the pack. The almighty yearbook was safely secure in the satchel slung over Lucca's shoulder.

"Didn't I say the cave was a good idea?" Palmer said, after a good half an hour of content silence.

Lucca started at the sudden speech from behind him. He smiled, but he didn't look back. "I guess you did."

"My master uses it all the time," Palmer said with a perky whistle.

Lucca shivered, despite the morning sunshine that shone on his back. He slowly spun around on his paws to face the diminutive dragon, seizing the opportunity to prise out more information. "Your master?"

"My master, yes. The one who owns me. Who gives me orders. Yannow, that sort of thing," Palmer replied. He waved his hands through the air.

"Who is your owner?" Lucca asked. He walked backwards to continue facing the dragon. He was curious to know where Palmer had come from. As much as he enjoyed the lap-dragon's company, he knew Palmer would eventually have to return to his true owner.

"You do not have permission to access that information, felian Silven."

The unfamiliar name almost caught Lucca out, before he recalled his false persona. "Aww, come on. You can tell me," he pleaded.

"Not happening," Palmer said, turning his head away from Lucca and folding his arms in an adorable pout.

"Fine then," Lucca said. He turned away from the dragon and started to stalk off ahead. The pack picked up its pace to keep up with the lion, carrying the lap-dragon with it. The lion glanced back at Palmer on occasion, chewing his lip as he pondered the mystery of the strange creature. He couldn't help but find himself amused and fascinated with the lap-dragon, but there was an uneasiness in his gut as he pondered the purpose for Palmer's excursion. Lap-dragons simply didn't wander the empty moors by themselves.

This continued for nearly twenty minutes as Lucca did his best to ignore the lap-dragon, all while internally debating with himself whether he should try to slip free from Palmer's constant attention. Every time he looked, the lap-dragon's sparkling blue eyes were fixed on him. Unblinking.

"I like you," Palmer said abruptly.

"What?"

"I like you. You're funny." Palmer's face showed a touch of sorrow as he spoke. His small wings drooped. He picked absently at some stitching on the pack with a single red talon.

"What's wrong?" Lucca asked. He slowed down to walk alongside the levitating pack.

"Nothing. I said I liked you. That's a compliment, isn't it?" Palmer said loudly, his voice rising in pitch as he got defensive.

Lucca raised his hands in front of his chest. "Alright, I'm sorry. I beg your forgiveness. And thank you. I like you too."

"No problem," Palmer chirped. All traces of sorrow and annoyance had melted away from his voice. The grin returned to his face, and his wings flicked out briefly. "Say. What do you think of a short-cut?"

Lucca stopped so abruptly that his pack bumped into his legs. "How much of a short-cut?"

"This road loops a lot to cross the Wolden River. My short-cut goes straight to where you need to go. It'll cut about a day off the journey. No one uses it either, not even bandits."

Lucca was tempted, especially at the thought of cutting a whole day off his endless hike, but he hesitated. The isolation of the trail didn't concern him. It wasn't like there would be many travelling in this weather anyway. Even the main road was likely to be deserted. "I'd rather stick to the road," he said, thinking of the mages who were meant to be travelling a few hours behind him. They might not realise he had taken a detour, depending on how regularly they checked his tracker. What if the thief caught up with him before he returned to the main road? Unless...

"I won't get us lost," Palmer said, tapping his head with a talon. His horns briefly flashed red. "I have a map up here."

Lucca bit his bottom lip in thought. He worried about a trap. Taking him off the road would be an easy place to ambush him. But no one knew about his journey. Certainly not about the almighty yearbook. No common thief or bandit would have had the chance to lay an ambush. Only the relic thief had the skills of apparent divination to know of his quest.

Either Palmer's diversion was a scheme somehow orchestrated by the relic thief, in which case Lucca would have the chance to complete his mission; or he would reach Emberfade a day early and avoid wearing out his aching paws. Both seemed an attractive proposition.

He took a deep breath and made his choice.

"Alright. Lead the way," he said, deciding that he could easily alert the following battlemages of his new path. After all, as Master Roe would say, he was only giving the relic thief another challenge to overcome should he not be behind this shortcut. No point making it too easy for him.

"Yah! Let's go then," Palmer cried. He dug his heels into the pack. With a quick gesture from Lucca, the baggage reared up like a horse. For a moment, Palmer looked like he was about to fall straight off, but then he plunged into a tiny trail that meandered through the trees.

Lucca placed a hand on a tree that bordered the trail. "*Verto dexter. Lucca,*" he whispered under his breath. The entire tree flashed red for a brief instant. Then it looked exactly as it had done before. There was no trace of the spell that Lucca had placed on it. None, that is, except for what the battlemages would see.

He patted his satchel to feel the tracking stone that would also guide the battlemages to him. The relic thief might be tested, but his distant escort would not.

Feeling pretty pleased with himself, Lucca followed the dragon down the trail.

The sun disappeared behind the canopy of leaves as the evening deepened, casting the fragments of trail in shade, the road already many hours behind them. The cold air chilled even further amongst the trees. The further from the road they went, the darker it became. Lucca couldn't tell whether the canopy was getting thicker, or if the sun had been swallowed by clouds again. The lion couldn't see anything more than a few feet on either side of the narrow path, the foliage pressing in on him, constricting him. He hurried after Palmer as a sudden desire to remain close to his companion struck him.

While Palmer rode the pack without care for the roots and vines that spread across the muddy trail, Lucca couldn't share the same luxury. Not only did he need to direct the pack to Palmer's instruction, he also had to constantly keep his eyes on the ground to avoid becoming entangled in them and tripping. That was then he noticed the tracks. The trail was used.

There were four sets of tracks going in both directions. As far as Lucca could tell, they were all from the same person, judging from the size and shape of the pawprints. All had been made since the rains of the previous night.

"Palmer, someone's been down here recently," Lucca said, slowing down a little.

No answer came. The lion looked up and stopped walking completely. Both dragon and baggage had disappeared from sight. He clicked his fingers to summon his pack.

The heavy bag bumped against a tree as it returned, almost bashfully, without its passenger. The lap-dragon was gone.

"Palmer? Palmer!"

Lucca held his satchel close to his chest. The only response was the faint echo of his own shout. He suddenly felt scared. Every noise was amplified in his ears: he could hear every rustle of the leaves as they swayed in the gentle breeze, every dry scraping of tree branch on tree branch. There was no sound of any living animal but for his ragged breathing.

The lion ran a cautious claw over the kinship rune on his cuff as he forced himself to control and slow his breathing. There was little he could do about the pounding of his heart, thumping away inside even his ears. "You're fine, Lucca. You're fine," he whispered to himself. His eyes flicked into the thick undergrowth, then back the way he had come. Already he lost the trail of his pawprints, quickly disappearing into the undergrowth. "You're just on your own, lost on a dark trail without knowing where the road is. Nothing to worry about.

"I'm sure the battlemages will find me tomorrow. Curled up under a tree. Maybe they'll walk past me without realising while I'm asleep." A hysterical chuckle burst from his lips. "Or they'll find my body after some common bandit has robbed me."

With the little dragon gone, and his companionable chatter with him, the forest seemed to grow larger. It was bad enough that Esfyr's Wold had a knack for making lost travellers feel like the only being in existence. To Lucca, that now felt like a reality.

"*Saph'ittur Lucca,*" the lion said out loud, trying to reassure himself in Winterpaw. He took a step forward, and then another. Before long, he worked up a snail pace down the lap-dragon's short-cut. Palmer couldn't have gone far.

Shadows reached towards him, twisting tendrils of darkness like grasping vines. Lucca tried not to see the shapes amongst them. Rows of monsters waiting to pounce.

Minutes passed, and the isolation stirred up a memory in the lion's head.

"*They will look after you there. They can teach you to control it.*"

The lion winced, baring his teeth as he fought back the memory of his mother's last words to him. It was one thing being alone. He didn't want to be miserable on top of it.

"*There is no future for your gifts here.*"

Something inaudible escaped the lion's lips. Something else from his eyelid.

"*Make us proud, Lu'Rahl.*"

Lucca stopped in his steps.

"*We love you.*"

Lucca slumped back onto his pack, head in his hands. How was it he thought he could do this? He was alone. A lost felian far from home. He had no map, no way of easily finding the road again, not without tramping through several hours of forest and hoping he went in the right direction. It would be better if this were a trap. Perhaps the relic thief could steal the book and point him in the right direction home.

A twig snapped somewhere close by.

Lucca opened his eyes, which blazed bright orange. He jumped to his paws, hands igniting with crimson flames. Shadows fled, back beneath the trees where they belonged.

"Don't hurt me, please."

The lion blinked at the familiar voice. He lifted his hand, letting his light extend deeper between the trees. Palmer cowered amongst the roots, wings covering his face.

"Palmer?" Lucca asked in surprise. He quickly brushed away the tears that wetted his cheeks, then flicked his wrists to rid himself of the illusory flames that twisted around his hands.

"Who else?" the lap-dragon asked, peeking through a gap in his wings.

"Where did you go?" the lion asked. He was still breathing heavily, but already the sense of profound isolation was starting to trickle away.

"Needed better reception," Palmer said vaguely. He tapped a talon against the side of his head. His red horns flickered with intermittent light. "Can't get any signal beneath all these trees."

"Reception? For what?"

"The warp. It's the telepathic communication network that all dragons and lap-dragons can access. Convenience and portability, all in one small lap-dragon form," Palmer chirped, sounding like a merchant pitching a new product. He grinned. "Had to make sure my maps weren't out of date. Don't want to be leading us in the wrong direction, yannow?"

"And is everything up to date?" Lucca asked.

Palmer nodded as he hopped back up onto the pack. "Yup. Everything is just perfect." The lap-dragon looked up at Lucca. "Hey. Do you mind turning off your eyes? It's a little bit creepy."

"What? Oh." Lucca blinked a few times to clear his eyes of the lingering tears, wiping them with the back of his hand. The heat on his face, some of it magical, some of it emotional, began to fade. His eyes returned to their usual pale amber.

"That's better," the dragon said brightly. "What was with all the glowing anyway? Do they help you see better in the darkness?"

Lucca smiled weakly. "Let's go with that, sure." He had no interest in explaining the true reason for his emotional distress, the memories of how his parents had put him on a ship to sail away to distant lands without them. Some things were better left alone.

Palmer shrugged his wings. "Right then. Shall we keep going? Still have some way to go."

Lucca looked down at the dragon warily. "You're not going to run off on me again, are you?" he asked, not wanting a repeat of the fear and loneliness that had almost overwhelmed him.

"I'll warn you next time," the lap-dragon said toothily.

"Thanks," Lucca muttered, not at all inspired by Palmer's assurances. Nevertheless, he shouldered his precious satchel and set off after the lap-dragon again. He just wanted to get to Emberfade as quickly as possible. There was still a niggling feeling of unease that Palmer's return had not been able to dispel. The forest had eyes that he could not see.

Holding his arms close, Lucca walked with his back slightly hunched. The casual, and at times inane, banter between him and the lap-dragon had ceased entirely. Palmer looked every bit as uneasy as the lion felt, but neither mentioned anything about it.. Lucca pulled his furs a little closer to his body in an attempt to keep warm. Palmer seemed unaffected by the chill.

As he walked, Lucca's mind began to wander. He imagined various scenarios about what would happen when the notorious relic thief finally caught up to them – assuming the thief was able to track them down this narrow trail, apparently unknown even by bandits. Should the relic thief catch him by surprise, Lucca knew he had precious little to defend himself with. The number of offensive spells he knew didn't even grace the plurals. Defensive and illusion magic was better than nothing, at least.

Though he had never met nor seen the relic thief before, the imagined image of him Lucca held was that of a light-furred otter with a devilishly handsome and mischievous smile. There was great life in his eyes. He was carefree and relaxed, but Lucca knew this fictitious version of the thief also possessed a serious side. He needed one to be the successful bandit he was.

Lucca's heart fluttered. He was nervous, he reasoned.

At the cusp of Lucca's hearing was a dull roaring noise. Initially he was unsure what it was, and he regarded it with a little fear. He really did not want something else to worry about.

The close trees masked the sound a little, for Lucca suddenly found himself standing in daylight, and virtually on the precipice of a sheer rock wall. About twenty feet below him was the Wolden River, pouring noisily over its rocky bed. The river was fairly narrow, but still wider than two leaps, let alone one.

"Mind yourself, felian Silven. Bandits like this area, and they don't take kindly to intruders," Palmer warned.

"I thought you said they didn't know about this path," Lucca accused.

"They don't, not up here. Down there," the lap-dragon said. He jumped off from the pack and pointed down towards the river. "There's a narrow path along the banks, and there are plenty of caves in the cliffs. Oh, and they're usually good archers, so you might want to step back."

The Lutrean River Rats weren't unheard of by Lucca and the Esfyr's Wold Chapterhouse. By and large, the two factions left each other alone. The River Rats chose easier targets than the chapterhouse, and the mages let the bandits operate so long as the thieves never targeted the guild. Sometimes, the guild moved in to stop some of the more disreputable acts to curry favour with the locals, but otherwise they had little to do with each other. Unlike the relic thief, the River Rats would not hesitate to kill for goods. He hoped they were not the bandits Palmer spoke of, as they were an entirely different class of criminal to the noble rogue. They came from his nightmares, not the dreams of adventure the relic thief dwelt within.

He had half a mind to turn tail and march right back to Master Roe, gilded yearbook and all. Only the thought of facing the battlemages halfway down the narrow trail kept him where he was.

Even so, Lucca did as the lap-dragon recommended and stood away from the cliff edge. He retreated to the tree line to look upon the panorama before him. As far as he could see to his right and left, the trees came right up to the edge of the ravine, at times to within a couple of feet of the sheer cliff. Beyond the river, there were no trees. Open grasslands were punctuated by low hedgerows every now and then, but there was little else to break the seemingly endless meadows. There was barely a hill to be seen.

Another thing distinctly lacking in Lucca's field of vision was a bridge.

"How do we cross, Palmer? Emberfade is on the other side of the river and I can't see any way to cross," Lucca said, exasperated. He did not much fancy having to walk all the way back down the narrow trail to the main road, just because the lap-dragon had forgotten there was no way to cross the river here.

"You're a mage, aren't you? A little hocus-pocus and you're right on the other side."

"Are you suggesting I portal? I wouldn't even know where to begin," Lucca admitted. That was an advanced technique that no second-level initiate could hope to understand. He hadn't even looked at the theory of it yet.

Palmer clicked his tongue irritably. "You will have to find a way across with magic, or you climb down and swim. There isn't any other way you can go."

Lucca shuddered at the mere thought of swimming. At this time of year, the river would be almost down to freezing temperature, fed as it was from the icy mountains to the distant north. There was nothing that would make him voluntarily enter that river, but he knew enough about lap-dragons to understand the concerns. They did not lie. Could not lie. Palmer had been quite clear. His options were to turn back or to find a way to cross the ravine.

The lion briefly pondered a levitation spell, but he quickly discounted it. Allowing a simple pack to defy gravity's pull was one thing. He had learned in the past that picking himself up with a levitation spell was about as easy as picking himself up physically by his own ankles. Levitating the pack with him resting on it, Palmer-style, was out of the question. His additional weight would be too much for the simple spell to support.

Lucca rubbed his muzzle. "Palmer, you might want to fly across with the pack. That would make it easier for me."

"That's not going to happen, felian Silven." The lap-dragon looked down at the ground and shuffled his paws awkwardly. "I can't fly."

"You... can't?"

"No, I don't have the necessary capabilities to do so."

"You don't have what? You have wings, don't you?"

Palmer flapped his wings, kicking up a small whirlwind of leaves and dirt. "Yeah, but they're really just an aesthetic feature."

"Aesthetic?"

"Yeah, yannow. For looks."

"I know what it means," Lucca snapped in exasperation. He ran his hands through his trimmed mane. "Let me just get this straight. You brought me down this path with no way across the ravine, and the nearest path with a bridge is the main road?"

"Yeah, that sounds about right," Palmer said brightly.

"Then how is this a short-cut?"

Palmer shrugged. "Not as many steps."

Lucca slapped his hands against his hips a few times as he looked out over the ravine. It was too far to jump, but there was no point in turning back now. He would waste too much time, and the battlemages would likely already be on the narrow path, ruining the chance to ambush the relic thief. Climbing down and swimming was out of the question. The water would be too cold, and the River Rats would almost certainly capture him.

The lion's eyes drifted down to the ground beneath his paws. Amongst the clumps of springy grass were a few rocks with unusually smooth surfaces. Lucca stood on the nearest one. With his paw right in the middle of the stone, there were a few inches of spare space either side. All the rocks looked to be about the same size.

"What's this? A rock balancing contest?" Palmer squealed in delight as he watched the lion balance on one leg. The lap-dragon clapped his hands together. "I'm really good at that."

"What? No. I just needed to know how big they were," the lion explained. He hopped off the rock and crouched down to dig his fingers beneath it. The stone lifted off the ground easily enough, though he did let off quite an ignoble sound as a woodlouse crawled across his fingers.

Palmer beeped and giggled. "Why do you need to know that, felian Silven?"

The lion tossed the stone up into the air and snapped his fingers. At his command, the stone stopped its inevitable plummet back to the ground and merely hung in the air. Lucca grinned. "Stepping stones."

Lucca jumped onto the floating stone. His arms spread wide as he tried to balance on one paw, but it didn't matter too much as the stone suddenly recalled its affinity with gravity. It fell back to the ground, and Lucca followed right after it.

"Was it meant to do that?" Palmer chirped.

"It was not."

"Because it probably should have stayed in the air."

"It should have done, but it's difficult holding myself up with my own magic. Like lifting yourself up by grabbing your own britches and belt." Lucca sat up and rubbed his hands through his fur. He'd gotten grass everywhere, and it would take ages to groom himself and his Winterpaw leathers clean again.

"But I don't wear any britches, felian Silven!"

Lucca chewed on his lip. He could see no other way to cross the ravine. No bridge in sight, and he would lose too much time doubling back or finding another way to cross. "Are you sure there's no other way around?"

"None that you should take," Palmer said, nodding sagely. "And there are bandits coming."

"What?" Lucca yelped. He jumped to his paws as though burned.

Palmer's eyes flicked to the ravine. His horns flashed red. "Yah. Lots of bandits. Coming right here. I don't think they would make very good friends."

"*Ka'heirbek!*"

Lucca grimaced, trying to work out what could be done. But he didn't know how to get away if he didn't know where the bandits came from. "You're able to scan using the warp aren't you? Can you check to see when they might get here?"

"Doot! That feature request is password protected," the lap-dragon chirped.

Lucca groaned and slapped his hand to his muzzle. "Of course it is. Can you at least tell me where they're coming from?"

Palmer chewed on his lip, then turned to point towards the forest behind them, down the narrow pathway the lap-dragon had assured the lion the bandits knew nothing of. "North! And on this side of the river. If they pick up your scent, they will find the path. You should cross the river, felian Silven."

Lucca felt himself go cold, despite his warm leathers. He snapped his fingers to summon his pack. "Get on," he commanded the small lap-dragon.

Palmer didn't need any further encouragement. He jumped up onto the floating pack. "Whee!" He dug his heels into the side of the pack, encouraging it to gallop ahead. Completely disobeying the wishes of its rider, the pack just languidly drifted across the ravine. Palmer's enthusiasm was not dulled.

The lion had to focus on the pack as it moved out over the ravine. It wanted to sink down to the distant river and keep hovering just a few inches above the water, but Lucca didn't let it. Having an excited lap-dragon bouncing around didn't make things easier.

With one hand extended, Lucca was able to deposit the pack – lap-dragon passenger and all – on the far side of the ravine. He severed the magic to the pack, and it fell to the ground with an audible thump. There was no sound of the bandits, but Lucca didn't want to delay.

The lion quickly dug up two more stones that looked wide enough for his paw, and smooth enough that he wouldn't hurt himself landing on them. He took a deep breath and prepared himself for the stupid thing he was about to do.

One at a time, Lucca tossed the stones out over the ravine. With a snap of his fingers, the three came to rest hovering at the level of the cliffs either side, far above the distant river surface. One close to him. One in the middle. One close to Palmer and the pack of supplies. They were his stepping stones. He would have about a second on each before he would have to jump to the next. Adrenaline pumped through his body. Anticipation already brought a sheen of sweat to the lion's brow.

"Here goes nothing," the lion muttered to himself. He braced his paw behind him, then sprinted for the ravine. He launched himself into the air, trusting that his magic would hold.

Right paw down. Jump!

Left paw down. Jump!

Right paw down. Jump!

The rocks wobbled and plunged down behind him. Lucca's legs wheeled in mid-air as he dove for the ravine cliff on the far side of the river. His chest crashed against the rock, and his hands scrabbled to find anything to grab hold of. He felt himself slipping, until his toeclaws were able to dig into a gap in the rock.

"You did it!" Palmer called out, still perched on top of the motionless pack of luggage.

"Not yet," Lucca gasped. He had been able to stop his slide down the cliff for now, but his hands still couldn't find anything to grab hold of to pull himself up. He lifted two fingers, and the pack burst open. The lap-dragon squawked as he was thrown clear. Another quick gesture from the lion's fingers and two lengths of rope spooled out from his luggage and wrapped tight around his wrists.

Using the weight of the pack as an anchor, Lucca hauled himself up the cliff. His paws struggled for grip, but the pack didn't move at all, even as all of his weight pulled on it. Slowly he made it up, and he collapsed down onto the grass with the ropes still wrapped tight around his wrists.

"Do you need any help, felian Silven?" Palmer chirped, prodding at one of the ropes.

Lucca shook his wrists, trying to dislodge the ropes, but they clung tightly to his arms. "Stop that," he growled.

The lion's claws unsheathed. The ropes hastily loosened at the threat. They wound back up into tight bundles and retreated back into the luggage, which snapped shut with a definitive click. The lion glared up at the small lap-dragon as he staggered up to his paws. "We'd better keep moving though before those bandits find us."

"What bandits?"

"The bandits you said were coming," the lion said uncertainly, waving his hand in the general direction of the ravine.

Palmer flashed a smile as bright as his eyes. "No bandits here."

Lucca frowned and rested his hands on his hips. "Are there any bandits here, or did you make the whole thing up?"

The lap-dragon nodded. "Of course. Big bandit stronghold. They're here every summer."

"And it's the middle of winter," Lucca said tersely.

"Exactly. Nothing to worry about," Palmer replied.

Lucca steepled his hands on either side of his muzzle. He breathed in deep several times, his breath escaping with a soft hiss each time. He closed his eyes as bile twisted in his gut, the adrenaline of his jump across the ravine still pumping through his blood. There had never been any danger but the one he had put himself into by using shoddy magic to cross the gorge. The danger Palmer had put him into.

Unable to trust himself to open his mouth, Lucca stomped away from the lap-dragon in a huff, crimson flame twisting between his fingers. Heat welled in his eyes, both from the anger that pumped through his blood and the shame of letting his imagination run wild, fuelled by the lap-dragon's deception. He didn't look back as he stalked away from the ravine, which had been free from bandits for at least two months. He didn't stop until he heard a whistle from Palmer.

"Felian Silven, you might want to help your luggage."

The lion turned back as he remembered he had removed the animation charm from his pack. With a snap of his fingers, his luggage jerked to life again. It rose off the ground with the lap-dragon quickly back in place upon his noble steed.

With a growl, Lucca waited for the luggage and lap-dragon to catch back up, taking the time to let the flames of his fury fade from his arms. "How much further is it from here until the main road?"

The lap-dragon pondered the question for a few moments. "Before nightfall. Good place to camp just before the main road."

"Camp? Oh goody. I can use my collapsible lodgings," Lucca said bitterly.

"You mean a tent?"

"Yes, I mean a... never mind. In-joke with myself," Lucca muttered sullenly to himself. It wasn't as enjoyable to make fun of Kyde if the otter wasn't there, or when his companions didn't know what he was talking about. He was sure the luggage would be laughing if it could. Or if it were alive.

There were not many hours of daylight left, with the afternoon fast waning. Lucca hoped that was enough time to reach the night's planned campsite. He looked forward to being back on the main road again, if only for the thought that Palmer wouldn't be able to fabricate any more danger for him to imagine.

Chapter Five

The air was getting colder, plummeting from 'chilly' to 'bloody freezing.' The sun had bid farewell to shine on greener, warmer pastures. A small glow in the clouds told Lucca that the sun was still, allegedly, there. The lion wasn't inclined to believe it. No matter how tight he pulled his thick, Winterpaw fur cloak to his body, the cold always found a way to get in. The wind was a monster with many gnashing teeth and claws that were determined to dig into his flesh.

Palmer and the luggage didn't seem to be affected by the cold at all. The lap-dragon still chirped incessantly, though he didn't try to talk to the lion at all. The luggage just drifted along as it always did, floating a few inches above the gently undulating ground.

"Is it much further?" Lucca called out eventually. The wind and cold whipped around him, and the lion couldn't help but think about his nice warm bed and a roaring fire. He longed for a hot chocolate. Or anything hot, for that matter. Instead, he just had his tent and a dragon who couldn't fly or breathe fire. A useless exchange.

"Soon, soon," the lap-dragon trilled out. "You're making very good progress, felian Silven."

"Feels like we're going around in circles," the lion grumbled. "I'm sure I saw that rock an hour ago."

"Nah, no circles here," Palmer replied. He looked back to the trudging lion, who had fallen behind even the slow hover of the luggage. "Nothing but straight lines, all the way through to your destination."

"This had better not be like the ravine," Lucca growled. He glanced back. There were only empty moors behind him. The same ahead and all around. He felt like he was miles from the closest village. Some short-cut the lap-dragon had led him on.

"No, not at all," Palmer trilled. The diminutive creature stood up on the baggage, balancing expertly on the uneven surface. "We are almost there."

Lucca exhaled softly. His paws were hurting and his legs protested every step. He wanted to rest, and he especially didn't want to think about how much further there was left to go before he reached Emberfade. He didn't know how much time Palmer's short-cut was meant to save. More than anything, the lion wanted to sit and rest, but he couldn't see anywhere that offered any shelter.

The narrow path Lucca followed cut directly across Esfyr's Wold with little protection from the elements. Nothing but endless rolling hills with the occasional copse of trees to provide meagre protection from the wind. At least it wasn't raining.

Thunder growled from the west.

"Well isn't that just peachy." Lucca gave the western horizon and its dark clouds a two-fingered salute. It made him feel better for a moment. The sky responded with a louder peal of deafening thunder. The lion held both hands up, beseeching whatever sky god he had angered that his act of defiance had merely been in jest.

"Not too far now," Palmer called back. The oncoming weather gave a little more urgency to Lucca's weary legs, and he hurried to catch up with the lap-dragon.

"But there's nothing here," Lucca protested. There was no shelter anywhere to be seen, but the little dragon just grinned his toothy grin.

"Nothing here, no. But we are not there yet, are we?"

"But there's nothing anywhere else, either," Lucca said, sweeping his arm around for emphasis. "There's a tree over there. It might have a leaf on it. Is that our shelter for the night?"

"Always complaining, felian Silven. Don't worry, there is a good place to shelter just five minutes away," the lap-dragon chirped back. He stood up on the pack, his paws sinking partially into the fabric.

Lucca resorted to grumbling beneath his breath, but he didn't complain any further. He had to trust the lap-dragon, despite the evidence that his eyes were providing. There was nothing but hills and hedges to break up the stark emptiness of the wold. There were no villages in sight, nor any places where caves would be likely. The only life Lucca saw was the occasional bird swooping overhead, and a dozen sheep grazing on the open grassland.

Despite his deception at the river, Palmer was still a necessary guide. Lucca had to trust that the lap-dragon knew of somewhere safe to camp ahead, even if those seeds of doubt had laid roots. At this stage, he didn't have any other choice. He wouldn't find any shelter by himself.

The winding path meandered between a few low hills. It was little more than a dirt track in the grass, beaten out by paws following the same route. It filled the lion with a little concern. For all of Palmer's assurances that the path was never used, the trail appeared to be well worn.

Still there appeared to be nowhere to rest. Lucca was starting to prepare himself for a night in the cold, exposed wold, before the ground suddenly opened up just before his paws. Hidden behind a row of bushes largely shorn of their leaves for winter was a deep ravine that snaked across the wold. It was as wide as the ravine he had crossed earlier, but this time there was no river flowing at the bottom. There was also a path that gently wound down the cliffs.

Lucca stopped and blinked in surprise as Palmer started to descend. "Huh."

"See, felian Silven? Palmer doesn't lie," the lap-dragon called out. "No caves, but shelter for your collapsible lodgings."

"You can just call it a tent."

"Doot. Collapsible lodgings."

Lucca rubbed a hand over his face. "Wish I'd never even brought that up."

Palmer just grinned from atop his noble steed of baggage.

The path gradually wound down the side of the cliffs, until it joined up with a second trail that followed the snaking course of the ravine. "Is this the main road?" Lucca asked, momentarily distracted by the presence of the other path. It seemed like a more traditional road, with a small wooden marker visible further down the ravine, though too far away for Lucca to read what it said.

Palmer shook his head. "Nah. Not the main road. That's a little further on. No good places to camp on the main road though." The lap-dragon kicked his feels into the side of the baggage. Lucca was surprised when it actually came to a halt. "Here we are though. A nice space for your collapsible lodgings."

Lucca blinked and looked around. There seemed to be nothing there but the road. It was not what he would call sheltered, despite the cliff walls either side of him. "Here? Really?" he asked, spinning slowly on the spot. When he faced towards the lap-dragon again, he was startled to find Palmer had vanished, and he had absconded with the luggage too. "Palmer?"

Fearful that the lap-dragon had disappeared again, Lucca spun around on the spot once more. He still couldn't see any sign of the lap-dragon, but there was nowhere for Palmer to have gone.

"In here, felian Silven." The voice seemed to come through the rocks.

"Where?"

The lap-dragon's head poked out from within the rock. He grinned toothily as Lucca warily approached.

The lion blinked a few times as he tried to rationalise what he saw. Then he tilted his head and saw the tell-tale shimmer of a broken illusion around the lap-dragon's neck. He took a couple of steps forward and reached out with his hand, pressing his fingers against what appeared as solid rock. The air crackled with magic. The lion closed his eyes and expelled his will into the illusion, which quickly gave way and crumbled around him to reveal a narrow passage through the cliff. Beyond that was a small hollow; a cave with a partially enclosed roof but still sheltered from the wind by the sheer walls that encircled it. From this side of the illusion, the way to the road was open and clear, with no cliffs to block the view.

The lap-dragon had been right. It was the perfect place to set up camp. It was so good that there was obvious evidence of others using it recently.

At the far side of the hollow, a wide cave a few paces deep sunk into the cliff wall. A few crates were stored inside, sheltered further from the weather by the cave and the loose canvas sheet draped over them. Metal pegs hammered into the ground secured the straps holding the canvas into place.

Lucca reached out with one hand to touch the nearest crate, but Palmer chirped loudly. "Please don't touch."

Lucca's hand snapped back to his side as though it had been burned. "Who camps here?" the lion asked nervously. Already he feared opening his eyes in the middle of the night to see a bandit holding a sword to his throat for trespassing.

Palmer shrugged his shoulders as he jumped down from the floating pack. Showing none of the reserve he had warned Lucca of, he pulled aside the canvas sheet and began to rummage through a couple of the crates. "My master usually," he said, his voice muffled slightly by the wooden crates. He poked his head back out for a moment, teeth showing in a wide grin. "He set up the illusion with that thing down there so only he and I can see it."

Lucca scratched behind his ear as he glanced down, following the point of the lap-dragon's tail. He had missed it earlier, but there was a small golden disc on the ground in the very centre of the hollow. He extended his hand towards it, feeling the magic tickling at his fur. An illusory disc. They were meant to be rare and powerful artefacts. Whoever resided in these caves knew their relics and was confident enough in the illusion to leave it unattended.

What if the caves weren't unattended? He lifted his head and sniffed at the air. A myriad of scents filled his nose. It was difficult to make out anything distinct, especially with a strong odour coming from some of the crates. If anyone else was present, then they stayed quiet and masked their scent well.

A twinge of unease tickled down Lucca's spine. There were few thieves who would use a relic to cast such a powerful illusion. The lion furrowed his brow. Master Roe had intended him as the bait. He feared the trap may have been sprung and he was unprepared.

He turned his attention back to the lap-dragon. "Who is your master, Palmer?"

The lap-dragon chirped. "Can't tell you that, felian Silven." He quickly disappeared amongst the stacked crates. Lucca peered curiously around, but he could only see the lap-dragon's tail wiggling as he tried to reach for something buried at the back of the stack.

The answer did nothing to ease Lucca's worries. He turned away as the back of his neck prickled, but there was no one else in the hollow. They were completely alone, and yet the feeling of being watched did not recede. There was nowhere to hide in the small hollow, though. And no one watched from the top of the cliffs either.

If this was a trap set by the relic thief, then the rogue had set it well.

Hoping to convince his tired mind that he was merely being paranoid, Lucca slumped to his haunches, summoning his baggage with an outstretched hand. He pulled out one of the boxed meals Kyde had prepared for him and held it in his hands for a few moments.

Lucca stared down at his food. A full day of walking should have built up his appetite, even for the endless fish and nuts, but the sudden sense of unease had quelled it. Ever since he had met Palmer, there had been a sensation of wrongness eating away deep inside him, but he had rarely allowed that to the surface. The companionship of the lap-dragon had been enough to overlook that unease. The lion stared at the wiggling tail of the little blue lap-dragon as he came out from behind the crates.

"Who is your master, Palmer?" Lucca asked. He put his lunchbox down and gently nudged his luggage away with a paw.

The lap-dragon chirped. "Can't tell you that, felian Silven."

Another question squirmed its way out of Lucca's lips. "Can I trust you?"

"You have been so far." The lap-dragon grinned a little wider. All of his needle-like teeth were on display.

"Should I be trusting you?"

"Depends who you ask." A new voice spoke that was full of contradictions. Deep yet light. Suave yet rough. Palmer squeaked and clapped his hands together.

Lucca's eyes widened as he stared around the empty hollow. It wasn't the lap-dragon who had spoken, but he could see no one else. "Who's there?" the lion barked out.

The air shimmered a few feet in front of Lucca. Reality seemed to split for a moment, and a ferret stepped out from the void. There was a tuft of dyed blue fur on his head, and most of his sleek white-furred body was covered in hiking leathers. A few patches of his summer coat still lingered around his exposed biceps. His blue eyes sparkled with flecks of golden light. A shimmering silver cloak was draped over one wrist. Lucca recognised it immediately.

"That's the Mystic Shroud of the Unseen Walker," he gasped, stammering slightly. He stared at the ferret that had emerged in front of him. "It's been missing for years. Everyone assumed Guildmaster Decard just forgot where he put it."

"That what it's called?" the ferret replied. He cocked his ears and grinned. "Just call it my invisibility cloak. Less wordy, don'tcha think?"

The cogs of Lucca's mind slowly turned. His eyes flicked between Palmer and the ferret. "Why do you have it? You're... are you...?"

The ferret reached out to cup a hand beneath Lucca's chin. "I have it 'cos I stole it. And that, my handsome friend, should tell you exactly who I am."

Lucca's mouth hung open, before he snapped it closed again. He swallowed nervously. "You're the relic thief."

"Russet, if you would be so kind," the ferret said, sweeping down into a deep bow before the lion. "And you must be the great Silven. Or would you prefer Lucca?"

Lucca licked his lips, his tongue feeling as dry as the deserts of Da'Manyr. "W-who's Lucca?"

Palmer squeaked and clapped his hands. "Oh, I can answer that one! Felian Silven is really called felian Lucca!"

Fear overwhelmed anger and shame. Tears sprung to the lion's eyes as he realised how easily he'd been manipulated. He could barely breathe as the ferret leaned in close.

The relic thief leaned down to whisper in the sitting lion's ear. "I believe you have something for me."

Lucca shook his head and held a hand over his satchel. Then he realised he was being too obvious. He lowered his hand again. Now that he was here with the relic thief, he wasn't so certain of Master Roe's plan. If the love charm had worked, it didn't seem likely to stop the ferret from getting what he wanted. "No. Nothing."

"Oh really?" Russet said. His long whiskers brushed against Lucca's. His breath smelled like mint. His hands rested on Lucca's shoulders. "What about if I ask really, really, *really*, nicely?"

Lucca let out a noise that wasn't quite a whimper or a squeak. Instead it ended up being something partway between the two. He knew what he had to do. He had to distract and delay the ferret for long enough that the battlemages could apprehend the relic thief. It felt like an impossible task already.

Then the ferret kissed him, and all his resistance crumbled away into nothing. He felt lost in the bright, gold-flecked eyes as their muzzles locked together. Hands stroked gently down his arms, teasing the lion's fur through his Winterpaw leathers. Fingers swirled around his elbow for a moment, before sliding away again.

Russet pulled away. In his hands was the precious registry.

"Give that back, please," Lucca said quietly.

The ferret smirked as he carefully opened the gilded book. His blue eyes widened as he saw what he held. "Oh, this is beautiful," Russet crooned. He flicked through some of the pages and winked to Lucca. "The book as well. Quite stunning. Rare, too. I ain't seen anything quite like this before."

"It's just a yearbook," Lucca mumbled.

Russet paused halfway through turning the pages of the registry. A smile slowly spread across his muzzle and a light, musical laugh broke from his lips. "A yearbook? I like that," he giggled. He snapped the book closed and held it up, though keeping it out of Lucca's reach. "An *almighty* yearbook. A truly great gift indeed."

Lucca swallowed. He felt like he was losing grip on the situation as quickly as he had lost grip on the almighty yearbook. His voice trembled. "I can't let you leave with it."

The ferret raised his brow. "Leave?"

"I was entrusted to courier the registry. I won't let you just walk away with it."

"Wasn't planning on leaving, Sweetie. I ain't even gotten to know you yet," the ferret replied. With the book tucked under one arm, he stepped closer to the lion again and cupped his hand against Lucca's cheek. The ferret's voice dropped down to a whisper as he leaned in close. "And I think there's a lot to learn about a felian like yourself."

Lucca stammered and blushed his way through an attempted response, but he was unable to properly force the words out. Everything would have been so much easier if the ferret wasn't so damned hot. It took a lot of effort to remind himself that Russet was only showing so much interest in him because of the love spell Master Roe had cast. The relic thief was charmed. None of it was real. It was all just an act, and he had a role to play.

Russet's hand stroked against Lucca's cheek for a few more seconds, before the ferret spun around on his toes. He clicked his fingers towards the small lap-dragon. "Run a scan of the area to make sure no one followed you."

"Doot doot. No one nearby within one mile," the lap-dragon quickly chirped. He tensed his hands and gave a little growl. "There is a raven in the trees that laughed at me though."

"Is it magical?"

Palmer shook his head. "No, Master Russet. No magical presence detected for at least one mile." The lap-dragon grinned at the lion. "Except for felian Lucca of course."

"Very good. Thank you, Palmer," Russet said. He patted the lap-dragon on the head, who squeaked in delight from the touch.

"I… I thought you needed a password to do a warp scan," Lucca spluttered.

Palmer squeaked. "Oh! Master Russet is an authorised user who doesn't need one."

Russet grinned. "We ain't been through everything for me to still use passwords." He passed the registry to Palmer, who scurried away amongst the crates with his precious cargo.

"So…" Lucca said uncertainly, keeping his eyes on Palmer as long as possible. "You're not going to be running away with the book?" Perhaps there was a chance Master Roe's plan could still work after all.

Russet shook his head and took a single step back. "No. There's much more interesting things waiting for me right here," the ferret said with a smirk. He gestured down to the bare ground between them. "Why don't you set up a fire, and I can arrange some dinner for us."

Lucca noticed the ferret never once mentioned that he wasn't allowed to leave. The lion knew he was able to leave whenever he wanted. He also knew that the moment he did so, he would have failed his mission. The relic thief would vanish with the registry in an instant, slipping through their fingers once more, and Master Roe would need to find a new way to ensnare the cunning ferret. His only hope of succeeding was to stall and distract Russet for long enough that the battlemages would catch up and capture the ferret. He could still feel the rough shape of the tracking stone in his satchel, so the ferret hadn't discovered that when snatching the registry.

The lion blinked out of his musings to see that the ferret was digging through some of the crates to pull out some food. Russet was bent over, tail raised up. Even through the leather clothes, Lucca could see that the ferret had quite a shapely rear. It was a nice one to admire, and the lion quickly found himself distracted by an empty mind, rather than one full of racing thoughts.

"Have you forgotten the spell, felian Lucca?" Palmer called out. The lap-dragon was perched on top of the closest crate. His legs were swinging as he beamed down at the lion. "I can look some up for you if you like. Roaring conflagration. Towering inferno. Forest fire. Oooh, fireball. The old classic. How about that immolation spell you used before?"

Lucca shook his head and forced himself to look away from the alluring ferret. It wasn't fair. Such a wonderful specimen of a male presenting himself in front of him, and the lion knew that he couldn't act on his desires, no matter how insistent Russet was. The ferret was charmed into being attracted to Lucca. It would be immoral to take advantage of that.

"What did I do to deserve this, old man?" Lucca muttered beneath his breath. He expected a very big favour from Master Roe if he was able to carry out the badger's devious scheme.

Desperate for a distraction from his physical temptations and thoughts of morality, Lucca quickly scanned the cave to see what material he had to play with. As much as Russet had assured him that he could start a fire because he was a mage, Lucca knew it was anything but that simple. Sparing a furtive glance towards the ferret to make sure he wasn't paying attention, the lion whistled softly to summon his pack.

He rummaged through the many pockets until he found the small box of firelighters stowed deep inside. Sparing one last wistful glance towards the ferret, the lion turned his back on his enamoured captor to hide his actions. Thankfully, there was enough kindling scattered around the cave to create a ruse he hoped would be enough to fool the relic thief.

After gathering together enough kindling, Lucca surreptitiously prepared the lighter and, after saying a few words that sounded like an incantation, he stoked the flames to life.

Sensing movement behind him, Lucca quickly stood upright and turned around, slipping the firelighter into his pocket. Russet stared at him, a cocked grin on his muzzle.

"Ain't never realised how useful a fire mage like you is," the ferret said. He caressed a hand down Lucca's arm. "I'm almost done with food. Be a dear and sit down and look pretty for me. Shouldn't be too hard for you."

Lucca snapped his jaw closed before he managed to say anything. His ears heated up far more than the small fire accounted for.

As the ferret turned back to preparing their meal, Lucca managed to step around the small fire and slump against one of the crates. This time, he wasn't berated or warned by Palmer, though the lap-dragon did slowly sidle across to him.

"I don't think I know that spell, felian Lucca," the lap-dragon whispered.

Lucca cleared my throat. Now his eyes burned, and he found himself unable to look towards the diminutive creature. He wiped at his eyes with the back of his hand, feigning smoke blowing into his face. "Oh, uh. It's one of my own making."

Palmer clapped his hands together. "You make your own spells? Wow!"

The lion put his head in his hands and tried not to groan. Already he felt like he had lost complete control of the situation. Lies and truths twisted within his gut. Desire swelled, both enticing and mortifying him.

Snatching on any opportunity to distract himself from the internal war, Lucca peeked through his fingers and wondered what food the ferret was going to provide. He imagined a rogue such as the relic thief would be used to fine dining, and even out on the road he would have access to some lavish meals. Then again, anything would feel like fine dining in comparison to the tinned fish and various fruits and nuts Kyde had provided for him.

Russet turned around with a couple of plates in his hands. On the plates was a pile of chopped fish and a serving of various fruits. Lucca struggled not to turn up his nose. Typical musteliads.

The relic thief stayed silent as he started to eat. There were no utensils, but the ferret didn't seem perturbed and just ate with his hands, scooping up the fish and fruits directly to his mouth. His eyes never left Lucca's face, and a half-smirk remained on his muzzle even as he chewed his food.

Lucca followed suit with his eating style, but he resolutely kept his eyes staring into the fire. The attention from the ferret felt awkward, especially as he knew it was merely a charmed attraction. The sky outside was beginning to darken, but thankfully the storm that had been threatening did not appear to be heading in their direction. They were sheltered from the worst of the cold winds too. With the fire, the temperature was almost pleasant, though Lucca didn't remove any of his thick furs.

The silence got ever more awkward as they ate. It felt like an unwanted guest sitting around the fire with them, but Lucca didn't dare speak up against it. To break the silence seemed like it would be ruder than letting it continue. All the same, the lion felt almost suffocated by its oppressive weight as it sat down between the lion and ferret. A blush burned the lion's cheeks, one he hoped his fur would be able to conceal.

Then Palmer let out a loud squeak of excitement to shatter the silence. He clapped his hands together. "This is fun!"

Russet grinned up at the lap-dragon, before he turned his attention back to the lion. "You are a quiet one, ain't you?"

Lucca quickly stuffed a few slices of apple into his mouth to give him the opportunity not to answer right away. He didn't know what to say. He couldn't admit what was truly on his mind. None of it sat right with him. He was even more uncomfortable about it all now than he had been when Master Roe had first mentioned the idea.

"Been kidnapped, haven't I?" the lion mumbled quietly, finally bringing himself to speak.

"Kidnapped?" the ferret replied, holding one hand to his chest. "You ain't been kidnapped. No one is keeping you here but yourself, though I do hope you stay."

"If I want to keep the yearbook though..."

"Well of course I ain't gonna let you take that." The ferret grinned widely. "Won't be much of a thief if I let you take that, would I?"

"I'm not leaving without it."

Russet smirked. The tip of his tongue stuck out from between his lips. "Then I guess you'll be staying here with me, won't you?" His tail swished and curled up over his lap. The ferret's hands slowly stroked over the soft fur. "Not kidnapped though. You can leave any time you like."

Lucca's eyes briefly flicked towards the small gap in the rock, leading back out to the road. He then sighed softly. Even if he had somewhere else to rest for the night, he wouldn't take the opportunity to leave. He owed it to Master Roe to try and keep Russet in one place for as long as possible.

"Do you treat all your victims like this?" Lucca asked. His voice quavered a little, and he found himself unable to properly look the grinning ferret in the eye.

"Victims? Tchh, you make it sound so cruel," Russet said with a shake of his head. The smirk didn't leave his muzzle. "I ain't some common thug. I have standards, you know."

Lucca stared down at the couple of slices of apple in his hand. He slowly placed one piece into his mouth and crunched down on the fruit. "Your standards are... giving your victims... targets. Giving your targets dinner?"

Russet shrugged his shoulders. He leaned back and teased between his sharp teeth with a toothpick. "Only the cute ones," he said nonchalantly. He winked towards the lion.

The lion almost choked on the slice of apple. He should have known such a comment was coming, but he still felt flustered at the thought. Few musteliads had ever complimented him in such a way. Usually he was too exotic for local tastes. The kind words only came from the charm, Lucca had to remind himself. He needed to temper his expectations, but there was still a role to play.

"You really think I'm cute?" the lion asked. The breathlessness in his voice came easily, a legacy from the shy and uncertain cub he had once been. And yet, despite all his confidence now, his heart still thudded in his chest as he felt a blush tinge his cheeks. Lion he may be, but the bumbling teenager blustering before his crush was closer to the surface than he realised.

Russet licked his lips. His gold-flecked eyes shone brightly in the flickering firelight. He held a hand over his chest. "I can honestly say I ain't ever met anyone as beautiful as you, my dear. Truly, you are a wonder to behold. The finest jewel of Da'Manyr."

Lucca held his mouth open. No one had spoken to him like that in a long time. His ears burned with the growing blush that heated his face. This dashing rogue was every bit what he had imagined in his dreams. The lion's head bowed slightly. Just a shame that the ferret was a fabrication of the love charm, just as much as the relic thief of Lucca's dreams was not real.

"Cat got your tongue?" Russet asked.

"Doot!" Palmer chirped, sitting cross-legged on his vantage point atop the pile of crates. "I can still see his tongue. He's still got it. Though felian Lucca is a cat, and he has his tongue..." The lap-dragon went cross-eyed.

"I'm just... No one has said something so kind to me for years," Lucca said. To his horror he found his vision blurring slightly as tears came to his eyes. He coughed a few times, pretending to choke on his apple to give himself an excuse for his watery eyes.

Not since the Winterpaw hunter, haltingly and through broken sentences and mime, had anyone been so eager to compliment him and his looks. Not since then had Lucca felt like a blushing fool, undeserving of the attentions bestowed upon him. Act had so quickly become truth. He no longer knew what was expected of him. He barely even knew what he wanted.

Lucca was surprised to feel a finger against his chin. The ferret had crossed the gap between them, looking up at Lucca right in the eyes. He was so close that Lucca could feel his minty breath on his face. Close enough that, if Lucca wanted, he could pull the ferret into another kiss. He could take advantage of the love spell right there; he could provide a long-lasting distraction that would allow the battlemages to catch up.

The lion turned his head away.

"Did I say something wrong?" Russet asked. He remained crouched by Lucca's side, though he did drop his hand down. His brow was cocked in confusion.

Lucca took in a deep breath to regain control of his emotions. He forced a smile back onto his muzzle. "No, you're fine. Just a bit of apple tried to go down the wrong way," he said weakly. He wasn't sure if the ferret would believe him at all.

Palmer chirped brightly. "Apple should only go down one way, felian Lucca. Otherwise it's going up!"

"Noted," Lucca replied. He shared a quick smile with Russet. A genuine one this time.

"May I?" Russet asked. The ferret's hand moved up towards Lucca's shortened mane. The lion nodded and leaned in, letting Russet gently stroke through his artificially green fur. "I like how this looks. Suits you."

"Yours too," Lucca replied. His eyes glanced up to see the small fringe of blue fur hanging down over Russet's eyes.

Russet flashed a quick smile. His ears flicked up and back, and his tail flicked back and forth a few times. "Thanks," he said quietly. "Just something I've always done."

Once again, Lucca was struck by the temptation to pull the ferret in close. It would be so easy. This was what Master Roe had chosen him to do. No one would think any less of him. No one but himself. Lucca would not be able to forgive himself for taking advantage of the charmed ferret in such a way, no matter how much his heart craved the attention and compliments the relic thief gave him.

The ferret leaned in, his lips brushing through the fur on Lucca's cheek. "Perhaps we should get to know each other a little more... physically," he whispered. He lightly kissed the lion.

Lucca tensed so that he didn't give in right away. He trembled. "I shouldn't."

Russet leaned back. Confusion and disappointment briefly flicked across his eyes, before he hid it behind a little smirk. "No? Why not?" the ferret asked, though there was a little uncertainty in that voice that hadn't been present moments earlier. Less surety. "I'm attracted to you, and I know you're attracted to me. What's stopping us from enjoying the night?"

The lion looked into Russet's gold-flecked eyes. He almost melted again and gave in, but he tensed his jaw. He tried to re-engage his usual mask of confidence he wore around the academy. He didn't know why it was so difficult to get it back in place. "I don't... not on a first date."

Russet's brow rose. "First date? I'm a thief, felian. Likes of me don't hang around for second dates."

Lucca managed to smirk. "Trust me, I'm worth it."

Russet laughed loudly. His eyes brightened as a wide smile spread across his muzzle. "Oh really?" The ferret leaned back in to lightly kiss Lucca on the cheek again, but he made no more physical advances. "Well then. Perhaps I can be convinced to stay for a second date."

Lucca's ears flicked up. His heart hammered in his chest. Perhaps this plan could still work. "You ever been with a felian before?"

Russet settled back and rested with his hands behind his head, looking out to the darkening sky. "I have not," he said, his voice almost distant as he gazed towards the darkness beyond the entrance of the hollow.

Lucca's attention followed the ferret's. The stars had been blocked out by the thickening clouds. An occasional flash of lightning lit up the sky, but otherwise the only light around came from the small campfire. Rain was in the air.

"I have heard good things though," Russet continued, still looking upwards. "But sadly there aren't too many of your kind out here."

Lucca shook his head and lay on his back beside the ferret. "My kind don't much like the weather," he said, gesturing with one hand towards the gathering clouds.

"Not keen on getting a little wet?" the ferret asked with a wink.

Lucca felt the blush returning to his cheeks. "Well, yes. I mean, no. Uh..." he spluttered, before choosing to just keep his mouth shut.

Russet grinned. "How about we get somewhere away from the rain?" he asked, before raising his voice to address the lap-dragon, still perched above them on the stack of crates, underneath the shelter of the cave roof. "Palmer, what do we have?"

"He's got some collapsible lodgings," Palmer replied immediately, swinging his legs back and forth as he gazed down at the ferret and lion.

Lucca groaned and placed his hand over his eyes. "It's a tent."

"Collapsible lodgings? That's some mighty fancy talk for a tent. Is that what the fine folk in the guild are calling them these days?" Russet asked. The tip of his tongue stuck out between his lips.

"No, that's what Kyde called it," Lucca said, rubbing his hand over his face. "She's one of the usual couriers."

"This Kyde person has a way with words then." Russet giggled. "Did she teach you any more tricks of the tongue?"

"I... What? No!" Lucca protested, almost rolling away from the ferret as he realised what the relic thief was insinuating. He could feel the blush burning up his cheeks again.

"No?" Russet asked with another wink. "Well don't worry, felian. No dirty tricks from me tonight. On my honour."

Lucca flicked his ears. "Thought thieves only had honour amongst other thieves."

"Know much about the thieves' code, do you?" The ferret tilted his head to the side. His eyes sparkled.

"Just heard a few stories. Mostly about you," Lucca admitted. He kept one wary eye on the sky, not wanting to be caught out in the rain again. He barely felt like he had fully dried off from the previous day.

"About me? Well, I think you have to tell me some of those," Russet said. The ferret rose to his paws; his chest swelled out. He posed with his hands on his hips. "Do I match up to my reputation?"

"You're cuter than the stories said," Lucca admitted. A moment passed by before Lucca realised just what he said. His ears curled back as they burned with embarrassed heat.

Russet chuckled. He relaxed his pose. "Glad to hear my good looks are appreciated." He brushed his hand through his headfur and smirked. "But why don't you make a start on your collapsible lodgings? I'd hate to have a wet cat on my hands."

"Tent," Lucca muttered to himself, but he knew it was futile to protest. He turned away from the teasing ferret and lap-dragon and crawled towards his baggage. He rummaged through until he was able to find the tent, then quickly pulled it out.

As Kyde had promised, putting up the tent wasn't much of a challenge. Finding space for it inside the cave, amongst the piles of crates, proved to be the tougher ask.

The canvas sheets and poles were easy to assemble and connect to each other, and he didn't even need to ask the ferret for assistance. Amongst his supplies was even a small mallet, which he used to hammer down the support pegs. He doubted the wind would get intense in the sheltered hollow, but it was one more distraction from the relic thief.

The tent was quite roomy considering how small it folded down. There was room for two people on separate bedrolls, plus the remaining baggage, without feeling overly cramped. The lion felt quite proud of his work, and he stepped back to admire the little tent. The entry flap was pinned open, overlooking the fire. He was just in time, too. A light mist had started to descend, with the smell of further rain tickling at Lucca's nose.

While he had been busy with the tent, Russet and Palmer had cleared away the mess left from dinner. They had further secured the crates furthest from the back of the cave with a second canvas sheet to protect their contents from any overnight downpours.

Lucca sat down on his bedroll. He stared at Russet for a few seconds. Somehow, it seemed like his ruse had worked. The ferret wasn't looking to flee into the night. Instead, they would share a tent together and wait until the battlemages came to apprehend the ferret. Lucca's tail thumped nervously against the bedroll. He would hate to see that, but he knew what had to be done.

All those compliments had felt nice, but Lucca knew he had to forget them. They weren't real, anyway. Just the result of a charmed mind.

Lucca managed to get the smile back on his face as Russet ducked into the tent. The ferret carried his own bedroll, which he quickly flattened out to lie next to Lucca's.

"I promise you nothing dirty tonight, as much as I'd want to," the ferret said. He reached out to touch Lucca on the shoulder. "But it ain't every night I get the chance to lie with a felian like you. The night's a cold one, and I ain't got a blanket."

Lucca lifted his brow. "The mighty relic thief, who has a solution for every problem he has ever faced, doesn't have something as simple as a blanket to keep warm at night?"

Russet put a finger to the felian's lips. "Shush. I'm trying to be romantic. Ain't my fault I'm a little rusty in the art."

The lion hesitated. His eyes flicked down to the ferret as he pondered his options. He hadn't slept in close proximity to anyone since his time on the Winterpaw excursion. Though the temptation would be to go further than just lying with his arms wrapped around the ferret, Lucca was sure that he would be able to resist his urges. It would also give him the opportunity to keep hold of the relic thief, to make sure he didn't slink away in the night.

Lucca held out his arms, and the ferret quickly slunk into place. Lucca's arms wrapped around the shorter musteliad, holding him close and sharing the warmth between their bodies. Both remained fully clothed, which Lucca was thankful for. Though his leathers could get a little uncomfortable, they would help minimise the temptation to break his morals.

Outside the tent, rain had begun to fall with increased intensity. Palmer had not joined them inside the tent, but Russet showed no concern for the lap-dragon's well-being.

Russet's hand lightly brushed around Lucca's wrist, where the Winterpaw runes had been stitched into the cuffs of his clothes. "Health? No, vitality... This one is kinship... I ain't seen this one."

Lucca tugged his hand away, moving it down to rest against the ferret's belly. He had never revealed the translation of the third rune, ever since he had found it in one of Master Roe's translation tomes.

"You read Winterpaw?" the lion said, hoping to distract the relic thief.

The ferret shrugged. "Some of the basic runes, that's all." He smirked. "But come on. I know you wanna say it."

Lucca cleared his throat. His ears heated, and he gripped his arm tighter around the ferret's body. "Uh, it doesn't really have a direct translation. But it's sort of like potency. Virility. Sexual competence, that sort of thing."

Russet whistled. The ferret lightly swatted a hand at Lucca's chest. "Naughty lion! Quite the impression you left up there."

"It was a long time ago," the lion said with a sigh.

"Perhaps if I'm lucky I can learn what prompted these runes," Russet said. He arched his neck to grin up at the lion, tongue sticking out slightly from his lips.

Lucca's hands slowly stroked over the ferret's chest and belly, unsure how to answer. His chin rested against the top of Russet's head, even with the ferret's paws not quite reaching his ankles. It would be so easy to give into his temptations, the ferret was certainly encouraging enough. His mind told him to resist. His heart wasn't quite sure on the matter. A little lower demanded that he give in. The lion closed his eyes and took a deep breath, but that only filled his nose with the slightly earthy scent of the ferret.

Suppressing a shudder, Lucca forced himself to relax. He had to keep things natural until morning and resist the urges of his body. Come daylight, the battlemages would catch up and all would be over. The ferret would be taken into custody, and Lucca would return back to his studies.

An errant thought passed through the forefront of Lucca's mind. He tried to ignore it, but the thought kept coming back.

If only...

Chapter Six

The funny thing about dreams was how they always seemed to linger and feel real for the first few seconds after waking up. Fantasy and reality meld for those precious few moments, and the waking dreamer can experience the delights of the imagination for a little longer before the cold harshness of reality sets back in. Lucca had a smile on his muzzle and he wrapped himself a little tighter in his blankets. His bed didn't quite feel as comfortable as it normally did, but the sheer joy of his dream meant that he couldn't worry about that.

With his eyes still closed, Lucca stretched his arms out. His hands brushed against canvas. That wasn't quite right.

Lucca sat bolt upright and opened his eyes. Memories slowly trickled back to him as he looked around the unfamiliar tent in surprise. This wasn't his dormitory, and he was out somewhere in the middle of Esfyr's Wold, with an important task to do. There was someone he had in his arms; someone who was not there anymore. He was alone.

"*Ka'heirbek!*"

Lucca fumbled around the tent as he tried to kick his blankets off. He was still clothed in his Winterpaw leathers, though they had become dishevelled in the night. For once he didn't bother about setting them correctly. He just needed to get outside so he could start tracking down the relic thief.

The lion burst out into the early-morning sunlight. He blinked in surprise when he saw the ferret crouched over the remains of the magical fire. The ferret had dressed in his breeches, though he remained bare-chested.

"Morning," Russet said brightly, a smile coming to his muzzle as he turned to face the lion. He held up a metal kettle that had been placed above the lingering fire, which sloshed around. "Tea?"

Lucca nodded dumbly as he sat down beside the smouldering embers. There was no sign of the lap-dragon. "I thought you'd left."

"After what you promised last night? Not a chance, Sweetie," the ferret said. He stuck out his tongue. "I ain't usually the kind of guy to stick around. Kiss and run is more my style, but you feel special."

"So... what happens now?" Lucca asked. His chest tightened slightly. If he was able to hold the ferret here for a few hours, then that would give the battlemages a chance to catch up and ambush the relic thief. The lion bowed his head and tried to hide his concern by straightening his cuffs.

Russet grinned widely. "Anything you like, my dear. I ain't got any pressing needs that can't be delayed. The day is ours to do what we will. We can have our second date."

"We can just stay here?" Lucca asked in surprise. Maybe things would be easier than he had expected.

Russet nodded. He rose up to his paws and padded across the clearing. Lucca's eyes followed the ferret all the way, but Russet just went to get a couple of cups and bags of tea leaves. "We can stay here as long as you like, my handsome felian. A mage like you probably isn't used to walking so far, and my Palmer did push you hard."

"Well I suppose my paws are hurting a bit," Lucca admitted. He stretched out his legs and leaned back, splaying his toes out in front of the lingering fire. "A rest would be nice."

"Then a rest you shall have," Russet said. The ferret grinned at the lion as he settled back down to brew their tea.

Lucca closed his eyes and tilted his head back. He wondered how long it would take for the battlemages to catch up. He almost didn't want it to happen, though he knew how silly such thoughts were. The romantic, dashing nature of the ferret was down to a magic spell and nothing more. There was no attraction there. Nothing real, at least. The lion let out a weary sigh.

"Something on your mind?"

Lucca flicked his ear up. He opened one eye to look across at the ferret, who held a pair of steaming cups in his hands. The lion gratefully took the offered cup. Though it was sheltered in the hollow, the air was still cool. It was nice to have something to warm his hands.

"Always something on my mind," Lucca replied, knowing the ferret would want an answer, and the truth wouldn't be tactful. Even a love spell wouldn't protect the lion should the truth slip from his lips.

"Must be hard, being so far from home," Russet said. His paw idly brushed against Lucca's leg.

The lion knew Russet didn't mean Esfyr's Wold. He sighed again and bowed his head, though internally he was glad of the lead Russet had given him. "I left Da'Manyr eleven years ago. I still miss them, but I wouldn't fit in there. Don't really fit in here either, but at least I can learn magic."

"Miss your family?"

Lucca nodded. "Always. But they knew this was best for me."

Russet's smile flickered. Sorrow entered his eyes. "Me too." His hand wandered. Slowly. Hesitantly. Until it found Lucca's. He squeezed tight.

Lucca froze. His eyes flicked down to the hand grasping his own. He struggled to resist the tremble that threatened to twitch down his arm. Also the urge to pull the ferret closer and kiss him.

The ferret took a deep breath, then smiled brightly again. "The past ain't what we should focus on. We have each other. And you must be hungry, am I right? I've been such a rude host. Not even offering you some breakfast. Why don't I whip out my finest wares for you?"

Lucca longed for the ferret's loving offer to be real, but he knew that Russet would want nothing to do with him should the charm be removed. None of this was genuine, as much as he desired it. Still, he had a part to play.

The smile came to the lion's lips with a struggle as he agreed to some breakfast, hoping that for once it wouldn't be fish on offer. He stayed sitting as he watched the ferret rummage through the crates for some breakfast supplies. The ferret refused to accept some help, politely telling Lucca to remain sitting down. He occasionally sipped at his steaming tea, but he preferred using the hot cup as a means to keep himself warm.

The 'finest wares' Russet had for breakfast turned out to be smoked salmon. While Lucca was initially disappointed to see yet more fish, it was sided with some bread that felt almost freshly baked, thick strips of ham, and slices of pungent cheese. Lucca had a cautious nibble of the cheese when Russet held some out for him. The flavour was rich and strong, and Lucca found himself liking it.

Lucca's hunger overcame his discomfort. He gladly devoured the offered breakfast, finding it to be a much less awkward affair than their dinner the previous night. Russet still didn't say much, just watching the lion with a constant smirk on his muzzle. The lion found himself blushing from the attention. He was able to put the battlemages out of mind again, allowing himself to just enjoy the moment. There would come a time soon when it would all start crashing down, but that was a problem for future-Lucca to worry about.

By the time breakfast was finished, there was a small noise from outside the hollow. Lucca was immediately on his guard, but Russet seemed completely unperturbed. The lion breathed a sigh of relief when he saw the familiar blue scales of Palmer.

"Any news?" Russet asked the lap-dragon, before Lucca had a chance to greet Palmer.

The lap-dragon nodded vigorously. "Yah! All went according to plan," he said brightly, bouncing on his toes in excitement. "They're already most of the way to Emberfade. They've checked in with Esfyr's Wold through the warp every evening like you thought. They don't suspect anything yet."

Lucca's ears perked up. "Emberfade?" A cold prickle of unease trickled down his back. "Who is almost there?"

Russet's smile remained as warm as ever. He approached the lion and gently took the cup from Lucca's trembling fingers. "Just the battlemages following behind you."

Lucca felt cold. He tried to force a laugh. "The what?"

The ferret leaned in to lightly kiss his cheek. "Don't worry, I understand. I know they used you. I know how they tried to ensnare me. I expected the guild to try something so desperate."

Lucca felt light-headed. He was glad he was already sitting down. "You knew?"

"Oh, Sweetie. You don't do what I do without suspecting everything and everyone. I knew you were bait. That's why I took you off the road before I made my move." He rummaged into a pocket and pulled out a few slivers of bark, which he tossed to the ground in front of Lucca. The bark had Lucca's magical signposts on them. "Was a smart idea to leave breadcrumbs for your mages, but you made one mistake. They were only on the bark. It was easy cutting them off and they've been following a false trail since then."

Lucca frantically ripped open his satchel and pulled out what he had thought was the tracking gem, but in its place was a simple stone wrapped in a copper wire. He took in a few deep breaths.

"Yeah, we got that too. Another thief owed me a favour, so he scampered down the road with the real thing. So many good ideas, but none we ain't seen before." The ferret grinned. He sat on Lucca's lap, perched on the lion's legs so he could lean in close. "Bit too trusting of Palmer, but otherwise a flawless display."

Lucca took another couple of deep breaths. This time he managed to open his mouth as well, but still no words came out.

"They chose their bait well, I'll give the guild credit there." The ferret kissed Lucca's cheek again. "I would have fallen for a cute face like yours even without a love spell."

"You knew about the spell?" Lucca asked. His voice was hoarse.

"I can still feel that unnatural desire, pulling at me," Russet said. His hands played with Lucca's clothes. "I crave you with every fibre of my heart. But there's one thing you didn't consider."

Lucca swallowed. "What's that?"

Russet stroked a hand over Lucca's cheek, before sorrowfully slipping off from the lion's lap. He stood up and held out his hand to pull Lucca up to his paws. "I'm a thief, felian. Love is a… complication. It makes people irrational. I ain't survived this long by falling in love."

"So… what happens now?" Lucca asked. His throat was dry. He wished there was still more tea in his cup, but he had already drained it. He swayed unsteadily on his paws like he was drunk. The ferret's grip on him was strong, keeping him upright.

The ferret traced a teasing finger over Lucca's chest. "Right now, I still need you. Keeping you close makes me… happy. I know it's just a spell, but my heart wants you by my side." He tapped another finger against the side of his head. "My mind compromised with my heart. I keep you around while I find a way to reverse it."

Lucca flicked his ear. "So I am kidnapped now?"

Russet blinked and jumped back a couple of paces. His eyes were wide. "No, not at all. If you ain't wanting to stay, then you may go," he said quickly. He held his hands up. "I ain't gonna force you to stay. I'll be miserable without you, but if you'll be miserable with me, then I ain't gonna tie you up or anything."

"He has some rope," Palmer chirped brightly.

"I don't think that will be necessary," Russet said with a smirk.

"What will you do?" Lucca asked sadly. His tail curled up, and he bowed his head. The guilt felt stronger than ever, now that he was aware Russet knew he was being deceived.

The ferret shrugged his shoulders. "Find someone who can reverse the charm."

Lucca narrowed his eyes as he stared down at the ground. "I think I know someone who can help. I don't think they're too far away."

Russet raised a brow. "Can I trust you, Sweetie? I'm madly in love with you because of this spell, but I ain't blinded by that love. I'll still know if you're trying to trick me."

Lucca shrugged his shoulders. "It's up to you if you trust me," he said slowly. He sighed and turned away from the ferret. "It wasn't my idea to do the love spell. I didn't like it. If I can help you remove it, then I feel like I owe you that."

"You owe me nothing, felian," Russet said simply. He didn't try to pull Lucca back. "The guild won't like you helping me."

Lucca grinned wryly to himself. He looked up to the grey clouds that hung low above the cliffs. "I'm not going to get the yearbook back. They don't have to know I helped you."

Russet was silent for a few moments. "Alright. Tell me about this person then."

The lion turned around to look towards the ferret. Russet's head was bowed, and he had clutched the tip of his tail in both hands. For a couple of seconds, he looked weak and vulnerable.

"I... one of my old teachers lives somewhere near here. Mistress Juri is her name. She lives in Melry's Reach," the lion explained. He flicked his tail nervously. He felt like eyes were watching him, though only Palmer and Russet were with him. Could the battlemages still hear him? If they could, they might think he was betraying the guild. Lucca doubted that. Any connection to the battlemages was likely severed when he lost the tracker.

Besides, this wasn't really betraying the guild, was it? Lucca bit his lip nervously. He was just correcting a wrong that had been done to the relic thief. The love charm had not worked. This wasn't going to change anything there. He might even be able to convince any rescuers that he stayed with the relic thief in case any impossible opportunity arose where he might steal back the precious book.

Russet clicked his fingers. "You still with me, cutie?"

"Sorry, was lost in my thoughts," Lucca said quietly. He scuffed his paws against the ground and looked up to the ferret. "What did you say?"

"I asked if we can trust this teacher."

Lucca frowned. "No more or no less than anyone else who can remove the charm. Unless you want to go to Master Roe, who created the spell."

Russet giggled softly and shook his head. "No, thank you. I ain't that stupid." He clapped his hands together and called out to Palmer. "Fetch the horses please, Palmer. Don't forget to give the fake name this time, not the real one."

"Doot! Right on it, Master Russet!"

The lap-dragon sped from the small hollow to do his master's bidding. The ferret himself remained behind and started to tidy up the crates. He glanced back to Lucca. "You might want to pack away your tent. It's good quality stuff. Would hate to leave it behind."

Lucca nodded. He got to work at packing everything down and returning it to his baggage. His head was in a daze. He had thought he had been about to betray the ferret, but now he found himself and Master Roe thoroughly outsmarted. The plan had come crashing down hard, and Lucca wasn't sure what he was meant to do next. He felt ashamed for his part in it, for bewitching the ferret and for acting on a love that wasn't real. Russet would be within his rights to hate him once the spell was lifted.

It wasn't long before Palmer returned. Not only did he return with a pair of horses, but there was a large wagon tethered up behind the two animals. They didn't fit into the hollow, but Palmer had the horses back the wagon up so it was as close to the cliffs as possible. Horses were one of the few pack animals used in Lutrea. They didn't have access to some of the more exotic creatures in places like Da'Manyr. Lucca doubted zebras or hogs would appreciate the cooler climate of the peninsula.

Lucca wandered towards the wagon. There wasn't enough room to squeeze through the narrow gap towards the road. Even still, he kept a wary eye on the horses. He knew they possessed quite a kick if angered.

"Where did you even get these from?" the lion mused. Neither of the horses looked damp. They hadn't been out in the rain.

Palmer giggled. "There is a traveller's lodge about a five-minute walk away." The lap-dragon paused and inspected Lucca, eyes wandering up and down the lion's body. "Maybe four minutes with your long legs."

Lucca flicked his ear back. "A traveller's lodge? Why didn't we stay there for the night? Wouldn't that have been more comfortable?"

Russet stumbled by, carrying one of the crates, which must have been lighter than it appeared, as the ferret didn't struggle much. He dropped it down on the back of the wagon. The axle creaked. As Palmer got to work on dragging the crate to the far end of the wagon, Russet turned and grinned. "More comfortable, perhaps. But ain't as romantic. Now, if you don't mind just looking pretty for a bit, I need to get this done with Palmer."

Though Lucca offered to help, Russet refused any assistance. One by one, he transferred his crates of presumably stolen goods to the wagon. Though the ferret didn't struggle with the weight of any of them, they made the wagon creak and lower on its heavy wheels. The last thing added was Lucca's baggage, before the back doors were closed and latched shut.

The bare rock walls of the small cave still dripped from the overnight rain, now exposed without the stolen goods to fill it.

Even the tarpaulin sheets were neatly folded and bundled into the back of the wagon until nothing remained.

Russet's hand touched Lucca's back, then slipped down to grope around the base of the lion's tail. "So this Mistress Juri is in Melry's Reach?"

"Yeah. She retired from Esfyr's Wold Chapterhouse last year to live in the Reach," Lucca replied with a nod. He struggled not to react to the ferret's wandering hand.

Russet clicked his tongue. "As luck has it, that ain't too far from here. Can get there by nightfall, for sure. Palmer, shout ahead to Tallie and let her know we're stopping by."

Palmer sucked in a deep breath.

"Through RedClaw," Russet said quickly.

Palmer deflated like a balloon. The lap-dragon pouted and closed his eyes. His horns flashed bright red as he began to communicate silently through the warp.

Lucca shivered as a cool gust of wind whistled around the horses and the loaded wagon. He was about to travel with the relic thief, the very ferret he had set out to help capture. He had to remind himself that this ferret was dangerous, even if he was enamoured with the love charm.

"You ready? We're waiting on you, Sweetie."

"Will I be safe with you?" Lucca asked nervously, his worries breaking to the surface before he could contain them.

Russet's hand squeezed around his. The ferret leaned in for a kiss, standing on the tips of his toes to reach the lion's muzzle. "You won't be in any harm while I need you. I ain't got a clue about this magic stuff, so I need you to convince Juri to help me. She ain't got reason to help any ferret off the street, no matter how handsome." Russet winked as he released Lucca's hand. He jumped up onto the front of the wagon, but Lucca still didn't move.

"And then?"

"I slip away into the night and start my plans to steal the next target. I'm a thief. Love ain't my thing, Sweetie. A pretty face ain't gonna change that." The ferret smiled sadly as he extended his arm out to the lion.

Lucca nodded his head. He knew that was what had to happen. He just hated hearing those words. Not only would Russet take that spark of adventure with him, but his departure would also mean his mission failed. The thief was too crafty to let Lucca even see the yearbook again. He would not be given the chance to steal it back.

With one last glance around the clearing, Lucca accepted Russet's hand to clamber up onto the front of the wagon.

Chapter Seven

Melry's Reach was a large village skirting the edge of the Esfyr's Wold region. On one side of the village were the open moors that gave way to the forests that surrounded the Esfyr's Wold village and chapterhouse. On the other side were seemingly endless farmlands. The divide between the wold and the farms was an ancient stone wall that had once been the boundary between two warring nations.

Lucca had delved into the history lessons of that era with relish. Everything had been new information to him, having never learned anything about Lutrea during his limited schooling in Da'Manyr. His fellow students had been bored by the same lessons, but the young felian had found them fascinating. War was something any felian was well-versed in, while the Lutrean peninsula had seen almost total peace for nearly a dozen generations.

Lucca had never been to Melry's Reach before. It was many miles away from the main road, a fact that helped Lucca realise just how far he had been led astray by Palmer. The battlemages would never have a chance to find him, unless Lucca managed to send a message without Russet realising, and then managed to delay the relic thief for long enough. It felt like an impossible task.

The village was surrounded by a low stone wall that was almost as ancient and crumbled as the boundary wall that divided the wold. A wooden scaffold had been built up around some parts of the wall where repairs were being run, though there was no one working on the ancient stonework as Lucca and Russet approached.

Melry's Reach was larger than the Esfyr's Wold village, a short walk away from the chapterhouse. A stone castle overlooked the village from a nearby hill. Everything felt quaint and quiet as the wagon approached the village. It had taken the horses most of the day to pull the wagon along the rough roads from Russet's safehold, and the sun was starting to set by the time they were nearly amongst the buildings of Melry's Reach.

Russet's hand had been on Lucca's leg for most of the journey, but the ferret had remained fairly quiet. Palmer had chirped incessantly, and the lap-dragon had been particularly happy to point out different species of tree as they passed them.

Most of the trees were of the same species.

Palmer had been happy to point that out too.

"People might be on the lookout for you," Russet said suddenly. The wagon was approaching the protective wall that surrounded the village. The gatehouse was wide open, and there wasn't any garrison or guard by it. "Lions are distinctive enough, especially one with your hair. Any chance you can change that?"

Lucca shook his head. "Not without the right reagents."

Russet clicked his tongue. "Shame. Can't be helped. I have a spare hood you can borrow as yours doesn't have one."

"Do you think I need one," Lucca asked in alarm.

"Ain't wanting any rogue mages recognising your lovely self." Russet leaned back and looked up to Palmer, perched above them on the top of the wagon. "Fetch a spare hood, would you?"

"Doot! Right on it, Master Russet."

Palmer vanished into the back of a wagon for a few moments, before returning with a dark silk hood. The lap-dragon held it out for Lucca to take, and the lion quickly secured it in place to cover his distinctive green hair. The hood didn't match his leathers, but it felt like it was made of quality material. He wondered who the original owner had been.

"Looks good on you," Russet said warmly. He smiled and leaned into the lion, who put his arm around the ferret before he realised what he was doing.

Lucca warred with himself. He didn't want to get too comfortable with the ferret, for he knew things wouldn't last. They couldn't. As soon as Mistress Juri was able to reverse the charm Master Roe had placed on Russet, then the ferret would be out of his life. He would never see the relic thief again. By all logic, he should still be trying to capture the elusive thief, or at least make sure that he was recognised. Even so, he didn't move his hand. He didn't lower his hood.

The horses stopped outside a small inn, located right in the middle of the village. A sign out the front proclaimed it as The Royal Egg. It was on one side of an open plaza, which looked like it was sometimes used as a market square. Directly opposite was a stone temple. The clang of a blacksmith's hammer rang out through the square, but otherwise everything was fairly quiet.

An otter hurried out of the inn. She stopped next to the horses and took their reins from Russet. "Wasn't expecting you for a few more days," she said. She flicked her ears as she looked up at Lucca, but she didn't comment on his presence.

"Plans changed. No message for me?" Russet replied. The ferret slipped down from the wagon.

Lucca scrambled down after the ferret. He wasn't sure how close he should stand next to Russet, and he awkwardly lurked a couple of feet away from the thief.

"Nothing, no," the otter said simply.

Russet flashed a smile. "Perfect. Just how I like it." The ferret slapped the side of the wagon. "Let me get my stuff out, then if you could lead the wagon to the stables?"

"You staying the night?" the otter asked. She unhitched the back of the wagon and swung open the doors, almost catching Lucca as they clattered against the wooden sides. She didn't even look at the lion as she hauled herself up into the back of the wagon and began to sift through the crates.

"Aye, if that works," Russet replied. He hung towards the back of the wagon, watching the otter from the road.

Lucca warily lingered by Russet's side, keeping one eye on the otter to make sure she didn't get too close to his pack of supplies. She left it well alone.

The otter seemed satisfied with what she saw amongst the crates, though she never opened any of them up. She hopped down onto the road again. "I'll have my guys take it through to the stables. Anything you need to take out, do it now."

"Right on it, Tallie," Russet said. The ferret let go of Lucca's hand to jump up into the wagon. Of all the crates present, there wasn't much in there that the ferret seemed eager to take out. Lucca moved forward to drag his pack closer towards him, but the ferret's paw pushed aside his hand. "Let me deal with this. Palmer will make sure it's stowed safely for the night."

"I think I'd rather keep it with me," Lucca said, trying once more to grab his baggage.

Russet grabbed hold of his wrist, his grip firm. "Palmer has it," he said. A touch of steel came into his voice as he looked up to meet the lion's eyes.

"Al-alright," Lucca stammered, taking a step back from the wagon. His tail curled. He didn't like the idea of leaving his baggage behind, but he could tell from Russet's tone that he had no choice in this.

Palmer clambered up onto the back of the wagon. The lap-dragon poked around some of the crates, before he jumped up onto the baggage. He kicked his ankles into the sides, but without Lucca's magic, the pack remained still and dead. "Aww."

Russet looked up towards the otter. "Tallie, you mind taking Lucca here inside? Table for two? I owe him a date."

"Table for two, right you are," the otter replied without any hesitation, as though such a thing was completely expected. She held out a webbed hand for Lucca to take.

"Thanks, Tallie. You're a saint," Russet called out.

"Oh, I know," Tallie replied with a smirk. She winked to Lucca as she led the lion away from the wagon, Lucca wondering just how many dates Russet brought back to the Royal Egg.

The smell of smoke was the first thing Lucca noticed as they stepped through the door. A pair of fireplaces happily burned inside the Royal Egg, which spewed out a thin film of smoke that lingered towards the ceiling, across which several massive beams of wood provided support to the level above. A dozen tables were neatly arranged over the floor, with a large bar dominating one side of the room. Another otter was behind the bar, mixing some drinks for a pair of weasel customers with a swirl of her finger, never once touching the cups.

Tallie didn't lead Lucca to any of the tables. Instead, she led him past the bar, where a small corridor led away from the main room. Tantalising smells of cooking food came through from another door to the side. A quick glance as they walked past confirmed that the door led through to the kitchen, but sadly that was not where the otter led Lucca.

Instead, he was led through a low archway into a second, smaller room. The lights were dimmed, with only a single fireplace providing heat. Four booths were situated in the corners of the room, with each providing a semi-secluded space for four people to sit together. None were occupied.

Tallie pointed Lucca towards the booth in the far corner, closest to the flickering fireplace. "That is Russet's favourite table. Feel free to get comfortable. Menu is on the table, and the specials are listed up here," she said, pointing to the chalkboard that hung just above the arched doorway she still stood in. "Can I get you a drink while you wait for Russet to finish his business outside?"

"I'm fine, thank you," Lucca said nervously. He was aware that he didn't have much in the way of money on him. He had some emergency funds in his pack, just in case he was forced to take a room for the night, but that had been provided by Master Roe. Lucca didn't want to spend the old badger's scalls on something as frivolous as a drink.

"If you need me, give the bell a little ring." The otter bowed her head and retreated back up the corridor, leaving Lucca alone in the small room.

Lucca glanced down. In the middle of the table was a small copper bell. He lightly brushed his fingers over the metallic surface, but he didn't pick it up. He doubted he would need anything until Russet arrived.

The lion slumped down on the wooden bench beneath the table. He removed the outer layer of his leathers, finding it a little too warm inside to keep all his clothes on. He wrinkled his nose as he ran his hand through the fur lining. They had never been worn for so long without a wash before. The leathers beneath the fur were dirty and scratched. He looked forward to getting back to Esfyr's Wold, where he could give them a more thorough clean and restoration than he ever could while on the road.

If he were even allowed back to the chapterhouse.

The thought crept into the back of his mind before he had chance to ignore it. The lion shuddered and gripped his hand tightly around one of the forks on the table. He was helping Russet escape the bonds of the love spell. He wasn't doing everything he could to attract the attention of the duped battlemages. He was helping the thief he had been sent to capture.

No one in the guild had to know that. It could be his secret. He would have to come up with a plausible story as to how he came to be in Melry's Reach with the relic thief.

The lion sighed and thumped his head against the table. Those were problems he could think about later. He had other problems to deal with first. Like how he was going to convince Russet to avoid the urges of the love spell for a second night? Would he be able to resist the ferret's infectious, if charmed, flirting?

What had he gotten himself into?

Russet didn't make Lucca wait for long. About ten minutes after Lucca had first sat down, the ferret joined the lion. Palmer was not with him.

The ferret had changed his clothes in that time. He still wore hiking leathers, but these were a deep ochre in colour, rather than the black he had been wearing before. The colour suited his almost pure white fur. Small patches of coloured fur still stuck out beneath the sleeves where the ferret hadn't fully moulted for winter.

Lucca idly rubbed the golden fur on his arms, glad that he didn't have any of the seasonal variance many musteliads had to suffer through. Some of his fellow students, and even some of the teachers, complained vociferously at the turn of the seasons.

Russet looked around the table. He frowned. "Did Tallie not offer you any drinks?"

"Yeah, she did. I don't have the scalls to get much though," Lucca replied. He grimaced and curled his ears down, a little ashamed to admit such a thing.

Russet waved his hand. "You ain't paying for a thing. The meal and room are covered," the ferret explained. He pushed one of the menus across to Lucca. "A felian like you ain't gonna turn down some steak, are you?"

The lion's mouth watered at just the thought. "They do steak?"

"The best steak outside Cofferknell, I'm told," the ferret said with a grin. "A felian like you should deserve the best."

"That's just the love spell talking," Lucca mumbled, feeling the shame rising through his body. His tail flicked against the back of the chair as he stared down at the table. He gripped the fork tightly and tapped it against the wooden surface.

Russet took hold of Lucca's hand. He kissed it lightly. "Can I give you a little advice?"

The lion tilted his head to the left. "Of course."

Every one of Russet's teeth was visible as he grinned. "Forget about the love spell. It's only gonna get in the way of a good time."

"But I feel ba-"

Russet held his hand up, placing one finger against Lucca's lips. "Don't worry about it. Not now. Let's just have fun, alright?"

Lucca bit his lip. "I can try," he said, but he couldn't shake the unpleasant taste he had in his mouth. He still felt like he was taking advantage of the thief by using the love spell for his own pleasure. Capturing the relic thief with the love spell had felt uncomfortable enough. This seemed so much worse.

Before Lucca could think much more about the worries running through his mind, Russet reached out for the copper bell and rang it. The ferret smiled. "I know what I want already, and you ain't gonna resist that steak."

Lucca nodded dumbly. He hadn't enjoyed a proper steak since he had left Da'Manyr, all those years ago. Lutreans just didn't understand the right way to cook meat that didn't come from the sea. He wasn't sure if he was able to properly enjoy the thought of another underwhelming effort to replicate his favourite meal from childhood.

Tallie didn't take long to come into the private room. "What can I get you both?" she asked.

Lucca flicked his ears back. "Russet said something about steaks? Done rare?"

The otter nodded. She scrawled quickly on the notepad she carried. "Steak, sure thing. I can make it a special too."

"I'll take the omelette," Russet chirped brightly. "You know how I like it. Bring us a couple of my usual drinks too."

"I'll get right on it," Tallie said, finishing off her notes of the order.

"You're the best, Tallie," Russet said. The ferret leaned back in his seat, dragging his eyes away from Lucca for a moment.

The otter didn't reply. She just smiled and winked to Lucca as she turned around and retreated up the narrow corridor.

Lucca waited until he could no longer hear her pawsteps on the smooth stone floor. "You seem to know her well. Do you come here often?"

Russet leaned forward again. He rested his elbows on the table and cupped his chin in his hands. The corners of his mouth twitched up into a brief smile. His gold-flecked eyes stared right into the lion's. "I ain't a stranger to these parts. Tallie and I have an... arrangement."

"She's like a..." Lucca said, tapping his hand against the table as he struggled to find the right words. "Broker? Fence? Distributor?"

The ferret stuck the tip of his tongue out. His eyes sparkled. "It's a love spell, Lucca. Not a truth spell. I ain't gonna tell you anything that you can take back to your guild. She's an old friend."

Lucca snapped his mouth closed. His tail flicked across to rest on his lap. "Wasn't trying to do that," he muttered.

"No?" Russet asked, still with that smirk. His head tilted to the side. "Any mage would. Is the smart thing to do, after all. Blinded by love, I might admit anything."

Lucca tapped the base of the fork against the table. "I'm not a smart mage. I have bravado and bluster, but not smarts."

Russet scoffed and laughed. "Seriously, felian? That thing you did at the ravine was smart. The stepping stone thing was great thinking."

The lion paused. He held his hand up and frowned. "Were you there? Were you watching me?"

"Of course," Russet said, spreading his hands out wide. "I weren't going to let you harm my Palmer, was I?"

Lucca opened his mouth, but no sound came out. His ears curled down as the fork clattered against the table, falling away from his slackened fingers. "If you were following me, how did you cross the river?"

Russet shrugged his shoulders. "I used the bridge that was just around the corner."

"But Palmer said that wasn't any bridge," Lucca gasped, his eyes widening in shock. "He said there... that there wasn't any way to cross. He told me that. I didn't think lap-dragons could lie?"

Russet grinned and shook his head. "They can't lie, but they can bend the truth if they see fit. Palmer was a little creative in his way of getting you to cross."

Lucca stared down at his hands. "I should have known. You must think I'm so stupid."

"That don't make you stupid." Russet touched his hand to Lucca's chin, pulling the lion's gaze back up. "Your only sins were being naïve and a little too trusting. That ain't a bad thing, unless you're in my line of work."

A shadow of a smile tugged at Lucca's lips. "You really think that was clever? It's not just the spell talking?"

"Thought I said not to think about that," Russet said, taking hold of Lucca's hands in his own.

"I know, but... I don't know if I can believe what you say, with, you know..." the lion said. He grimaced and tried to pull his hands away, but Russet's grip tightened around his wrists.

Russet looked Lucca right in the eye. His mouth tightened. "It ain't the spell talking. Alright? Trust is a rare thing for me to see. It's nice seeing someone naïve. Don't get that much."

"Thieves don't trust each other?" Lucca asked, knowing not to mention the spell further. He tried to believe Russet, but a little voice nagged at the back of his mind. Nothing the ferret said could be taken truthfully.

"Only if there's something to gain from it," Russet said, his grin back in place.

"Then how can I know I can trust you? What can you gain from all of this?" Lucca asked, pulling his hand free from Russet's and gesturing to the table.

Russet smirked. "Told you that you've got smarts."

Lucca was fully aware that Russet hadn't answered the question at all, but he was distracted by the arrival of their food. The smell alerted him first. The scent of steak drifted down the corridor just before he heard Tallie's pawsteps.

The otter carried a large tray in both hands. Two plates and a pair of glasses filled with amber liquid were placed down on the table. Everything had been so quick to cook. Lucca briefly wondered if the inn had a mage in the kitchens to speed up the process, but he didn't ask the otter.

On Lucca's plate was a massive steak topped with various types of seafood that the lion didn't recognise, all covered in a rich sauce. Russet was given a large omelette with small chunks of fish and vegetables stirred through. The drinks were set down between the two plates.

"Enjoy your meal," Tallie said, inclining her head in Lucca's direction. She tucked the tray beneath her arm and retreated back from the private room.

Russet jabbed a fork at Lucca's steak, spearing one of the pieces of sauce-covered chunks of seafood. "Oh, Tallie does like you," the ferret said brightly. He held the fork out for Lucca to take the oceanic meat in his mouth. "Proper calamari is hard to find around the peninsula."

Lucca cautiously bit down on the offered seafood. Many years in Lutrea had given him a tolerance to the constant supply of seafood and fish, but nothing had ever tasted like the piece of calamari. The lion wasn't sure if it was the sauce or the seafood itself, but it was one of the best things he had ever eaten in Lutrea. It was surprisingly meaty, and a rich array of flavours burst across his tongue.

"That's so good," Lucca said in surprise after he'd swallowed the calamari. He stared down at his steak in wonder. If that had been how good the seafood was, then he couldn't wait to dig into the actual meat. He licked his lips in delight.

"Don't let me keep a lion from his food," Russet said. The ferret leaned back in his chair and turned his attention to his own meal.

Lucca eagerly dug into his food. Not only was it a rare treat to get a steak like he used to get in Da'Manyr, but it was also the first substantial meal after a few days on the road. The rations Kyde had provided had been reasonable for a smaller musteliad, but they had still left the felian feeling a little hungry. Now he had a plate that looked big enough to feed two and still have leftovers.

The felian was grateful for the opportunity to eat without distraction. He occasionally glanced up to Russet, but the ferret appeared to be focused on his meal as well. They made eye contact on a couple of occasions, but Russet didn't react except for a small smile.

The drink, which Lucca realised was an apple cider, was sweet, but not overpoweringly so. Lucca found that he rather liked it, especially when it gave him a slight buzzing sensation in his head. Initiates were rarely given the opportunity to drink alcoholic beverages, and when they were, it was usually just a dry, watered down wine. Cider provided a welcome change from that.

"Tell me about this Mistress Juri," Russet said, once he had set down his cutlery on his mostly empty plate. He cupped his glass of cider in his hands.

The two plates had been pushed into the middle of the table. Neither had quite been able to finish their food, but Lucca knew that he couldn't eat any more. It felt like a waste of the best steak he'd ever experienced in Lutrea, but the thought of another mouthful was almost nauseating.

Lucca closed his eyes for a moment. "Mistress Juri was my first teacher, back when I was a little cub," the felian explained. He drank down another mouthful of cider. "It's a school as well, you see, the chapterhouse. Students don't go there just for magic, but for numbers and writing and history. All sorts of things. It's only when you turn eighteen that you can become an initiate in the Mages' Guild."

"So she ain't a mage?" Russet asked.

"Oh no, she is," Lucca quickly said. He tapped his hand against the table. "She was very good with all kinds of charms. The other students didn't really appreciate it, because they saw it all the time. But for me, simple young Lucca from across the sea, I lapped it all up. I adored her, and she seemed to appreciate my wonder."

"Magic was new for you?"

Lucca nodded. "I'd heard about it. I knew I had this weird power inside me, but I didn't know what it was. I didn't know how to control it. I had to come here, though I never belonged."

"You ever think you made the wrong choice?"

"Never. My life would have been worse there. Mistress Juri helped me understand that. Later, Master Roe helped as well. He's not just my mentor and teacher. He's the closest I have to a friend there."

"Know many felians since coming here?"

Lucca sipped some more of his cider. "Nah. Saw a couple of tigers, once or twice. A leopard visited last year for a day. But never had the chance to actually speak to anyone. Certainly no felians who had recently been to Da'Manyr."

Russet's smile became slightly strained. "I only know one other. He's..." The ferret glanced sharply over Lucca's shoulder, then fell silent. "Nah, best not to say, sorry."

Lucca frowned. "Is everything alright?"

Russet's ears twitched. "So this Mistress Juri, what did she teach you?"

"She taught me about dragons," Lucca said slowly. Something had unsettled the ferret again, but he knew not to ask about it.

"Seen any of them?"

Lucca shook his head sadly. "No. Lap-dragons were always fairly common with visiting scholars and masters, though I only ever saw them from a distance, but never any true dragons. Mistress Juri was always good with the lap-dragons though. I think they were a bit of a passion project for her, and she often knew more about them than their owners did."

Russet perked up. His mouth was held partially open, brow furrowed in thought. "Did she now?" he pondered, but he didn't explain what path his thoughts had taken. When he looked up to Lucca again his eyes were bright. "I envy you, Lucca. Sounds like you learned a lot there."

"I suppose so. Didn't you get any of that?"

"Nah, not me. I came from the rough area of Nesterslip. Weren't much hope of me getting into a fancy school like yours," the ferret explained. He stretched his arms above his head and slipped down in his chair slightly. His paws nudged against Lucca's ankles beneath the table.

Lucca gently moved his paws, maintaining the contact with Russet. His eyes flicked down to stare at the table, a hollow sensation in his chest. "I've heard of that place," he said quietly. "Makes Da'Manyr feel like a paradise."

"It's a hell-hole. I hope you never had to go there," Russet said. He reached out for his glass of cider. A frown lingered on his brow. "I was lucky to get out, but it cost me more than I realised at the time. It was only a couple of years ago that I learned my letters and numbers. Still struggle with them, sometimes. I ain't smart that way, but I know how to survive."

"How did you get out?"

Russet stared down at his cider. He swirled the amber liquid around the glass. "I was... rescued."

Lucca didn't think that was the first word the ferret had been about to say. He knew better than to press further. Instead, he picked up his own glass of cider. The liquid had warmed since it had first come out from the kitchen. It didn't taste as good when it wasn't chilled.

The lion chanted a Winterpaw phrase and felt ice course through his blood. His fingers froze around the glass as ice began to permeate his cider, chilling it perfectly. He withdrew the magic before the liquid began to freeze.

"Uh, any chance you can do the same for me?" Russet asked, lifting his half-finished glass up.

Lucca repeated the spell, reaching out to send the magic through Russet's drink. He waited until he could see the frost creep up the inside of the glass before he stopped the stream of magic. The lion could still feel the chill of the spell circulating through his body, only slowly beginning to fade as his body warmed again.

"Should've known you'd know some Winterpaw magic," Russet said. His ears perked up as he tentatively sipped at his chilled cider.

"Yeah. About the only magic I've been able to be good at, other than illusion," Lucca admitted. He rubbed his fingers together to get some more warmth back into them, before picking up his glass. The cider had developed a slight crispness to it after being chilled again, and he eagerly gulped down a couple of mouthfuls.

"Not one of them fighty mages then," Russet said with a grin.

Lucca shook his head. "No. I'm never going to be a battle-mage, that's for sure, even if I wanted it," he said with a sigh. He leaned back and swirled his drink. "Illusion magic can be used to attack, but the Winterpaw ice magic is the only time I've been able to use a properly offensive spell."

Russet shrugged his shoulders. "Everyone's got their talents in different places," he said. He lifted his glass of cider to his muzzle, but he didn't drink anything. He paused completely and frowned. The glass lowered without a single sip being drunk. "I have a proposition for you, Lucca."

Lucca had not expected that. He gripped his glass in both hands. "Oh? What sort of proposition?"

"A job," Russet said. He sipped at his drink. "There's another mage in the village. Name of Erasmus. He ain't guild, as far as I can tell."

Lucca shook his head. "I've heard of him. He's definitely not guild. He's got a bit of a reputation for flaunting the rules the guild stands by."

"Like love charms?" Russet asked with a wink.

"Thought we weren't mentioning that," Lucca mumbled, quickly lowering his gaze. "Wasn't my idea anyway."

"I know, I'm just messing with you," Russet said with a grin. He drummed his fingers against the table. "Now, Erasmus has this artefact I really want, but his defences can only be opened by a mage. That's where you come in, my lovely felian friend."

Lucca swallowed, even though he had no cider in his mouth. "You want me to steal something for you?"

"With me, but yes. You've already promised to help me once. What's a second time?" the ferret asked. His paws lightly tapped against Lucca's ankles beneath the table.

"The guild will kick me out if they knew," Lucca said, a little fear starting to rise in his voice. His heart pounded inside his chest. The thought of an adventure with the roguish thief sounded wonderful in principle, but he knew what the risks would be.

Russet flicked an ear. "I ain't gonna get us caught. You do this for me, and I provide evidence that I forced you to help me. You had no choice. You go back to the guild sweet and innocent as always. No fear of being kicked out."

"And if I don't help you?" Lucca asked. His mouth felt dry, but he didn't take another drink.

Russet shrugged. "Then I leave you as soon as we've seen this Mistress Juri, and you go back to Esfyr's Wold to tell whatever story you want."

Lucca swallowed nervously. "What makes you think I'd be any good at it? I'll only be a liability."

The ferret shook his head. "Nah. Palmer weren't just leading out astray on the road. I wanted to test your skills too."

The lion lowered his eyes and clicked his tongue. He knew the risks involved. If he were caught, then he would never be allowed back into the chapterhouse. But if they pulled the heist off, then he would get a little taste of that adventure from Russet's stories. He might even get the chance to take back the yearbook while the thief was distracted by the mission. He already knew he wouldn't get any other opportunity.

The lion finished the last of his cider. "I'll do it."

Russet's eyes widened. His grin followed a few moments later. "You will? We should go and get some rest then. I want to start scouting and planning tomorrow."

"Do we need my tent?" Lucca asked, unsure if they needed to return to the wilderness to camp.

"Nah," Russet replied with a quick shake of his head. He drained his cider glass, before rising to his paws. "Tallie's got a room prepared for us. Perhaps you can give me a quick groom up there. My winter coat ain't come in fully yet, and the shedding is a chore to deal with."

"Uh huh, sure. I can do that," Lucca replied, sliding out from behind the table and rising up to his paws. His eyes flicked down to the last remnants of their meal, but his stomach protested the thought of even having another mouthful.

Lucca followed behind Russet. His paws stumbled. Thoughts continued to whirl towards the back of his head. He had agreed to a plan to commit crimes against a mage. A non-guild mage, but still a mage all the same. He was risking his future, and for what? A cute ferret he could never be with; a ferret he was exploiting through a love spell? The slimmest chance he could recover the yearbook?

Lucca could only hope that he was making the right decision.

Chapter Eight

To Lucca's surprise, nothing had happened between him and Russet the previous night. The ferret hadn't even attempted to appeal to Lucca's urges. Lucca had groomed the ferret, brushing through some of the lingering patches of summer fur, but the two had otherwise just enjoyed the quiet of each other's company, before falling asleep together on the bed. Lucca's arms had been wrapped around the ferret all night, and this time, Lucca had woken up with the ferret still there.

There had been time for breakfast and a shower each, but after that, Russet had been right to work. Lucca had been amazed by the change. The ferret was completely serious, discussing a few details with Palmer, but otherwise speaking through his plan to break into Erasmus's mansion on the outskirts of the village.

Russet planned everything to a meticulous detail and didn't move on until he was sure Lucca had fully understood what was being said. Palmer had drawn up a number of maps, which were all sprawled out across the floor of the rented room in the Royal Egg. Lucca sat on the edge of the double bed, his head swirling with all the information being given to him.

Only one thing was never mentioned. Lucca still had no idea what kind of artefact was to be stolen.

"Do you have all of that?" Russet asked, looking up at the lion from the middle of the maps. He had drawn on a few scribbled lines indicating possible points of entry or resistance.

Lucca wrinkled his muzzle. "I think so, yeah."

The ferret held up his hand. "No. No 'I think so.' You either know, or you don't. Erasmus ain't gonna be playing around. Nor can we."

Lucca hesitated. He bit down on the immediate response and furrowed his brow in thought. He mentally went through the plan Russet had detailed to him, making sure he understood each and every step. He slowly nodded. "I understand it."

The ferret cocked his brow. "Definitely?"

"Definitely," Lucca repeated, nodding again.

Russet clicked his tongue against the back of his teeth. "Now, I ain't sure exactly what nature all these defences are. Erasmus has all that information locked down tighter than Palmer can loosen, the cod-choker. But, what I have learned is that the final defence we must break is magical in nature. I suspect it is some form of illusion. If you say you ain't much good at that now, then we don't go in."

"I can do illusions," Lucca said, suppressing the immediate urge to shiver.

"Sure?"

Lucca kept his mouth shut. He nodded.

The ferret clapped his hands together. "Good. Now I hate leaving things to chance, but ain't no way around that with this job. I know what we're facing until that last barrier. Then it will be up to you to break the illusion."

"Got it."

Russet beamed, his smile spreading across his muzzle. He held out his hand for Lucca, using the lion as leverage to get back to his paws. "Perfect. Time for a quick lunch, then we start a rec run."

"Rec run?" Lucca asked, flicking his ears.

It was not Russet who answered, but Palmer. The lap-dragon squeaked in excitement. "Rec run. Recon. Reconnaissance. Scouting. Spying." Palmer bared his needle-like teeth. "Do you need any further definitions, felian Lucca?"

"I think that will be fine," Lucca said, waving his hand towards the lap-dragon. He understood what Russet had meant now, and the thought of it did make him nervous. He tried not to think too hard about what he was about to do with the ferret.

"Anything else you need to know?" Russet asked. He gathered together the papers that had spread out across the floor, stacking them in one pile on the desk.

"Did you want to see Mistress Juri before we start?" Lucca asked, watching the ferret's movements with interest.

Russet's eyes flicked towards Palmer for a moment. His ears twitched. "Nah. Not yet. We'll do that tomorrow, alright?"

"Should we delay it?" Lucca replied, confused that the ferret wouldn't want to see his old teacher right away.

Russet held his hand up, lightly pressing a finger against Lucca's mouth. "Tomorrow, alright?"

Lucca still didn't understand why Russet would want to delay, but he didn't continue to protest. He was almost looking forward to removing the love spell from the ferret, so he didn't continue to feel guilty every time those gold-flecked blue eyes gazed with adoration at him, every time the ferret complimented him over something small and trivial. They were all falsities created by the love charm and nothing more.

"Anything from Cofferknell?" Russet asked, glancing back down to the lap-dragon.

Palmer had been chasing a small moth around the room, scampering between Lucca's legs in his haste to grab the fluttering bug. As soon as Russet asked the question, he came to a sudden halt and grasped his hands behind his back. "Doot! No messages, Master Russet. Would you like me to send a request for a message out?"

"No no, that will be fine," Russet replied. He turned around and ran his hand over the top of the papers he had stacked up. He glanced back at Lucca and grinned. "You wanna get rid of these for me, Sweetie? Just a little bit of fire."

Lucca took the offered stack of papers in his hands. He knew what the ferret expected of him, and it felt like a betrayal of that when he simply tossed the paper into the fireplace. He tried to escape the bemused and slightly disappointed look from Russet by turning to stoke the flames, ensuring that there were no remnants of their written plans.

"That ain't how I thought that would go," Russet said. He rubbed the side of his muzzle, teasing out a few strands of lingering brown fur with his claws. He then shrugged. "Either way, it works. Best not to leave plans lying around. Even Tallie ain't gonna look away if that happens."

"Your arrangement doesn't go that far?" Lucca asked, his ears pinned back as he turned his attention away from the fire, hoping that the ferret wouldn't question him further. He looked around the small room. None of his possessions had ever made it into the rented room; wherever Russet had stored his pack, it hadn't been there.

"Not quite," Russet said, bumping his hip against Lucca's as he gathered the last of his belongings. All the ferret gathered from the room was some scalls, a leather pouch that clinked when moved, and a ring he had taken off his finger the previous night. As far as the lion could tell, Russet carried no weapons. None that he had seen, at least. “Come on. We’ll still have a few hours of daylight to rec the land.”

With Palmer scampering at his paws, Lucca followed Russet out of the rented room. He closed the door behind them.

Erasmus had a large mansion on the northern edge of the village, in the shadow of the crumbling castle that overlooked Melry’s Reach. The mansion itself looked almost as grand as Lucca imagined the castle must once have been. The expansive and perfectly manicured grounds were locked behind a tall fence, partially obscured by bushes and trees that grew on the outside of the fence. Lucca could see no obvious way in, but Russet insisted on walking a complete circuit around the property on three occasions.

The ferret occasionally paused to check something, asking Lucca to check for any evidence of illusions or other defensive charms. There was never any trace of magic protecting the manor. The defences were entirely mundane steel bars that made up the tall fence.

The sun began to drift down towards the horizon. Lucca’s paws ached, and he longed for an opportunity to sit down and rest, but he knew nothing was forthcoming. There had been no sign of activity within the mansion grounds, though they were far enough away from the building that it was hard to see inside the windows. No one walked the perfect lawns. The front gate remained firmly locked. Lucca wasn’t even sure Erasmus was home.

Finally, Russet took them away from the property, towards the old wall that surrounded the village. There, the ferret found a small nook to sit on, and Lucca eagerly settled down by his side. Palmer chased a butterfly.

“Soon as it’s dark, we go in,” Russet said. The ferret bounced a small piece of stone in his hand as he peered in towards the centre of the village. No one walked the winding road, though sounds of activity could be heard further towards the village square.

"I didn't see anyone at all," Lucca said, warily looking back in the direction of the mansion. He couldn't see the tall fences around Erasmus's property, as a few of the smaller houses nearby obscured the view. "Are we sure there will be anyone inside?"

"Oh, there will be someone. There always is. Be alert and follow my orders without question or hesitation. Alright?" Russet replied. He reached out to take Lucca's hand.

"I will," Lucca said. He tried to swallow down the nervousness that threatened to rise into his throat. A nasty taste settled on his tongue. He was sure someone inside Erasmus's mansion would be able to hear the frantic pounding of his heart.

"I'm serious, Sweetie. This ain't your world anymore. This is all mine," the ferret cautioned. His hand squeezed a little tighter around Lucca's. "My world is a dangerous place."

"I won't do anything you don't tell me to do," Lucca replied. He leaned back, resting against the crumbling wall. The stone felt rigid and uneven against his furs, but he managed to find a small nook to support his head and neck.

"That ain't quite what I'm asking," Russet said quietly. His fingers gently stroked over Lucca's palm. "There might be a time you need to think fast, without my orders. But when I do give instructions, you are to follow them."

Lucca nodded. He closed his eyes, shielding his vision from the descending sun as it threw dazzling colours of orange and red across the sky. "I understand, don't worry. I won't let you down."

Russet's hand kept rubbing Lucca's, though the ferret remained quiet for a few minutes. Neither spoke to each other. There was nothing else for them to discuss for the moment, giving Lucca's mind a chance to frantically run through everything they were about to do. He couldn't believe that he was getting the chance to run a job with the notorious relic thief, the very rogue who had so captivated his imagination. His experience with Russet had not been quite what he had imagined. Even if he managed to overcome the guilt that rippled beneath the surface of every action, he was coming to realise that the life of a thief was a lot less glamorous than the stories told.

The ferret's voice cut through Lucca's thoughts, but Russet hadn't been addressing the lion. "Palmer, can you check for any RedClaw or warp activity inside the mansion?"

Lucca squinted open his eyes, shielding his face with his free hand from the low sun. He glanced down at Palmer, who had snapped to attention. The butterfly he had been chasing was perched languidly on the lap-dragon's right wing. "No activity within the last three hours. I can't access most internal networks, but I can turn on his intruder alarm. Would you like me to do so?"

"No, Palmer. I want you to ensure that never turns on. Understand?" Russet said, rubbing his muzzle wearily.

"Doot! Unable to comply, Master Russet. I need administrator controls for that," Palmer chirped. He fluttered his wing, but the butterfly resolutely remained perched on the lap-dragon.

"If he's able to tell you all that, what am I here for?" Lucca asked, looking down at the little lap-dragon. He fiddled nervously with his tufted tail.

Russet grinned. "Don't worry, Sweetie. I ain't just bringing you along for eye-candy. Erasmus is a sneaky one. There's more defences inside that Palmer ain't able to warn us about. He certainly can't override them. For that, I need a mage. And here you are. After what I saw of you on the road, I know you've got just what I need."

Lucca averted his gaze from even the lap-dragon. "I'm not special or powerful."

Russet lifted the lion's head up. He gazed into the feline's eyes. "I ain't needing special. Don't need powerful. I just need someone who has a handle on illusions and can do the job. You're exactly what I need for this."

It wasn't a rousing vote of confidence, but Lucca knew he didn't deserve that. He had shown moments of skill on the road. If that was all Russet needed, then he would be able to provide that. So long as what they faced was illusions. Anything more and the lion knew he was out of his depth.

The lion knew anything more he could learn about the job might help soothe his nerves. Or it might make them worse. He opened his mouth before considering which one he might prefer. "And just what is it we're... you're trying to steal?"

"It's a... bracelet, of sorts. Looks like it's made of pewter, about two fingers wide." The ferret glanced at Lucca's hands. "My fingers." He took a deep breath, his grin fading as his face turned dark and serious. "We already know which room it's in, so follow my lead and act when you need to, and you won't need to know what it looks like. We'll find it just fine."

"And what does this bracelet do?" The lion was sure this bracelet had to be magical. Probably powerful. Why else would a mage like Erasmus have it? Why else would the notorious relic thief want it?

The ferret's grin returned. He tapped his nose. "Need-to-know basis. Come on. The sun is low enough now. We'd best start moving."

The rest had not been as long as Lucca would have liked, but his paws were grateful for the short time sat down. They still protested walking again, but not enough that Lucca regretted offering his help to the relic thief.

Russet led the lion around to the side of the expansive property, away from the front gate. A narrow strip of greenery separated the mansion's fence with the surrounding properties, giving a little shelter amongst the trees. Dead leaves squelched underpaw, bringing up moisture from the soil beneath the layer of foliage. A small trail had been cut through the worst of the fallen leaves and branches on the ground, beaten out by the three on their previous laps of the property. There was no evidence of anyone else traversing the undergrowth.

Halfway up the property, almost level with the front of the mansion, was a small ditch. Ankle deep water pooled in the bottom of the ditch, which cut perpendicular to the fence. Russet stopped by the ditch, casting a quick glance through the bars of the fence into the gardens. There was still no movement inside.

"Alarms still active?" the ferret asked, glancing down to the excited lap-dragon at his paws.

"Uh huh. All alarms still active. None patrolling nearby. Musteliad Erasmus is reportedly upstairs," Palmer chirped. He swished his tail as he approached the edge of the ditch. The butterfly was still perched on his wings.

"Alright. Here we go then," Russet said. He jumped down into the ditch, splashing in the stagnant water. There was no gap between the bottom of the fence and the lowest point of the ditch. There would be no easy way through into the gardens.

Lucca reluctantly followed after the ferret. Russet had told him they would be entering here, but the ferret had not mentioned how. No mention had also been made of the water, even if there was only enough to cover his ankles. The lion grimaced as he slipped down the banking of the ditch, landing with a splash. He could feel his paws sinking in the sodden mud.

Russet tapped his fingers against the metallic bars of the fence. His movements seemed random to Lucca's eyes, but the ferret's brow was furrowed in thought. His fingers danced back and forth across the six bars, with each one ringing out in a different musical note. The ferret finally held onto one of the middle bars at the same moment a wave of magic rippled out from the fence.

Lucca held his hands to his chest, his eyes wide as he looked around the ditch. The magic extended outwards, surrounding the lion, ferret, and lap-dragon. It filled Lucca with warmth, and small sparkles of red light danced around him. The magical illumination focused on a square against the wet banks of the ditch.

As Lucca watched, an indentation formed in the mud, pushing deeper into the ditch bank. Stone steps formed in the void, leading down into the darkness beyond the magical light.

Russet stepped away from the fence, releasing the bars. Light continued to dance around his fingers, before slowly fading into darkness. He placed one hand against the top of the entry into the side of the ditch, one paw on the top step inside. "Took me months to learn that pattern," the ferret said, his face etched in a victorious grin. "Come on. Down we go."

"What is this place?" Lucca asked, warily following after the ferret as he descended into the dark.

"Emergency escape," Russet said, not looking back. "Best to keep quiet though. Only speak if it's urgent. Alright?"

Lucca opened his mouth to respond, before snapping his jaw shut again. He just nodded, hoping the ferret would take his silence for understanding. Even Palmer remained quiet as they moved further away from the sunset light above.

Russet didn't stop until he reached the bottom of the stone stairs. The further away from the light, the darker the underground passage got, and the less Lucca could see. Each step was a test of faith, unsure exactly where the stair would be.

At the bottom of the stairs was a narrow tunnel that cut directly towards the mansion on the surface. Absolute darkness soon fell as the entry sealed itself once more. A tingle of magic flared against Lucca's fur close to his side. Moments later, Russet's hand found his and a sudden light illuminated the passage. The ferret held a ruby gem in his other hand, blazing with enchanted light. Lucca had to bite his tongue to stop himself identifying the gem as an Eye of Revelation, one of a dozen matching artefacts created generations ago. All that mattered for the moment was that the gem lit up the tunnel ahead. Better still, no one else would see the light unless they made contact with the bearer.

The ground underpaw was damp earth, but the walls and low ceiling were reinforced with wooden struts. The dull, earthy smell filled Lucca's nose, forcing out every other scent. It was so pervasive he could almost taste the dirt on his tongue.

There were no branching pathways. The tunnel cut perfectly straight through the ground, not once deviating in direction or elevation. Lucca wondered how it had been created. The walls were too smooth to have been cut by hand. There had to have been magic involved, but the felian could not feel any lingering sense of that sorcery.

Russet led the way, holding aloft the magical gem in his hand. Nothing moved. There were no sounds but for their pawsteps, muffled by the soft dirt. Even the air did not move at all.

Lucca knew they had to have passed underneath the foundations of the mansion. Occasional jutting pieces of stone sunk out of the ceiling, making Lucca duck beneath them lest he hit his head. The shorter ferret ahead had no such concerns.

Stone steps, like those at the other end of the tunnel, began to rise up as the passage slanted back towards the surface. Walls of dirt and wood were replaced by stone and brick. All light was extinguished as Russet closed his hand around the Eye of Revelation. Lucca placed his hands out, brushing his fingertips alongside the wall to ensure he wasn't surprised by any sudden turn in the staircase. Each step was mercifully even, meaning he didn't stumble or trip on any unexpected indent or outcrop.

New light began to filter down from above. A small, thin strip of light shone brightly, but illuminated little. A shadow moved across the strip as Russet moved closer to the light. The snick of metal in a lock sounded out, almost deafening to Lucca's ears as he strained to hear any noise from outside the door.

The ferret worked with the lock for a few seconds, before the door silently swung open. Russet peered outside, into the ornate corridor beyond, then held his hand up. "Wipe your paws," he whispered, doing so himself to clear the worst of the mud.

Lucca nodded and repeated the gesture, before he followed the ferret nervously. He held his hands close to his chest as he placed his paws on the soft, carpeted floor. Once Palmer followed behind him, he pushed the door, which was disguised as a bookcase, almost fully closed. Even while slightly ajar, Lucca couldn't even tell there was a hidden passage there.

Russet silently gestured for Lucca to follow him. The lion tried to recall the maps of the mansion Russet had drawn up for him. He knew the target was in a study next to Erasmus's entertainment rooms. If Lucca's understanding was right, then they were on the lower level by the front foyer. Judging from the smell of baked goods, they were close to the kitchens on the east wing. That meant they still had to cross into the other wing of the mansion and break through the magical defences that surrounded the study.

The ferret moved with silent ease down the corridor, with Palmer scampering by his side. Lucca followed a few paces behind them, focusing hard on where he was putting his paws. The carpet was soft enough that his claws didn't make a sound, but he dreaded what might happen should there be somewhere without the sound-dulling carpets. He had never been so conscious about how much noise his leathers and furs made as he walked. A faint whirring buzzed at the lower end of his hearing.

Despite the number of valuable goods scattered around the mansion, Russet had no interest in any of them. The ferret ignored several priceless pots and works of art. Even the display of jewellery hung in the foyer beneath the stairs didn't even get a second look. They must have been worth thousands of scalls each. Even Lucca was tempted to wander over to them. Shinies were shinies, after all.

Resisting the urge to investigate, Lucca followed Russet away from the stairs towards a doorway on the far side of the foyer. Lucca's eyes were briefly attracted by the ornate golden banisters that lined the two flights of stairs, one at either side of the expansive foyer. A diamond chandelier provided light for the room, sparkling with its own magical glow. Artwork of a succession of badgers lined the foyer walls. The names beneath each portrait were meaningless to Lucca, though one had a familiar name and face. Erasmus.

Lucca had seen the badger at the Esfyr's Wold chapterhouse before, on occasional visits. The mage was a distant relative of Master Roe. That had all been before Erasmus's expulsion from the guild. Lucca had not heard the details about why Erasmus had been expelled from the guild. Rumours swirled about immoral and nefarious practices, but nothing had been definitively proven. In the public eye, anyway.

A door opened and closed.

Lucca froze and turned to look upstairs. He couldn't see any movement, but that had definitely been where the sound had come from. The back of his neck prickled with unease. His breathing sounded so loud to his ears that he was sure they echoed off the far wall. Most mansions this large would be bustling with servants and wait staff, but this was the home of a mage. They didn't need servants when magic could perform most of the duties. That meant anyone in the mansion was likely to be someone that lived there. The door could only have been opened by Erasmus himself.

"Psst!"

Lucca shook his head and backed away from the stairs. He hurried towards Russet, who had waved him through the door at the side of the foyer. There were no pawsteps coming from upstairs yet, so perhaps their presence had not yet been discovered.

Russet pulled Lucca through the door firmly. Just in time, too. The whirring that had been irritating Lucca's ears increased several pitches. The lion glanced back into the foyer to see a large purple security gem floating down the far stairs, like the ones at the chapterhouse. The gem flashed occasionally as it bobbed up and down, languidly drifting towards the lower level. It turned down the corridor towards the kitchens. The whirring began to fade again.

Lucca turned away from the door. He found himself in a large dining room. A massive table with over two dozen chairs around it was situated in the middle of the room. He couldn't help but hesitate. The table was larger than the one the students sat around at the chapterhouse. The walls were gilded with silver and gold ornaments.

At a pull from Russet's hand, Lucca wrenched his eyes away. He hurried after the ferret, following him through a small oak door that he hadn't initially noticed. The door led to a narrow, dark corridor that did not share the wealthy aesthetic of the dining room. The walls were bare grey stone, and the floor wasn't carpeted. The lion's claws clicked with each step as his claws kept unsheathing with his anxiety.

The far end of the corridor had a second small door. Russet peered through the keyhole to ensure the way was clear before pushing the door open. This room was another luscious affair, with wide silk curtains masking one wall, through which the evening sunlight filtered. Various couches and seats filled the room, gathered together around small circular tables. A second set of wide double doors were closed to Lucca's left. That was the only other way in or out.

Russet did not go towards those doors. Instead, the ferret hurried across to the far wall, the one covered by the silk curtains. The ferret pulled the cascading fabric aside, behind which was a bare stone wall with no further adornments or decorations beyond the obscuring curtain.

"Just here," Russet whispered, beckoning Lucca closer and pointing towards the featureless wall.

The lion frowned. He could see nothing unusual about the wall. All around the room he could see valuable items, from the gold candlesticks to the silk napkins draped across the armrests of every chair. Lucca could imagine this place full and bustling of the wealthy, exchanging conversations with each other.

Lucca shook his head. He had other things to worry about. He reached out and placed his hand on the wall. A rush of magic ripped through his body. He quickly withdrew his hand. Distressed whirs from a security gem increased in pitch briefly, before fading to near silence.

Palmer chirped quietly. "Security alarm nearly activated," the lap-dragon said quietly.

"Careful," Russet warned, holding on to Lucca's shoulder.

The lion shuddered. The lingering magic dispelled from his body as he held his hand out again. This time he didn't touch the wall, instead holding his fingers an inch away from the surface. He slowly walked along the corridor, feeling for the differences in magic that protected what lay beyond. The lion imagined a hidden room or secret door, protected with enchantments and magic.

A flare of magic caught his attention. Lucca paused mid-step. He looked at the uninteresting piece of stone wall, exactly in the middle. The air shimmered in front of him. "This is it," he muttered. The magic felt like just a simple illusion cast over the doorway, but one that would trigger the alarm if Lucca interacted with it. They couldn't simply walk through the door, even if he knew exactly where it was.

Floorboards in the ceiling creaked. Pawsteps moved upstairs.

"You got this?" Russet asked, leaning close to whisper in Lucca's ear.

Lucca set his jaw and nodded. He reached out with both hands, bracing his paws against the soft carpet. Slowly, he extended his magic outwards, feeling over the gentle cascade of the illusion set before the wall. His magic probed against the illusion, trying to find any weak point or way he could unravel the spell. He could find nothing at first, but then he noticed a couple of spikes in magical pressure. He flicked his ears and tried to make sense of the strange sensations.

The lion then realised what he needed to do. Turning his wrists, he began to pull at the middle of the illusion, right where he knew the door to be. Slowly, golden light shimmered as the illusion stretched, before splitting around a small hole barely large enough for a hand to slip through. Through the hole, Lucca could see the handle of the hidden door.

"Lockpick, quickly," the lion gasped. He didn't know how long he would be able to hold the magic at bay. He could already feel warmth spreading through his hands and up his arms. The whirring of a gem increased in his ears.

Russet carefully pushed his lockpick through the magical gap and into the lock behind. The ferret stuck the tip of his tongue out as he worked, while Palmer stood a few paces away and kept watch. The pawsteps from upstairs had gone away again, with no further sounds coming from the upper level.

The lock clicked. Russet pulled his lockpick out. The whirring reached a fevered pitch.

Lucca transferred his magic from maintaining the hole, towards pushing on the unlocked door. The illusion snapped back into place, but Lucca could hear the hinges of the door moving behind the curtain of magic.

For a moment, nothing happened. Lucca's ears and tail curled as he thought he might have been wrong, but then the illusion began to splinter and fragment. Cracks of golden light spread across the illusory wall, before the whole thing shattered with a rush of magic. The whirring fell into silence again as the door revealed itself.

A chair scraped against the floor upstairs.

Russet hurried into the study, pulling Lucca along with him. Palmer followed them, hesitating only to keep the door propped ajar. Without the illusion to mask the doorway, any onlooker would be able to see it had been tampered with; however they hadn't wanted to risk the illusion restoring with a closed door, lest they trigger the alarms on their escape.

Lucca looked around the small study. The room wasn't large, but it was filled with so much equipment that Russet and the lion could barely fit inside without touching each other. Four wooden desks were squeezed against the walls, which were themselves covered in rows of shelving that rose all the way up to the ceiling. A small window provided illumination, and that was the only part of the wall that was actually visible. Each of the desks were covered in papers and arcane equipment. Crystals were scattered across one desk, thrumming with magical potential. Another desk had a sapphire orb resting on a gold plinth.

Russet turned away from them all. The ferret had eyes only for one thing; a small bracelet of dull pewter. He snatched up the bracelet and held it up in front of his eyes, checking the symbols around the band. He grinned and slipped the uninteresting jewellery into the satchel at his hip.

"How we looking upstairs, Palmer?" Russet asked, still keeping his voice quiet.

"Movement, but not towards us," Palmer replied. The little lap-dragon looked up, his eyes flicking around as though he was able to see right through the ceiling to the mage above. "Some security gems patrolling nearby."

Russet breathed out slowly. "See? Easy," he whispered, taking hold of Lucca's hand. "You did good. Now let's get out of here."

"That's really all you wanted?" Lucca asked in shock. He looked around. Even in the small study he could see so much that would surely be worth more than the pewter bracelet.

"Ain't for me," Russet replied. The ferret glanced at the window, but quickly shook his head. "Back through to the escape tunnel. Keep an ear alert. I ain't wanting to give Erasmus a chance to find us."

Lucca felt that tightening around his heart again. He nodded and bit his lip, trying not to breathe too quickly. His hands curled up into fists. "Let's go then."

Russet pulled open the study door. The room outside was quiet still, with no sounds of movement throughout the mansion and only the gentle hum of a gem in a different room. If it was Erasmus upstairs, then the badger didn't know about the thieves in his home.

The ferret cautiously crept back through the maze of couches and tables. They didn't bother closing the door behind them. Without any way of restoring the illusion, they couldn't make the study look like no one had broken in.

Lucca followed just behind Palmer. His fingers itched at his sides, longing to touch some of the valuable shinies all around him. He had rarely gotten the chance to sit in the chapterhouse great hall, where they dined with the richest of the cutlery and rubbed shoulders with the guild elite. Students were not given that privilege often. Lucca only got that chance when the guildmaster wanted to show off the exotic felian to a visiting governor. The lion's lip curled at the memory.

Lucca bumped into a table. A golden candlestick rattled and wobbled, before evading Lucca's desperate grasp and falling to the floor. The carpet muffled most of the sound, but the dull thud still sounded so loud to the lion. A gem beeped from outside the main doors.

Russet whirled around on the spot. The ferret had already made it across the expansive room, his hand almost on the small door to the narrow corridor. He bared his teeth and hissed and the lion, beckoning frantically for Lucca to hurry up. Even Palmer was already by the ferret's side, waiting to continue.

Lucca picked through the remaining tables, making sure not to hit anything else on his way through. He needed to focus. This wasn't some playful jaunt with friends. He was in the home of a non-guild mage without permission. His company was the notorious relic thief, who had stolen something from

Erasmus. Who had stolen so much from the guild. There were consequences to being caught.

No more sounds came from upstairs, but that worried Lucca. Everything seemed so easy, and it wasn't just because of Russet's skill. The prickle down his neck sunk a little lower.

Russet paused by the far door, which hung slightly ajar. The ferret pulled the door open a little more, peering out into the ornate dining room. Lucca watched over his shoulder. A gem hovered into the dining room, flashing purple light against the cream walls. The ferret pushed the door closed, holding down on the handle to make sure the catch didn't make any noise. Purple light continued to radiate through the crack at the bottom of the door.

The ferret held his finger to his lips. Lucca didn't need the warning. His hands were clapped over his mouth and nose, trying to muffle the sounds of his frantic breathing. The gem whirred and chirped in the dining room, sometimes sounding like it was right on the other side of the door. Lucca didn't want to know what would happen should the gem detect them.

The whirring slowly descended in pitch and volume. The purple light faded from the cracks around the door. The gem was gone.

Russet slowly pushed open the door. Silence greeted them in the dining room, though the lingering flash of purple light still lit up the wide double doors leading towards the foyer. The ferret held himself low to the floor as he slunk forward.

Lucca padded after the ferret, feeling deeply conspicuous in comparison to the quick, agile movements of the relic thief. Even Palmer barely made a noise as he scampered after Russet.

The gem was still in the foyer. It whirred and chirped as it drifted towards the stairs, the purple light radiating outwards in regular intervals. Russet held his hand out, warning Lucca to stay back. The lion didn't need the warning. He wasn't going to move anywhere while the gem was still in the foyer.

Lucca's focus was solely on the movement of the gem. The whirring was still loud in his ears, but he could only hear the one security gem. Any others that patrolled the mansion were in other parts of the building, with none close to the foyer. A whisper in his ear and a rustle of fabric almost distracted him, but he kept his eyes on the gem as it bobbed up the stairs.

The lion reached for Russet's hand, but he felt nothing behind him. With a cold shiver, Lucca dragged his attention away from the gem. He was alone. Russet was already halfway across the foyer, with Palmer at his heels. The gem had not reacted to their presence.

Lucca's breath caught in his throat. His heart pounded. His eyes flicked between gem and ferret. He had to do something, but fear froze him to the spot. If he moved, then surely the gem would notice him. Only when Russet reached the far side of the foyer did he find the confidence and desperation to wrench his paws from the floor.

The lion pushed himself forward. He stumbled forward into the foyer, both eyes looking up to the gem as it neared the upper landing.

Lucca's paws stumbled over each other. He kicked his own ankle and tripped himself up. For a moment, he thought he would be able to stay upright, before collapsing to the carpeted floor with a painful hit. His elbow took the brunt of the impact, sending a jarring pain through his arm and shoulder.

A hissed gasp from Russet reached Lucca's ears moments before the whirring of the gem changed pitch. A beeping chirp emanated from the upper level. Lucca looked up to see the gem descending again.

Lucca scrambled to his paws and ran after Russet, no longer even trying to keep quiet. Fear gave him strength and urgency, narrowing his focus down to that one open doorway, while he still listened for the growing sounds of the security gem.

The ferret didn't wait for him. Russet ran down the corridor, only stopping when he reached the bookcase. He pulled on one of the books and opened the hidden door. Only then did he look back, meeting Lucca's eyes. The lion was nearly there.

A bright flash emanated from the gem, summoning a barrier of purple light that burst from the floor. Lucca crashed into the magic barrier and fell back, dazed by the impact. The whirring of the gems turned into a loud wailing.

Russet held out his hand. The ferret's eyes widened. Palmer plucked at the ferret's trousers. The hand fell.

Russet pulled the bookshelf closed behind him. The ferret was gone.

Lucca pulled himself up to his paws. His mind felt foggy and dazed, barely able to comprehend what he had just seen. If he could just get through to the bookcase, he might be able to catch Russet up... That would be what the ferret wanted him to do. Russet was waiting for him still, just on the other side of the bookcase.

He didn't want to believe the alternative. Russet knew he was as good as captured. The thief was gone.

Lucca lifted his hands. The gem was not in sight yet. The flashing of its purple light shone against the open door into the foyer, but the gem itself hadn't come around the corner. There was nowhere to go, though. The barrier was behind him, and there were no other passages or doors off the corridor.

The lion's eyes fell on a long table that ran half the length of the corridor. An embroidered cloth covered the table, sinking almost all the way to the floor. He didn't know if his idea would work, but he had nowhere else to go. Before he had the chance to confirm the stupidity of his actions, Lucca slipped beneath the table, hoping that the cloth would be able to hide him from view. He did not want to use magic in the presence of the gems, which would likely be able to detect any spell he attempted.

The purple light of the gem grew stronger, before stopping close to the table. No more magic attempted to trap Lucca in place. The wailing alarm irritated Lucca's ears. He clenched his jaw and held his hands over his mouth.

Pawsteps approached. "What is the meaning of this?" a deep voice growled.

Lucca resisted the urge to answer. He could see badger paws approaching beneath the hem of the cloth cover. The voice was vaguely familiar. This was Erasmus.

"Intruder detected," the gem chirped brightly, its voice surprisingly lilting for a construct.

"Are they still inside?" the badger asked.

"Affirmative. They are here."

The badger's paws scuffed on the carpet. "Where are they now?"

"They are here," the gem repeated.

"Ugh, cheap rubbish," the badger muttered. He snapped his fingers. "Double all patrols. Guard every exit. Don't let them escape. You have authority for lethal response should you see this intruder."

"They are here," the gem repeated again.

"Yes, I know," the badger snapped. "If you see them, kill them. Until then, don't disturb me. I'm busy."

"Affirmative."

Erasmus turned away and prowled back towards the foyer. The gem did not follow the badger. Instead, it just remained close to Lucca's hiding spot. The whirring of several other gems filled the air, patrolling towards the kitchens, and back in the foyer.

A door slammed upstairs.

Lucca didn't dare move. He felt sure the gems knew he was still here, but Erasmus's wording had saved him. If the gems couldn't see him, they wouldn't attack him, even if they already knew he cowered beneath the table. He briefly considered an invisibility charm, but he doubted that would fool the gems for long enough. Could he outlast the gems? He didn't think he would be able to do that. They would not stop until they found him.

The lion rubbed his eyes, fighting off the moisture that built there. He should never have come with Russet. What was he even thinking? He wasn't cut out for this sort of adventure. His exams were enough excitement for him.

If he was even going to be allowed back to the chapterhouse. If Erasmus caught him, then he would either be dead or disgraced. There would be no going back to Esfyr's Wold now.

Lucca suppressed a sob. The noise died at the back of his throat before it could give away his position. Perhaps he could escape and barter for passage back to Da'Manyr.

The gem fell to the floor with a clunk.

Lucca clapped his hands over his mouth to stop the scream of panic. The light had faded from the gem. Its smooth surface cracked slightly.

Breathing so fast he was practically panting, Lucca reached out with one trembling hand to touch the gem. It didn't react at all. The whirring from the other security gems had all fallen to silence.

The bookcase creaked.

Erasmus's voice bellowed from upstairs. "What's going on now?"

Lucca peered out from beneath the table. He heard a chair crashing over from upstairs. Pawsteps quickly followed.

Palmer peered around the corner of the bookcase, which had been pushed open slightly. The lap-dragon wore the pewter bracelet around his wrist. Lucca hurried to his paws, smacking his head against the underside of the table in his haste. The barrier of light had faded with the deactivation of the gems, leaving Lucca with an unhindered run to the hidden passageway.

The lion hurried inside. The bookcase was closed behind him, plunging the passage into darkness. A hand closed around his own and dragged him down the stairs. The badger's shouts echoed through the back of the bookshelf, but they slowly got quieter as they silently ran down into the darkness, quickly banished by the Eye of Revelation.

Lucca didn't dare look up until he felt dirt beneath his paws again. He got a brief look at Russet's face before the thief turned away to guide the way.

The ferret was furious.

Chapter Nine

Other than to send Palmer back to the Royal Egg, Russet had not uttered a single word since leaving the mansion. The ferret had taken hold of Lucca's hand the moment they had emerged from the damp ditch beside the fence, but he had remained completely silent. Through their contact, Lucca could feel the ferret shaking.

Russet led Lucca away from the village, out into the moors that surrounded Melry's Reach. Only then did the ferret release his hand, prowling away into the darkness, taking with him the now-hidden light of the Eye of Revelation.

The moonless night cast shadows over everything, meaning Lucca could no longer see Russet clearly. The ferret appeared as little more than a gloomy silhouette, even to the lion's strong night vision.

They climbed one of the hills that surrounded the village. Russet moved easily through the night, magic to guide him, while Lucca stumbled through the darkness. Unsure if they were safe from Erasmus's gems, he didn't dare light the way with magic of his own. The ferret stopped and turned when they reached the summit. He looked down to the glittering lights of Melry's Reach.

"I told you to obey every command," the ferret whispered. His voice shook as much as his hand. "I told you to listen to me."

"I did," Lucca protested, holding up his hands. He saw the anger in the ferret's eyes, reflected in the pale light of the stars. He quailed and lowered his head. "I tried to."

"Try ain't good enough," Russet hissed. He took a couple of steps away. He stepped forward and reached out, almost close enough to touch the lion, but his hand fell away again. Shadows cast across the ferret's face, but Lucca could still see the bright gleam of his eyes.

"I'm sorry, alright? I tried my best," Lucca said. He kept his head low, not wanting to see the frustration and anger in Russet's eyes. Even worse, the disappointment.

"You don't understand," Russet growled. His voice slowly grew louder and louder with each word. "I'm such a cod-choking fool. I thought I could... argh!" The ferret threw his arms up in frustration.

"You got what you needed, didn't you?" Lucca asked. He felt like sitting down and turning his back on the ferret, but he stayed on his paws for the moment.

"You think that's why I'm angry?" Russet asked. He laughed bitterly. "I could've lost you. You could've died in there. Because you didn't listen. Because I put you in danger."

"We both know you wouldn't have cared about that," Lucca said dully.

"I... what?" Russet said, surprise draining the anger from his voice.

Lucca placed his hands on Russet's shoulders, the night suddenly ablaze with light once more. He blinked into the ethereal glow, able to see every strand of Russet's fur and the teardrops that balanced on his whiskers. "This is the love spell talking. You don't really feel this about me," he said. He tried to smile, but instead felt like crying. "It's not real. I'm a complication, remember?"

Russet reached up to hold onto Lucca's hand. "Oh, Lucca." All the anger had drained from his voice, replaced by sorrow and shame. "There never was a love charm."

Lucca's head spun. He felt dizzy as his thoughts crashed down around his mind. They all made a lot of noise, but he could not make sense of a single one. "But… but I was there. Master Roe… he cast the spell. He…" This time, Lucca did sit down. He did so slowly, before he could collapse, engulfing himself in darkness once more as he released Russet's hand. Even on the ground, his head continued to spin.

Russet crouched down in front of the lion. He reached into the front of his leathers and pulled out a small necklace. On the end of the chain was a pink amethyst, glinting in the soft starlight. "A good thief thinks of everything. I ain't survived this long without that." A weary smile came to his lips. "Ain't many thieves who would think a mage would use a love charm, but I ain't like them. I got counter charms for every damn spell I could think of. Never thought this would be useful 'til I felt it go off in the middle of the night. Knew then someone was trying to trap me with a love charm."

Lucca had to marvel at the foresight. The Mages' Guild really had underestimated the thief. They had been beaten long before they realised a game was afoot, though Lucca did have to wonder just how Russet managed to carry so many charms. It was a miracle he wasn't rattling with every step.

But the revelation opened a new path for Lucca's thoughts to delve down. One far more pressing than wanting to see the myriad of charms.

"Then why any of this?" the lion asked. He tried to keep his mouth closed, but it kept wanting to stay hanging open. His throat felt dry.

Russet hissed quietly to himself. "No one but me would think someone would use a love charm to snare a thief. That meant no one would think it weird that I got hit by one," the ferret said slowly. His tail swished as he slowly paced through the shadows. "Gives me a chance to deviate from the plan."

"So, everything that happened between us was, what?" Lucca asked, frowning. His ears curled in.

"An act," Russet said, laughing bitterly. "All an act. I thought I could have a bit of fun that first night, but you resisted. That caught my intention. I was intrigued. Thought I could have some fun of a different kind."

Lucca bowed his head. He tore up a small clump of grass and twisted the blades around his fingers. "So if it was all an act, why did you come back for me? You could have just left me there. You'd never have seen me again."

Russet slumped down on the grass beside Lucca. "Because you became a complication."

Lucca looked across to the ferret. "Oh."

"Yeah. Oh." Russet grinned wryly. His ears pinned back. He tapped a hand to his chest. "I had this feeling in my heart. Never really felt it before. Never let myself feel it. Call it infatuation if you like. I call it complication."

"So what happens now?" Lucca asked. He turned his head again to look up at the cloudy sky.

Russet breathed out deeply. "I don't know. I thought I could just leave you. I could throw off the act of the love spell and just go. You're right. I would never have seen you again. Free of complications," the ferret said, before sighing again. "But I realised I couldn't do it. I had to turn back."

"Because I'm a complication." Lucca wasn't sure whether that was a good thing or not. He didn't know what to believe.

Russet's hand sought out Lucca's. The Eye of Revelation flooded bright once more, illuminating the ferret in a spotlight glow. "Yeah. I don't know what to do now. Reason screams at me. Go. Go now. Leave you behind before you can complicate things further."

"Will you?" Lucca asked nervously. He already knew what the answer was going to be.

"I think I'm gonna have to," Russet admitted. He rolled over onto his side and kissed Lucca on the cheek. "Complications ain't good for a thief. It would be dangerous for you."

"And that wasn't?" Lucca asked, rolling his head to gesture in the direction of the mansion.

Russet said nothing for a few moments. His hand idly rubbed over the lion's belly, teasing at the leather. "I ain't just talking about being caught. A thief like me ain't able to have any weaknesses. We're not allowed to be vulnerable. Love is a complication because it's a distraction, but also means my enemies can get to me through my love."

Lucca rested his hand atop Russet's. "Sounds lonely."

The ferret sighed softly, head resting against Lucca's shoulder. "Why do you think I jumped at the chance to have fun with the love charm?"

Lucca rolled over so he could pull Russet into an embrace. He enjoyed the comfort of the ferret's body pressed against him. Russet was warm while the night air was cool. "I'm sorry for that. It was wrong. I should have told Master Roe it was a bad idea."

Russet placed a finger on Lucca's lips. "All is forgiven. I know it weren't your idea. You didn't give in when you could've taken advantage of me."

"Even though you wanted it," Lucca said. He smirked, though internally berated himself. He could have given in, after all.

"I had everything planned out. Everything was perfect," Russet said, pulling Lucca into another kiss. "I was gonna lure you in with my wiles and charms, have some fun for a night, and then disappear into the morning with whatever prize the mages dared to dangle in front of me."

"Sorry to ruin those plans," Lucca said wryly. He arched his neck to lightly touch his nose against Russet's. "If I'd have known the love charm hadn't worked, I would never have held myself back."

"And yet, here we are. Lying beneath the stars and no reason to leave until dawn. What do you say? Catch up on lost time?" Russet said.

"Here? Now?" Lucca asked. His heart fluttered with excitement as he gazed at the ferret, the idol of his suppressed adventurous spirit, now in his arms at last. He wrapped the ferret into a tight embrace, hand resting on the back of the musteliad's head.

"We can go back to the inn first." The ferret smiled, but there was a sadness in his eyes. He turned his head aside and rested his head on the lion's shoulder. "But we have to promise each other. We ain't gonna think with anything but our heads tomorrow."

Lucca purred and kissed the ferret on the top of the head. "If this is to be our only chance to have fun together, let's make it a good time."

Lucca woke the next morning with the sun in his eyes. He groaned softly and kept his eyelids squeezed shut, not wanting to move at all. He didn't want to get up and close the curtains across the window, nor did he want to escape the warm embrace of the blankets over his naked body. The arms wrapped around his torso were comfortable, as was the feeling of another body behind him.

The lion's hand slowly moved up to cup over the one resting on his chest. Movement stirred behind him, and he felt a kiss to the back of his neck. He slowly blinked open his eyes, still squinting in the morning light.

"Finally awake are you?" Russet mumbled sleepily.

"I thought you'd have left already," Lucca said. He hadn't expected to wake up with the ferret still with him. They were in the Royal Egg room, alone. Palmer had not been there when they had returned the previous night, and he still hadn't made an appearance.

"Not just yet," the ferret said. Lucca could feel him breathing slowly and deeply; the ferret's chest pushing into his back with every breath. "Wanted to wait a little longer."

Lucca slowly rolled over in bed. The ferret's white-furred body was on full display for him to enjoy. They had barely slept at all, having enjoyed each other's company long into the night. Despite that, Lucca still felt oddly refreshed. He felt happy, though his joy was tinged with the sorrow of knowing he would never see Russet again.

"Where will you be going after today?" Lucca asked. He leaned in to kiss Russet.

The ferret stuck the tip of his tongue out. "Still trying to get my secrets?" he said with a wink. He kissed the lion back, silencing his spluttered apologies. "Cofferknell. Got business to attend to there. I've already sent Palmer upstairs to get everything prepared with Tallie so I can leave as soon as possible."

"I don't know if I want this to end," Lucca said, slowly shaking his head. He trembled as reality started to seep into him. He would never see the ferret again, reduced to hearing stories and hearsay once more.

Russet touched his brow against Lucca's muzzle. "You must be looking forward to going home again, at least."

"Everything is going to feel boring without you," Lucca said. How could he go back to the academic routines of life at Esfyr's Wold after this? He could never call his life mundane, not since leaving Da'Manyr, but there would be no more adventures. No more relic thief.

He rested his head on the pillow and stared at the ferret, trying to commit to memory every last detail of the thief. He wanted to remember him as he was, the true ferret behind all the legends. Those memories would be the only memento he would take, unlike the Winterpaw hunter whose precious gifts he still treasured.

"Boring? At the chapterhouse? Nah, I doubt that. But it will be safe," Russet replied. He smiled, before sitting up and stretching his hands above his head. "Will be best to forget about me as soon as you can."

"I don't think that's going to happen," Lucca replied. He blushed a little. "I think I've been a little bit in love with you since I first heard your stories."

The ferret bared his teeth. "You never did tell me any of those stories. Do I still live up to your expectations?"

"I think you exceeded them," Lucca said. He lifted himself up onto his elbows.

"Flatterer," Russet said. A pink tinge blushed beneath the white fur on his cheeks. "I'm glad they sent you. If things were different, if I were... ah, best not to think about it."

"Think about what?" Lucca asked, flicking his ears back.

Russet kissed Lucca. "Best not to think about it. As much as I hate the idea, we should get ready. Still want to see Mistress Juri before I go."

Lucca blinked. "You still want to see her? Why? We don't have to remove the love charm."

The ferret frowned. He shifted his paws up and hugged his legs close to his chest. "You said Mistress Juri knows lap-dragons better than anyone else, right?"

Lucca nodded. He tilted his head to the side. "Yeah, I think so. Why?"

"Then we have a different reason to visit her. One last thing for me, alright? Then you're free to go home," Russet said. He reached out with one hand to take hold of Lucca's. "I promise. I'll have that evidence to give your battlemages and I won't ask anything of you again."

Lucca wasn't sure if he wanted any of that. He forced a smile to his face anyway. "Then let's get dressed."

Lucca didn't know exactly where Mistress Juri lived now, but Tallie did. The otter innkeeper was able to give directions to a small cottage on the outskirts of the village, uncomfortably close to Erasmus's mansion. Though Lucca had so many questions to ask Russet, he kept quiet. He feared losing the ferret but could think of no casual conversation to bring up. He wanted to tell Russet all about his experiences in Lutrea, but they just didn't seem interesting to him anymore. The thief lived a life of adventure. Lucca had gotten a taste of that. It had been terrifying but thrilling.

The little cottage looked much like all the others. The grey stones had been painted white at some point, though much of that paint was starting to fleck away. Not many flowers in the garden had survived the coming of winter. Most were withered and wilted. Compared to the ostentatious manor Erasmus owned, this was mundane and almost disappointing. Lucca had hoped for a little more from a mage's home.

"Ain't much of a gardener, is she?" Russet said. It had been the first thing he had said since leaving the Royal Egg Inn.

Lucca shook his head. "I don't think she ever was."

"So long as she's a better mage, I'm fine with that."

Lucca chanced a question. "What are we here for? You don't need the love spell reversed."

The ferret sucked in his breath. His hand rested on the gate that led through to Mistress Juri's garden. His eyes flicked around the narrow, winding road. There didn't appear to be anyone around. "Palmer is a spy. He ain't to blame. It's just what he is. But he spies on me and reports back to his other master."

Lucca's eyes widened. "Who is his other master?"

Russet bowed his head. "His name is Sama'Rey. He runs the Thieves' Guild in Cofferknell."

"Sama'Rey? That sounds like a..."

"A felian, yes. He's the one who rescued me from Nesterslip."

Lucca took a deep breath. He wasn't sure he understood anything about what was going on. "So you want Mistress Juri to... stop Palmer reporting back to Sama'Rey? Is that why you made sure he stayed with Tallie?"

Russet nodded, but he couldn't say anything else. The door to the cottage opened, and an elderly otter stepped out. She squinted as she approached the gate. Lucca recognised her immediately, but the feeling didn't appear to be mutual. Not until the lion lowered the hood he had wrapped around his mane.

"Well here is a face I didn't think I'd see again. Hello, Lucca," Mistress Juri said. She held out her hand to take Lucca's, shaking it briefly. "To what do I owe the pleasure of this unexpected visit?"

Lucca placed his hand on Russet's shoulder. "This is my... friend. He needs your help on something. May we come inside?"

"My help?" Mistress Juri asked in surprise. "I'm just an old otter, but I can do what I can. Come in and sit down. Would you care for some tea?"

The inside of Mistress Juri's cottage was just how Lucca remembered her office to be. Almost every surface was crowded with tapestries and cloths, all embroidered in bright, gaudy colours. Glazed commemorative plates hung from the wall, and a small bookshelf was squeezed into one corner. A framed parchment held a position of prominence on the main wall. Lucca approached it curiously to see that it was a certificate of authenticity for her qualifications and rank within the Mages' Guild. It had been signed by the archmage who had preceded Mafren's predecessor.

Russet sat down on one of the available chairs while Lucca remained standing. Mistress Juri bustled around in the kitchen as she prepared tea for them all. The ferret's legs kept bouncing, and his hands twisted at his tail. Something bothered him, and Lucca doubted it was being around his old teacher that caused the visible anxiety. Was it this other felian, this Sama'Rey, who Russet feared? Or, given the way the ferret's eyes kept flicking towards the window, was it the proximity to Erasmus's mansion?

The more Lucca pondered Russet's fear, the more his own began to rise. The badger had not seen either of them, but there might still be other ways to tell who had broken into his mansion. Other magics that Lucca had not yet been taught. Every shadow across the window turned into the badger coming to track them down and soon his hands twisted at his tail as much as Russet's did.

Lucca was grateful when Mistress Juri returned. She carried a tray with three steaming cups on it, as well as a plate of biscuits. Lucca held his cup in both hands, letting the steam from the hot tea wash over his face. Small drops of condensation beaded on his whiskers, but he largely ignored them.

"This does seem like an interesting visit," Mistress Juri said. She settled down in a comfortable armchair in front of the fire, which burned with emerald flames. "How do you feel I can help you? Is one of the masters in trouble back at the Wold?"

Lucca turned to Russet. He knew the ferret would do much of the talking, but for the moment Russet just stared into his drink.

"It's nothing to do with the Mages' Guild," Lucca started to say, but he was silenced by a sharp gesture from Russet's hand.

"It's all to do with me," the ferret said. He looked up to the elderly otter. "I have a problem with my lap-dragon, and Lucca told me you were skilled with them."

Mistress Juri flicked up an ear. "I do know a lot about them. I can try to help, but I see you didn't bring your lap-dragon to me, so what I can do may be limited."

"I didn't want to have this conversation in front of Palmer. He's being used to spy against me, and I can't let... this other person know that I'm aware of it."

Mistress Juri cupped her hands together beneath her chin. "A difficult proposition. Lap-dragons should be immune from being used in such nefarious ways. It is not so easy to undo such things, short of disconnecting them entirely from the warp, but this can be quite traumatic for them. Your lap-dragon would likely suffer from any prolonged time disconnected like that."

"I don't want to hurt him. Palmer ain't to blame for this," Russet whispered. He bowed his head again and stared at his tea. "Is there a way to break the connection just to the paired lap-dragon?"

"There is, but it takes a mage to do it. I can't guarantee it will work, but if you know the true name of this other lap-dragon, then there is a spell I can teach you that should be able to sever the connection between them," the otter explained. She leaned forward in her chair and held up one webbed finger. "However, you must be warned that the other lap-dragon will know this connection is broken. If this other person is spying on you, then he will know that you have broken the link."

Lucca's eyes flicked across to Russet briefly. The ferret still stared down, his tail drooping across the chair. He wanted to reach out and place a hand on Russet's knee, but he wasn't sure how the ferret would react to that.

"Is there no way we can make it so Palmer reports things that ain't real?" Russet asked.

"Not without damaging your lap-dragon, no," Mistress Juri replied. "I don't know what sort of business you've ended up in, but modifying lap-dragons like this is risky and dangerous. There is no easy way to do this. It's not what they were created for."

Russet slowly exhaled. "I know that. I just dunno if it's worth this risk. This person is not someone I wanna cross."

"I can teach you the spell, but I will not advise you on whether you should use it or not," Mistress Juri offered.

Russet said nothing, so Lucca looked up to the otter. "I'd be the one to use the spell. You can teach me."

The ferret opened his mouth, but he kept silent. His eyes were wide as he stared at Lucca. The lion did his best to ignore the attention being given to him.

Mistress Juri pointed to the bookshelf in the corner, closest to Lucca. "There is a book in there. You'll know which one it is. There's only one about lap-dragons. Bring it to me please, Initiate Lucca."

Lucca smirked as his old teacher started to revert back into her old ways. He obediently rose to his paws and crouched down in front of the bookshelf. The otter had been right. There was only one book that looked like it would be useful, and he carefully pulled it out from the shelves. He held it in his hands for a moment and ran his hand over the cover.

The lion muttered a quiet spell beneath his breath.

The satchel over his shoulder burned briefly as magic flared through his book contained within.

Lucca's tail twitched. Neither the ferret nor otter appeared to have noticed the spell. He rose to his paws and held the book out for Mistress Juri to take.

The otter took the book and flipped it open. She flicked through the pages until she found what she wanted, then held it back out for the lion. She tapped a webbed finger over a phrase, which glowed with a golden light at her touch. "Learn this phrase, Initiate. Substitute in the required names, and it will do what you request."

Lucca stared at the book with wide eyes. "What language is this in, Mistress Juri?"

The otter grinned. "Old draconic, converted to the Lutrean alphabet. Quite the tongue-twister, isn't it?"

The felian chuckled nervously. "Just a bit, yes. There's not many vowels in this."

"Correct pronunciation is important, Initiate. If you feel like you can't remember it, you may write it down before you leave. I have spare parchment and a quill you may borrow," Mistress Juri said.

Lucca nodded. "I think that would be for the best."

"All spells to do with lap-dragons are spoken in old draconic. It helps prevent security breaches in their magic, as few can actually pronounce what they intend to do. I will teach you how to pronounce this spell, but I will not perform it myself. I have no wish to alter a lap-dragon I do not know."

"I understand, Mistress Juri," Lucca said, bowing his head to his old teacher. "I appreciate how much you're doing for us."

The otter smiled. "Anything for one of my favourite students."

"Favourite?" Lucca squeaked in surprise.

"You were more attentive than any other. Maybe it was because you were raised in such a savage place, but you drank in every scrap of knowledge I had to offer," Mistress Juri said. "It took you no time at all to catch up to the other students, and soon you were racing ahead. It doesn't surprise me now to see you interested in how lap-dragons work."

"I appreciate that, Mistress Juri," Lucca replied. He couldn't help but smile, as well as feeling a little burning blush run up the back of his neck.

Mistress Juri hesitated. She wrung her hands. "What was that name you were called when you first came to us?"

Lucca's smile faded. "Lu'Rahl."

Mistress Juri nodded. "That was it, Lu'Rahl. I'm glad you changed it. Lucca suits you so much more."

The felian's tail twitched, but he kept his silence.

"Now, shall I teach you these words?"

Russet didn't lead Lucca back to the inn. Instead, the ferret guided him towards the crumbling wall and stopped outside the remains of a gatehouse. The mossy stone fortifications had cracked in places, with some parts of the old tower fallen completely. A few rusted iron bars jutted out of the stonework, where once wooden platforms had been constructed on the inside of the wall.

"It's best if I leave you here," the ferret said, not meeting Lucca's eye. He clenched his fist around an amulet, the silver chain dangling between his fingers.

"What? Why? Aren't we going to try this on Palmer first?" Lucca asked in surprise. He had hoped for a little more time with the relic thief. He didn't want to let the ferret go now.

Russet shook his head. "Naw. I thought it would be the answer, but it ain't. It was a foolish hope, but it ain't gonna help me."

Lucca tried to grab hold of Russet's hands, but the ferret kept stepping backwards. "You haven't even told me what you need help for," Lucca said, pleading with the ferret, but giving up trying to grab his hands.

Russet smiled sadly. "You don't want to know, Sweetie. Trust me. I appreciate the sentiment, but it ain't something you can help me with."

"It's something to do with Sama'Rey, isn't it?" Lucca asked. He folded his arms across his chest and scuffed his paw against the ground.

Russet nodded once. "Yeah. But that's all I'm telling you. It ain't safe for you to know more."

Lucca clenched his jaw. He looked at the ferret and saw his vision blurring. Dampness trickled down his cheeks. "So this is goodbye then, is it?"

"It can't be any other way." Russet leaned in to kiss Lucca on the cheek. The ferret's face was damp too. A sad smile spread across his muzzle. He slipped the amulet he carried into Lucca's hand. "Now, I ain't much good with how this magic works, but this amulet should give you the protection you need. Say the love charm backfired and hit you instead. This amulet should show that."

The lion slowly opened his hand. In it was the pale pink amulet the ferret usually wore. He forced his grimace into a smile, though doubt already plagued the back of his mind. He didn't expect the charm to hold up to anyone who investigated the claims. After all, if the charm was meant to reflect the magic back, then it would have done so already. "Thank you," the lion whispered, hoping those claims would never be tested.

Russet smiled. "Goodbye, Lucca. Wait here. I'll send Palmer with your supplies."

With that, Russet turned and walked back into the village. Lucca slumped against the aging stonework and watched him leave. The ferret didn't once look back.

Chapter Ten

Lucca had not moved from the gatehouse. No one had passed by. The road was empty of travellers. The lion had sat with his back to the stone, looking out over the deserted wilderness. A couple of eagles soared overhead, clearly visible against the backdrop of the pale blue sky. Nothing had worked the way it should have. He was going to return to Esfyr's Wold a failure. The registry had been lost. Russet had left his life. Lucca felt more alone than ever.

The lion's hand moved to the satchel he had carried all the way from Esfyr's Wold. Once it had carried the registry, but now it was just the textbook he had brought with him in case he had a spare minute to brush up on some of his study. He reached into the satchel and pulled the book out. For the first time, he could see that the illusion spell he had cast in Mistress Juri's cottage had worked. Instead of a book on alchemy, he looked down at a tome on lap-dragons. The duplication would not last long, but he had thought it would last long enough to help Palmer.

The lion flicked open the book to a random page. The spidery writing was almost undecipherable, saying nothing of the tongue-twisting language that was written there. He traced his finger over a word and tried to force the word out. "Regrill? Regharyl? Righryl? Ugh, why don't you have any vowels?"

"Rghryl?" a familiar voice called out.

Lucca looked up to see Palmer standing just beside him. He hadn't heard the lap-dragon approaching at all. Following just behind the tiny dragon was Lucca's pack, hovering a few inches above the ground. The lap-dragon still had the pewter bracelet around his wrist.

"How did you do that?" Lucca asked in surprise.

Palmer plucked a small gemstone from the front of the pack, which instantly slumped lifelessly to the ground. "Master Russet has a few little charms, yannow. He said everything in here will get you home. Lots of food. Your collapsible lodgings too."

Lucca smiled weakly. He opened his arms out to Palmer, who gave off a little squeak and jumped forward to be embraced by the lion. "I'm going to miss you, Palmer."

"I'll miss you too, felian Lucca. You're good fun, and Master Russet likes you too." The lap-dragon's eyes briefly fell across the book clutched in Lucca's hand.

Lucca nodded. "I like him too. You look after him, alright?"

Palmer squeaked. "I always do, felian Lucca. I would do anything to help Master Russet be happy."

Lucca pulled back from the embrace. He smiled sadly and placed his hand on Palmer's cheek. "I'm glad he'll have you around at least."

The lion closed the book and started to return it to the satchel over his shoulder, but the lap-dragon swayed on the spot briefly. He closed his eyes, before reaching out to lunge for the book. He snatched it from Lucca's surprised hands.

"Quickly, felian Lucca," the lap-dragon hissed. He spoke in a voice that was not his usual bright tone. Gone was the brightness, instead there was a desperate urgency. He held out the book, a claw tapping against one of the spells. "He is disconnected, but only for a moment. Quickly."

"Who is?"

"Tella. Master Sama'Rey's other lap-dragon. Please. I can't block him for long." The little lap-dragon trembled.

Lucca hesitated. "Are you sure?"

"Yes," Palmer squeaked urgently. "Quickly, please. Master Russet needs you, not Master Sama'Rey."

Lucca's eyes flicked down to the book. It was not the spell Mistress Juri had taught him earlier. None of the words matched, and the lion didn't know how to pronounce them. He looked back to Palmer. The lap-dragon trembled where he stood, his hands held to his head.

The lion traced a finger over the activation phrase. He sweated on the pronunciation. He made a sound not unlike coughing up a hairball.

"Doot!" Palmer's back straightened up and his hands snapped down to his sides. The little lap-dragon remained completely still. He stared straight ahead, his eyes glazed over slightly.

Lucca swallowed nervously. He knew he needed to get the pronunciation right, but he'd never even seen most of the words before. There weren't enough vowels. He looked to Palmer's still body and gritted his teeth. The lap-dragon had trusted him to get it right. He quickly read through the spell, sounding out the alleged words in his mind.

After taking another deep breath, Lucca slowly spoke the spell. A cough threatened to burst from his throat halfway through, though the lion was sure it wouldn't sound out of place. His hackles rose as he spat out the last couple of challenging syllables.

"Doot! Accepted!" Palmer chirped. The lap-dragon fell flat on his face.

"Palmer?" Lucca asked warily. His throat felt sore. He snapped the book closed and returned it to his satchel as he crouched down in front of the prone lap-dragon. With one finger, he gently prodded Palmer, but the lap-dragon didn't move at all. "Palmer? Oh no."

Lucca carefully rolled the lap-dragon over, but Palmer didn't resist the moment at all. There was no life in him at all. The lap-dragon's eyes were open still, but they appeared to be glazed over and sightless. Lucca scooped his arms beneath the lap-dragon and lifted him up. With a snap of his fingers, Lucca summoned his luggage to follow him back into the village.

Russet was going to kill him.

No one paid much attention to the hooded lion, even with the magical pack following his heels. If there were any reports out for a missing felian mage, then they hadn't yet reached Melry's Reach. Even with his green mane kept hidden, he couldn't imagine he blended in too well.

There wasn't much activity around the Royal Egg Inn. There was no sign of the ferret as the relic thief prepared to move on to his next destination. Lucca didn't know where to find Russet, but he knew how to find someone who could. He pushed open the door to the inn and stepped inside, hoping to find Tallie.

He found them both. The ferret was sat at the bar in conversation with the otter, his back to the door. Tallie looked up and lifted a brow.

Russet reacted to the pointed glance from the otter, turning around on his chair. He almost fell off. "Lucca?" he gasped. His eyes flicked from the lion to the lap-dragon. "What did you do with Palmer?"

"I didn't mean to," Lucca said with a whimper. The weight of Palmer felt heavy in his arms as he looked down at the lap-dragon. "He said you needed me, not, you know. The other felian."

The ferret shared a quick glance with Tallie. He slid her a couple of scalls before hopping down from his seat. He pushed past Lucca, almost tripping over the lion's floating baggage. "Follow me. Quickly."

Lucca hurried after the ferret, a click of his fingers having his baggage follow, rising to float vertical in the confined space. Russet led him around the side of the inn, away from the street. A narrow alley led between the inn and the next building, which led through to the gardens at the back. Trees clustered close to the tables of the outdoor dining area, but that wasn't where Russet was going. He pulled open a cellar door.

A narrow staircase cut into the ground beneath the inn. Although it looked like a cellar, Lucca could smell no evidence of anything stored down there, and there were no scuffs around the stonework that indicated anything heavy like wine barrels had ever been carried down.

Russet pulled the doors closed behind them, plunging everything into total darkness. The ferret's hand rested on Lucca's shoulder, giving him a gentle nudge to keep moving forward. Slowly, they descended down the stairs and further into the dark.

Beneath the inn, it was not only pitch black, but also wet. There was a constant drip of water somewhere, and the scents of mould and mildew filled Lucca's nose. It made him feel like sneezing constantly. A couple of loud thumps emanated down through the oppressive stone ceiling.

"Where are we going?" Lucca asked nervously. Even his strong night vision could see nothing down here. He lifted his hand, tempted to summon magelight to his fingers, but the ferret spoke before he could.

"My hideout. It's just through here. I'll get a light going," Russet replied. Lucca couldn't tell what emotion was in the ferret's voice. Anger? Fear? Worry? Relief? It could have been all of them, or none of them.

Stone grated just ahead. Before Lucca could utter the words of an illumination charm, a faint light began to glow, then an oil burner flared to life. A door opened up in the stone wall of the cellar, leading through to a small room where the burner had been lit. Cautiously, the lion stepped forward to peer inside.

The stone walls felt close inside the room, and there were no windows to outside. A couple of small vents at the ceiling carried the smoke from the burner lamp away. An unlit fireplace could also be used for heat and light. A small bed took up one side of the room, and a narrow desk cluttered with papers and scrolls filled one corner. Wooden shelving took up most of the remaining space on the walls, covered in various trinkets and possessions.

"This is your home?" Lucca asked.

Russet crouched next to the desk. "One of them," he said, rummaging through a couple of boxes. "Put him on the bed, please?"

Lucca did as he was asked. Palmer was placed on the bed. The lap-dragon remained perfectly still.

Russet stood empty-handed. He grimaced to himself and placed his hand on Palmer's forehead, before he glanced back to the lion. "He's in hibernation. What did you do?" he asked, his tone veering from curious to accusatory.

"He saw the spellbook, and..."

"Which spellbook?"

"The one from Mistress Juri's house. The one about lap-dragons."

"You stole it?" Russet asked, grinning at the lion. He slapped Lucca playfully on the back. "Good work."

Lucca wasn't sure he liked the change in tone to admiration. He quickly shook his head. "I duplicated it. My spell won't last long, but I thought it might have more in it to help Palmer..."

Russet lifted his brow. "This is helping him?"

Lucca sighed. "He saw the book, and he got really frantic for a moment. He pointed out the spell and told me to hurry. He said he was blocking Sama'Rey's access, but he couldn't hold him for long. Palmer wanted me to do this."

"Palmer... asked you?" Russet asked in surprise. His hand kept stroking at the still lap-dragon's shoulders. "Why would he ask you to do that?"

"I don't know, but he did it after he said he would do anything to make you happy. He said... he said that you needed to be with me, not Sama'Rey," Lucca said hesitantly.

Russet ran a hand over his muzzle. "That ain't possible. He *belongs* to Sama'Rey, not me. It's just what he is, I can't blame him for that. But he can't choose me over him."

Lucca glanced down to the bed. "I think he just did."

The ferret sighed and slumped onto the floor. His head bumped back against the mattress. "Everything was so simple before I met you, felian."

Lucca grimaced. "Should I just leave you both?"

"No," Russet said sharply. The ferret took a deep breath and softened his voice. "No, please. I dunno if Palmer chose me. I think he chose *you*. He sees something in you."

Lucca ran his hands nervously through his mane. "What do we do now? We have to help him."

"We?" Russet said sharply, looking up to the lion. "Are you sure this is a 'we' situation?"

Lucca gestured to the lap-dragon. "You said Palmer seemed to think it is."

Russet scratched at his chin. "You have to go back to the guild. You stay with me, and you may not be able to go back," he said. He sat on the edge of the bed, one hand resting on Palmer's arm. His fingers traced around the pewter bracelet still secure at the lap-dragon's wrist. "I'm a thief. One your guild wants to catch. You can't be seen helping me."

"Then we make sure we aren't seen," Lucca said with a shrug. "No one knows where we are. The battlemages are in Emberfade."

"That's just the thing," Russet said. He thumped his tail on the bed and looked down at Palmer. "I ain't got the equipment to restore Palmer here. My closest hideout with that is at Emberfade. That's where I need to go."

Lucca placed his hand on Russet's knee. "Then that's where I go too. I did this. I have to help fix it."

Russet twitched his muzzle. He rose to his paws and looked Lucca in the eye. "This ain't your world, Lucca. This is like Erasmus's mansion. My world. My rules. You listen to what I have to say, alright? You obey every order, without question."

Lucca bowed his head. "I understand."

Russet lifted Lucca's chin, forcing the lion to keep his gaze. "If I say run, you run. You don't look back. You abandon me to whatever fate takes me. Do you understand?"

The lion shivered. He cautiously placed his hand on Russet's hip. The ferret didn't pull away. "I'll do my best."

"Is all I can ask," Russet said quietly. He leaned in to give Lucca a quick kiss on the cheek, before turning away. "Did you say you had some rope in your pack?"

"I do, yeah," Lucca said. He glanced back to see his pack had dropped to the ground behind him, barely visible in the gloom.

"Can you tie Palmer to your bag, then wait for me out the front? I've got some things to pack. Then I'll get some extra food from Tallie," the ferret said. He tapped his paw against the floor and looked around the small, dark hideout. "We've got a long walk ahead of us."

Lucca knelt down next to his baggage, rummaging around inside until he found one of the lengths of rope. He groaned. "We're walking? We can't take the cart?"

"Tallie ain't gonna let me take it that far, but the road's easy enough," Russet said with a shake of his head. He helped Lucca move Palmer down onto the top of the baggage. They secured the lap-dragon in place with the rope. He smirked. "You ain't bad with knots. I might have a thing or two to teach you about them though."

It took Lucca a moment to realise what Russet insinuated. He stammered, unable to form a proper response.

The ferret's grin grew wider. "Tongue tied? Didn't realise you were so eager to begin."

Lucca sought any distraction he could find, and his eyes soon settled on the pewter band around Palmer's wrist, gleaming softly in the light from the oil burner. He could still sense faint traces of magic from it, even after the lap-dragon had fallen into hibernation. "What does that even do?" he asked, trying to change the subject quickly.

The ferret ran his finger around the bracelet. "This? It's a little trinket that gives a lap-dragon access to stronger abilities. This allows one to break into magical defences."

"So that's how Palmer broke the security gems?" the lion asked. His tail thrashed behind him.

Russet grinned, showing off his sharp teeth. "Exactly. Now, go on. Wait for me out the front. I won't be long."

Lucca nodded and stepped away from the ferret. He snapped his fingers and summoned his pack. The luggage levitated off the floor, with Palmer securely balanced on top. The lap-dragon didn't move at all, even as the luggage began to drift along behind Lucca. The lion didn't look back at the ferret as he climbed back up the darkened stairs, then opened the cellar doors to step outside. He knew Russet would catch up before long.

The lion's heart hammered in his chest. He looked up to the blue sky to avoid looking in the shadows for fear that thieves were lurking in them. He didn't know what he had walked into, but he knew that it was surely above his head. He could still run. He could leave and go back to Esfyr's Wold. When Lucca reached the street, he looked in that direction. The village walls were out of sight, but he knew the rolling moors were out there, beyond the stone buildings.

Lucca then looked left. That way was Emberfade. He would reach the port town after all, but he wouldn't be doing it alone. Russet, the ferret he was sent out to capture, would be his companion on that road now.

There had been an excuse before. Lucca had been able to justify overturning the love charm that had never taken hold. That innocence was gone now. There were no excuses to hide behind. Lucca was helping the relic thief and not even the flimsy exonerating evidence Russet had given him would save him. Should the guild learn of his actions, then his hopes and ambitions for his life on Lutrea were over. The Mages Guild would not forgive him for this.

Lucca set his jaw. He just had to make sure they never knew what he was doing.

Chapter Eleven

The road to Emberfade was reasonably busy. Merchants travelled in both directions, though most were heading in the same direction as Lucca and Russet. Those on horseback were able to overtake them easily enough, though the ferret and lion walked faster than most of those on paw. The clear weather held for the remainder of the day, but clouds began to gather as the sun sunk down to the western horizon.

For most of the day, Lucca had idly chatted with Russet about his studies. The ferret had never had the chance to learn any magic, and he had been interested to learn some of the theory behind it. He had not shown any aptitude for learning the skill though; one of a small percentage of musteliads who possessed no skill in magic. Russet also showed little interest in the history of the region, which Lucca had voraciously studied, especially in the peaceful centuries of development that had followed the last conflicts on the peninsula.

As evening deepened, the road became clearer as fewer travellers remained on it. Though they passed by a few villages, Russet never stopped at them. He kept walking through, ignoring the various inns and places to stop. The ferret never gave a reason why each village was unsatisfactory, but every time Lucca suggested they stop, he just shook his head and continued on his way.

Lucca's paws were beginning to hurt. The air was cooling drastically as clouds began to cover the sun, and they were approaching a thick forest that seemed to stretch from horizon to horizon. Hills loomed large to their right, while farmland dominated the left side of the road. The lion couldn't see a village between them and the boughs of the forest ahead.

The road delved into the forest. Beneath the trees was dark, and it put Lucca in mind of the forest that surrounded Esfyr's Wold. Most of the trees were barren of leaves, but the branches were close enough together that they almost completely hid the sun as it lowered towards the horizon.

Lucca glanced back. He could see nothing but trees in both directions. Were it not for the road beneath his aching paws, he was sure that he would get lost amongst the trees. Birds chirped in the bare branches above them, and small creatures darted out of view before Lucca could properly find them. A stream bubbled not too far away, though the lion couldn't actually see the water.

Finally, Russet placed his hand on the lion's elbow and guided the lion from the road. They traipsed a short way through the trees, their paws crunching on the dry, dead leaves that scattered across the ground. A small clearing opened up between the trees, with the narrow stream flowing around the edge. The stream was only a couple of feet wide, and the muddy water slowly flowed through the trees.

The ferret crouched down by the bank of the stream. He wrinkled his muzzle. "Ah, I had been hoping the water would be clear enough to fill our skins. Unless you had a spell to filter out mud from water?"

Lucca gratefully collapsed down to the ground. He didn't bother himself with looking at the stream. He just lay back amongst the leaves and stretched his legs out. The luggage gently lowered to the ground beside him, with Palmer still securely in place on top. "I can try if we get desperate," the lion replied. "But I haven't been taught one."

"Shame. We've got enough to get to Emberfade. Just would have preferred to fill up here," the ferret said with a shrug. He turned to grin at Lucca. "Before you get too comfortable, let's set up your collapsible lodgings."

"Ugh," Lucca groaned. He wasn't sure if it was about having to get up, or the continued teasing about the collapsible lodgings that was more annoying. He shouldn't be the one getting teased for Kyde's term. He would have to work out a way to get back at the otter when he returned to the chapterhouse. If he returned. Lucca forced that thought to the back of his mind for now. There would be time enough to worry about the guild in Emberfade.

Russet's suggestion had been a good one. Barely had the tent been raised before rain started to fall through the trees. It wasn't a heavy downfall, but Lucca was glad that he had somewhere to shelter from it. The tent didn't have much room with two packs and Palmer squeezed inside, but the two were able to comfortably sit next to each other. The ferret had also produced a thick canvas sheet, which he was able to secure to the nearest trees. It provided them with a small dry area outside the tent. Lucca soon had a fire burning to warm their hands.

A kettle whistled over the fire. Russet prepared a hot drink for them both, while Lucca rationed out his supplies from Kyde to provide a simple meal for them both, leaving Tallie's supplies for the next day. As the lion looked down at the fish and couscous, he tried hard not to think about the steak he had enjoyed two nights earlier.

"Well, here we are again," Lucca said as he passed Russet his meal.

"Just you and me alone in the woods. What could possibly happen?" the ferret replied. Despite his wink, Russet stayed sat down on the opposite side of the fire. Rain drummed off the canvas sheet just above his head, and water trickled to the ground behind him.

Lucca paused from eating his first mouthful of couscous. He stared at the simple meal, then out to the forest beyond the protection of their tent.

"Something on your mind?" Russet asked, speaking around a mouthful of fish.

Lucca put his food down. He had barely eaten all day, ever since their quick breakfast in the Royal Egg, but even so the questions burned at his throat until he could no longer contain them. "Who is Sama'Rey?"

Russet slowly lowered his fork. He swallowed his mouthful. "He's the guildmaster of the Thieves' Guild," the ferret said slowly. "I told you that before."

Lucca shook his head. "Why is he important? Why would Palmer do this?"

The ferret tucked his paws in beneath his legs. He wrinkled his muzzle and frowned. "If I tell you and the guild, my guild, learns about it, there ain't no going back. They won't let you."

"If I'm helping you, I deserve to know why," Lucca replied. Instead of hunger, he felt a little nausea welling in his stomach. His hands trembled.

Russet bit his lip. His tail swished over his lap. "I grew up in Nesterslip. My parents weren't rich. Quite the opposite. Ain't much work in a place like that. By the time I was six, I was already a great pickpocket. Thieves' Guild already knew about me. When I was eight, my parents were accused of attempted murder. Tried to kill a local lord."

"What happened to them?" Lucca asked. His hands tightened around the small container of food, though the fish and couscous remained uneaten.

Russet shrugged. "Dunno. Never saw them again. Probably killed. But this lord somehow knew they had children. He wanted me as payment. I was to be his bonded servant." The ferret paused. He smiled bitterly. "That's where Sama'Rey comes in."

"He paid out your bond?" Lucca asked. He wanted to reach out and take Russet's hand, but the ferret still held onto his food container.

Russet nodded. "He promised me that as soon as I paid him back, I would be free to do what I wanted. Until then, I'm his. If I run away, then every crime I ever did comes to light. He turns me into the Cofferknell guard. I take the fall for every crime *he* ever did too."

"He can do that?" Lucca whispered. His eyes flicked towards the shadows outside, fearful that Sama'Rey himself might be lurking in them.

The ferret's gaze followed Lucca's. "I dunno," he admitted. He curled his ears down. "I ain't willing to test him, though."

"So how can you escape him?" Lucca asked. He dragged his eyes away from the darkness outside.

"I pay my bond. He dies. I die," Russet said, holding up a finger for each option. "That's it. He uses Palmer to spy on me. I hoped that maybe I could disconnect Palmer for a bit and run, but that weren't gonna work. Then Palmer went and did his thing anyway. I just hope he's got some plan for all this."

"What's your debt with him? I have some savings from little jobs I've done around the chapterhouse," Lucca offered.

Russet laughed and shook his head. He smiled warmly as he looked up to the lion. "Oh, Sweetie. Unless you have sixteen million scalls rattling around your pockets, I don't think you have enough."

Lucca almost choked. "Sixteen *million*? That would be enough to buy all of Esfyr's Wold many times over!"

Russet shrugged again. He poked his fork at his couscous. "I was young when I accepted Sama'Rey's offer. Eleven years now and I've managed to knock a couple of mill off it. For a few years I thought I'd get to pay it off. Now I know I never will."

Lucca stared down at his food. "So, you've been stealing artefacts to take back to him? That's how you're paying the debt?"

"He gives me a list of what he wants. If I can get it, I steal it," Russet admitted. He started to eat again, shovelling a mouthful of couscous onto his fork again. "He targets the Mages' Guild mostly. Wants stuff from them."

"And the yearbook was part of that?" Lucca asked.

Russet nodded. "He mentioned it two years ago. Never had a chance to get it before you came along."

Lucca groaned and rubbed his forehead. Master Roe had chosen the perfect bait indeed. "What does Sama'Rey need it for?"

Russet's muzzle flicked. He waited until he'd finished some couscous before answering. "I ain't too sure. He's felian, like you. Hates magic, and especially your guild. The yearbook's just part of his plan against your archmage."

Lucca set his jaw. "Then we have to make sure he doesn't get the book."

The ferret chuckled. "You're cute when you look all serious," he said with a smile. "But until I'm free from Sama'Rey, I have to assume I'm bound to take the book back to him."

"I don't understand why..."

"I'm good at what I do. Very good. Ain't no one better," Russet said, puffing out his chest a little. His smile lingered, but it didn't quite light up his gold-flecked eyes. "But I only survive because of the Thieves' Guild. Hideouts like the Royal Egg and people like Tallie give me refuge. If I run from the guild, that all goes. No more safe spaces. Oh, and every guard on the peninsula will be looking for me."

Lucca dropped his eyes. He prodded idly at his serving of fish. "We'll work something out."

"It don't have to be a 'we', Lucca. You can leave if it's too much. You have the evidence that'll clear you," Russet said. He still smiled, but Lucca could see the sorrow in his eyes.

Lucca chose to ignore that. He didn't know how to answer it and remain truthful, given how ineffective he believed that evidence truly was. He wanted to help Russet, but there was a growing fear within his gut that still partially suppressed his appetite. "Why me, though? Why did you stay with me that first night?"

Russet took a while to answer. He ate some of his couscous, staring intently at the container of food. "I'm a thief. It's a lonely job. Can't trust anyone. Can't get close to anyone."

"Apart from Palmer," Lucca said, his eyes flicking towards the tent, where the lap-dragon's still body rested.

"Yeah, of course. But he ain't the same as you or I. He's a lap-dragon. He don't know how people like us work," Russet explained. He took a moment to eat some of his fish. "It's difficult for him. Difficult for me."

Lucca nodded. He scraped up the last of his couscous. "I know what it's like to be alone."

"I just wanted the chance to spend some time with someone and have fun. No risks. No complications," Russet said with a laugh. "Then you didn't take advantage of it. You intrigued me. I played along, but then I..." The ferret speared the last piece of fish on his fork. He chewed on the seafood.

"You got in too deep," Lucca said, finishing the sentence for the flustered ferret.

"Yeah. Thieves don't take well to complications. You gave me the taste of a life without Sama'Rey. I got infatuated with the idea. With you. I'd forgotten how much I wanted something else," Russet admitted. He took a deep breath and sighed. "I ain't got a life outside of this. Dunno what I'd do."

"I don't know what I'd do if I wasn't a mage," Lucca said. He finished the last of his meal and closed up the lunchbox with the fork inside. He leaned back to rest on his elbows, looking up at the canvas sheet that protected them from the light rain. His tail swished idly. "Magic is all I've ever known, since I was a kitten."

"Perhaps I'd be an honest merchant," Russet said. A sly grin broke across his muzzle, and his eyes lit up. "I know all the best suppliers. I know who's in the pocket of the Thieves' Guild."

Lucca blinked. "Some merchants pay the Thieves' Guild?"

"How else do you think their merchandise don't go missing?" Russet grinned. He crawled over to Lucca's side of the fire and rested against the felian. "Or they might want a rival's shipment to get permanently delayed."

Lucca's hand moved down to stroke over the ferret's shoulders. "Couldn't they just hire guards to protect their stock?"

Russet shrugged. "Cheaper to pay off the thieves. Guards are expensive."

The felian frowned. "If mages placed wards on them?"

"Ain't that what got us into this mess to begin with?" Russet giggled. He spread his arms wide as he rested his head in Lucca's lap. "The mighty thief ward! It will bring the Thieves' Guild to its knees overnight. We'll never steal anything again!"

Lucca rolled his eyes. "Master Roe told me it was impossible to make one. I think you'll be safe for a while."

Russet's muzzle twitched in amusement. "Oh good. Perhaps my stealing days ain't over yet."

"I think you've got other things to worry about, rather than Master Roe's next grand scheme," Lucca said. He gently stroked Russet's chest.

"Don't underestimate Sama'Rey, alright Sweetie? He's had years of experience running the guild," Russet warned, reaching up with one hand to lightly touch Lucca's chin.

"He's never come up against many mages though, has he?" Lucca asked, wondering if he could work out a weakness in this mysterious foe.

"Dozens. Beaten them all," Russet said, smirking despite the disappointing news.

Lucca frowned. "Oh. Well not a felian mage."

Russet raised a brow. "I dunno if there are any other felian mages. Didn't believe you were until I saw your magic tricks."

Lucca lightly tapped his fingers against Russet's belly. "So, Sama'Rey might look at me and see a felian, and not a mage?"

Russet shrugged. "Yeah, I guess. Especially if you ain't wearing any robes."

"I should disrobe before I see him?" Lucca asked, sticking his tongue out.

Russet snorted in laughter. "Wouldn't recommend it. He might not appreciate you like I do."

"Pity," Lucca said with a smirk. "Everyone should. I'm majestic enough for it."

The ferret paused. His smile flickered as he looked right into Lucca's eyes. "Maybe I don't want to share that."

Lucca flicked an ear. "Am I yours to share?"

Russet's hand stroked up Lucca's belly, sneaking in beneath his Winterpaw leathers. "Maybe. Depends what happens. Like I said… complication."

"And what if I were to just tie you up and take you back to Esfyr's Wold now. Would that still be a complication?"

Russet sat up and smirked to Lucca. The ferret's teeth gleamed in the firelight. He held up his hands and pressed his palms together. "Go on. Try it. Still got some rope, ain't you?"

"I… what?" Lucca blinked.

"Try tying me up. See how far it gets you."

Lucca flicked his ears back. "Are you sure?"

"You got your skills. I got mine. Test them."

Lucca frowned slightly, but he rose up to his paws to retrieve the remainder of the rope from his pack. Some of it had been used to secure Palmer, who remained completely silent and still inside the tent. The lion looked down sadly at the lap-dragon. Palmer was one reason why he'd never stop Russet from getting back to Emberfade, and some of his good mood trickled away. There could be someone at the guild chapterhouse who could help Palmer, but the felian doubted Russet would want to risk going anywhere near there. They had to get to Emberfade.

The lion was smiling again when he turned back to the fire with the spool of rope wrapped around his hand.

Russet was on his knees, hands still pressed together in front of him. "Come on then, felian. Or are you scared you can't do it?"

Lucca scoffed and approached the ferret. He wrapped the rope around Russet's wrists, keeping his palms tight together. The rope then wound around the ferret's elbows, before Lucca tightened it around the ferret's torso as well, keeping Russet's arms pinned to his chest. For all of it, Russet remained completely still.

As the lion tied the final knot, he ran his hand over the rope. It shimmered with light for a few brief moments. A bright flash lit up the small clearing, and when the light faded the rope had sealed to itself, leaving no knot behind.

"There you go. All tied up," Lucca said with a smile. He knew there was no way the ferret would be able to wriggle free.

"Nice trick with the knots," Russet said. He sounded impressed, and his arms struggled fruitlessly in the ropes. "You mind fetching my hood for me? Should be just inside the tent."

"What do you need that for?"

"Wanna show you something."

Lucca tilted his head, but he turned his back on the ferret to retrieve the hood. He saw it right away, draped across Russet's small pack. There didn't appear to be anything interesting or unusual about it, but he took it in his hand. He turned back to face the ferret and froze.

Russet was sat in front of the fire, his arms outstretched. He was completely free of the rope. "Ta-da!"

"H-how..." Lucca stammered. "You said you can't do magic."

"It ain't magic, Sweetie. Least, not the kind you do."

"Then how did you do it?"

Russet tossed the rope over to Lucca, who struggled to catch the flailing length. It was still looped to itself, his magic keeping it bound together. "I'm a ferret. It's in my blood."

"Huh." Lucca frowned and ran his fingers over the rope. It had not been cut in any way. "What else can you do?"

"With a rope, or without?" The ferret bared his teeth in a wide grin.

"How about we start without?"

"*Start* without?" Russet asked. He smirked and crawled closer to the lion. "Don't put it away just yet then, in case I need it later."

"Oh, I didn't mean..." Lucca started to protest, but his words faded away into a fierce blush as the ferret pulled him back to the fire.

"Why don't you show me what you meant?"

Anything further the lion had to say was silenced by a firm kiss from Russet. The ferret's hands tugged on Lucca's leathers, pulling him down. Together, they sank to the ground.

The sound of rain enveloped them. Nothing else in the world mattered anymore.

"You said we should reach Emberfade before nightfall?" Lucca asked.

The two had been walking all day. They had woken with the rising sun and enjoyed a quick breakfast, but their rest didn't last as long as Lucca wanted. His legs were still tired from the previous day, and he hadn't slept too much after their late night in each other's arms. There had been no end to the forest either. Despite the sun having already gone beyond its highest point, they were still beneath the leafless canopy of the forest. Without any way to see the landscape, Lucca couldn't tell just how far they had been walking.

"At our pace? No problem at all," Russet called back. The ferret had been walking a few paces ahead of Lucca for most of the day, occasionally reaching back to give the lion an encouraging tug on the hand. He didn't let their pace drop too much though.

"And what's our plan when we get there?" Lucca asked wearily. He hoped that there would be time to rest for a couple of days. He almost envied Palmer, getting to miss all this walking. The lap-dragon was still secured to the floating pack, which drifted along at the same pace behind Lucca's heels.

Russet shrugged his shoulders. He spun around on his toes and walked backwards. "Depends on what Palmer says when he wakes up. If Sama'Rey can't use him, then maybe we have a chance to get away. If not, we may need to head to Cofferknell."

Lucca shuddered. That was the answer he had been most worried about. He wasn't sure what would happen in the capital city. "Palmer would have had a reason for choosing that spell."

"I sure hope so," Russet said. The ferret grimaced. "We'll need to be on our guard in Emberfade. Sama'Rey might have sent someone there to look out for me."

"Friendly?"

Russet shrugged. "Maybe. Maybe not. Guess we'll find out when we get there."

"That's comforting."

The ferret flashed a smile. "Don't worry, Sweetie. I've got your back."

"Promise?"

"I promise," the ferret replied, placing a hand over his heart. He then tensed slightly and looked up to something beyond Lucca's shoulder.

The lion felt a cold shiver pass through his spine. He chanced a quick glance, but he couldn't see anything untoward. A few crows were perched on the trees above him. They cawed softly amongst themselves. There was no one on the road behind them.

Russet's hand closed around Lucca's. "We should hurry. Sama'Rey has eyes everywhere."

"He's watching us now?" Lucca asked. He was careful to drop his voice low.

"He might be. I ain't sure. Just a feeling I had, and this time I ain't got Palmer to scan for me."

"Will we be safe in Emberfade?"

Lucca wished he hadn't asked. He would have preferred the question had remained unsaid. Instead, the answer never came. The lion looked back up to the three crows. They each let out another loud caw before taking to wing. He soon lost them amongst the trees, but they had flown away in the direction of Emberfade.

Lucca held the tip of his tail in his hand. He felt like they were walking right into danger.

Chapter Twelve

Emberfade was a large, sprawling town on the estuary of the Lutrea River. The settlement spread out across the flat plain between the ocean, river, and the forest which ended abruptly a few miles from the shore. There was no protective wall around the town, with no defined boundary between the buildings and the countryside surrounding the settlement.

Long ago, it had been the capital of the local region, when the peninsula had been split into warring factions. Trade had always flourished with a natural harbour gradually built upon over the many years. Lucca had learned much about the history of Emberfade and the importance it had held in the burgeoning united peninsula, bringing through food and materials from lands even as distant as Da'Manyr. Over time though, its use had faded to newer and more modern ports that had sprung up in the area.

Lucca eagerly recounted this history to the ferret, pointing out a few of the older buildings that spoke of the town's crumbling past. Russet did not speak much, letting the lion blurt out his excitement in a constant stream of words.

Once the road into the old port town emerged from the forest, it angled close to the river as it wound towards the ocean. Buildings crowded in close to the main road, and soon smaller roads led off to the left, with the river remaining a constant distance to the right. The wind blew a strong scent of fish and salt across the air. Lucca had wrinkled his nose, though Russet appeared to be delighted by the fresh scent.

Russet nudged Lucca off to the right of the road. Behind the single row of stone buildings was a dock. A wooden walkway stretched out into the river. Several small fishing boats were tied up to the dock, and a couple of otters had even sat on the planks with fishing rods lazily dangled into the fast-flowing water. A few boats were out on the water, crossing between the two shores. A second, smaller dock perched onto the opposite bank. Behind the far docks, the land rose up into a steep hill. A sheer cliff face pockmarked with small caves overlooked the town.

"Been to Emberfade before?" Russet asked. He kept his hand on Lucca's as they started to walk down the docks. The wood clunked and thudded beneath every pawstep.

In the distance, Lucca could see a few larger ships. One towering ship had only just moored, as its sails were still billowing in the breeze. "Once," the lion replied. He pointed to the massive ship. "Came to Lutrea on a ship like that."

The ferret whistled in admiration. "Now that's a proper boat. Don't see many sea-going ships here. They tend to come in at Copper Bay to the north. The ones that don't come in on Reef Point, that is."

"There's a harbour at Reef Point?"

Russet grinned. "Nah. That's the point though."

"Oh." Lucca's eyes widened as he realised what the thief was insinuating. "You do that too?"

"Not us. That's the River Rats. They give us a small cut though, and we don't go for their usual targets. Fair's fair."

"Except for the ships they wreck."

"Apart from them."

No one turned an ear at their conversation. The few musteliads who passed them didn't even look in their direction. Lucca didn't know whether such conversations were expected on the docks, or if it was just the general noise and activity around them that managed to mask them from attention. The lion wasn't sure he wanted to ask the ferret, in case merely pointing it out was enough to break the illusion.

"Where do we go now?" he asked instead.

Russet pointed to one of the small boats crossing the river. His finger then rose to the hill that overlooked the river. "Got a small cave up there. It ain't a fine inn like you mage types are familiar with, but it's got a lovely view."

"And you can fix Palmer there?"

"I certainly hope so."

"Better keep moving then. Hope it's not too steep a climb."

"Nah, it ain't too bad. Come on, before the next ferry crosses. I'd rather not wait around too long."

Lucca nodded. The docks were full of activity, with large crates of materials being moved around the wooden walkway, levitated by charms much like the one that animated the felian's baggage. Some were being transferred from boat to boat, while others saw their loads being moved onto wagons that would carry the goods into the town and the lands beyond. Those which would be transported further distances would be taken to the train station in the outskirts on the far side of town.

To Lucca's unfamiliar eyes, everything seemed orchestrated perfectly. It was a dance of movement, with a cacophonous roar of shouting as the melody that held it all together. Were it not for the constant smell of salt and fish, and the fast-flowing river just to his right, Lucca might almost have enjoyed the experience.

"Apple?" Russet asked. He offered the lion the fruit in his hand. He brandished a strip of dried meat in his other. "Or would you prefer the jerky?"

Lucca blinked. There had not been any apples or jerky in their supplies. He would have seen them at breakfast. He glanced back to see a barrel of apples a few paces behind them. The wooden barrel was branded with the mark of one of the peninsula's finest producers of cider. A few paces beyond that was a crate of dried and salted meat. His eyes flicked back to the offered food. "Did you...?"

The lion decided it was a question better not asked. He fell silent and took the jerky from the ferret. Lucca had known what he was getting into. He had already stolen for the ferret. This was no time to think about the moral quandaries that came with that decision. He chewed uneasily on the salty meat while Russet happily crunched his way through the crisp apple.

The ferry arrived at the dock just as Lucca and Russet reached the boarding ramp. The vessel was little more than a small rowing boat, barely big enough to fit a dozen people. The single oarsman was an otter with powerful shoulders and thick arms that Lucca was quite sure would crush him. The otter wasn't wearing much, despite the cold air. His dark brown fur glistened with sweat.

Three weasels and a badger stepped off the boat after the oarsman secured the vessel in place with a thick rope wound around one of the dock's support posts. There was no one other than Lucca or Russet waiting to get on.

The lion almost lost his balance as the boat pitched in the water. He clung onto the ferret in fear and took a seat as close to the middle of the tiny craft as he could. His luggage slumped down between his paws on the damp wood at the bottom of the boat. His tail lashed nervously as he thought about anything other than the boat sinking.

"We wait a few minutes in case there's others," the otter grunted as the two stepped onto the boat. Lucca imagined the otter's voice sounded similar to something scraping through the riverbed.

Russet handed a small silver shell-shaped coin to the oarsman. "Can we make it now?"

The otter grunted again. He pocketed the scall, then started to unwind the rope from the moorings. The boat rocked as the otter pushed them away from the dock and out into the mercy of the rapid river current.

Lucca clung to his seat. He kept his eyes fixated on the solid ground they were leaving behind, but then he saw a sight that chilled him more than the river. He chanced loosening his grip on the boat to pull down his hood to cover his face. He turned his head to the side.

"Everything alright?" Russet asked.

"Look up to the docks," Lucca said quietly. He hoped the otter would be busy enough with the oars to not listen in. "Do you see those three mages up there?"

Russet's hand tightened on Lucca's thigh. "I see them."

"Do you think they saw us?"

"If they did, I dunno if they were suspicious. They ain't looking at us now. They're going back to the town."

Lucca hissed softly beneath his breath. "I recognise them. They're from Esfyr's Wold. Probably the battlemages who followed after me. I guess Palmer's shortcut wasn't much of one after all."

"Think they're still looking for you?"

"Absolutely. I'd have thought they'd be searching the road first. Must mean your friend made it all the way here before they realised something was wrong."

"Just another thing to be careful about. We'll be fine," Russet said. His hand lifted Lucca's chin. He smiled. "They don't know you're here, and they certainly don't know where we're going. Trust me."

Lucca exhaled slowly and nodded. "I trust you."

Russet flashed a smile. "Ain't many people who say that. I'm glad you do."

"Why don't people trust you?"

"Part of the job description, ain't it? Not exactly the most honest job. We have our codes, but they ain't always followed."

"Oh, right. Yeah," Lucca muttered. He felt a little foolish for even asking the question. The ferret's casual charm kept disarming him, making the lion forget just who he travelled with.

Lucca squeaked as the boat pitched in the wake of a larger craft. The bigger boat was slowly heading upstream. Its hull was laden low with goods. Two massive waterwheels churned through the river to power the boat against the current, but that left some rough waters behind it. The otter oarsman barely reacted.

Once the turbulence cleared, Lucca was able to relax a little again. Water always set his fur on edge. It had been one of the many ways he had been set apart from the locals. The otters especially adored the water, but even the ferrets, weasels, and badgers had been quite happy to get their fur wet. Lucca had never enjoyed it, but for where the water was nicely contained with a visible depth, like in the bathtub. Water magic could have helped him, but he had never managed to get a good grasp on the element, unless it was frozen.

Finally, the boat pulled up next to the docks on the other side of the river. The otter held out his hand as he tucked the oars against the bottom of the boat, warning the other two to remain seated. The oarsman then secured the little boat in place and pulled down a wooden ramp to provide a walkway for the two passengers. Lucca held onto Russet's hand as they stepped off the boat.

The docks on the other side of the river were much quieter. There weren't as many boats moored to the docks, and fewer buildings sat on the shore. In the distance, Lucca could see sandy dunes rising up, but he couldn't see the ocean just yet. It still remained hidden behind the town and a bend in the river.

"Come on, this way. Not too far." Russet pulled on Lucca's hand, and the two made their way through the docks. The town was left behind them, on the other side of the river.

A tiny trail meandered up the hill. It was little more than a dirt path beaten down through the grass by hundreds of feet. Several copses grew alongside the path, but the way up was mostly clear. A small sign at the bottom of the hill advised that it was the route up to the Emberfade Lookout.

Despite what Russet had promised before, the climb was not an easy one for Lucca's aching legs. The slope was steep, despite the path winding around the worst of the incline. Lucca's chest and thighs burned with the exertion.

Close to the top of the hill, the grassy terrain gave way to rocky crags. No more trees grew around the path. The summit was in sight, but Russet slowed down and glanced back down the hill. Lucca followed his gaze. No one followed them.

"Down here," the ferret said. He didn't even sound out of breath as he guided the lion from the path.

The ferret took Lucca down one of the small crags that opened up either side of the path. Stone walls quickly swallowed them up. The crag led through to the open cliff that plummeted down to the distant ground below. It was the far side of the hill to Emberfade, with just rolling hills and the ocean to look upon. Lucca didn't take in the view. He just stared with wide eyes as he found himself standing on a small ledge of stone with nothing between himself and a terrifying fall. He held tightly onto Russet's hand.

"Mind your step. Just around here."

Lucca didn't need the warning to mind where he was stepping. He shuffled after the ferret, moving around the cliff on the narrow shelf of stone. His focus was entirely on his paws, making sure that there was solid ground beneath him with every step.

After just a dozen steps – each of which feeling like a lifetime to the terrified lion – Russet pulled Lucca into a wide cave. The lion collapsed to the floor instantly and curled up, glad to be on safer terrain. He didn't look back, even as he heard his luggage thump down just behind him. He was vaguely aware of scattered belongings through the deep cave, which sloped downwards slightly, away from the sheer drop at the mouth.

"This the place then?" the lion said quietly. He remained sprawled out on the rocky ground, not even caring too much that he wasn't too comfortable. He was just glad he was safe.

"Yeah, this is it. Someone else has been here recently. Can you smell it?"

Lucca flicked his ears and glanced up. "I don't think I can smell anyone else."

The ferret bit his lip. "Maybe it's not smell. Maybe it's just a feeling..."

"You know someone's probably looking for us, so maybe it's just paranoia," Lucca said nervously, speaking mostly to reassure himself as well as the ferret. He knew most musteliads had a better sense of smell than his.

Russet shook his head. "No. I ain't survived this long without a healthy sense of paranoia. Someone was here. You know any warding spells?"

"No warding ones, but I know a few illusions that might stop anyone trying to get in," Lucca said.

"Can you do that while I get everything ready for Palmer?"

Lucca nodded and wearily pulled himself back up to his paws. With one hand held against the inside of the cave, he slowly shuffled towards the mouth of the cave again. His eyes widened as he looked over the great drop again, but this time he focused more on the incredible view. He didn't have many good memories of the ocean. The voyage from Da'Manyr had been rough and traumatic, with a powerful storm whipping up gigantic waves that had crashed against the side of the ship.

The view of the gentle shore was most unlike that horrific memory. Small lines of white arced along the shore where the slate-grey waters met the dirty yellow beaches. From this height, everything looked calm and tranquil, even out towards the flat horizon. He knew better than to look for Da'Manyr. He was looking roughly north, and his homeland was to the distant south. It had taken over a week to reach Lutrea from the sun-baked islands of his homeland.

He shivered as a cold wind blew around him. He still remembered stepping onto that ship. He remembered standing on the deck and looking down at the docks, where his parents had stood. They had waved to him. He had waved back. There had been no tears. Those had already been shed, though many more were yet to come. The young felian had brought nothing with him other than the clothes he had worn. He had owned nothing then. The mage who had come to take him to Lutrea had placed a hand on his shoulder then, and Lu'Rahl had been led inside.

No one had called him Lu'Rahl since.

Remembering he had a task to do, Lucca shook his head and blinked away the wetness in his eyes. Nothing but the cold wind had caused that, he tried to convince himself.

Lucca looked down to the small shelf of rock that provided the only access into the cave. He extended his hand out and barked out a quick spell. With another gesture from his hand, the rock was erased from view, leaving just a terrifying view of the distant ground below.

Extending a paw out, Lucca prodded gently at the seemingly empty space in the air. He could still feel the rock beneath his toes, but he didn't dare place any weight down. The illusion was his own magic, but his eyes still demanded that he not stand on the invisible rock. As an added flourish, Lucca added some cracks to the shelf where the path emerged from the narrow crag. He didn't know if it would be enough, but he hoped it would deter anyone who may try to follow after them.

Turning away from the cliff and the impressive vista, Lucca looked back into the cave. Russet had already unstrapped Palmer from the back of the lion's luggage. The lap-dragon lay on a small blue mat. An azure gemstone the size of Lucca's fist had been placed in the lap-dragon's hands.

Lucca crouched down beside Russet as the ferret stroked his hand over the lap-dragon's brow. "Is there anything we need to do for him?"

Russet shook his head. "Nah, not now." He tapped a finger against the crystal in the lap-dragon's hands. "This is what's important. They're paired to a specific lap-dragon and helps them heal, in their own way. They're helpful when they get damaged or broken in some way, but I dunno how they work beyond that. Something about restarting their mind. I got a few of these at some of my more regular safehouses."

"How long does it take?"

"Shouldn't be long. Just a few minutes at most. You fixed up out there?"

Lucca nodded. "Anyone will think twice about it, at least."

Russet peered over Lucca's shoulder. "An illusion, I hope? Or else we ain't getting back out."

"I can reverse it when we need to leave," Lucca assured the ferret. The lion took another step back away from the edge. The height made his head spin, though he could certainly appreciate the view of the coastline as it swept out towards a distant headland. He sat back and rested his hands on his knees. "Who do you think may have come here?"

Russet sat down beside the lion. "Has to be someone from the guild. Nothing is missing, so they must have come for me."

"Does that change anything?"

The ferret ran his hands over his muzzle. His fingers twirled around the blue tuft of fur between his eyes. "Might do. Sama'Rey knows Palmer was disconnected. He must think it's suspicious."

"Will they... will they try to kill us?"

Russet's silence went on for much longer than Lucca liked.

"I don't think so," Russet said slowly, uncertainly. He bit his lip and flicked his ears. "We're thieves, not assassins, and it ain't Sama'Rey's style either. He prefers to humiliate, rather than kill. That said, I ain't putting it past him either."

"How comforting," Lucca muttered.

Russet placed his hand on Lucca's shoulder. "I promise you, I ain't gonna let anything happen to you. His argument is with me. He ain't got anything on you, so long as you don't give him anything to hold."

"He already does though," Lucca said sadly.

The ferret blinked. "What does he have?"

"He has you."

Russet sighed softly and stroked his hand down Lucca's arm. "You have to be ready to leave me, Lucca. At any moment. Don't matter what we both want."

"We both?" Lucca asked, perking his ears up.

Russet grinned bashfully. His cheeks reddened beneath his white fur. "I, well… yannow. If we do, then perhaps we can…"

A small chirp sounded behind them. "Doot."

Russet rose to his paws and spun around.

Lucca followed just a moment later. He turned to see Palmer had sat up.

The lap-dragon clutched the azure gemstone in one hand. He rubbed his eyes with the other. "That was a nice sleep. Did I miss anything fun?"

Russet crouched down beside the lap-dragon. "How are you feeling? Can Tella still connect with you?"

Palmer tilted his head to the side. He bit his lip and tapped a claw to the side of his head. "Won't know until he tries," he said. He frowned slightly and lowered his hand. "The warp feels foggy. I can't reach it properly."

"Was that meant to happen?" Lucca asked nervously. "I didn't say it wrong, did I?"

Palmer shook his head. The bright smile returned to his face as he looked up at the lion. "Master Lucca, you did stay! You did what you needed to do, I think." The lap-dragon lowered the gemstone gently to the ground, then stretched out his arms. "Are you mad at me, Master Russet?"

The ferret shook his head. "I ain't mad. I just don't know why you did it."

Palmer shrugged. "Felt like the best thing to do, yannow. Big Master is nasty to you."

Russet held out his hands to pull the little lap-dragon into an embrace. "You shouldn't have done it without asking me, you silly thing."

"But if I had asked you, you'd have said no. And Master Sama'Rey would have known and sent someone after you," Palmer said. His brow was furrowed in thought as his hands rested against Russet's sides. "I just want you to be happy, and felian Lucca makes you happy."

Russet opened his mouth. He hesitated. He covered his eyes with his hand. "I ain't that obvious, right?"

Lucca knelt down beside the two. He rested his hand on Russet's shoulder as he felt his heart thudding away inside his chest. Palmer knew how they felt about each other. That had been why the lap-dragon had taken matters into his own hands. He briefly made eye contact with the ferret, and they both smiled.

"Very obvious, Master Russet. Your fur always goes white when you're happy," Palmer said brightly.

Russet blinked. "Winter, Palmer. It goes white in winter."

Palmer nodded eagerly. "Yah. And you love winter."

"Sound logic there," Lucca said with a giggle.

"Glad you think so, felian Lucca," Palmer said, turning towards the felian. His eyes shone brightly. "You make Master Russet happy like winter does. Although Master Russet doesn't stare at winter so much. Or release so many pheromones around it."

Russet reddened. "I thought we agreed not to talk about my pheromones," he muttered.

Palmer chirped and nodded. He hooked his hands together behind his back. "I believe you did, Master Russet."

Lucca tried to suppress his continued giggles.

The ferret groaned and covered his face. "Well, do you even have a plan? Sama'Rey ain't gonna sit back and do nothing," he said with a weary sigh. He leaned back and looked down over the lap-dragon.

Palmer nodded. "I think so." He drew away from the ferret and slumped down on the mat. "My head feels all fuzzy. Makes things feel a bit... slow. Dunno how you deal with it."

Though the lap-dragon smiled widely, the smile didn't quite reach his eyes.

"Alright. Hit me with it then. What's this mighty plan of yours?" Russet said. He sat down in front of Palmer, crossing his legs and resting his hands over his knees.

This time, Palmer's grin did reach up to his eyes. "I can make Master Sama'Rey think you're dead. Maybe. If he's not looking too hard."

Russet scratched behind his ear. "Uh huh. Sorry Palmer. I think there's a reason why I come up with our heist plans," he said uncertainly. "Make it look like I die, and the moment anyone from the guild sees me then it's all over."

Palmer clicked his tongue. "True. Didn't think about that."

"Any other master plans in that head of yours?" Russet asked.

"We make Master Sama'Rey think he's dead," Palmer chirped brightly.

This time Russet didn't even dignify Palmer with a vocal response. He just raised a brow and shook his head.

Palmer's enthusiasm didn't wane. "You turn yourself into the Mages' Guild and offer up Master Sama'Rey in exchange for your freedom."

Russet flicked back his ear. He grimaced. "Hate the thought of turning myself in. But what do you think, Lucca? Would the mages accept that?"

Lucca furrowed his brow. He wanted to say yes. The simple solution presented itself to them, but he knew to agree to that plan would be a lie. He slowly shook his head. "Archmage Mafren made it the guild's task to capture you, specifically. Yes, he'd love to be the one to bring down the Thieves' Guild, but he won't throw away the chance to say he captured the notorious relic thief. He'll want you both. He won't bargain for your freedom."

"The cod-choker sounds too much like Sama'Rey for my liking," the ferret growled. He snapped his fingers. "Alright, Palmer. One more. What else have you got?"

"We give Master Sama'Rey something more valuable than your service," the lap-dragon said. He bounced slightly, wings fluttering.

"Could that work?" Lucca asked. He remained standing, a safe distance away from the mouth of the cave. He leaned against the stone wall, with one paw tapping nervously against the ground. "I mean, you're in his debt financially, aren't you? Sixteen million scalls, didn't you say?"

"Ain't anything worth that much, else I'd have stolen it already," Russet replied. The ferret didn't even turn to look at Lucca, though Palmer's wide eyes did gaze at the felian.

"What about the yearbook?"

That got Russet's attention. The ferret snapped around to glare up at Lucca. "Thought you said you didn't want him to get anymore relics?" he asked suspiciously.

Lucca spread his hands. "What other option is there? It's valuable. Sama'Rey will know that. I can convince him that it's worth enough to free you from his bonds."

Russet ran a hand through his blue-tufted hair. "All due respect, Lucca. I prefer Palmer's plan."

"Thank you, Master Russet," Palmer squeaked.

"That wasn't a complime— ah, never mind," Russet said with a wave of his hand. He shook his head and grimaced. "Lucca, look. This book is clearly important to you. To your guild. Why would you suddenly be alright with Sama'Rey getting it?"

Lucca scuffed his paw on the ground. "I'm not," he admitted quietly. He frowned. Cogs slowly turned in his mind. "But I think there might be a way..."

"Oh, Sweetie. The only other way is for you to run. For you to leave and pretend you never met me," Russet said with a sad sigh.

"Too late for that," Lucca replied. He smiled wryly. "We have to go to Cofferknell. I think you know that."

"I do know that. Don't mean I have to like it."

Lucca slid his hand into Russet's. "We'll make it work. Somehow. You, me, and Palmer."

"If you knew Sama'Rey, you wouldn't be so confident. You ain't seen him. You don't know what he can do."

Palmer chirped brightly as he took hold of Russet's other hand. "Felian Lucca is a mage. He can fix anything."

Lucca grinned nervously. He couldn't be sure how serious Palmer was. "I don't know about everything."

Russet's muzzle twisted into a bitter smile. "You really wanting to do this? Go to Sama'Rey and hope he accepts this book as payment for my debt? It ain't much of a plan."

"Did he know that you were going to steal the yearbook? Does he know anything about it?"

The ferret shook his head. "Nah. Didn't have chance to tell him. Palmer, what about you? Did you report to Sama'Rey what I stole?"

The lap-dragon tapped his claws to his chin. "I hadn't done a full report, no. And Tella only gets alerted when I hear key words."

Both ferret and lap-dragon stared at each other for a few moments, before Palmer's eyes widened. "Oh! Some of my restrictions have been removed! I normally can't mention what I had to spy for."

Russet looked away. His fist clenched around the tip of his tail.

Lucca leaned back against the cliff wall and closed his eyes. His brow furrowed in thought. "And does Sama'Rey know about your defensive charms? The love spell one specifically?"

Again, eyes turned to Palmer. The lap-dragon scuffed his clawed paw against the stone. "He knows Master Russet had defensive charms, but he never cared to know the specifics. He never likes hearing about much magic. It's possible his lap-dragon has a summary of them all, but I doubt Master Sama'Rey himself knows about the love spell countercharm."

"If he doesn't know, then that's good. That could work." Lucca tapped his fingers against the stone. "We present something else to him as the relic I had been carrying. The book? That's something else. A gift from me to him as payment for your debt."

Russet managed a grimace. He sucked in his breath. "It really ain't much of a plan. It's the briefest flirtation with a plan. The concept of a plan. I ain't got much faith in it, Lucca. I'm sorry."

"I do," Palmer chirped. The lap-dragon beamed widely as he looked between lion and ferret. "I think it could work."

Lucca shrugged his shoulders. "We'd have a few days to refine the idea," he said, unsure if he really believed that himself. He couldn't think of any other way to help Russet though. He doubted they would be afforded much opportunity to sit down and wait until they thought of a better plan.

Russet sighed. The ferret pulled his hands free and slapped them against his thighs. "He's not going to let me go that easy. And remember, he wants this book. He's gonna bring down your guild with it. Would you do that to them, just for me? Because I ain't worth that."

Lucca grimaced. "I'll think of something to stop him. Could tell my guild where he is," he muttered, thinking to himself.

Russet held up one finger. "Firstly, if Sama'Rey thinks you're doing that, you ain't getting out of there alive," he said tersely. He held a second finger up. "Secondly, there are magical defences there stopping you mage folk scrying the hideout so not only can they not locate it, the wards stop you jumping in with those portals you like using." A third finger raised. "And finally, he has personal protection from magic. Charms bigger and better than mine. Mages can't touch him."

"Alright, so that won't work. But we can think of something," Lucca said. He resisted the urge to grip hold of his tail and twist it between his fingers. "The three of us. We can think of something."

"I have an idea!" Palmer said brightly. He bounced on his toes and looked between the ferret and felian. "We make Master Sama'Rey think he's dead... oh wait, no. I said that one before."

Russet rubbed his muzzle. "Can't believe I'm even saying this, but what's to lose? Sama'Rey might slap on another few mill to my debt, but I ain't ever gonna pay that off anyway."

A smile nervously spread across Lucca's muzzle. "You'll do it then?"

Russet threw his hands up. "It's a fool's plan, but we're all fools. I guess we're doing it. We have a few days to refine the details. Or come up with any details."

Lucca beamed as wide as Palmer as the felian pulled Russet up to his paws. He wrapped his arms tight around the relic thief. "I won't let you down, I promise."

Russet kissed Lucca lightly on the cheek. "I know. It ain't your dedication I'm worried about. Sama'Rey's got his claws in deep."

"Then we'll get them out, one at a time if we must," Lucca replied. He kissed Russet again, pulling the ferret in close.

Russet wriggled his way out of Lucca's embrace. The ferret's tail tucked low, and his hands nervously fiddled with a loose thread from his clothes. "The best way to Cofferknell is up the river, especially if we want to avoid the portals. Those are all locked down tight by your guild. Staying around here too long will be dangerous. So, if we're going, then we go tomorrow. I got a few contacts in town. I'll get us a boat."

"Do you want me to come with you?" Lucca offered.

Russet shook his head. He rummaged through his pack and pulled out his invisibility cloak. "Nah. You stay here. Safer that way. Don't want those mages to see you." The ferret flashed a nervous smile.

"If you're sure," Lucca said uncertainly. The lion took a step back as Russet approached the mouth of the cave. "Did you want me to lower the illusion?"

"Nah, I got this," Russet replied. His paw scuffed around what appeared to be empty air as he found the narrow ledge. He slowly slipped outside, testing every step before settling his weight. Before leaving completely, he poked his head back inside and jabbed a finger first towards Lucca, and then to Palmer. "Both of you stay there. Alright? I'll be back by sundown."

Lucca nodded his head. He could barely dare watch as Russet carefully left. The ferret appeared to walk on empty air, and even the knowledge that Lucca's own illusion hid the shelf of stone did little to alleviate his worries. Then the sounds of Russet's movement faded into nothing as the ferret moved back onto solid ground, leaving Lucca alone in the cave with Palmer.

The lion sank down to his haunches. He didn't know what he had gotten himself into. The plan sounded as weak as Russet had claimed. Lucca could only hope that it could work.

The voice of the lap-dragon cut through Lucca's thoughts. "Well, this is going to be fun!"

Chapter Thirteen

Russet did not return before sunset. The ferret had promised to be back by the time the sun sunk below the horizon, and the lion had grown steadily more nervous as sunset neared. Dazzling light of gold and red had filled the cave, but that had only been a brief display of beauty before gloomy darkness enveloped everything.

Palmer hadn't said much. The lap-dragon had spent most of the time curled up in the corner of the cave, with one small wing held over his head. Lucca would have thought the lap-dragon to be asleep, but for the occasional gleam of yellow eyes between the wings.

Lucca didn't try to speak to the lap-dragon. Instead, he sat as close as he dared to the mouth of the cave and watched the sunset. His ears strained for any sounds outside, but nothing sounded like Russet returning. Instead, all he could hear was the distant sounds of the ocean waves, and the occasional shout from the nearby town.

Once darkness fell, Lucca rose to his paws and began to pace around the small cave. He feared something had gone wrong, but he didn't know what. Nor did he know how he could do anything about it.

"I should go down there and find him," Lucca said nervously. His tail curled close as he padded around. There wasn't much room to pace, and Lucca had to make sure not to stand on Palmer's outstretched tail.

Palmer moved his wing. "Find him?"

"Something has gone wrong. He should have been back before now," Lucca said. He paused his pacing to look down to Palmer. "I need to make sure he's alright."

Palmer frowned. He gently held his claws against his forehead. "Master Russet told me to wait here. I shouldn't go anywhere until he gets back."

Lucca grimaced. "Just tell me where he might have gone. Who would he have gone to see?"

Palmer whimpered softly. "My maps are all out of date. I can't access the new ones," he squeaked softly. His claws drummed a nervous beat against his scales, and when he looked up at Lucca, his eyes twinkled as though with tears. "If I accessed the warp, then I could find him. But then Master Sama'Rey would find me."

"Just tell me where he normally goes. I'll be able to find it," Lucca replied. He crouched down in front of the lap-dragon and gently rested his hand on the diminutive creature's head.

Palmer remained still for a few moments, before he suddenly jerked upright. He scratched his claws into the light sandy dusting over the rock floor of the cave. At first, Lucca couldn't tell what the lap-dragon was doing, before he recognised a forming map of the town. The lion stepped back, making sure not to trample over the map.

Palmer took a few minutes to construct his map. Once he had finished, he took a step back, then pointed with a single claw to one end. "That's the main harbour, with all the big ships," he said, a touch of brightness returning to his voice. His claw slowly moved, tracing a path through some of the narrow streets. "This is the inn where Master Russet does his business. You might find him there."

"What's the inn called?"

Palmer clicked his tongue. He furrowed his brow. "The Merry Drunkard."

"Sounds classy."

"Yah, it is," Palmer said. A bright smile spread across his face. He nodded eagerly. "Master Russet always finds so many friends there. Sometimes they give him shinies."

Lucca took a deep breath. He looked out towards the darkness again. He could see no lights at all, with nothing visible at all in the gloom. The distant, gentle rush of ocean waves across the sandy beaches told Lucca where the sea was, but he couldn't see the divide between land and sea.

"You should wait here," Lucca said, glancing back to the lap-dragon. He pulled his Winterpaw leathers a little tighter around his body to protect him from the coastal winds that blew in from the ocean. "I'll keep the illusion up so no one else but us can come in."

Palmer nodded vigorously. "I'll wait here for you and Master Russet," the lap-dragon said brightly. He sat back, and his tail softly swished through the map he had scrawled into the sand. He waved at the lion. "Be safe, felian Lucca. Emberfade has lots of nasty people."

Lucca's ear flicked. "Thanks for that," he said nervously. He hoped not to find any of those nasty people. His hand stroked through his shortened mane. His green hair would be distinctive on the streets of Emberfade, but he only had the hood he had borrowed from Russet to conceal himself.

"Have fun, felian Lucca."

"Fun, yeah. This is going to be just peachy."

The first step Lucca took terrified him. Though his own illusion hid the rock beneath his paws from view, he still couldn't shake the feeling that he had nothing beneath him. His claws dug into the rocky face beside him as he shuffled forward, never fully taking his paws away from the rock. His toes made sure he was never about to step out into the void his senses kept telling him was there.

Lucca's knees felt weak as he finally made it back to the crevasse that led away from the sheer drop. He staggered forward, still keeping one hand on the rock beside him. His other hand extended out in front of him. With a quick word of power, he summoned a ball of magelight to illuminate the way.

The path down the side of the hill looked different at night. Shadows loomed in the light of Lucca's mageball. They seemed to jump out at him, making the lion quail in fear. He kept one paw stepping down in front of the other as he stumbled down the narrow, winding path. The sounds of the ocean grew louder and louder, until he felt like he walked right on the shoreline.

One great obstacle still kept Lucca away from Emberfade. He pinned his ears down as he thought about the great, wide river that flowed between him and the town. Over the gentle rush of waves crashing against the nearby beach, he could hear the flow of the river. He couldn't hear any paddles in the water.

Lucca's worst fear was realised when he reached the small dock on the river bank. He could see lamps twinkling in the town opposite, with some lights gleaming off the inky blackness of the river. No movement blemished the surface. No ferries crossed at this time, and Lucca's mageball didn't illuminate any ferry master waiting to ship him across.

Instead, the magelight shone on something else. A small rowing boat had been tied to the docks, drifting languidly in the current.

Lucca fretted to himself. He could see or hear no one on the docks on either side of the river. No one was there to see him take the boat, but still the lion hesitated. He was just borrowing the boat. That was all. He'd make sure it was secure on the other side. If he got there. First, he needed to subject himself to the wiles of the water.

The lion perched on the edge of the dock, looking down to the small wooden boat that bobbed in the river current. Two oars rested inside the little vessel. He had everything he needed to get across the river but screwing up the courage to jump down into the boat eluded him. Getting closer to the water was not something he wanted to do. Unfortunately, he knew no spells that could see him cross the river without getting wet, and he could recall no bridges close by.

With a soft whimper, Lucca eased himself down into the boat. The vessel rocked and bucked beneath his paws as they settled against the wood. He kept his hands firmly gripped onto the dock behind him as he tried to keep his balance.

After taking a deep breath, Lucca dropped down fully into the boat. The vessel lurched with the sudden weight, throwing the lion against the side. He yelped and scrabbled for balance, the boat splashing in the river. Once he knew he wasn't about to topple overboard, he crouched down low, his hands resting on the bottom. He could feel a little moisture beneath his fingers, but no flood of water as the boat sank. The boat remained afloat, but Lucca didn't move for a few dozen seconds as he braced himself mentally and physically.

Lucca grabbed hold of the oars as the boat rocked uncomfortably beneath him. His fingers clenched tight around them as he slowly lowered them into the water. A sharp word of command loosened the knots securing the boat to the dock, and the rope spooled into a neat pile inside the vessel.

Immediately, Lucca could feel the current take hold of the boat. The lion splashed the oars into the river, trying to get some sort of rhythm to his movements and mimic the otter who had ferried them across earlier. The boat swirled and started to spin in the current as it was pushed downriver.

Lucca felt like he made no progress at all. In the darkness, he could barely see what he was doing. His oars flailed and splashed in the water as he struggled to correct the course. Panic threatened to overwhelm him, and several times the oars almost wrenched from his hands. Only his iron-hard grip around the paddles kept them from being ripped away in the current.

The lion couldn't be sure just how long he flailed at the water. He imagined himself drifting out into the ocean itself, but before he felt the turbulence of waves passing beneath the little boat, he heard something grinding underneath him. An oar struck sand, and finally the paddle was pulled from his grip. The wooden oar splashed into the water and was lost to Lucca's grasping hand.

The little boat scraped over more sand. With a sudden judder, the boat came to a halt as it beached on a riverbank. Lucca scrambled forward in the boat and tossed the remaining oar to the side. He jumped overboard and instantly regretted it. Instead of nice, solid ground, his paws splashed down in the river. He sank to his knees, forcing him to wade back to shore.

Lucca's Winterpaw furs quickly felt heavy and sodden in the water. The lion's muzzle wrinkled in distaste as he trudged up onto the shore, feeling wet sand beneath his paws. A few lights twinkled ahead of him, and the shadows of buildings loomed close by. With the ocean still to his right, Lucca knew he had successfully crossed the river, and hadn't just looped around in his clumsy attempts to row.

The lion held his arms close to his body. A cool ocean breeze cut through to his fur, despite the thick leathers wrapped around him. The sodden leathers did little to retain heat. His legs especially felt the bite of the wind.

Lucca felt miserable as he clambered up the sandy bank, tugging the boat behind him before finding a place to tie the vessel with the damp rope. Soft, wet sand gave way to cut stone as he soon stepped onto the streets of Emberfade. A row of low buildings stretched out on the opposite side of the road, though none of them had any lights shining within.

Lucca knew he had to be close to the main docks on the shoreline. Palmer's maps placed the inn close to those docks, so Lucca knew his best way of finding Russet's tracks would be to make his way into town from beneath the shadows of the docked ships.

Wet pawprints trailed behind Lucca as he made his way towards the docks, peering through the gloom to make out any signs that could point him in the right direction. Movement caught his attention from the ships. He cowered back into the shadows. Patrols kept watch on both the ships and the harbourfront.

There was little Lucca could do to avoid standing out. A lion like him was always going to be recognised. He reached for his hood to at least disguise his mane, but he found nothing. He hissed to himself. He was sure he had grabbed it from the cave. He must have lost it in his dash across the river.

"Just great," he whispered to himself. He closed his eyes for a moment. There still was one thing he could do to protect his identity a little, though he wasn't keen on the idea. He sighed to himself. At least it would only be temporary.

The lion closed his eyes and focused his magic. He visualised what he needed and raised his hands to his forehead.

A rush of heat flooded through his head as an illusion spread over him.

He opened his eyes and sought out a window to peer at his reflection. He grimaced. He did not like the boring and dull auburn mane that now graced his head.

"At least no one will recognise you now," he muttered quietly. At least, he hoped no one did. He didn't want to be seen looking so ordinary.

Feeling a little better about his ability to remain hidden – though he wouldn't have minded being drier and warmer – Lucca made his way towards the harbour. The silhouette of a ship in the distance, blotting out some of the stars. The smell of fish and salt filled his nose, and the soft rush of waves over stone guided his ears.

Nothing on the ground looked the same as the map Palmer had drawn up. Lucca found the docks easily enough, but he struggled to work out which street he had to take deeper into down. He paced up and down a couple of times, casting his magelight out to read the road signs. The large ship in the port barely seemed to move at all, despite the gentle waves that splashed against the stone dock wall.

Wooden boards provided the walkway beneath Lucca's paws, which had finally started to dry. A couple of carts had been parked close to the dock wall, ready to transfer cargo come the morning. But for the patrols, the entire harbourfront felt deserted. Occasional pawsteps reached Lucca's ears, but no one approached him.

Several narrow streets led away from the docks. They slipped between the low buildings that faced the waterfront. A couple of lamps illuminated the path from their iron perches on the corners of each building, allowing Lucca to extinguish his magelight. The fiery lanterns all provided rings of flickering light to see by, the smoke drifting up into the clear night sky.

Lucca chose one of the streets at random. He could feel eyes on him as he made his way down the narrow street. The cobbled path wound between the close buildings. Each door had been closed for the night but scraped markings on the stone road told the lion they would usually be thrown open, with stalls on display for residents to hawk their wares. At night, though, all remained quiet and still.

From the second storey windows, Lucca could see a few eyes looking down at him. He couldn't tell what species his watchers were, but in Emberfade he knew most of the residents would likely be otters. They tended to dwell in coastal towns like this one, and this had once been the capital of their territory.

The narrow alley opened up into a small square. A statue of an otter lit by more lanterns stood in the middle of the square. A small pool and fountain surrounded the statue. A copper plaque had been embedded into the stone wall of the fountain pool.

A lone ferret stood by the fountain. For a moment, Lucca thought it might have been Russet, before he realised the ferret was female. She turned around as Lucca stepped into the square and beckoned the lion closer. She had fully moulted into her winter coat, though a few darker patches remained around her eyes. Two golden studs gleamed in her right ear. "What brings you to Emberfade, stranger?"

Lucca flicked his ears. "I'm looking for a ferret."

"You've found one," the ferret replied. She smirked as she looked over the lion. "Or was it a specific one you sought?"

"A specific one," Lucca quickly clarified. His eyes quickly scanned around the rest of the square. No one else was present. "Have you seen any around?"

The ferret grinned. "Plenty. What does this one look like? As it so happens, I'm looking for one too. Perhaps we can look together."

A small chill ran down Lucca's tail. He turned his eyes away from the ferret and stared down into the bubbling fountain pool. "What ferret are you looking for?"

The ferret leaned in close. She whispered into Lucca's ear. "A thief of some renown wanted by the Mages' Guild." She flashed a bright grin. "That's who you want, isn't it?"

Lucca raised a brow. "What makes you think that?" He still tried not to look to the mysterious ferret.

"Mages' Guild battlemages were sent out from Esfyr's Wold to hunt down the relic thief," the ferret said, still keeping her voice quiet. "I saw that bit of magic back there. That's not some simple cantrip, so you must be with the guild. Not many mages grace Emberfade."

Lucca slowly turned to the ferret, brushing his hand through his mane. "Who are you? Why have you been following me?"

The ferret held out her hand. "The name's Mera. I'm with the Cofferknell Investigation Board. Following people is my job, and catching the relic thief is our highest priority. If you're with the Mages' Guild, then why don't we scout through the town together?"

Lucca had never heard of such an organisation before. He narrowed his eyes slightly, and his brow furrowed in thought. He didn't want anyone else finding Russet before him. He needed to find a way to throw Mera off the trail. "I heard he's got a hideout on the outskirts of the town," he said slowly, keeping an eye on Mera to gauge her reaction.

"I had the same information," the ferret replied. She showed no sign of surprise on her face. She barely reacted at all. Her eyes gleamed in the firelight of the lanterns surrounding the otter statue. "To the north, in the hills."

"I heard the east, in the forest."

"Really? Where did you get that information from, mage?"

"We have some tracking spells in place." Lucca scuffed his paw against the ground. "We haven't been able to get an accurate position though, but he's definitely in the forest."

Mera idly toyed with her gold studded ear. "Interesting," she mused.

"Would it be worth splitting our search?" Lucca suggested. He tried to keep his back straight and tail still, so as not to project his discomfort around the ferret. "If you search the forest, I can track any leads through the town."

"Why do you wish me to track through the forest?"

Lucca shrugged his shoulders. "We have already done a sweep through the forest, but found nothing. We know he must have some den there, but he is hiding from us. Perhaps a fellow ferret can have better luck."

"Sounds fair," Mera replied. She flicked her ears. "Do you know of the Merry Drunkard? Meet me there in two hours if you find any trace of the relic thief."

"Two hours to sweep the forest at night? Will you be that quick?"

Mera grinned, showing off every one of her teeth. "No. I will be quicker. I was adding time for you. Do you need longer?"

Lucca wanted to question her, unsure if she told the truth that she could search the forest in less than two hours. But in the end, it didn't matter whether her boasts were true or not. All that mattered was that she had given him two hours to get Russet out of her claws. He slowly shook his head. "No. Two hours will be fine."

Mera held out her hand. "Good. Then two hours it is. Happy hunting, mage."

Lucca squeezed tight around Mera's hand as they shook in agreement. "I'll see you at the Merry Drunkard in two hours."

The ferret flashed one last smile before she turned around. With a flick of her tail, she scampered across the square and disappeared into the shadows. Lucca stayed still for a few more seconds, before he turned and left the square down a different alley. He glanced back to make sure he wasn't being followed. He couldn't see anything, so he turned his attention to what lay ahead. He needed to get to the Merry Drunkard quickly.

A tiny alley led off from the narrow road. No lights lit up the small alley, barely wide enough for Lucca to squeeze through. This time, he didn't feel safe summoning his magelight, unsure of who else might be watching him. Buildings loomed up either side of him, and his shoulders bumped against jutting stonework with almost every step. At the far end of the alley, Lucca could see an open door. A few puffs of thick smoke drifted out from inside the darkened interior.

Lucca had found the Merry Drunkard. A small sign above the door confirmed that this was the inn. The lion ducked his head as he entered the darkened room. He waited a moment for his eyes to adjust before he looked around.

A narrow bar took up most of the far end of the room. A dozen tables had been squeezed into whatever space was available. A staircase to the right of the bar led up to the next level, while a second stairwell on the other side led down.

Every table was occupied. Otters, weasels, and badgers sat around them. Most were drinking in conversation, though some played card games. One dealer used simple magic to direct cards around the table without touching the deck.

No one looked up to Lucca, and no one broke conversation. A constant bubble of chatter filled the smoky room; too much for Lucca to properly understand anything that was being said. He tried to listen out for any mention of Russet's name, but nothing caught his attention.

Lucca approached the bar, behind which stood a badger, whose narrow eyes glared around the room. The barkeep's sharp teeth were bared as he looked to the lion.

"You're not another one of those mages, are you?" he growled. His voice sounded like a heavy cart dragged across gravel. His thick, meaty hands tightened against the bar.

Lucca held his hand to his chest. "I'm not with them, I promise," he said quickly. He did not want to be associated with the battlemages, lest the badger or anyone else inform them that a lion was asking interesting questions. Already he realised he was putting himself at risk, and he struggled to wet his throat. "Where... where did they go? I'd rather they not know I was here."

"They went out an hour ago," the badger spat in derision. "Paid up for three more nights, so if you have business that doesn't want their attention you may wish to keep yourself scarce."

Lucca flicked his ears. "Thank you, I will be sure to avoid them."

The badger's lip curled. "Be sure you do. Mages are bad luck at the moment. I won't have you trying to cheat me of my scallops."

Lucca took a half step back. Usually, disgust towards him was because of his felian nature, but this seemed different. He had never known distrust of mages on the peninsula before. That had been behaviour he had thought left behind on Da'Manyr.

"Did they do something wrong?" Lucca asked, his ear flicking back.

The badger scoffed. "The Mages Guild were meant to protect my last shipment of ale, but it was stolen. Same as half of the last dozen or so." The barkeep's shoulders hunched over, and he jabbed a thick finger in Lucca's direction. "Sooner I see the back of them all, the better. Don't know what beef you have with them, but I'll have none of their troubles brought here."

Lucca's eyes flicked around the smoky tavern. He regretted coming to the Merry Drunkard. The badger intimidated him, and he didn't like the prickling feeling down the back of his neck, like unfriendly eyes were constantly watching him. He shuffled back towards the bar and lightly rested his hands on the dirty, sticky wooden surface.

"I'm just looking for someone," he said quietly, speaking quickly before the badger turned away. "If you help me find him, I'll be out of your tail."

"I don't know where the mages are."

"Not them," Lucca said, shaking his head. "I'm after a ferret. Winter coat, but a little blue hair on his forehead."

The badger's brow rose. "Why would you be seeking him?"

Lucca's mouth hung open for a moment as his mind raced. He didn't know if he could trust the badger with the truth. He didn't know how believable it would be. A lie popped into his head, and before he had the chance to think things through, it had spilled from his lips. "Sama'Rey sent me."

The badger's demeanour changed in an instant. He leaned back, and the furrow in his brow smoothed out. His hands, which had been held defensively in front of his chest, dropped down to hang passively by his sides. "Well why didn't you say so in the first place, friend?"

"I'm trying to be careful," Lucca said nervously. His tail tucked close to his legs. "Hard to know who I can trust."

"Well you can always trust old Long Tooth," the badger said, tapping a hand to his chest. He grinned widely. The teeth that may once have been long were almost all cracked and broken. "Sama'Rey has finally grown tired of his ferret toy, has he?"

Lucca nodded. "He wants the ferret brought back to Cofferknell. Have you seen him?"

Long Tooth tapped a finger on the bar. He grimaced. "Yes. But not for nearly half an hour. He left with an otter for the docks."

Lucca bowed his head. "Thank you." He took a couple of steps away from the bar, resisting the urge to wipe his hands over his furs. The feeling of the sticky grime on his fingers disgusted him. The lion bumped into an otter behind him. He squeaked an apology as he turned around.

Long Tooth kept his eyes on Lucca. The badger's shoulders dropped again, and his thick hand dipped beneath the bar.

Lucca felt a surge of magic radiate out against his back. He tensed and glanced back to the bar, but all he could see was Long Tooth. The badger's cracked teeth were all on display. "Anything else?" the barkeep asked, speaking loudly so his voice could be heard over the rest of the noisy bar.

"No, nothing," Lucca replied. His tail flicked. He couldn't be sure exactly what he had felt. Something magical had spread through the bar, and he had been sure that the surge of magic had come from the badger. A prickle of unease spread down his back as he stepped outside. The smoke didn't clear right away, but Lucca felt an immediate change in the open air.

At the far end of the alley, Lucca could see a shadow slip by. The lion tightened his furs around his body and hunched down. His senses had been overpowered by the smoke, and he couldn't smell anything ahead.

Lucca crept forward. His nose couldn't detect anything, but his ears still could. The sounds of conversation faded behind him, and the occasional rattle of a cart slipped through the tightly-packed buildings. Plates clattered and chairs scraped, but nothing seemed to be on the streets of Emberfade.

A hand grabbed hold of Lucca's shoulder.

Lucca yelped and spun around; his hands raised.

"What are you doing here?" a familiar voice hissed.

Lucca blinked to see Russet standing there, between him and the Merry Drunkard. "What are *you* doing here?" the lion repeated with a yelp. His heart hammered a rapid beat inside his chest.

"Long Tooth lies to anyone looking for me," the ferret said. He pulled Lucca back towards the inn, away from the larger road the lion had been about to step into. "Where did he tell you to go?"

"The docks," Lucca replied. He frowned and looked back to the Merry Drunkard. "You were inside all along?"

Russet nodded. "Was finishing up a meeting in the back room. Why are you here? Is Palmer alright?" He squinted up at Lucca. "And what did you do to your mane?"

Lucca's worries suddenly felt so meaningless. "I, uh... I was worried you were in trouble." He shoulders slumped as he let the illusion covering his mane splinter and fade. "I didn't want people to recognise me, especially the battlemages. I thought an illusion would be the best thing to do."

The ferret smirked. "I ain't in trouble, and those battlemages ain't gonna see either of us. They're on the far side of town so they ain't gonna find me here."

"And what about that ferret from the Cofferknell Investigation Board?"

Russet blinked. His hand gripped tight around Lucca's. "Who?"

Lucca tilted his head back. "There was a ferret I met on the way. Said her name was Mera, and that she was with-"

"I know who she is, and that means we need to scarper," Russet said, cutting the lion off. He pulled on Lucca's arm, dragging the lion back towards the smoky inn.

"You've seen her before?"

"Oh yeah. She's guild. There ain't no Investigation Board. Nothing real, anyway," the ferret replied.

"So she's..." Lucca said hesitantly.

"Here to get me," Russet confirmed.

"I got her to go to the forest," Lucca said, uncertainty rippling through his voice. He stared down the alley, but everything was dark and partially obscured in smoke that drifted from the inn.

Russet barked in laughter. "She ain't gonna fall for that. She'd have used you to lure me out from Long Tooth." He squinted down the dark alleyway. "She won't be far off. Best to get inside. Now."

Lucca didn't hesitate. He stepped back inside the inn, with Russet following right behind. The ferret's hand rested in the middle of his back, guiding him to the stairs leading down from the main room.

Long Tooth grunted in their direction. If he even noticed the lion's mane had changed colour, then he showed no reaction.

"Mera's here," Russet said, speaking quietly as they hurried past the bar. "Delay her."

The badger nodded, but he said nothing as he started to wipe clean a dirtied glass.

The stairs led down to a dark corridor. Closed doors lined the corridor, which had only a couple of lights to provide illumination. Smoke still drifted down from the main room, mostly lingering by the wood-beamed ceiling.

Russet ignored every door. The ceiling slowly sloped down towards the far end of the corridor. A closed cellar door blocked further passage, but this didn't deter Russet. The ferret unclasped the lock and pulled the door open, revealing the coal-black void beyond. A cool breeze drifted up from the cellar.

Lucca stepped through first. Weathered stone steps led down into the darkness, and the lion carefully placed his paws as he descended. The light didn't last long as Russet closed the cellar door behind them.

"Keep going down," Russet said, his voice cutting through the darkness as he gently pushed his way in front.

Lucca suppressed a shiver as he groped forward in the darkness, unable to find the ferret again. "Do you have the Eye of Revelation?"

"Yeah, give me a moment," Russet replied. Metal jangled, charms and necklaces clinking over each other as the ferret rummaged through his pockets. The sound grew further away, descending the steps.

Lucca resisted the urge to summon some light with magic, trusting the ferret to warn of any dangers in the darkness. He could hear Russet ahead of him as he slowly, carefully made his way down. Each stone stair was weathered smooth beneath his paws.

"Here we are. Come forward a little more and take my hand," Russet said.

The lion stumbled as he reached the bottom of the stairs. A flat stone floor spread out beneath him. His hands flung out, trying to find something to support him. His fingers brushed over a wooden barrel before he found his balance.

Russet's hand closed around his wrist. Darkness melted into magical light, only visible by their eyes. They were in a long, narrow cellar with the far end lost in shadows beyond the range of the Eye.

Russet grimaced, looking back over the lion's shoulder. "Follow me. It ain't far."

"Where are we going?" Lucca asked.

"Out. Somewhere safe."

"Are you sure?"

"Nope."

Lucca shivered. The relic thief sounded flustered, and that did not fill the lion with confidence. He glanced back. Only darkness followed them. Only darkness lay ahead, beyond the ring of light created by the Eye of Revelation, held aloft in Russet's other hand.

Wherever they were going, Lucca knew he had to trust Russet. The ferret knew where to go and how to escape Mera, wherever she was. All that remained to worry about was the whereabouts of the battlemages who had been sent after Lucca for his protection. The lion shivered. He doubted they would care about the changed plans. They would fight to defeat Russet and retrieve the yearbook. If Lucca got in their way, then they would fight him too. That was a battle Lucca knew he would never be able to win.

The cellar extended some way. Big barrels lined the stone basement. A layer of grime and dirt coated the stonework floor. Lucca could feel the muck beneath his paws. Small scuff marks of cleaner stone marked a path through the darkness. Lucca tried to stick to that path, but even in the light summoned by the Eye, it was difficult to see where to put his paws.

"How much further is it?"

Russet didn't look back. The ferret held up the Eye a little higher as though it was a common lantern, sweeping aside some cobwebs with his hand. "Ain't far. Should be a ladder..."

The light shone off a couple of rusted metal bars.

The cellar door creaked open.

Russet's hand closed around Lucca's mouth to stop him from crying out at the sound.

"Climb," Russet whispered, right in Lucca's ear. He then released his wrist, plunging the cellar into total darkness once more. "It's her."

Lucca didn't question how Russet knew that. He trusted the thief. He groped through the pitch darkness for the ladder, trying to rely on his memory for just where it was. On the third attempt, his hands closed around the rusted metal. The ladder creaked and buckled slightly in his grip, but he trusted his weight to it as his paws scrambled for a lower rung.

Slowly, the lion began to climb. He could hear Russet follow right beneath him; the ferret's head between his paws. Normally, Lucca would blush at the thought of the ferret positioned like that, but instead all he felt was fear. A pinprick of light shone in the distance, further back in the cellar.

As Lucca climbed, he expected to bump his head against the ceiling, but the contact never came. The distant light vanished as the lion felt the darkness constrict around him. He didn't extend his hands away from the rusted ladder, but he could feel the close confines of a stone chute as he slowly hauled himself up.

Lucca lost track of how far up he climbed. His arms burned from the exertion, and his paws ached as he struggled to find grip on the narrow rungs of the ladder.

The ladder ended suddenly. Lucca reached out for the next rung, but his hand fell into empty air. He nearly overbalanced, before gripping tighter onto the ladder with his other hand.

The lion fumbled around for a few seconds, but Russet's urgent nudges beneath him forced him to continue.

Lucca pulled himself up, finding himself in a corridor with a flat floor. He quickly pulled himself away from the ladder, letting Russet come up behind him.

With Russet's hand to guide him, Lucca hurried down the darkened corridor. Even with his shoulders hunched over, the lion could feel the low ceiling brushing against his ears. He could only hope there were no low hanging pipes or protruding chunks of stone, for he could see nothing at all, even after a few minutes for his eyes to adjust.

"Hurry," Russet whispered, making sure Lucca kept up with him.

The lion hadn't slowed down at all. Despite his fear for what lay ahead in the darkness, he remained alongside Russet. They didn't go far. A heavy iron door blocked their way, but Russet's hands took just a few moments to haul it open. A small amount of light shone down from a little point above them.

The iron door screeched on its hinges. Lucca grimaced and looked back into the darkness. He could see nothing there, but he thought he could hear the soft grunt of someone climbing the ladder.

Russet closed the door behind them, but there appeared to be nothing they could use to seal the door shut. Instead, the ferret grabbed hold of Lucca's hand and dragged the lion down the corridor again. This time, Lucca could feel the floor sloping upwards slightly, towards the dim light above.

Without looking back, Lucca hurried up towards the light. Another ladder waited for them, leading up a vertical shaft down which shone the light above. A flickering flame lantern shone down, fixed to the wall a few feet above Lucca's head.

Just above the lantern, a wooden trapdoor blocked off the shaft.

Russet pulled himself up the ladder first. With one hand, he held onto the ladder while he pushed up the trapdoor. Lucca followed just behind. Before he could wriggle up through the trapdoor, he heard the screech of iron behind as their pursuer passed through the metal door further back.

Lucca scrambled up to his paws as Russet closed the trapdoor. The lion looked around quickly. They had come up in the middle of a cellar with only one way out. A stone staircase ascended upwards. Though Lucca quickly scanned the room, everything was either too heavy to move or too light to provide a barrier against the trapdoor.

Again, the ferret went first. Russet scampered up the stairs seemingly without any concern that anyone above would be able to hear them. Lucca kept glancing back, but his view of the cellar quickly disappeared. At the summit of the stairs was an open door, which led out to a small foyer. To the left, another flight of stairs led up to a second level. Directly in front was a door leading through to more rooms, while the main doors to the building lay to the right.

Moonlight shone in from outside through the main doors, which had been flung open wide. Lucca pushed the cellar door closed behind him, but he grabbed hold of Russet's hand and froze before the ferret dashed outside.

"What are you doing?" Russet growled.

"I feel something," Lucca replied warily. A prickle of discomfort trickled down his neck as his fur stood on end. Magic filled the air. A shadow moved on the street. Robes fluttered in the breeze. "They're here."

"Who?"

"The battlemages."

Russet swore.

Lucca pulled the ferret away from the door, towards the stairs. "Hurry."

"Not upstairs," the ferret said, shaking his head.

"Don't have much choice," Lucca replied. His strength won out, and he pulled the ferret up the stairs. The building appeared to be deserted. All of the rooms were completely empty, with the doors all open.

A door crashed downstairs. Someone shouted. Russet's eyes flicked back to the stairs. "We're trapped up here," the ferret whimpered.

Lucca pulled Russet into one of the empty rooms. He quietly closed the door behind them and sent his magic into the wood, whispering a quick word of power to make it swell and stiffen on its frame. The battlemages and Mera wouldn't be held long, but Lucca hoped to delay them for a few extra seconds.

While Russet remained almost frozen in the middle of the room, Lucca hurried to the lone window. He glanced down to the street, close to a dozen feet below. Probably too far to drop down, but the building opposite was much lower, with only one storey. The sloped roof overhung the street, leaving a jump of only six feet.

Lucca crouched on the windowsill.

"Are you mad?" Russet yelped.

"Got any better ideas?" Lucca asked. He tensed his paws against the windowsill and judged the gap he had to clear. "It's not too far."

With a spring of powerful muscles, Lucca leaped out into the air. He easily cleared the distance and landed on the tiled, sloping roof opposite. The lion's paws found no grip on the smooth surface, and more a moment he found himself sliding back. He dived down onto his belly, gripping his sharp claws in a gap between two tiles to steady himself. He pulled himself up, clearing some room for the ferret to follow.

Russet stood on the windowsill. The ferret's tail lashed nervously. His hips wiggled. He swallowed nervously. Someone bashed on the door, almost knocking it from the hinges. They were out of time.

The ferret jumped from the windowsill.

He plummeted straight down, never getting close to the opposite roof.

Lucca tried to reach out for the ferret, but he was powerless as he heard Russet land with a pained thud. The lion scrambled down to the edge of the roof as he heard someone strike the door inside again.

Russet lay unmoving on the cobbled street below. Lucca dropped down beside him. The impact against the stone jarred his ankles, but he was able to keep his balance and land safely.

Above them, the door splintered with a loud crash. Heavy pawsteps approached from both sides.

Lucca fumbled over Russet's body, tugging out the invisibility cloak that was tucked beneath the ferret's belt. The cloak was barely big enough to cover them both, even crouched and huddled close together. Lucca couldn't be sure his paws were covered.

Both battlemages were otters. One came from either side.

"Thought we had him," one of the otters barked.

"He has to be here somewhere," the second otter said. She approached the cowering lion, invisible by her paws. She stopped just a couple of paces away.

Lucca didn't dare look up to see where her eyes were focussed. All he could see was her paws beneath the hem of the invisibility cloak.

"Are you sure he's down here?" the first otter said. He approached to stand next to his companion.

A third voice called out from above. Mera. "You cod-chokers lost them? How could you lose them?"

"He can't have gone far," the second otter said. Her paws retreated a couple of steps.

"Well find him," Mera growled. A door slammed a moment later.

"Why are we taking orders from her again?" the second battlemage muttered quietly to her companion.

"Someone from the sheriff's office, isn't she?" the other replied.

"Never heard of her before."

"Must be a new hire. Rough around the edges still. Let's just find that felian and be done with it."

Pawsteps slowly retreated and faded into silence. Lucca barely dared move until he could be sure the mages were gone. He cautiously unfurled the cloak from around them and looked down to Russet. The ferret's eyes were open, but he had remained silent and still in Lucca's embrace.

"What was that about?" Lucca hissed under his breath.

Russet shrugged. "I'm a ferret. We ain't good jumpers."

"You're a thief! Aren't you meant to be good at running away?"

"Running, yeah. Climbing? Sure. Jumping? Not so much. I stay on the ground when escaping."

Lucca rolled his eyes as he rose to his paws. He held his hand out for Russet to take. The ferret accepted the assistance and tentatively braced his paws against the stone street. He winced slightly.

"Bruised ankle. Should be fine," the ferret explained. He leaned heavily against Lucca as the lion started to walk. "We should get back to Palmer."

"Will we be safe up there?"

"No. We'll need to find somewhere else to sleep tonight." Russet grimaced as he flexed his foot. "We may have to brave it on the moors tonight."

Lucca bit his tongue to stop his immediate response. "And tomorrow?"

"We got a boat upriver to Cofferknell."

"Can we trust them? They might be working for Mera too."

Russet shook his head. "This guy ain't guild. He ain't got reason to turn us over."

"I can only hope you're right," Lucca said quietly. The lion kept one arm protectively around Russet as they slowly walked down the narrow street. Lucca's ears and eyes were strained for any signs of the two battlemages and Mera. He knew a third mage had to be present somewhere in town, but he couldn't be sure where they were. Every dark shadow seemed to contain danger to Lucca's mind. The sound of his beating heart had to be heard as far away as the distant docks.

Russet leaned into Lucca as they walked forward. The ferret limped, keeping his weight off his left ankle.

"We should get off the streets," Russet said. He glanced back a couple of times. "My cloak ain't big enough for us both, is it?"

Every time Lucca looked back, he could see nothing in the darkened streets. Lit lanterns shone down on the cobbled streets, casting a flickering light between the looming buildings. Plenty of shadows still remained, but Lucca's eyes were sharp enough to peer into the gloom without seeing any movement.

"Not when we're both standing. You think we're being followed?" the lion asked warily.

Russet nodded. "Mera ain't a fool. She'll be on us quickly."

Lucca's eyes drifted upwards. "Then we go somewhere she can't follow."

Russet looked up, following the lion's gaze. "I ain't able to go up there either. Don't think I can put much weight on my ankle right now."

"Any better ideas?"

The ferret clicked his tongue and shook his head. "I still ain't able to go up there though."

Lucca swept the ferret up into his arms. Russet squeaked and squirmed in surprise, before settling down and wrapping one arm around Lucca's neck for support.

Before Lucca could do anything with Russet in his arms, a small stone struck the wall just behind the lion. He jumped back and spun around, almost dropping Russet in the process.

"*Effini invisibilis*," the lion whispered, shivering as he felt a trickle of magic running through him. He tensed and turned slowly on his toes to find Mera stepping out of the shadows. She carried a sling in one hand.

"That was a warning shot, felian," Mera said. She took a step forward, raising her sling again. Another small pebble had already been secured inside the sling, ready to be fired again. "Give yourself in. Russet comes with me. You go back to the mages."

"Why does he want us?" Russet barked out. He wriggled a little, but he didn't try to jump away from Lucca's grip.

Mera shrugged her shoulders. "I don't question Sama'Rey," she said coolly. She raised her arm. "Come with me now and we don't have to make this difficult."

Lucca flicked his ears. "You don't know me, but I live to make things difficult," he said. As Mera's attention turned to him, the lion took another step backwards until his back pressed against the stone wall behind him.

"Don't try anything funny, felian," Mera warned.

Lucca took a step to the left, moving away from the illusion of himself and Russet he had created moments earlier.

His real self, and Russet in his arms, was completely invisible. Mera's eyes remained fixed on the illusion.

Lucca's toeclaws retracted as he padded silently across the cobbled street. He never stopped looking at the ferret, who remained glaring at the apparition Lucca had left behind. Her eyes never even reacted to the lion's movement.

"There's nothing you can do. Give yourself up, felian. My patience is limited," Mera growled. She lifted her slingshot again, but no response came from the illusion. Her temper grew to an end, and she fired the pellet in her sling. The shot passed right through the leg of the illusion to strike the wall behind. It would have been a disabling shot had Lucca actually been there.

Lucca turned to run as Mera snarled in anger. He dove down a narrow street, making sure not to strike Russet's head against the stone as he ran. Though his invisibility charm remained active, he could hear Mera not far behind. In his urgency, he made no attempt to conceal the sounds of his paws, and she would be able to smell him too.

"Left," Russet whispered, giving quick directions to the lion.

Lucca didn't hesitate. He darted to the left, slipping into another narrow alley. He didn't know where he was going, but Russet seemed to know the way. The ferret guided Russet through the narrow, twisting streets that all looked the same to the lion.

They couldn't shake Mera. The other ferret remained close behind. She was fast.

Lucca's shoulders and chest burned with the exertion. His legs ached. He didn't know how much longer he could keep running. He staggered, but with his arms wrapped around Russet, he couldn't brace himself.

"Climb up here," Russet hissed.

Lucca looked to the right. A stairway led up the side of a house. A balcony opened up at the top of the stairs, which provided access to a door, and a small jump across to the next roof.

Lucca's paws dragged against the stone stairs as he hauled himself up. He could hear Mera not far behind. She shouted out, but her slingshot didn't fire again.

Lucca didn't hesitate. He reached the top of the stairs and launched himself over the gap between the buildings. His paws briefly hung in the air, before he thudded down on the opposite roof. He struggled to find his balance without his hands to support him, but he just about stayed upright.

The lion scrambled up the sloped roof. His claws dug in between the slates as he stumbled along. He didn't look back, though Russet poked his head above his shoulder to watch behind.

Mera didn't attempt the jump. She swore loudly, but she had no parting shot for the lion as he slid down the other side of the roof.

"Where now?" Lucca asked. Before them, a sea of slate grey tiles rose up and down. Small gaps lay between them as the narrow streets wound between the houses of Emberfade. Shrouded against the starlight, the surrounding hills loomed over the town. Lucca couldn't see a clear path across the roofs, and nor did he think his shoulders could last much longer with Russet in his arms.

"Get across another couple if you can," Russet said. His voice quavered a little. "Can you... make me see myself again?"

"*Aufusi*," Lucca said. Magic trickled away, and the lion became a shadow on the roof. He grimaced to himself, not looking down at the ferret in his arms. "Sorry. I forget how disconcerting that can be."

"Thanks. My invisibility cloak ain't so uncomfortable," the thief admitted. He pointed towards the looming hills. "We need to go that way."

"Shouldn't we try to lose Mera first?"

"Nah, she knows all my hideouts here. We need to get out quickly."

"Couldn't we stay invisible and lose her?"

Russet barked in laughter. "She's better than that. She ain't gone just yet. Now hurry. We only got a few moments."

Lucca sucked in his breath. He scrambled down the roof until he stood on the verge. Below his paws was a short drop down to the street. As Russet had already proved, the fall could be a painful one.

The lion took just a few moments to judge the gap, before leaping across. This time, he landed with more grace. His paws braced against the tiled roof, and he leaned forward to stop himself toppling back over the street.

A few shouts echoed around the streets. Lucca didn't recognise the voices. Some of them might have come from the mages. Others may have been Mera. Most were probably residents expressing their anger at his unconventional passages across town. All the lion knew to do was keep his head down and clamber up another roof.

Lucca could barely believe what he was doing. Dashing across a roof with a thief held protectively in his arms; a second thief and at least two mages pursuing him through the streets. He briefly wondered what Master Roe would think of him at the moment.

A tile shattered beneath Lucca's paws. The lion's mind snapped back to the present. He couldn't allow himself to get distracted.

"Down here," Russet said. He pointed to a street that ran parallel to the docks, with only one row of buildings to shield the street from the open port.

Lucca gently let Russet down. The two sat together on the edge of the roof, with their paws dangling down. "Will you be able to drop down?" Lucca asked, glancing to the white-furred ferret.

Russet looked down. He twitched his nose. "Should be fine. After you?"

Lucca smirked. He enjoyed being able to showcase skills that were superior to the ferret's, especially ones that had nothing to do with magic. He lowered himself down into the street, with his hands holding onto the slates on the edge of the roof. When he let go, he fell only a few feet before his paws touched the cobbled ground.

Only shadows filled the street. No one walked through it, though in the adjacent waterfront, Lucca could hear the voices of sailors and traders arranging the loading of one of the ships. Lucca couldn't see the mages or Mera anywhere nearby, and nor could he feel the tell-tale trace of magic in the air.

Russet dropped down by Lucca's side. "Both paws on the ground, where they belong," the ferret muttered. He grabbed hold of Lucca's hand. "Come on. This way."

Though the relic thief still limped slightly, he led the way around the docks. Lucca kept looking back at any sound nearby, but he never saw anyone pursuing them.

The river approached. Lucca could hear the waters flowing, as well as the gentle lapping of waves against the docks. The lion wrinkled his nose at the thought of crossing the river once more. In Esfyr's Wold, he had never had to worry about too much water around. But for the small stream that wound around the village, there were no large bodies of water. In Emberfade, water was everywhere.

Russet held out a hand to stop Lucca. For a moment, the lion feared that they had been found, but the ferret only poked his head out around a corner to look down a larger road they had come across. The closest bank of the river encroached up towards the far side of the road, with the stonework of the docks just a few feet to their left.

They soon found the small boat Lucca had earlier commandeered, still tied up where he had left it.

"The boat to Cofferknell better be bigger than this," Lucca muttered in distaste. His muzzle wrinkled as he slowly lowered himself down into the small boat. The wooden hull creaked at his weight, and the lion almost pulled himself back up onto the docks. Russet coaxed Lucca's fingers free of the wooden planks, before slipping down into the boat himself.

The boat barely rocked as Russet settled down. "Don't worry. I ain't gonna force you into anything too small. We've got a proper narrowboat to go up the river."

Lucca hugged his knees close to his chest. "You'd better not be lying to make me feel better."

Russet flashed a bright grin. "When have I ever lied to you, Sweetie?"

The felian raised his brow. "About the love spell?"

"Oh, yeah. Apart from that, though." Russet leaned across to give Lucca a light kiss. "Don't worry. I got this."

Lucca wrapped his tail around his legs and tried to ignore the river as they began to cross. He could only hope Russet was right. Fear gripped him and he wondered if he had thrown himself into something he had little knowledge about.

The lion looked up to the darkened sky. Clouds had started to gather over the ocean, obscuring the stars. Rain was in the air.

Just what he needed.

Chapter Fourteen

Palmer squeaked in excitement as Lucca and Russet made their way across the precarious ledge leading into the ferret's hideout. Lucca's illusion had survived, keeping the last section of rock hidden from the eye. As far as the lion could tell, no one but Palmer had been up the side of the cliff since his departure. The lap-dragon didn't mention any intruders, though Russet didn't question him about any.

"Get all your things and prepare to leave," Russet said quietly, glancing back to Lucca just behind him. He flicked a tail out at the lion. "Mera knows we'll be up here. Don't want her to catch up."

Lucca shivered. "No. Definitely not. Out to the moors?" He crouched down and started to crudely pack his bag, not worrying about getting everything neat and tidy.

Russet grinned. "Nah. I thought it over some more. The docks. Captain Periwinkle should allow us to depart early."

"And if he doesn't?"

The ferret shrugged his shoulders. "Not like I ain't stolen a ship before."

Palmer squeaked in delight. "Oh, I remember that! Didn't you steal a pirate ship?"

"Merchant ship. We were the pirates."

Palmer squeaked and clapped his hands together. "That's right! Though don't you need a wooden leg to be a pirate?"

"Nah, though I found they ain't adverse to another kind of wood," Russet said, winking back at Lucca. "Works every time. Usually."

Lucca blushed and put his head down, doing his best to ignore the teasing comments from the ferret. "I hope that won't be necessary this time."

"Well, if it ain't your thing to share an otter," Russet said, still grinning widely. He snapped his fingers towards Palmer. "Don't forget to bring your charge mat."

"Won't we be coming back, Master Russet?" the lap-dragon squeaked.

For the first time, a touch of sorrow dipped into the ferret's words. "No. Not for a long time. Maybe never." He tightened the strings around his bag. He had managed to fit a lot in, but there was so much still scattered around the cave.

The ferret started to haul the bag up onto his back, before Lucca held out his hand. The bag slipped from Russet's hands and floated towards the lion's outstretched hand. The ferret's pack joined Lucca's own luggage, which sprung to life and hovered just above the ground. "Save your back, at least," Lucca said. He half-turned, looking out into the night. "You going to ride it again, Palmer?"

The lap-dragon squeaked in delight and jumped up onto the top of the luggage. In his arms, he carried the rolled up mat he slept on, but had no other belongings at all. "Mush!" he called out, but the luggage didn't move at all. "Uh... what is it I'm meant to say?"

Lucca snapped his fingers. Immediately, the luggage jumped up to float beside Russet's bags. "Do you have everything?" the lion asked, glancing back at Russet.

The ferret managed to put a brave smile on. "Ready to go. Best make it quick, before Mera thinks to check up here again."

Lucca didn't want to run into the other ferret again. He quickly glanced around the cave, making sure he had not left anything behind. He could see nothing. He patted his hand over the satchel he carried over his shoulder, feeling the one book inside. He hadn't seen the mystical yearbook since Russet had taken it from him. Only his alchemy textbook remained.

The lion left first. He cautiously placed his paws on the invisible rocky shelf outside, confident that the luggage would follow behind. The bulky packs didn't have to worry about where to place their paws. The felian envied that.

Lucca didn't stop until he had both paws back on solid ground, away from the ledge of terror. The winding track that led up to the summit of the mountain remained empty and quiet, though Lucca expected nothing else so late at night. He turned back to see Russet hadn't followed him.

"Russet?" he called out, holding his hand up to stop the luggage.

Palmer pouted and kicked his heels against the luggage, but the pack didn't obey his commands. The lap-dragon seemed unconcerned that his master hadn't come with them.

Lucca took a step back towards the crevasse, but as he did so, Russet emerged from around the corner. The ferret ran his hand along the rocky wall beside him. His tail had drooped, but that quickly perked up when he realised Lucca was looking at him.

"Come on then. No use waiting around," the ferret said brightly.

Lucca could see the ferret's smile never made it up to his eyes. The lion turned and hunched his shoulders, suppressing the weary sigh. He wished he knew if he was doing the right thing or not. If they failed, then both the lion and ferret would be in serious trouble.

He just had to make sure he didn't fail. He could only hope Russet trusted him enough to do what had to be done.

For one last time, Lucca and Russet crossed the river in the same small, rickety boat they had made their other crossings in. Raindrops had started to fall from the sky in a light drizzle, but there was no sign of an oncoming storm. The rain would remain light, but Lucca still had no desire to be left outside in the cold and damp.

Russet constantly looked around, remaining alert for anyone who potentially approached. If Mera was still searching for them, then neither Lucca nor Russet could see any trace of the other ferret. She had melted back into the night, lost in the winding streets of Emberfade. Russet kept silent; not telling Lucca anything about where they were going, other than to head towards the docks.

Even as Lucca's paws clattered against one of the wooden jetties stretching out into the bay, the lion still didn't know which ship they were going for. Three big-masted ships loomed at the end of the jetty. Each one looked larger than the one Lucca had come to Lutrea on. One appeared to be a military vessel, with cannons on display out the open portholes. The other two appeared to be merchant ships. At first, Lucca thought the ships were deserted, but the longer he looked, the more shadows he noticed patrolling the decks. He hastily looked down again, not wanting to draw attention to himself from the night watch.

"This one here," Russet said, taking hold of Lucca's hand and pulling the lion to the side of the jetty.

Lucca's eyes slid away from the three ships. Below the level of the jetty, bobbing lightly in the movement of the water, rested a fourth vessel. A canal boat had been tied up, dwarfed by the massive ships.

"Really?" Lucca asked, taking a step back from the edge of the jetty.

"Yeah. Ain't got a problem, have you?" Russet replied, a mischievous smirk on his face. The ferret slipped off the side of the jetty, holding onto the wood with his hands, before he dropped down the remaining couple of inches onto the flat deck that ran around the narrowboat. "Pass down the first pack, would you?"

Lucca stared. The narrowboat looked about as wide as he was tall, though about ten times that in length. The boat floated low in the water, with the deck protected by a low fence. In the middle of the narrowboat rose a cabin. Candlelight flickered in the windows.

"Come on. Quickly now," Russet encouraged.

Palmer jumped down from the luggage and leaped onto the boat. The lap-dragon landed with a bump. He rolled up against the far fencing with a giggle.

A second bump echoed out from within the cabin.

"Lucca. Come on," Russet hissed. He held his arms out, waiting to take hold of the first pack.

The lion sighed. He clicked his fingers and pointed towards the boat. The two packs of luggage drifted off the jetty, ignoring Russet to gently drift down to land on the deck.

Lucca dropped down after the luggage. As he fell, he heard a door open. By the time he lifted his head up again, he realised he was staring at the pointy end of a crossbow.

On the other side of the crossbow was an otter.

The otter growled as he looked between the ferret and lion. He seemed not to notice the lap-dragon. "Thought you weren't coming 'til sun-up."

"Plans changed, Peri. Any chance we can leave now?"

The otter lowered his crossbow. He sneered. "You're lucky the tide's still good for it."

Russet grinned. He moved to slap the otter lightly on the shoulder, but he held his hand back at the last moment. "You're the best, Peri. You know that?"

"Don't push your luck."

Russet held both hands up. "Wouldn't dream of it."

The otter pushed open the cabin door with his tail. "Get in there. You're lucky I wasn't running any other errands, so everything inside is ready for you. Near bed is mine. Get comfortable at the far end."

"More than one bed? That ain't like last time, Peri," Russet said. He took a couple of steps back as the otter prowled past. The ferret flashed a grin to Lucca. "Come on. Let's get out the rain."

Lucca ducked his head low to slip inside the cabin. Inside, he barely had room to walk. The low ceiling meant he had to keep his shoulders hunched over. A narrow bed took up most of the space directly to his right, while a couple of chairs circled around a table in the middle of the cabin. At the far end were another pair of beds, with a stairwell leading up to the front deck beyond them. Cupboards and storage units clustered over almost every free space, providing a cramped, claustrophobic environment.

The lion shuffled forward, struggling not to knock anything over with the sleeves of his furs. Behind him, Russet followed. The two packs of luggage squeezed behind the ferret, with Palmer back on his usual spot atop Lucca's bulging pack.

At the otter's request, Lucca ignored the first bed, and instead made his way through the cabin until he could sit on one of the far beds. Russet took a seat opposite him, giving Lucca the opportunity to magically lift the two packs onto the mattresses beside them. Though they both sat as far back onto the beds as they could, their knees still touched in the middle of the narrow walkway.

"How long will we be on here for?" Lucca asked. He looked around the cluttered narrowboat warily. He didn't like the feeling of being so constricted, not even considering the fact he was stuck on a boat. His paw tapped nervously on the floor.

"Ain't gonna be longer than a week, if the current's good. There's a couple of places we can stop along the way to get supplies if we need them," Russet replied. The ferret wiggled back and rested his head against the side wall, between two of the curtained windows.

Lucca suppressed his shudder of distaste. A week between Cofferknell and Emberfade was still much faster than they could manage on paw, or even by horse. With the portals locked to them, that left the river as the fastest route, but that didn't mean he had to be happy about the arrangement. His tail lashed against the bed.

"You're sure this otter can be trusted?"

"I said I couldn't trust anyone. He's the exception."

Lucca bowed his head and frowned. He had no choice but to trust Russet's judgement.

The narrowboat began to vibrate. Lucca's ears immediately perked up and his eyes widened. He felt a tingle of magic flow through the wall behind him. "Is that a thaumaturgical engine?"

"Is that a what?" Russet asked, tilting his head to the side.

"A thaumaturgical..." Lucca paused when he saw Russet's brow rise. He sighed. "It's a device the Mages' Guild created.

It powers ships without needing to use the wind or oars. I've never known one to be on a boat so small."

"Uh huh. Sure, let's call it that, if you want," Russet said. The ferret lifted his paws up onto the rigid mattress. He rummaged through his luggage and pulled out a small pack of biscuits, which had only mostly been smashed up. He offered one to Lucca, who refused them. The vibrations through the canal boat sputtered out.

A few seconds later, the door at the rear of the narrowboat opened. The otter poked his head in. "Either of you familiar with a thaumaturgical engine?"

Russet's paw nudged against Lucca's.

The lion lifted his hand. "I know some of the theory. Why?"

"Engine's buggered. Needs two people to fix it," the otter said gruffly.

Russet's ears flicked up. "What do you mean, buggered? You said you were ready to go, Peri."

The otter narrowed his eyes. "You said you weren't needing to leave 'til tomorrow. I had a thaumatist coming at sunrise." Captain Periwinkle's eyes flicked to the felian. "You think you can help fix it?"

Russet leaned forward before Lucca could answer, pushing his leg across the gap between the two beds and preventing the lion from moving far. "Does it have to be now? We're being chased. He's recognisable."

Captain Periwinkle shrugged his shoulders. "If you want to leave tonight, it has to be done now. You're just lucky I've got enough fuel for a few more days."

Russet hissed softly. He leaned forward and tossed a spare hood to the lion. "Hood up. Head down. Alright? Mera's still gonna be out there. Peri, you mind if I borrow your crossbow? I'll keep watch while you work."

The otter grunted. "Sure, if you like. Though it doesn't actually work."

"What do you mean, it doesn't work?" the ferret spluttered.

Captain Periwinkle grabbed the crossbow and tossed it across to the thief. "I mean it doesn't work. Don't need it to. Intimidation gets the point across just fine."

Russet muttered to himself, running his hands around the crossbow. He aimed the weapon towards the window and squeezed the trigger. Though Lucca yelped and ducked away, Periwinkle didn't even flinch. Sure enough, the bolt remained fixed in place.

"Well, come on," the ferret grumbled. "Let's go and I'll *intimidate* anyone away while you work."

Lucca reached back for his hood. He pulled it up and tightened the drawstrings so it mostly covered his alchemic-altered green mane. There wasn't much he could do about his felian appearance. He made his way back through the cabin, before pushing open the far door.

The lion's curiosity about the thaumaturgical engine managed to distract him from the rocking of the narrowboat as it slowly drifted in the water. Sheltered by the massive ships all around, the water didn't rock the boat too much. He still needed to use one of the railings on the side of the boat for support as he staggered from the cabin towards the engine housing. They had drifted a short distance from the docks, but the boat had little momentum against the waves.

Captain Periwinkle hunched over the engine, which looked like a large, square box at the back of the boat. A deep thrum of magical energy sputtered from the engine, but not at the power level Lucca expected to feel.

The otter ran his webbed fingers over the side of the engine. With a whir and a click, the black box began to unravel itself. Small strips opened out and expanded, forming a series of steps to reveal the inner workings of the magotech device. A dozen small crystals floated in the revealed space, all slowly circling around a larger crystal in the middle. Hundreds of small filaments of blue light connected each of the crystals to each other in a gently glowing lattice. Other tendrils of light extended out to touch against the outer shell of the engine.

Lucca could immediately see the problem. The central crystal should have been glowing with an intense blue glow, but it was muted and almost dark. "That shouldn't be like that," the lion pointed out.

The otter glanced up. "Thankfully I managed to work out that part," he said. He pointed to something on the other side of the small deck. "Pass me the probe from the toolkit behind you."

Lucca looked back. He found the open toolkit on the floor close to Russet's paws as the ferret kept his eyes on the shadowy docks. He crouched down and rummaged through, vaguely familiar with what the probe should look like. He found something that matched his expectations, a slender metallic stick with a blue light on one end and held it up for the otter. Captain Periwinkle snatched the probe from his hand with a small grunt.

The otter prodded the glowing end of the probe into the engine. The blue light flashed bright, attracting the glowing tendrils to the point. Dozens of tendrils appeared to have fallen loose and were waving around amongst the gems without a connection to anchor both ends of the light string.

"Is that what's causing the problem?" Lucca asked. He tried to recall the diagrams he had seen of thaumaturgical engines, but a diagram in a textbook was wildly different to looking at the real thing.

"Yeah. Now, there should be a second probe in there. Purple tip. I need you to use that one," Captain Periwinkle said.

He shook the blue-tip probe and squeezed his thumb against the side. The loose threads of light detached from the tip and rippled in the air like leaves on the surface of a lake.

Lucca found the second probe and held it tightly in his left hand. He found that when he squeezed a small indentation on the side, the purple light at the tip flared a little brighter. A small tingle of magic itched through his fingers each time.

Captain Periwinkle tapped the end of his probe against the crystal in the middle of the engine. "When I connect the strands, you seal them with yours. Got it?"

"I think so," Lucca said. He was distracted by some movement out of the corner of his eye, but he didn't have the chance to look. Instead, he just bowed his head and looked down towards the engine. The back of his neck prickled. His hackles rose beneath his leathers and hood. Someone was watching them, and Lucca thought he knew who it was. He had to hope Russet's intimidation with the crossbow would be enough to keep their pursuers away.

"Focus, kid," Captain Periwinkle said. He already held the probe in place, ensnaring one of the blue tendrils within the thrumming engine.

Lucca shook his head to clear his thoughts. He struggled to ignore the sound of pawsteps on the dock. At the otter's instruction, he pressed the purple tip of his probe to the central crystal as Periwinkle manipulated the loose strand of light against it. A flare of magic shuddered through Lucca's hand. When the probes moved away from the crystal, the strand of light remained in place. There were dozens left to go.

The lion looked up. A dark figure paced along the dock, pausing at each boat moored to the stone walkway. Lucca couldn't see any identifying features through the darkness, but he knew who was following them. Mera. Their boat was still close enough to the jetty that she might be able to reach them. They didn't have time to fix the engine the slow way.

"Felian," Captain Periwinkle growled. He had his probe prepared for the next strand.

Lucca flicked his tail. He tried to focus on the memory of exactly how the magic of the thaumaturgical engine had felt in his hands. If he was able to recreate that exact magic, then he might be able to fix the engine quickly.

The lion pushed aside Periwinkle's hands. Before he could regret his decision, he laid his hands down on the central crystal and summoned his magic. Immediately, Lucca felt the buzz of raw magic roaring through his hands and into his arms. The loose tendrils of magic tickled at his hands. Lucca saw stars of twinkling blue light dance around his head.

Focusing his magic down to the crystal at the heart of the engine, Lucca summoned the same power he had felt in the tip of the probe. He spoke a single word of command, focusing his magic through his hands. His ears flicked and twitched as he closed his eyes, seeing an imprint of the engine on the darkened inside of his eyelids. Through that after-image, the lion was able to manipulate all the individual strands at once, pulling them taut and stretching them out towards the central crystal.

A second flare of magic burned through Lucca's arms as the tendrils sealed into place at the lion's vocal command. A burst of searing light followed, almost blinding Lucca even through his closed eyelids. He heard the otter hiss out in surprise.

The low hum of the thaumaturgical engine grew louder. Lucca tentatively opened his eyes and pulled his hands back from the engine. The moment his hands were clear, the grey casing began to fold inwards and seal away the crystals, which all shone brightly where before they had been dull and listless.

Small sparks of blue magical energy flicked out the back of the engine, settling on the water like a trail of dust.

The boat started to creep forward, aimed for a gap between two large ships. Beyond those, the little boat would be able to traverse out to open water.

Lucca's attention turned to the dock, looking over Russet's shoulder. The silhouetted figure stood at the end of the jetty. Her eyes gleamed in the gentle light of the thaumaturgical engine. Lucca pulled up his hood a little tighter, though he doubted that would do much to hide his identity. Mera turned and started to disappear into the darkness.

Captain Periwinkle tapped his finger against the side of the engine. Three red indicators flashed up at his touch. The otter slowly dragged his finger up the indicator. Lucca felt the boat begin to pick up speed. Only then did Russet lower the useless crossbow, though he still stared towards the dock.

"We ain't lost her yet," Russet cautioned.

"What's your name, kid?" the otter asked gruffly. His attention was focused the other way, not taking his eyes off the water ahead of the boat.

The lion leaned back against the side of the boat, gripping his hands tightly around the protective railing. "Lucca."

The otter glanced across at the lion. "Battlemages were asking for you. Offering a lot of scalls."

Lucca quailed backwards, leaning away from the otter. He suddenly regretted giving his true name, though he doubted there were many other felian mages. Especially those with a short, green mane.

"Relax, felian. I have no need for their coin," the otter said. He extended a webbed hand. "I'm Captain Periwinkle. For as long as we're on the water, you're under my protection."

Lucca breathed a sigh of relief. He steadied himself against the railings as a small wave rocked the narrowboat. They were close to the large ships, near the rougher water beyond their protection.

"Do you need help navigating?" Lucca offered, wanting something to distract himself from the rocking motion of the boat.

"You've clearly got some skill with thaumaturgy, but the port is not a place for beginners and this boat is designed for canals and rivers," Captain Periwinkle replied. The otter showed off a toothy grin. "I'll let you practice when we're on calmer water. Deal?"

Lucca nodded. He kept his hands tucked into the sleeves of his Winterpaw furs. The boat rolled across a large wave as it emerged from between the two ships. The wide bay came into view, mostly shrouded in darkness. The bright beam of light from the lighthouse provided some illumination, standing tall on the headland overlooking the town.

Two stone breakwaters blocked open access to the ocean, instead filtering any vessels through a narrow gap between the pair of concrete structures. The canal boat lifted up and dropped uncomfortably in the open bay. The waves coming in between the breakwaters lifted the prow into the air, before crashing back down again with a wild splash. Even at the rear of the boat, Lucca felt some of the spray drifting back into his face.

The lion's stomach churned. "It won't be like this all the way, will it?" he pleaded.

"Only until we get into the river," Captain Periwinkle replied. The otter seemed completely unconcerned by the motion of his boat. "If you're going to lose your dinner, do so over the side."

Lucca held his hands to his muzzle. He closed his eyes and leaned back against the cabin, resting his head against the damp wood. He tried to breathe deep and ignore the jolts that jerked through his body each time the narrowboat slapped down onto the rough water. A gentle hand rested against his shoulder as Russet stood over him.

Once the boat drifted out beyond the breakwaters, the rough water only got worse. This time, they rocked from side to side as Captain Periwinkle navigated the boat around the headland, towards the mouth of the river. Lucca felt like he was a pendulum, struggling to stay upright. With his eyes squeezed closed, he could no longer be sure exactly which way up was. He had to trust gravity to keep him standing and out of the angry ocean.

The waves beneath the boat changed again. The rocking slowed as the canal boat turned further, instead starting at the rear and slowly rolling towards the front. Lucca fluttered his eyes open.

The narrowboat approached the boardwalk that ran alongside the town. Several times already, Lucca and Russet had crossed the river from the boardwalk, and now they drifted past on the river, slowly moving upstream. The occasional wave still caught up to them, but mostly the uncomfortable rocking had come to an end.

Light pawsteps thudded against the boardwalk. Lucca sharply looked up to see a shadow sprinting along, coming from the docks.

The lion tensed.

Russet drew in his breath. "We're too close to the boardwalk. Can't you move us away?"

"Not quickly," the otter replied. His attention had turned to the sound of running too.

"This would be a nice time to have a crossbow that works," Russet hissed.

The canal boat didn't move fast enough for Lucca's liking. He felt like it crawled along, though the running shadow could only barely close in on them. The lion took a deep breath, running through the list of spells he knew. Not much could help. He couldn't just cast an illusion or summon a burst of light to disorient the pursuer. He was sure they were smart enough to avoid that.

Unless...

Lucca's eyes briefly flicked to the left, towards the far end of the boardwalk. He looked back towards the shadowy runner, and quickly worked out just how far they'd want to run before making the jump onto the narrowboat deck. He grimaced. This plan would only work if they had to run all the way to the end.

The lion extended his left hand and took a deep breath. He summoned his magic, then released the growing power with a few muttered words. Magic rushed through him, extending his awareness out to the end of the boardwalk.

Lucca didn't need long before he clenched his hand closed and severed the flow of magic. He looked up to the boardwalk. The runner had gotten a little closer, but still not near enough to make the leap.

A flash of light illuminated the runner. Lucca grinned to himself. Mera. Now he knew his plan had to work. If she was anything like Russet, then she would want to run all the way to the end of the boardwalk so she didn't have to jump as far.

Lucca straightened his back. He lowered his hood, but immediately regretted that as the rain washed through his mane. The downpour had started to increase in intensity, plastering his fur down against his head. He flicked his ears in annoyance and kept his eyes on Mera.

The chasing ferret picked up her speed. Lucca's heart hammered as he watched her gain on them. She had almost made it alongside the back of the narrowboat.

"Can't we go faster?" Lucca asked.

“’Fraid not,” Captain Periwinkle replied gruffly.

Lucca took a step back, pressing up against the cabin. He raised his arms nervously, though he wasn’t sure what spell he could prepare to prevent Mera from jumping.

The ferret closed in. She swung her arms back, ready to leap…

Mera fell through the boardwalk and splashed into the river with a strangled squawk of surprise.

The illusion Lucca had created, extending the boardwalk by a few feet, flickered and faded.

Lucca breathed a sigh of relief as Mera’s head bobbed back up to the surface, now quickly receding into the darkness. The river angled away from the road, curving around a bend. Mera was soon obscured from sight.

“Smart thinking,” Captain Periwinkle said gruffly.

Russet exhaled sharply. “I’d hoped to get away without her noticing. Can’t be helped.”

“Will she know where we’re going?”

Russet shrugged. “River goes through plenty of towns. She ain’t got any way of knowing for sure, but she’ll probably guess.”

“Does that change anything?” Lucca asked nervously.

“I’d have liked her not to know, but she probably ain’t getting to Cofferknell ahead of us without using the portals, and there ain’t many thieves who will trust those.” The ferret shrugged his shoulders. “She might send a message ahead if she can access RedClaw to send a d-mail.”

“What about another boat with an engine like this?”

Russet furrowed his brow, tapping his clenched knuckles against his chin. “Ain’t likely to be many about, and they’ll be expensive to hire. We only got this ‘cos Peri owes me some favours.”

"But if she does get one?" Lucca asked. He glanced back to the ferret.

Russet leaned back against the door. He flicked his tail to the side. "Not much we can do about it."

"Won't she make problems for us?" Lucca asked, surprised that the ferret was taking this so nonchalantly.

Russet grimaced. "She'd cause us problems either way. All we could control was her catching up to us, so good work in delaying her there."

The lion's chest puffed out in pride. Despite the miserable weather; despite the proximity of the river to his paws, Lucca felt pride and happiness welling within him. He grinned at Russet.

The ferret winked back, before disappearing back inside to the dry cabin. The door snicked closed quietly. Lucca was tempted to follow after Russet right away, but he remained next to the thaumaturgical engine for a moment longer. He looked back down the river. Already, Emberfade was lost to the darkness and the forests. They had escaped.

Lucca's attention turned to the front of the boat. Cofferknell awaited. He dreaded what was waiting for them there.

Chapter Fifteen

Three days passed by on the river. Lucca had been taught how to navigate the narrowboat upstream, fighting against the constant current of the Lutrea River. A map on the cabin wall showed the route he needed to take, avoiding the tributaries that merged with the river, branching their way across the peninsula. The Wolden River, which led closest to Esfyr's Wold and home, was part of a separate system of water, on the far end of Lutrea.

Day and night passed by, and not once did the canal boat stop. Enough supplies were onboard to last for several weeks, should they need it. The four settled into a routine, with Lucca and Captain Periwinkle taking most of the responsibility for looking after the thaumaturgical engine. Palmer spent most of his time curled up on Russet's bed, while the ferret sat outside and watched the scenery drift by, often muttering to himself in thought as he planned out how to survive their arrival in Cofferknell.

There was little time where Lucca and Russet had the chance to spend time together inside the cabin, with one or the other usually with Captain Periwinkle to ensure there was always someone to guide the narrowboat upriver. On those few occasions, they spent that time sharing the small bed, Lucca always feeling like he was one wrong move away from rolling off onto the floor.

When they did not develop their schemes for Cofferknell, hands wandered as they explored each other's bodies, often to relieve the tensions that arose whenever their plotting resulting in no answers. Despite Russet's teasing insinuations, Captain Periwinkle was never invited to share in their nightly activities.

Lucca was sure the otter had to know what took place within his boat, but the captain never commented. He just gave the lion a few pointed looks and gruffly continued his tutelage, letting Lucca take control of the thaumaturgical engine more frequently.

Small towns and villages were left behind on the riverbanks. At their highest concentration, the canal boat passed a village every half an hour. About a dozen boats of all shapes and sizes passed in the opposite direction each day, most laden down with goods from the capital city, ready to be transported to the many villages and towns across the peninsula. They overtook a couple of boats when they had stopped at the various villages to unload their cargo.

If Mera still followed them, then Lucca had seen no evidence of her. The river behind was almost always empty, with only the occasional narrowboat or fishing vessel in sight. The weather had cleared after the first night too, with beautiful sunny, but cold, days. Though most of the nights had been cloudy, they had also been dry. Hardly any rain had fallen, much to Lucca's relief. The water on either side of the railings no longer filled him with dread, but he was still glad not to get wet.

Lucca used his time alone with the engine to think of ways to outsmart the mighty Sama'Rey in Cofferknell. He and Russet had not been able to come up with anything that resembled much of a plan, with so much relying on chance and opportunity. Russet had been snappy and terse a lot of the time, and that was when Lucca was happy to navigate the narrowboat up the river.

Shadows of ideas and plans were not going to be enough. But that was all they had.

The sun lingered low towards the horizon. Another night had come to its end; one more day closer to Cofferknell as the chill of the night slowly melted away like the frost coating the ground. The narrowboat rounded another gentle bend in the river. A village began to emerge from behind the trees. Stone buildings encroached on the river; old, crumbling fortifications surrounding the homes beyond. A guard tower rose tallest, but the roof had fallen off, with large chunks of masonry scattered around the base.

Lucca held his arm up, letting his hand drape through the branches of an overhanging willow. A gentle wind blew through the trees, which grew right up close to the banks of the river. Red and orange leaves still littered the banks and the river, with few still on the trees.

The lion slowed the narrowboat as they approached the village, easing off the speed to ensure their wake didn't disturb the boats docked on the waterway. The thaumaturgical engine responded easily to Lucca's command.

As the narrowboat slowed, Russet poked his head out of the cabin and yawned. His eyes widened when he saw the guard tower. "Oh. We're at Willowbanks already? I asked Peri to warn me when we were approaching."

Lucca glanced up to the trees. He brushed his hand through the overhanging branches. "If these are anything to go by, I'd say so. I don't know this area too well."

"I have a safehouse here. I… hang on."

Russet disappeared back inside the cabin. He returned a few moments later still wriggling into his hiking leathers. "Can you dock, please?"

"Should we be doing that?" Lucca asked, lifting his brow in surprise.

"Probably not," Russet admitted. He stumbled and almost fell as he tried to pull up his breeches and secure his tail in place. "But like I said in Emberfade, I have safehouses everywhere and we need some supplies. If we're going to Cofferknell, I'd rather not go with just a single knife."

Lucca sucked in his breath. "What if Mera catches us? She might not be far behind."

"I only need a couple of hours. Alright?"

The cabin door opened again. Captain Periwinkle came out and peered towards the village. "If you need to dock, you'd better pull in now."

"Pull her in then," Russet said, approaching the side of the boat.

Captain Periwinkle shrugged his shoulders. "Gives me a chance to top up on fuel as well. She'll get me to Cofferknell, but not much further than that."

"If you're going, then I'm coming with you," Lucca said, looking back to Russet.

The ferret held his hands up. "No, you stay here where it's safe."

"How is the boat any safer than out there? Mera knows what it looks like," Lucca retorted. He turned away from Russet so he could navigate the boat closer to shore. A stone docks jutted out into the river, with several empty moorings, but the length of the boat made entry difficult for Lucca. The lion felt a hand over his as Captain Periwinkle took over control of the thaumaturgical engine.

"We can't know what's waiting for us," Russet said. He took hold of Lucca's hand as the lion moved back from the engine. "Mera might have got word out. The battlemages might have tracked us."

"I don't want to leave you by yourself out there," Lucca said firmly. He pulled his hand away from Russet's and folded his arms across his chest.

"I'm a big boy, Sweetie," Russet said with a smile. "I'd take Palmer if I needed someone to look after me."

"He's still not fully right after being disconnected from the warp," Lucca replied, speaking quickly. "Best if you take me."

Russet sighed. "You're gonna be insistent, aren't you?"

Lucca nodded.

The ferret rolled his eyes. "Alright. But you stay with me. And keep that hood up."

Lucca lifted his hood to cover his mane. He swished his tail with nervous energy. He had always liked visiting new towns around Esfyr's Wold when he had been younger. This gave him another opportunity to see somewhere new. That didn't relieve the prickling down the back of his neck. He glanced downriver. No other boats followed them, but they had no way of knowing how far behind Mera was.

The narrowboat bumped lightly against the stone docks as Captain Periwinkle guided the boat in. Another otter tossed a rope down to the captain, who used it to secure the vessel in place. He tied several sturdy knots in the rope to keep tight against the docks. The boat rocked as a third otter jumped down to the front and lashed the other end to the docks as well.

"You say you'll be a couple of hours?" Captain Periwinkle asked gruffly, watching the process with a stern eye.

Russet chewed his lip in thought. "About that. You ain't gonna leave on us, are you?"

Captain Periwinkle nodded. He shut off the thaumaturgical engine with a couple of fingers pressed against the side of the grey box. "If you're not back here by midday, I'll assume you're not coming back."

Russet flashed a grin. "We ain't gonna be that long."

The ferret pulled himself up onto the docks, then turned around and offered Lucca a helping hand.

Lucca looked around from his higher vantage on the dock. A single pathway led onto shore, where the village crowded close. Only one building that he could see rose higher than the crumbling ruins of the guard tower. A church spire dominated the village, almost twice the height of any other building. Instead of stone, the church spire had been constructed to look like a spiralled shell. White marble gleamed in the evening light. The church itself was hidden behind a row of houses.

"Where is it we need to go?" Lucca asked, keeping his voice low as he walked by Russet's side.

Russet pointed straight ahead, directly to the church. "In there."

"The church?" Lucca asked in surprise. His ears flicked up as his eyes narrowed, sure that the ferret must have been pointing to something else close to the towering spire. He could see nothing else.

Russet grinned. "I might want to give thanks to the Fisherman."

"You don't strike me as being the religious type," Lucca said slowly.

"I ain't been in my work for this long without a few prayers here and there," the ferret replied. He bumped his hip against Lucca and leaned his head against the lion's shoulder.

Lucca frowned. He didn't have a response to that. He scratched behind his ear and glanced around. Most of the villagers were otters, though a couple of ferrets and sables also wandered through the village. Lucca even caught sight of a winter fox. He had only seen a vulpun once before, and the unexpected sight caught the felian by surprise. The winter fox had already disappeared around a corner before he had a second look.

Most Lutrean villages were centred around an open square in the middle of the settlement, around which were the three most important buildings. The church, a residence of the local government official, and the inn. Willowbanks was no different.

But for the church spire, much of the village had been built from stone, with little constructed with wood. The streets were narrow between the houses, and the cobbled stone beneath Lucca paws was rough. A small gust of wind blew through the village, rippling at Lucca's fur. A slate tile slid from a roof and smashed against the road, heralding a chorus of angry shouts from a group of otters.

The walk through the village took almost fifteen minutes. The roads were busy, and a large crowd had gathered around the village square. Movement was slow. Though Russet tried to show some urgency, he struggled to push his way through the crowd. No one showed any eagerness to move out of the way.

The reason for such a crowd became clear as they finally moved into the village square. A huge market had been erected in the square. Hundreds of stalls had been squeezed close together. Thousands of Lutreans wandered up and down the many rows, far more than Lucca believed possible to live in the small village.

"Willowbanks markets," Russet muttered to the lion.

Lucca could barely hear the ferret over the noise of hundreds of stall owners, all shouting out to hawk their wares. This was not a place that enjoyed a sleepy and slow dawn. "They seem popular."

"Biggest markets outside of Cofferknell. Should have known they'd be this morning, but we can use the crowds to our advantage. More people to blend in with," Russet replied. He took hold of Lucca's wrist and guided the lion through a small gap that had opened up in the crowd.

Lucca's attention was briefly caught by a stall showcasing glittering amulets and pendants promising magical protection and boons, but before he had a chance to explore further, he found himself on the stairs before the church. Fewer musteliads crowded near the church, giving Lucca the chance to breathe again.

Russet pushed open the ornate doors of the church. They scraped against the stone floor, having worn out a curved path of scratched markings. The ferret pushed the door closed after Lucca, struggling against the friction from the swollen wood on stone. The door shut with an echoing bang that felt like it reverberated through the church several times, before the sound came to rest in Lucca's chest.

Candlelight kept the church lit, as there were no windows to let in any of the diminishing evening light. A couple of otters sat in the pools of water sunken into the floor, but there appeared to be no service ongoing. The sounds of the market were silenced, leaving a hushed quiet through the church.

Russet pulled Lucca through the church, stepping around the pools in the floor. The lion caught the muttered prayers from the otters in the water. He tried not to listen. Quiet prayers always seemed something that should remain private. He felt like he was prying into their secrets if he listened to what they shared with the Fisherman.

Cloth draped down at the far end of the church, woven to look like strands of seaweed floating in the ocean. Russet glanced back as he approached the artificial seaweed, but none of the otters in the church even looked up.

Behind the cloth, a stone staircase led down, illuminated by more candles held in sconces on the walls. Russet started to descend.

Lucca hesitated at the top of the stairs. "Isn't this down to the crypts?" he asked.

"Scared of a dead body?" Russet replied, flashing his usual smile at the lion.

Lucca squirmed. He wrung his hands in front of his chest. "They creep me out."

Russet ascended the stairs again, reaching his hands out to hold onto Lucca's. "Don't worry. I'll protect you."

The lion frowned. "You're mocking me, aren't you?"

Russet giggled. "Wouldn't dream of it." He reached up to kiss Lucca on the cheek. "Ain't nothing down here to worry you."

"Somehow I doubt that," Lucca muttered to himself. Despite his worries, he followed Russet down into the darkness.

The air felt cold in the rooms beneath the church. Shadows danced over the dark stone in the candlelight, and the drip of water constantly trickled down from the ceiling. Sconces of magical flame burst into flickering light as they approached, fading away again into darkness behind them.

"These are the tombs, right?" Lucca asked, realising the ferret still hadn't actually answered his question.

"And a few more things," Russet replied. His hand squeezed a little tighter around Lucca's. "Churches tend to have a few secret passages beneath them. Old tombs that were never used. Sometimes even a siege shelter, like this one used to be. They don't smell pretty, but they make a good hidden lair."

"How many of these do you have?"

Russet paused at a fork in the underground passageway. The path branched off into opposing paths, both leading down a flight of stairs. He placed his hand on a chalk marking on the left passage. He started down those stairs. "I dunno. Ain't ever counted. About twenty? Thirty, maybe?"

"And they're all stocked with useful items?"

"Some of them. I ain't able to keep all of them well-supplied. Can't get to them all in time." Russet barely paused in his stride, even as more splits in the passage approached. Each time, he found a mark of chalk to guide him. Lucca quickly lost track of how many chalk markings they passed, or how deep they had gone.

"How far do we need to go?" Lucca asked. His voice wavered a little, no matter how hard he tried to stop it. He tried to ignore the rapid beat of his heart. He especially tried to ignore the looming weight of stone above him. Just how deep did these crypts go? They had to have been underground for almost half an hour already.

"We're there," Russet said brightly. He tapped his finger on another chalk mark. All the others had just been a line of white, but this one was different. This was a chalk cross. The ferret walked a little further down the passage with his hand rubbing against the stone wall, seeming not to care about the built up of dirt and grime. He tapped a claw against each individual brick until he came to a sudden halt. "Stand back."

The ferret pushed hard on the stone brick, which scraped as it slid back deeper into the wall. The brick moved to the side to reveal a small, brass handle. Russet pulled on the metal handle to a loud clunk. Stone scraped against stone as an alcove slowly formed, revealing a narrow passage that led down into a dark, unlit chamber beyond. The air was cold and dusty, tickling Lucca's nose.

"Any chance of a light?" Russet asked, squeezing his hand around Lucca's elbow.

"What about the Eye of Revelation?" Lucca asked, holding his hand to his muzzle and trying not to sneeze.

The ferret grinned. "I'll need both hands free in a moment, and the Eye is attuned to my touch so you can't use it." He glanced back up the passages. "Besides, it ain't like we need to creep around down here. No one's gonna disturb us."

The lion warily looked into the darkness. He extended one hand out and barked out a single word of power. A ball of magelight emerged from his palm, illuminating out into the darkness as it rose to hover above his head. A narrow staircase descended down, with well-weathered steps of stone.

Lucca led the way down, directing his magelight forward with a flick of his wrist. At the bottom of the stairs, a small chamber opened out. A narrow bed squeezed into one corner, with a couple of wooden boxes stacked together. Beyond them all, Lucca's light shone on a stone coffin. Of all the hideouts of Russet's the lion had seen, this was the smallest and emptiest.

"Shine your light over here, would you?" Russet asked, slipping past the lion and placing his hands on the coffin.

As Lucca shifted his magelight to shine on the stone, he could see a figure on an otter engraved into the stone. "Who was this?" the lion asked, unsure if he felt curious or mortified that he was looking at the burial coffin of an otter.

"Watermaster Reedflower, apparently. Dunno who he was though," Russet replied. He didn't turn back to Lucca, instead just running his hands over the stone until he found a couple of notches to slip his fingers into. He pushed hard with both hands, using all of his strength to push aside the heavy slab and reveal a dark void below.

Lucca's chest tightened. "You can't just do that," he squeaked. His eyes widened as he turned, imagining a cold breeze on the back of his neck. Thoughts of the otter's spirit rising to exact vengeance on them for disturbing his tomb filled Lucca's mind.

"Why not? Don't hear him complaining," Russet replied. He clicked his fingers. "Light though, please."

"We have stories in Da'Manyr of curses if you disturb the dead," Lucca said. The light wavered as the lion lifted his hand again. Though he knew he should be looking away, his eyes were drawn directly towards the opened tomb. He could see nothing inside. Even Russet's arms were swallowed by darkness when he reached inside.

"Ain't nothing but stories and tall tales." The ferret rummaged around for a few moments. He crowed in delight and pulled his hands back out.

Lucca squinted. He struggled to see what Russet had in his hand. The void of darkness was so complete, so empty, that his eyes watered simply trying to focus on it.

In Russet's hand was a dagger, but the weapon was like none Lucca had ever seen before. Instead of metal, the blade appeared to be made of pure shadow. Even the pommel seemed to have no substance to it at all, like the ferret grasped at pure darkness. He had heard of only one such weapon before, in one of the encyclopedias he had borrowed from Master Roe's library to read into the small hours of the night.

"Is that the Vulpun Blade of Shredding Darkness?" the lion stammered in wonder.

Russet shrugged. "Might be. Call it my nightblade. Like it?"

"That's been missing for five years," Lucca gasped.

"It ain't been missing. It's been right here," Russet said, patting the open top of the tomb.

"What do you need it for?" Lucca asked. His eyes were drawn back to the tomb, which was now lighter than it had been before. He thought he could see part of a bone. He quickly looked away again.

"To kill things. What do you expect?" Russet said, not quite succeeding in suppressing some laughter.

Lucca felt foolish. He scuffed his paws against the dusty stone floor. "I thought you said thieves don't kill."

"They don't," Russet said tersely. All humour had been sucked from his voice. "But right now I ain't a thief. I'm an outlaw, and they've gotta do whatever they can to survive."

Lucca lashed his tail behind him. "You got anything for me, by any chance?"

Russet patted Lucca on the arm. "Sorry. Just the one. Ain't any other like it."

"I thought that would be the case," Lucca mumbled. He took a step back, letting Russet take the lead back up the narrow stairs. The lion kept his hands illuminated to light the way, only extinguishing them once they both stepped back out into the church crypts.

Russet pulled on the brass handle, and the stone began to screech and scrape as the alcove closed over once more. Only a few seconds passed before the wall had rebuilt itself, with no evidence of the pathway down to the hideout.

The ferret opened one of the small pouches hanging from his leathers and placed the shadowy form of the nightblade against the opening. Though the pouch was too small to take the entire weapon, both blade and pommel were sucked inside the darkness.

"That's incredible," Lucca whispered, eyes wide. "I didn't realise it could go that small."

Russet clipped the pouch closed, with just the tip of the pommel still visible. "Shadows are remarkably compact," the ferret said with a grin. "Thought magical items were your area of expertise."

Lucca pinned his ears down. "I only know what they list in the encyclopedias. I've never had a chance to see it myself," he protested, raising his hands up. "It's incredible. Like a legend come to life."

Russet grinned, baring his teeth. "Well, this one's mine. I can't use magic like you can, so I need to use relics like these to protect myself. Thankfully, I've made a bit of a name for myself for using them all the time."

The lion blinked. "You're called the relic thief because you *use* relics, not because you steal them?"

"A bit of both, really. I got the name in the Thieves' Guild because I always used relics, but the name stuck when my infamy grew," the ferret said with a shrug. He patted the pouch that contained the nightblade. "It means I have my weapons, and you have yours." He gestured up to the ball of bobbing magelight.

"I don't have any offensive spells. Just tricks and illusions," Lucca admitted.

Russet raised his brow. "What about your fire magic?" he asked.

Lucca summoned a ball of flame in his hand. The fire warmed his palm. "Hold out your hand," he said.

The ferret hesitated before extending his arm. His palm was outstretched as Lucca spilled the flame over to the ferret. Though Russet flinched and winced, almost instinctively, he was not harmed by the flame. "It's... not hot."

Lucca shook his head. "I can summon warm fire. It's like Captain Periwinkle's crossbow. Good for intimidation, but it's not an offensive spell."

"Well what about your ice magic?" Russet suggested. He stared at the ball of fire in his hand, prodding at the magical energy with the fingers of his other hand.

Lucca cupped his hands over Russet's. The flame extinguished. "I suppose they could be used offensively. But I'm better with illusion magic."

"Then just use those," Russet said. He kissed the lion on the cheek again. "Illusion can be just as effective, especially when our target is immune to offensive magic. We ain't gonna beat him with weapons. It has to be our ways, with tricks, illusions, and our minds."

Lucca wished he could be so certain. He couldn't stop the discomfort trickling down his spine.

The ferret patted Lucca on the cheek. "Reckon we've been gone close to an hour. We'd best get back before Peri gets wet paws." He started back up the passage, following the chalk markings once more.

"Think she'll be here?" Lucca asked quietly. He had to move quickly to keep up with Russet's rapid pace.

The ferret glanced back. "She? You mean Mera?" Russet shrugged as the lion nodded. "She's resourceful. If anyone was going to keep up, it's gonna be her."

"What will we do if she does?"

Russet grinned. "We make sure she doesn't keep following us."

Lucca warily eyed the pommel, sticking out of Russet's pouch. "Is that what the knife is for?"

The ferret blinked. He frowned and shook his head. In the flickering light of the magical sconces, Lucca thought he could see the ferret on the verge of tears. Then the moment was gone. He bared his teeth in amusement. "Nah. That ain't for her."

Lucca fell back into silence. He tried to ignore where they were. Everything filled him with worry in the crypts. Even the spiderwebs in the corners of the passage made him nervous. His imagination kept creating sounds following them. The whoosh of air. The clank of chains. The pawsteps of ancient ghosts, angry at their presence...

The passage behind was empty. Every time Lucca looked back, he could see that no one followed them. Still, he couldn't shake the feeling.

Finally, they reached the surface once more. They left behind the flickering lights of the crypts and emerged back into the church. A dozen otters still sat partially submerged in the pools, though Lucca couldn't tell if the same ones still lingered. None lifted their eyes as Russet and Lucca slipped back through the veil of seaweed.

Lucca hurried past Russet as they moved around the prayer pools. He pushed open the heavy doors and stepped out into the open air. The sunlight bathed down on him, filling the lion with its warmth. After an hour in the crypts, he felt like a flower turning to the morning sun. He took in several deep breaths, enjoying the chaotic scents that came from the market.

Russet pulled on Lucca's hand. "You coming? Or you wanting to have a tour of the village first?"

Lucca shook his head. "I'm coming."

The lion slowly followed after Russet. He hugged his arms close to his chest and glanced down at the stones beneath his paws. The fur on the back of his neck prickled, but whenever he glanced back, he could see nothing untoward. The feeling of being watched never quite left him. The ghosts couldn't have followed them from the crypts, could they? Russet showed no fear, but the ferret never did.

Lucca had never known the discomfort of being watched before he had left Esfyr's Wold on Master Roe's crazy scheme. Now, Lucca felt like he was in a constant state of looking over his shoulder. He hunched over a little more and he pulled the hood over his mane. He knew such attempts to disguise himself were useless. Felians like him would be as rare as vulpuns.

At first, Lucca thought the docks looked much the same as they had before. He noticed the new boat just as Russet pressed his arm against Lucca's chest, pushing him away from the stone jetty.

"This way," the ferret hissed.

"We can't get around this way," Lucca protested, but he allowed himself to be pushed along the riverbank. A second jetty extended out into the river, but didn't reach as far as the first, on which their boat had been moored.

Russet crouched down behind some crates that had been stacked on the smaller jetty. The ferret hissed at Lucca to follow suit.

"Can you see her?" Lucca asked, not daring to poke his head above the crates.

"Nah, but I could smell her. She's here," Russet replied. He peered up over the crates again. He hissed softly and loosened the nightblade. "Only one new boat. I'm gonna check on Peri. I need you to check the other boat. Alright?"

"I thought you said you weren't going to kill her," Lucca warily.

Russet hesitated. He looked up at the lion. "Never said anything about killing. I just need to know she's not got Peri or Palmer," he said. He peered around the crates. "And I need you to check she's not still on that boat."

With a low growl to try and lift his faltering confidence, Lucca pushed away from the crates. He silently padded towards the boats, creeping after the ferret.

Russet had already reached Captain Periwinkle's boat and had quietly slipped on board. Lucca couldn't see any sign of Mera, but he thought he could pick up two instances of a ferret's distinctive scents. One he knew had to be Russet, but the other was probably Mera.

The second scent definitely came from the new boat moored at the docks.

With a cautious glance around him, Lucca approached the new boat, which was a narrowboat much like Captain Periwinkle's. This one was a smaller, faster, but otherwise similar design. A thaumaturgical engine had been fixed to the back of the boat. The felian slowly approached, making sure there was no ferret close by.

An otter was sat on the deck, with her back to the jetty. In her webbed hands, she was fixing a broken net. "This boat's already taken," she said, without looking up or around at Lucca.

Lucca's shadow cast across the deck, thrown by the low-lying sun. The lion grimaced to himself. "May I ask where you're heading?"

The otter looked up. "Why do you care? I have a passenger. She pays well. I don't need another."

Lucca held up his hands. "My apologies, I didn't mean to pry. I just expected a friend of mine to be coming by here today. Thought she might have been your passenger. She's a ferret."

The otter thumped her tail against the wooden deck. "Might be, though she didn't mention any friend. She's gone into the village for some business. She said she wouldn't be long."

Lucca grinned. "Thank you. I'll see if I can catch up with her," he said, taking a few steps away from the narrowboat.

"Better be quick about it," the otter quipped. She turned away again and returned to her task of fixing the net.

Lucca spun around on his toes. A shadow of an idea formed in the back of his mind. He already felt bad about it, but he knew something needed to be done.

Russet hopped out of their narrowboat. He hurried towards Lucca. The nightblade was still tucked into his pouch. "Any luck?"

"She's in the village," Lucca said quietly, quickly padding away from Mera's hired transport. "She's probably looking for us."

Russet raised his brow. "Well, I know she ain't tried to get onto our boat. Peri hasn't seen her." He held out his hand to take hold of Lucca's. "We'd better make a move and hope she isn't able to follow us."

Lucca scuffed his paws. "I can help there," he said. He clenched his fist tight, feeling the flow of magic through his fingers. His hand trembled. He had always struggled with physical magic, but in his mind, he could feel wood creaking.

"*Expunsius*," the lion muttered.

Magic rushed out through his body. He staggered forward, leaning against Russet for support as the pressure within his mind broke. Wood creaked and cracked as the targeted planks began to swell and buckle, growing into each other and fast running out of space. The sealant between them fractured and water inevitably flooded into the void created. Mera's transport listed in the river. The otter captain yelped and jumped to her paws, but there was nothing she could do to seal the damage the lion had caused in the matter of an instant.

"Hurry," Russet said. The ferret's eyes were wide as a small crowd of people rushed forward, offering their assistance to the distressed otter.

Lucca took the hand of Captain Periwinkle, who had come to peer at the disruption just in front of his boat. The lion hopped down onto the deck, feeling the boat move in the water. He tucked his tail in close, keeping his eyes away from the chaos just a few feet away. He hoped the other narrowboat would not sink, but he was sure there would be several hours of repairs needed first.

The lion distracted himself by helping Captain Periwinkle and Russet to loosen the ropes from the jetty. The thick ropes were unknotted and unwound, setting them adrift on the river once more.

Lucca kept his head bowed as the narrowboat slowly drifted past the stranded craft, his hood tight around his mane. The otter captain didn't look up as she struggled to keep her vessel afloat.

Captain Periwinkle got the thaumaturgical engine powered up, picking up their pace and pulling away from the Willowbanks docks. Only then did Lucca look up again, as the stone jetty began to disappear around the next bend in the river.

Amongst the chaos on the docks, one lone figure stood calmly. Lucca tightened his hood, but he knew it was too late. The ferret standing on the end of the jetty had already seen him.

Mera raised her arm in farewell.

Russet gave her a two fingered salute in response.

Then she was gone. The overhanging willows over the river swallowed up the view of the village and the docks.

Lucca sighed and turned around. He placed his hands on the side of the boat and looked forward. An empty, murky brown river lay ahead of the narrowboat, the current working in a futile attempt to turn the boat around.

Unless there were any more unexpected stops, they were just a couple of days out from Cofferknell. He could only hope Mera wasn't able to catch them before they reached the city. She had already caught up to them once. She seemed resourceful enough to have the capability of doing so a second time. Even worse, she could have managed to get a message through to Sama'Rey. The Thieves' Guild could already be waiting for them and delaying Mera had succeeded in nothing at all.

Lucca stared down into the river. Several days on the narrowboat had suppressed some of his fear about being in such close proximity to a large volume of water, but the sight of his shimmering reflection still sent a chill up his tail.

"You've got this, Lucca," the lion muttered to himself. "You know what to do."

The felian wondered why he was trying to lie to himself.

Chapter Sixteen

Two more days on the river had passed without incident, and though the worry of Mera following them from Willowbanks still lingered on the back of Lucca's mind, there was never any sign of pursuit. Lucca had spent most of the days navigating the boat up the river, ever edging closer towards Cofferknell. Traffic on the river had begun to increase, however. Captain Periwinkle had taken control of the narrowboat from Lucca, preferring an older, more experienced hand on the engine to avoid any unnecessary collisions. That had given Lucca the opportunity to go below deck with Palmer and Russet.

The ferret paced nervously around the tight confines below deck. He didn't look up as Lucca closed the door, instead just biting his lip and prowling in the opposite direction.

Palmer sat on the edge of Russet's bed, the little lap-dragon's legs swinging freely. He did acknowledge Lucca's presence by beaming up with his usual wide smile. "Master Russet is just running over the plan again," the lap-dragon said. His tail thumped against the course mattress.

"How's it going?" Lucca muttered, taking a seat beside the lap-dragon.

"I'm not authorised to repeat such words," Palmer said gravely.

"That well, hey?"

Russet spun around on his toes and growled softly. "We're going to Cofferknell. We need to know our whole plan. We need to be prepared that Sama'Rey knows what that plan is. We need back ups for our back up plans. We ain't got that. For all our talks. For all our planning. We got nothing."

Palmer chirped. "Do you want me to work out how successful our plan could be?"

"No thank you," Russet whispered. He ran his hands over his muzzle. "I don't think it has any chance of working."

Palmer squeaked and clapped his hands together. "Hey, that's exactly what I worked it out to be!"

Russet collapsed on his bed. "I'm having doubts, Lucca. We reach Cofferknell tomorrow."

Lucca took a deep breath. He clasped his hands together and leaned forward. "We know how we're going to get in," he said slowly. His tail swished against the bed. He swallowed down a rising sensation of nausea and fear. They had spent much of the last three days discussing the plan, working out how they would be able to free Russet from his obligations beneath the guildmaster. Those discussions had not always ended well. "We know how we're going to speak to Sama'Rey."

The ferret leaned back and covered his face with a pillow. "He might speak to us, but ain't gonna to believe anything we say," he said, his voice muffled beneath the pillow. He held his arms over his hidden face.

"We don't need him to believe us," Lucca said. The plan would be easier if Sama'Rey did believe them, but he kept that thought silent. "We just need to get into this hideout."

Russet threw his arms up, though he didn't move the pillow at all. "Where we disable Sama'Rey's charms, then lower the magical shields around the hideout," he said, exasperated. "Ignoring the dozens of things that'll go wrong with each step."

Lucca sat on the edge of Russet's bed. He plucked the pillow away from the ferret's face and tossed it to the side. "We just have to trust each other," the lion said. He tried to smile warmly but was afraid that it came out more as a grimace. "We all know what we need to do."

"Doot! One percent chance. Maybe," the lap-dragon said. He swung his paws over the edge of the bed and grinned.

"Trust you?" Russet said warily. He looked Lucca in the eyes for a moment, before turning away.

"You do trust me, right?" Lucca asked. He lightly touched his hand to Russet's chin, but he didn't try to pull the ferret's head back around.

Russet sighed. He grabbed hold of the pillow again, but he didn't cover his face. Instead, he dropped the pillow over his lap. "I told you that a thief don't trust anyone." He squeezed Lucca's hand in his. "Guess that means I ain't a thief no more. I trust you. We'll do this. One way or another."

Lucca pulled the ferret into a hug. He lightly kissed Russet on the cheek, before the ferret twisted his head to kiss him on the lips. "I won't let him keep you," the lion said. He pressed his forehead against Russet's. "And I won't let him keep the registry, either."

Russet laughed and cupped Lucca's cheek in his hand. "If it were that simple, I'd have done it years ago," he said. He smiled weakly, then kissed Lucca again. "I need to speak to Peri quickly. Wait down here, alright?"

Lucca nodded and leaned back onto the bed to allow Russet to slip past. He dropped down onto the rough mattress and tucked his legs close.

Palmer crawled across to drape himself over the lion's paws. "Is two percent a good chance of success?" the lap-dragon asked, as soon as Russet had closed the door to the rear deck.

"Not really, no," Lucca replied with a laugh. He reached down to stroke Palmer on the head. "But it's better than no chance at all."

"Oh." Palmer glanced down. "Perhaps if I could access the warp again, I might be able to work out a better way."

Lucca shook his head. "No. Not yet. You know what you need to do, right?"

Palmer squeaked softly. "I remember, yah. I'm looking forward to when I can access the warp again. I feel weird without it there, yannow?"

"You're being really brave for us," Lucca said with a smile. He kept stroking over Palmer's head, between his small horns. "You just need to be brave a little bit longer."

"I do my best, Master Lucca," the lap-dragon said quietly.

Lucca's ears perked up. "Master Lucca?"

The lap-dragon squeaked and nodded. He leaned back, then reach up to take Lucca's hand in both of his. "Master Russet is everything to me, and I hate that felian Sama'Rey uses me like he does. But if you can stop him, then you make Master Russet happy. That means you're more important than the old big master."

"Will he still be able to control you when you reconnect to the warp?"

Palmer released Lucca's hand. He pulled up his legs and hugged them close to his chest. His wings fluttered. "I think so. At least, I can hide things from Tella. I should be able to give you enough time."

Lucca put his hand between Palmer's faded red horns. "I'll do my best to free you both from Sama'Rey."

The lion hoped he would be able to keep that promise, but he still worried what would happen with Palmer. Russet could be freed from his debt with Sama'Rey, but Palmer could be a different matter entirely. Despite Palmer's obvious love of Russet and loyalty towards the ferret, the lap-dragon would still be an unknown once reconnected to the warp. Palmer might believe himself to be strong enough, but Sama'Rey's influence could prove too strong to break. Everything depended on Palmer being able to resist that.

Cofferknell was a city unlike any other on the peninsula. The sprawling metropolis spread out for many miles surrounding the central districts of the city, all connected by a vast network of canals and roads. Stone buildings with thatched roofs stretched out almost from horizon to horizon, coming close towards the riverbanks but providing few places for boats to moor. A maze of villages was tightly packed into the land around Cofferknell. Most of the settlements could barely be separated from each other, without barely any bands of nature between the endless expanse of buildings.

The river was full of traffic. Long, narrow canal boats and more conventional vessels struggled to move past each other, with a heavy flow of movement in both directions. On more than one occasion, their boat had been struck by another. That had always resulted in some angry words exchanged between Captain Periwinkle and the skipper of the other boat.

Lucca had spent several hours trying to modify an old set of Captain Periwinkle's leathers, which he now struggled to squeeze into. The leather was ill-fitting and stank of fish.

"You look ridiculous," Russet said. The ferret stepped back and grimaced, before coming forward again and trying to adjust the leathers. "But they ain't going to get any better. Just don't know why you won't wear your own."

Lucca tried moving his arms. The shoulders of the leathers caught and restricted his movement, but it was better this time. "My Winterpaw gear is for mages and shamans," he explained. He hitched down his breeches, trying to stop them pinching. He had run out of time trying to adjust them. They were as good as they were going to be. "If we can convince Sama'Rey I'm not a mage, things might go smoother."

"That's not gonna convince anyone," Russet muttered. "Especially if Mera got a message through."

Lucca shrugged. "Worth a try, isn't it?"

"So long as you're not gonna cut off the blood to your arms, sure," the ferret replied.

"Not sure it's my arms I'm worried about," Lucca mumbled, re-adjusting his breeches again to stop them pinching around his crotch.

Russet raised his brow and stuck out his tongue. "Well *that* we've definitely gotta keep safe."

Before Lucca could reply, the boat bumped up against the Cofferknell docks. Lucca could see the marina through the smudged and dirty windows. Several hundred boats were secured at the marina, which stretched out almost all the way across the river. Only a small channel on the far side of the river was left for boats to travel further upstream.

Lucca clambered out the boat and onto the jetty. He felt slightly naked without his thick fur-lined Winterpaw leathers, and his nose constantly wrinkled at the scent of fish coming from his borrowed clothes. The lion carried no luggage but for his small shoulder satchel, which contained nothing but the two books he had left Esfyr's Wold with. He held his hand over the bag. The registry was back in his possession at long last, but the thought of fleeing Russet didn't even cross his mind.

As he waited for Russet and Palmer to finalise their plans with Captain Periwinkle, Lucca turned his attention to the city. Captain Periwinkle had agreed to stay in Cofferknell for a few days to provide them with a quick escape if needed, and to keep hold of their heavy luggage. Lucca was glad of that, as he had no desire to carry around his pack without the use of magic to help him.

As far as the lion could tell, Cofferknell had been built over a series of low hills clustered close together. The lowest areas of the city, nearest the river that bordered the south and west of Cofferknell, appeared to be where most of the merchants and shops were located. Most of the buildings Lucca could see on the riverfront were trade stores or banks, with the occasional tax office crammed in the middle. He could see no warehouses or storage facilities – a few warehouses perched right on the waterfront housed those goods that could not go directly to the merchants of Cofferknell.

Further up the hills, on higher ground overlooking the sprawling suburbs, were the large buildings for the rich folk that made up Cofferknell's elite. Even from a great distance, Lucca could see the gated walls that surrounded the larger properties, and the spires of ornate buildings that looked more at home on the dozen churches that rose up from the masses of houses in the city.

From the jetty, Lucca could see that most of the people in the city were native Lutreans. Otters were, as usual, the most common species. Weasels were also more prevalent than they were in the southern regions of the peninsula. A dozen stocky badgers worked near the docks. They usually acted as the stronger physical labour, assisted with featherweight charms to move heavy cargo from boat to wagon. Lucca couldn't see a single felian, though a few cainids towered over the native musteliads, with vulpuns and even an elusive thylacin from far-distant lands mixed amongst the cosmopolitan crowds.

Russet placed his hand on Lucca's shoulder. "Ready to go?"

The lion nodded. "Yeah, let's get this over with."

Together, the three made their way towards shore. The lion kept his eyes open, looking out for the narrowboat he had partially sunk in Willowbanks, but he couldn't see it at all. If Mera had been able to leave the small village in a hurry, then she had not made it as far as Cofferknell yet. Lucca could only hope that gave them an advantage still.

Sama'Rey might not yet know they were coming.

Lucca almost laughed at the thought. The guildmaster of the Thieves' Guild would surely already be aware of them.

"Where do we need to go?" Lucca asked. His eyes were wide as he looked around, taking in all the sights and smells of the city. Some were good. As they stepped off the docks, he could smell fresh bread in a nearby bakery, but just a few steps later he managed to catch the scent of rotting fish coming from the river.

"We don't need to go anywhere," Russet replied. "They're gonna find us sooner or later. Did you want something to eat?"

"So long as that something isn't fish, sure."

To Lucca's delight, the ferret led him towards the nearest bakery. The lion was then horrified to discover that nearly half of the baked goods still featured fish in some way. He picked out a sweetroll, after making sure with the baker that there was no fishy content. Russet followed his lead, and the two soon made their way back outside to enjoy they food. Palmer scampered around their heels, before darting off to chase a couple of pigeons that had dared to land nearby.

The road followed the curve of the river. The waterway remained on their right side, unimpeded by any buildings at all. Heavy horse-drawn carts clattered their way over the cobbled stone road, with a large crowd of musteliads bustling in both directions on the verges. Only a small strip of muddy grass separated the road from the bank of the river.

"Doesn't the river ever flood?" Lucca mused aloud, speaking in between bites of his sweetroll.

Palmer let out a little doot. "Yeah!" he replied exuberantly "The river flooded in... oh. I can't access the information at the moment," he added sadly.

Russet smirked and pointed to a small bronze plaque, embedded at shoulder height in the side of the closest building to them.

Lucca had to squint to make out what was written on the plaque. "Height of floodwaters; 17th of Harvest, 212. That was only thirty years ago."

Russet nodded. He swallowed a mouthful of sweetroll. "Yeah. Those floods displaced a lot of people. My parents amongst them. They'd never have ended up in Nesterslip were it not for those floods."

"I'd have thought water mages could have done something to stop that from happening," Lucca said with a frown.

Russet laughed. "Oh, they did. Once the water started to lap at the mansions, anyway."

"That's horrible," Lucca muttered. He bowed his head and looked towards the river. The water looked brown and murky as it flowed past the city, carrying some sticks and leaves in addition to the myriad of boats that drifted by.

Russet shrugged his shoulders. "That's life in the big cities. The rich have the power, and the poor struggle to get by. Is why I like the little villages so much. There ain't any of that nonsense."

Lucca leaned into the ferret. "Then maybe you can come to Esfyr's Wold with me once this is all done."

Russet smiled. For all the talk they'd had on freeing the ferret from his bonds with Sama'Rey, they hadn't actually discussed much about what they might want to do afterwards. "I'd like that," the ferret admitted. He leaned back against Lucca. "I'd like that a lot. But we ain't close to that yet. Gonna take more than taking down Sama'Rey to clear my name."

"I know. We'll work something out," Lucca replied. He held his hand draped around Russet's shoulder for a moment, before pulling away and looking out to the river. Dozens of boats were coming in and out of the docks at any given moment. The lion had been trying to keep an eye open for Mera's transport, but he had no hope of spotting a single specific boat amongst the constant movement on the wide river.

The slate-grey sky was beginning to darken overhead. But for a brief period of brightness at sunrise, Lucca hadn't seen the sun all day. Rain was coming, and Russet seemed to have noticed too. The ferret placed his hand on Lucca's elbow.

"There's a park nearby with shelter. We should wait there for a bit," the ferret said. He leaned in close to the lion. "Plus it's close to one of the guild entrances."

Lucca flicked his ears. "Why don't we just go straight to the guild?"

Russet chuckled softly and shook his head. "Nah. They ain't gonna let me in without an escort. They'll just beat us up and drag us in if we go to them. Gotta let them come to us first."

"And they won't beat us up that way?"

Russet shrugged his shoulders. "Fifty-fifty chance?"

"Great," Lucca said quietly. His tail flicked from side to side. "Getting beaten up by the Thieves' Guild wasn't on my to-do list."

Russet grinned widely as he leaned in to kiss Lucca on the cheek. The two turned away from the river, with Palmer scampering ahead down a side road. "And yet you were willing to be bait for me."

"Master Roe said you didn't steal that way," Lucca said. He allowed himself to be guided by Russet, feeling the ferret's hand on his waist. "He promised I wouldn't end up hurt and bleeding in a ditch somewhere."

Russet chuckled. "This Master Roe seems to know a lot about how I work."

"He was working on that thief ward to stop you."

Russet barked out in laughter, so loud that he briefly attracted the attention of a couple of weasels on the other side of the narrow road. "Still can't believe they tried that," the ferret said, grinning madly. His tail swished around to brush over Lucca's. "Must've been getting desperate."

Lucca nodded. "Archmage Mafren certainly was. I dunno the full story, but I think there were rumours of him being stood down if he didn't do something to stop... well, you."

Russet's ears perked up, a little pinkness colouring the skin beneath his white fur. "Always nice being talked about in such high places."

"This was serious," Lucca protested. "If the archmage was deposed, it could have caused a civil war in the guild that could have ripped it apart."

The ferret stumbled. For a moment, Lucca was convinced Russet was about to fall, but he regained his footing at the last moment. "I wonder if maybe that was the intention."

Lucca twitched his tail. "I'm somewhat hoping it is." He tapped his hand over the satchel draped across his shoulder. The weight of the almighty yearbook felt good back in its correct place. "He might accidentally turn himself in for us."

"I don't think that's likely," Russet said warily. He tightened the grip of his hand around Lucca's waist. "I know you're hoping he might underestimate you, but please Lucca, don't underestimate him. He ain't gotten to be the guildmaster without cunning and intelligence."

Lucca nodded. He peered around him. The narrow streets looked much the same as they did in any town of village he had been to. The difference with Cofferknell was how many of those streets were all connected together. The lion couldn't see the entirety of the city in one look, but the occasional glimpse he got of the taller mansions on their hills reminded him of just how far the city reached.

Otters, weasels, and badgers all strolled past, with the general flow of the crowds walking towards the river. Few paid any attention to the ferret, but some glanced in Lucca's direction and scampered to the other side of the road. He pulled his hood up to hide his green mane, then quickly realised how pointless the act was. Here in the city, it wasn't his mane that made him distinctive. But for the few cainids, he was taller than anyone else, and there were no other felians to hide amongst.

Palmer scampered ahead and disappeared around a corner. The little lap-dragon's excited chittering could still be heard, long before Lucca and Russet followed down the smaller side-street.

Buildings loomed tall and close to the narrow street. The ruts in the middle of the cobbled street had been worn smooth by the regular flow of wagon traffic. The stones beneath Lucca's paws were a little damp, though he couldn't recall any rain in the past couple of days, and the light drizzle currently falling wasn't strong enough to form puddles.

Lucca wrinkled his nose and avoided standing in the fouler-smelling of the puddles. Most of them formed beneath windows of the surrounding houses. It wasn't rain that formed those.

The park was around the next corner. Palmer darted forward, only just avoiding a horse-drawn cart in the process, running onto the small square of grass. Two wooden benches sat beneath a gazebo, which provided a little shelter from the intensifying rain.

Showing a little more caution than Palmer, Lucca and Russet crossed the road and took shelter inside the park. But for the benches and the square of grass, nothing else filled the small park. It was little more than a glorified gap between the houses where a small amount of nature had been able to cling to existence.

Russet wiped one of the benches clean with his hand, sweeping aside the crumbs and leaves that had gathered there. He sat down and draped his arms over the back of the bench. "We won't have long to wait."

"They'll know we're here?"

"They'd have known since we got off Peri's boat, if they were having a bad day."

Palmer darted up to sit by Russet's side, while Lucca remained standing. The lion wanted to feel ready and prepared. No one would sneak up on him as he slowly turned around on the spot, making sure to keep an eye on all four of the winding streets that approached the park.

"Lookie here, boys. Who do we have here?"

Lucca whirled around. An otter leaned against the side of the gazebo, where moments ago there had been nothing but empty space. Lucca had been sure of it. The otter wore leathers similar to Russet's.

Russet stayed sitting down. He didn't even look up to the otter. "Nyle. Nice of yous to join us. 'Bout time, ain't it?"

"Shut it, Russie. Boss don't wanna hear it from you," Nyle replied. He carried a small blade in his hand, but the otter seemed more intent on staring at his reflection in the metal, rather than threatening Russet or Lucca with the weapon.

Russet spread his hands. "I need to speak to him, though. Be a good lad and take me through. We're wanting no trouble, a'ight?"

"He wants yous. Your pet, too," Nyle said, jabbing a finger in Lucca's direction. "Boss wants yous dealt with."

The lion opened his mouth to protest, but quickly shut it again after a quick gesture from Russet's hand.

Rough hands grabbed hold of Lucca from behind. The lion yelped in surprise. His ears hadn't picked up any pawsteps from behind. He glanced back to see a pair of identical weasels. Both were mottled with their winter coats. One pushed Lucca's head back around to look forward. His arms were pulled back behind him.

Cold steel touched Lucca's wrists. The weasel behind him twisted the key in the lock of handcuffs with a quiet snick. He kept his hands tightened into fists as the two weasels stepped around to stand one on either side. The top of their heads only came to Lucca's shoulders.

Russet bowed his head to the two weasels. "Tel. Let. How's your lil' sis holding up?"

The weasel to Lucca's right hissed.

"You said it, Tel," the one to his left said. Let's hand gripped onto Lucca's wrist. "We got nothing but disgust for you."

Russet slowly rose to his paws, keeping his hands held high and away from any pockets. "I ain't wanting a mess of this. We gots something Sama'Rey wants. A'ight?"

"What kinda thing?" Nyle said, narrowing his eyes. "We ain't falling for any funny stuff."

"Magic stuff," Lucca said, speaking through a tight throat. The lion was acutely aware of the knives the weasel twins both carried.

Nyle scoffed. The weasel twins laughed. "Felian like yous? How'd yous know magic?"

One of the weasels slapped Lucca's side. "Only magics he knows is the tip of a blade."

Russet glared at the weasel. "You ain't quite understood what magic is," he said, before holding his hands up when the weasel's twin raised his knife. "A'ight, you made your point. Eloquent as always."

"Show us this magic thing. Then I decide if you see Sama'Rey," Nyle growled. He jabbed a finger at Russet.

The ferret kept his hand raised. He edged towards Lucca. "It's in the felian's bag," he said, fending off a sudden movement from one of the weasels. Tel and Let stepped away from Lucca; close enough they could still grab him in a moment, but giving Russet the space he needed. The ferret's movements were tense as he opened Lucca's satchel.

Russet pulled out the registry and showed it to Nyle. He opened the book, showing the otter the signatures within.

Nyle's ears flattened back. The otter swore loudly. He held his hand out. "Give it me. I'll take it to Sama'Rey."

Russet snapped the book closed and returned it to Lucca's satchel. "Not happening, Nyle. We take it. Not yous."

The otter scoffed. He took a step towards Russet. Lucca felt the point of a knife press against his back.

"There's a curse on the book," Lucca blurted out quickly. His breath hitched in his throat as all eyes turned to him. Even Russet looked surprised for a moment.

"Explain, felian," Nyle said. He waggled his knife in the lion's direction.

Lucca thought quickly. He tried to smile, but the expression didn't quite come. "Some mages told me that if someone takes the book by force, that thief will be struck down with terrible magic. Very painful, they told me," he said, managing to keep his voice even. "Are you wanting to risk it?"

Nyle's muzzle wrinkled. His brow furrowed as he tapped the blade of his knife against the claws of his opposite hand.

Lucca didn't dare to breath as he waited for the otter to make some sort of decision. Even Russet remained perfectly still, standing between the otter and the lion.

Nyle clicked his fingers at Tel. "Bring 'em. This ways."

Lucca stumbled forward as he was shoved hard from behind. One of the weasels roughly gripped around his wrist as Nyle grabbed hold of Russet and dragged him from the bench.

"Quick and quiets now," Nyle growled.

Though Lucca knew he could physically overwhelm the weasel behind him, he allowed himself to get shoved and pushed from the park and into the narrow alleys of Cofferknell. He tried to ignore the knife he knew was uncomfortably close to his back.

Russet muttered beneath his breath as the weasels led them down a twisting path, overhanging buildings casting long shadows. Nyle led the way, his rough grip on Russet never ceasing. Nor did Tel or Let, whichever weasel had hold of the lion, ever loosen their hands on his wrist.

They finally stopped when they reached a nondescript building, looking much the same as all the others they had passed. Nyle glanced up and down the alley before an old door barely staying on its hinges. Satisfied no one overlooked them, he pushed open the door and slipped inside, dragging Russet with him. Let and Tel shoved Lucca hard to get him to follow.

Lucca was met with Nyle's wide grin, the room beyond so dusty and gloomy he couldn't work out any of the details.

"Give 'em the hoods."

Russet flicked his ears. "Hoods? Plural?" A nervous smile spread across his muzzle. "Nyle. I'm guild. I ain't needing one of those."

Nyle's hand whipped out, so fast that Lucca didn't even see the otter move. He slapped Russet hard across the muzzle. "No, Russie. You ain't guild no more."

Lucca saw no more as a hood was pulled over his head, the grip on his wrists finally released. He could see nothing through the thick fabric, and even his breathing was restricted. A collar tightened around his neck, securing the hood in place. Sight was robbed from him, and his senses of smell and hearing were heavily muffled. Through the hood, Lucca could still hear Russet protesting.

A fist struck flesh again, harder this time. The protests ceased.

Hands patted down over Lucca's body. At first, he wasn't sure what they were doing, but when they tapped over his hips, he realised. They were searching for weapons. Lucca was glad he carried no weapons in his borrowed leathers. All he had were some coins and the books. None of those were deemed a threat to the weasels.

Lucca kept his hands tightened in a fist. The urge to use magic flared strong within him, but he kept his silence. He couldn't let the Thieves' Guild know he was a mage; not yet at least. The lion took a couple of steps forward at the push of a hand in the small of his back.

Walking without being able to see terrified Lucca. His tail thrashed from side to side as he shuffled forward, guided by the hand on his back, and another on his waist. He quickly lost his bearings; unsure where he was being led, and even in which direction they were going in relation to the door they had just passed through.

A stone floor gave way to wood beneath Lucca's paws. There was a downwards slope to the floor, and several times he was shoved left as his shoulder bumped against a curving wall. He longed to see where he was, to understand what he walked along, but the world was merely a field of darkness to his eyes.

Muffled voices followed Lucca. He could hear Nyle speaking, but he couldn't quite make out the words being said. Instead, he focused on putting one paw in front of the other, making sure he didn't trip over any unexpected obstacles. He doubted the thieves would be considerate enough to warn him.

A hand tugged hard on his tail, warning him to stop. A brief pause and more muffled voices followed. Lucca yelped as he felt himself spun around quickly on the spot, pushed around by four hands until he felt dizzy inside his hood, and with no knowledge at all of which direction he was now standing.

Russet's yelp of surprise told Lucca that the ferret had been subject to the same treatment.

"I know where we're going, cod-chokers," the ferret said, sounding as awful as Lucca felt.

More laughing voices. Then stone grated against stone. Lucca's tail curled between his legs.

A hand pressed into the lion's back and pushed him forward. He took a couple of steps, only to jolt forward as the ground fell away beneath his paw.

Laughter howled around the lion as two hands grabbed hold of his elbows, stopping him from falling over. Stairs descended even further beneath the city surface, and Lucca carefully stepped down each one, making sure to shuffle forward with his paws to find the edge of each step before committing his weight forward.

Lucca lost track of how many steps he had to blindly find his way down. The stone started out being smooth beneath his paws, but after a while they became rougher.

Finally, Lucca found himself on even ground once more. The stone felt slightly damp as he took a couple of steps forward. The hand at his back disappeared, and the lion froze.

Hands fumbled around his neck, and the collar loosened. Moments later, the hood was removed from his head.

Lucca found himself in a dark corridor of carved stone. A sloped, arched ceiling didn't give much room above his head, with small, swinging light fixtures hanging down. The light flickered unevenly through the passage, irritating Lucca's eyes almost immediately. He didn't look behind him, but he couldn't see any evidence of natural light flooding down from the stairs.

Ahead of the lion stood Russet. The ferret's hood was removed. Russet had a little blood trickling from his mouth, and his eyes looked slightly dazed in the flickering light, but he otherwise seemed unharmed.

Palmer stood with his hands behind his back, rocking back and forth on his paws as he waited for the others. He didn't appear to have had a hood on at all, unless his was removed first. Lucca hoped that meant the thieves still believed Palmer to belong unequivocally to Sama'Rey.

"Never wanna do that again," Russet muttered quietly. He swayed on his paws, before Nyle roughly took hold of him.

"This way."

The weasel twins took care of Lucca. One walked either side of the lion as they guided him through the long tunnel. Occasional passages branched off from the main tunnel, but Nyle and Palmer both walked unerringly, without pausing at any of the junctions.

Lucca's eyes flicked up occasionally. The ceiling curved into a perfect semi-circle, the brickwork reinforced with an occasional arch and column. He had to wonder just where they were. He knew they were underground, but he didn't know how far, or where these tunnels led.

The march felt like it went on forever. Lucca lost track of time, just as he had lost track of how many stairs he had come down. So many questions lingered at the tip of his tongue, but he held them all back. He didn't like the look on Tel or Let's faces.

Lucca's paws ached. He nearly stumbled a few times, despite the smoothness of the damp stone he walked on. His thoughts raced. He didn't know what would be waiting for them at the end of the endless corridor. Would Sama'Rey believe their lies? Would he take the bait? Could they even break the enchantments around the hideout and the lion himself? Lucca didn't know the answer to any of those questions. If they failed just once, then all would be over. Everything had to go perfectly.

Finally, the passage came to an end. A pair of oak doors blocked further passage. The doors looked like they did not belong in the tunnel, as a few inches gap separated the tops of the doors to the ceiling. The door on the right hung slightly crooked on the rusting hinges.

Nyle left Russet alone for a moment so the otter could step forward and open the doors. He struggled with them for a moment. The hinges were stiff, and the wood slightly swollen in the damp. They scraped open, running along deep scratches that had been left in the floor from previous times they had been opened and closed.

Lucca stepped forward with the weasel twins into a massive chamber. The ceiling was higher; twice Lucca's height, and the dark walls were far enough away that the lion didn't feel so claustrophobic. No natural light filtered into the chamber, leaving the only light sources as the flickering torches ensconced on the walls. Two rows of a dozen pillars stretched down the length of the chamber.

In the middle of the chamber was a raised dais, upon which was a large sandstone seat. Lucca was put in the mindset of a throne; the likes of which he hadn't seen since his childhood. His tailtip thrashed as he recognised some of the iconography on the pillars around the throne. Da'Manysque lettering had been carved into the stone. On the thrones of his homeland, these had been used to display the stories and tales of a ruler's legacy. They projected strength and honour, letting all subjects know why the lion who sat on the throne deserved the title of leadership.

A lion emerged from behind the throne, stepping out of the shadows. Even from a distance, Lucca knew Sama'Rey towered over him. The lion's leather clothes bulged with powerful muscle, and his long, thick mane put Lucca's past attempts to shame, even before he started to clip his short. A scar ran up the side of his muzzle, stopping just short of his left eye. He wore an ornate golden necklace with a purple gem sitting centrepiece on his chest. Lucca had expected the guildmaster to be somewhat like Russet; slender and agile. This lion was a pride leader, not someone who appeared capable of sneaking around in the shadows.

Sama'Rey stepped ahead of his throne. Curious musteliads watched on; four of them gathered around the bottom of the dais. Palmer scampered forward to perch on the edge of the bottom step beneath the throne, squeaking excitedly with a second lap-dragon, which was a lighter shade of blue. That must have been Tella. Palmer beamed widely as he looked back to Lucca and Russet, leaning against his companion with a flash of red horns. The pewter bracelet around his wrist caught the light that flickered from the ceiling.

The lion's attention was solely on Russet. He spread his big, meaty hands wide. "Russet. Welcome back. Word has reached my ears that you might have been misbehaving a little since we last spoke. Would you care to explain your actions, my most favoured thief?" Sama'Rey's voice growled deep, sending reverberations through Lucca's chest with every word.

Russet's head was bowed. He stared down at Sama'Rey's paws with his hands still bound behind his back. "I ain't done nothing but what you asked of me, Guildmaster."

"Hah!" Sama'Rey barked out with laughter, which then rippled around the onlookers. The musteliads gathered around to watch had smug smirks plastered across their muzzles, and one leaned in to whisper something to their nearby companions. Their eyes were all on Russet.

Sama'Rey seemed aware of where all the attention had fallen. He clapped his hands together once and roared. "Away!"

The musteliads gathered around the dais quickly leapt to their paws. They fled towards the doors on the far side of the chamber, with none even looking back. Only Nyle, Tel, and Let remained. The two weasels stood either side of Lucca. Nyle stayed beside Russet.

Sama'Rey slowly stepped down from his throne, almost kicking Palmer as he moved past the lap-dragon. He towered over Russet. "I think you have been very naughty, Russet. I asked you to claim relics and artefacts from the Mages' Guild for me. You did this dutifully, until, quite suddenly, you fall silent. And then I find out you damaged one of my lap-dragons, and were caught gallivanting around with this felian? I didn't ask you to do any of those things, dear Russet."

"I..." Russet said, but the words seemed to catch in his throat.

"It was my fault," Lucca said, speaking quickly before anyone could interrupt him. He clumsily dropped down onto one knee and bowed his head. He wanted to bring his hands in front of his chest in the traditional display of submission towards a felian leader, but they remained bound behind his back.

The fierce eyes of the guildmaster flicked to Lucca. His mouth pulled up in a sneer. "Well then. I planned to get to you later, fellow felian, but perhaps I should start now. What is your name?"

"Lucca, sire."

The thick hand slapped across his face before he even knew it was coming. Lucca recoiled and was nearly thrown from his paws as pain stung through his face. His eyes watered.

"I asked for your name," Sama'Rey snarled. "Not what they call you here. Your name, cub. Give it to me."

Lucca felt a little blood trickling from his nose, but he couldn't wipe it away. "Lu'Rahl," he gasped, the name sounding foreign to his lips. "My name is Lu'Rahl."

Sama'Rey cupped his hand beneath Lucca's chin. His touch was gentle, despite the fury he had shown moments earlier. "Lu'Rahl?" the lion asked tenderly. "That's much better, isn't it?"

Lucca nodded his head. He didn't attempt to cringe or pull away from the other lion's touch. "Yes, Pridelord."

Sama'Rey exhaled sharply, though Lucca couldn't tell if he did so in amusement or derision. "Tell me then, Lu'Rahl. Why did you waylay my best thief and delay him?"

Lucca warily raised his eyes. He briefly looked into the amber eyes of the guildmaster. "I came into possession of something you may be interested in."

"Lucca..." Russet warned. Sama'Rey lashed out at the ferret, catching him across the jaw with one hand. The ferret fell back into Nyle and whimpered.

"Go on," Sama'Rey prompted.

Lucca's eyes flicked down, looking at the small bag draped across his chest, held up by the single shoulder strap. He had carried that bag with him all the way from Esfyr's Wold. "Inside this bag are two books. One of which will be something you desire."

"If this is a trap, then I will know about it," Sama'Rey growled. His hands twitched against Lucca's chin. "And you will suffer greatly for it."

"No trap, Pridelord," Lucca squeaked.

Behind him, he could hear the pained whimpers from Russet, but the ferret's warnings had been silenced.

Sama'Rey's hands slowly moved down. His fingers closed around the clasp, undoing the bag in a moment. The lion reached into the bag and started to pull out one of the two books inside.

"Not that one," Lucca said sharply. He grinned bashfully when the eyes of the guildmaster returned to glare at him. His ears flicked back. "That's just a textbook from school. You want the other one."

Sama'Rey snorted. His hand moved to the other book. Slowly, he pulled out the gilded cover of the registry. The lion turned over the book in his hands, and his eyes widened in surprise. Lucca could hear the sharp intake of breath.

"You bring a mighty gift, Lu'Rahl," the lion rumbled. He started to turn around to face his throne.

"I ask only for one thing in exchange," Lucca said quickly.

Sama'Rey paused. He glanced back, but he didn't say anything.

"I ask for my freedom, and that of Russet," Lucca said. He kept his eyes low, and his voice quiet and calm. "With that book, you can do anything. You can rid yourself of the Mages' Guild. You can declare yourself King of Lutrea. Whatever you can imagine is possible with that book. What is one thief in exchange for that?"

Sama'Rey curled his lip. "What is one thief, indeed." He tightened his fingers around the registry. "A shame then, that you did not bring one. You brought merely a traitor and a deserter. Lock them both away."

"Wait, no!" Lucca cried out, but he was too late. Hands grabbed hold of his arms and dragged him away from the guildmaster.

Sama'Rey leered down at Lucca. "I do thank you for your noble gift. I might consider some leniency when I verify the worth of your offering and decide what to do with you both."

Palmer squeaked and waved, jumping up on the bottom of the throne with the other lap-dragon. "See you later, Masters Russet and Lucca!"

Lucca was dragged away, towards a different door to the first one. Russet and Nyle were just ahead of them. The lion's eyes frantically flicked from side to side, seeing the weasel twins dragging him away from the throne. His shoulders slumped, giving up resistance as he was taken out into a new dark corridor. They passed through a couple of other doors. Some musteliads looked on, but none dared to approach.

Finally, they were taken into a corridor that slowly angled down, spiraling in a long circle. No doors led off this passage as it sloped down. Few lights swung from the ceiling, shrouding most of the passage in darkness.

Russet struggled and squirmed in Nyle's grip, but the otter had a fierce grip on Russet's bound arms. Lucca didn't even attempt to escape. He knew there was no point.

At the bottom of the spiral passage was a small, straight corridor. Eight cell doors opened into the narrow passage. The doors were made of a heavy metal with thick bars, looking strong and solid. All eight were empty and unoccupied.

Russet was thrown into the first cell. The ferret yelped in pain as he struck the back wall.

Lucca followed moments later, tossed into the opposite cell with so much force that he crashed against the stone.

Before either of them could react, the cell doors were slammed closed. Keys snicked loudly in the locks.

Nyle leaned against the cell bars. His hands rested on the metal. "The great and mighty Russet, brought to his knees. Never thought I'd see the day."

"Shut it, cod-choker," Russet snarled. The ferret stumbled to his paws, one hand resting against the stone wall for balance. His fur stood on end.

"Tsk tsk, such words from an egg sucker," Nyle retorted, wagging his finger in disapproval. "Only one who's gonna hear them now is your pet felian."

"Don't let Sama'Rey hear yous calling a felian my pet," Russet warned.

Nyle laughed. "I ain't the one who should worry about what Sama'Rey thinks. I hope yous rot down here for years."

Russet hissed in anger, but he had no verbal comeback. Nyle just laughed again. The otter turned aside. The weasel twins had already left the corridor, though Lucca could just about see the white fur of one just outside the heavy oak door that had been propped open.

Nyle mock saluted Russet, then pulled the oak door closed. It slammed shut, and another click of a lock echoed through the empty cell block. The cells of Sama'Rey had claimed two prisoners.

Chapter Seventeen

Russet slumped back and leaned against the bare wall of their cell with his hands still awkwardly bound behind his back. He stretched out his jaw and shook his head. “Well, that could have gone a bit better,” he muttered. His arms wiggled and squirmed as his hands groped amongst the shadows.

“Could have gone worse,” Lucca replied. His jaw still ached from Sama’Rey’s backhanded blow. He hadn’t been expecting that.

Metal clattered against stone as Russet’s handcuffs dropped to the floor. The ferret winced and rubbed his wrists. “Think you can handle yours?”

Lucca wiggled his wrists, trying to imitate what he had seen the ferret do. The cuffs remained stubbornly tight against his fur. The lock was resolutely secure. “Don’t think so.”

“A’ight, just sit tight for a few,” the ferret said. He prowled up and down the small confines of his cell, pausing occasionally to tap his claws against the narrow bars. His ears twitched with each sound coming from beyond the door.

The lion looked around the dark dungeon. The other six cells were bare, though the faint smell of damp and mould lingered in the air. The only light across the cells came from two small swinging lights near the ceiling, putting out a flickering glow that was starting to irritate Lucca's eyes.

Lucca rested his head on the bars as he watched the ferret. His jaw ached and the coolness of the metal soothed that pain somewhat. "You think he bought it?"

Russet scoffed quietly. He kicked aside the discarded pair of handcuffs and stood by the bars, coming to rest at last. He glanced left and right, but he didn't say what he was looking out for. "I dunno. He'll test that book first."

"Palmer knows what he needs to do to delay Sama'Rey," Lucca replied. He tried to wriggle his hands free of his cuffs again, but he couldn't get his wrist through the band of unyielding metal. "Will he be alright up there?"

"He'll have everything under control," Russet said. His tail swished as rested his head against the bars, mirroring Lucca from the other side of the dungeon. "Maybe. This is Palmer we're talking about here. He's either got everything under control, or he's telling Sama'Rey all our secrets. I ain't doubted his loyalty on any of our other jobs, but with this? This is the only time where he may be a liability, and it tears my heart to think he might betray me without knowing."

Lucca glanced to the door. "He's been with you that long?"

The ferret smiled. He lowered his gaze. "Yeah. Since the first job. He's as much the relic thief as I am."

"And... how?" Lucca swallowed nervously as the ferret's eyes snapped up to meet his from across the dungeon. The lion licked his lips and struggled not to step back from the force of that blue-eyed stare. "I mean, you know. How did you do everything? The relics were meant to be impossible to steal, even before the thief ward."

The strength of Russet's gaze faded to warmth as he smiled and shook his head. "Still trying to get my secrets?"

Lucca shrugged, difficult to do with his arms still bound behind his back. "We're in it together now, aren't we?"

Russet laughed. "For better or worse, hey." He spread his hands wide. "Truth is, your mages are so protective of the vault and so scared of things going missing, every relic going in or out is registered. Who took it. Where it's from. Where it's going. Palmer managed to break into that register a few years ago. It gives a thief like me everything I need to intercept the nicest relics on the road."

Lucca blinked. He tilted his head. "That's it? No incredible schemes or plots? Just... wait until the mages accidentally tell you where everything is?"

The ferret snorted in amusement. His eyes twinkled brightly. "Oh, the scheme to get that exploit was incredible. Daring and brave just like all the stories tell. But, if we're asking each other questions about our guilds," Russet said, a frown creasing his brow, "how did you work out the thefts were all by one person? Could have been dozens of us."

Lucca flexed his fingers, trying to find a comfortable position for his arms as he shrugged again. "The notes you left. They were all signed by the Relic Thief. Thought that was the point of them."

"Notes?" Russet's jaw hung slack. Then he groaned and palmed his hand to his forehead. "Palmer. I bet all my scalls on it."

The lion smiled, which slowly faded as his eyes drifted up, towards the grimy and dark ceiling. "Speaking of him, we don't want to leave him up there alone for much longer."

Russet swished his tail. He looked across at the lion. "This'll be like the Erasmus job, alright? You do what I say, when I say it."

"I won't get distracted this time," Lucca promised. He knew he would have to focus. Any lapses in concentration could get them both killed.

"Good," Russet replied. A small needle of shadow grew between his fingers, which slowly morphed and elongated out into his nightblade. He spun the shadow around in his hand. "Now, let's get out of here, shall we?"

Lucca stepped away from the cell door, watching as the ferret pressed the shadows of the nightblade against the sturdy bars.

"You're lucky they didn't find that on you," Lucca said, keeping a wary eye on the wooden door on the other side of the chamber. The quiet murmur of conversation drifted around the cracks in the door.

"Lucky? Hah," Russet replied. He paused and grunted as he pressed hard on the nightblade's pommel as the blade sliced through the metal. "Bit hard to find a shadow, don'tcha think?"

The ferret worked at the bars until the door broke away from the lock, slowly swinging open with a quiet screech. Both ferret and lion looked to the door, but there was no movement from beyond the dungeon. No indication their escape had been noticed.

Russet quickly scampered across the dungeon and set the nightblade to free Lucca from his cell. The shadows made quick work of the door, and the ferret slipped inside the cell.

"Let's get this off you," Russet said, his hand gently pulling at Lucca's wrists.

Lucca took in a deep breath as he felt the icy touch of the blade against his fur. He suppressed a shiver, trying to keep still lest he distract the ferret. A moment later, his handcuffs fell away, bouncing against the straw-dusted stone floor.

The lion rubbed his wrists and flexed his fingers, glad to be able to move his arms properly again. Russet did not remain idle. He turned his focus to the broken bars, slicing off a new segment about the length of his forearm. He held out the bar for Lucca to take hold of. "In case you need a weapon other than your magic," he said. He grimaced at the mutilated doors. "Just so you know, I ain't usually so... crude. Normally I'd have my lockpicks, but Peri's got them all. Weren't wanting their grubby hands on them or any of my other relics."

Lucca warily tested the weight of the metal bar. He struggled to move it quickly, but the ferret was right. He felt a little better carrying it, rather than nothing at all. His magic wouldn't be able to protect him from a knife or sword. He doubted he would last long in a fight even with the bar in his hands, but that time might be all he needed before Russet came to help him.

Free from their cells, Russet moved forward to the oak door that sealed them inside the small corridor. From the other side of the door, Lucca could hear the murmured conversation between the otter and two weasels. Though the lion couldn't hear exactly what was being said, there was no urgency to their words. They had not yet realised their prisoners had broken free.

"Is there any other way out?" Lucca asked. He looked around the small chamber. The remaining seven cell blocks were all open. They looked identical, with no furnishings in any of them. Only bare stone and metal was down here.

"Ain't gonna be a good prison with more than one way in and out," Russet replied. The ferret leaned close to the oak door, pressing his ear against the wood. He held out his hand, warning Lucca to stay back.

"How are we going to do this?" Lucca asked nervously. Combat was not something he ever expected to take part in. Sometimes he had been bullied on Da'Manyr, with the other cubs taking turns to push him around, but that had been the closest to a fight he had ever been in.

"Nyle's a good fighter. I'll take care of him first," Russet explained. He kept his voice low, making sure he couldn't be heard on the other side of the door. "The twins will fight for each other. Don't be fooled by their names. Their parents weren't imaginative, but they are. If they see a weakness, they'll exploit it."

"So what should I do?" Lucca asked. He tightened his grip on the metal pipe.

Russet grinned. "Let me do the work. Watch my back."

Once more, Russet slipped the nightblade into the lock. Once again, he did not bother with finesse. He simply wrenched the blade around and pulled back hard. The lock splintered as Russet withdrew the shadowy relic.

The ferret kicked the door open and leaped forward before the three guards could do anything to react.

Russet's nightblade slashed and parried. The ferret himself was a whirl of movement. He kicked and slashed at the three musteliads. The nightblade sliced Nyle across the forearm, and the otter yelped and dropped the sword he had only just begun to draw.

Tel and Let hastened to stand between Russet and the spiral passage that led back up to the main part of the underground complex. The weasels had both scrambled to ready their own weapons, though both warily eyed the intense darkness of the nightblade.

Russet's attention turned solely to the weasel twins. He grinned a savage smile. His ears perked up. "This ain't gotta be anything bad. Step aside and let us go."

"You think Sama'Rey's gonna let yous leave?" Tel spat.

"He's gonna have your hide for this," Let added.

"I'll take those chances," Russet replied. He shuffled forward half a step. The weasels did not move.

Lucca edged forward, standing in the doorway. His eyes flicked to Nyle, who cowered beneath the sloping ceiling, right in the far corner of the small watch area. The otter's eyes were solely on Russet's back, paying no attention at all to the lion.

The clash of steel against the nightblade rang out between the close stone walls. Russet spun away from the double attack from the twins. He kicked out with one paw, forcing Let back a couple of steps.

With the ferret distracted, the otter moved out from the shadows. His blood-soaked hand tightly gripped a dagger.

Lucca didn't think. He jumped forward with the metal pipe raised in both hands. He smashed the makeshift weapon down onto Nyle's shoulder, who reacted too slow. The otter grunted in pain, before Lucca brought the crude club around to hit the otter's chest. Nyle crumbled with a pained wheeze.

The lion heard the patter of claws on stone. He whirled around quickly, keeping his pipe raised. A weasel's blade struck the pipe, almost dislodging the metal from Lucca's hands. His wrists ached from the impact.

Tel snarled and slashed at Lucca again. The lion stepped back quickly, until he bumped against the stone wall.

Every time Lucca tried to strike the weasel, the musteliad had moved out of the way. His attacks were slow and clumsy compared to the weasel, and twice he felt the bite of the sword strike his borrowed leathers. Each time, the blade failed to pierce through, but Lucca winced and tried to retreat, but he had nowhere to go.

"*Conger geminus effini*," Lucca gasped. He felt the flare of magic run through him, before he dived to the side to avoid Tel's blade. The knife crashed into stone. The musteliad leapt back with a yelp as three copies of Lucca rose up again.

The weasel's eyes flicked between the three lions. His mouth hung slightly open. He then braced his paws against the stone and regained his composure. His eyes narrowed as he leaped forward, slicing his blade through Lucca's shoulder.

The illusion flickered and faded. The weasel, losing his balance with nothing to thrust against, stumbled forward and smashed his shoulder against the wall. The two remaining lions both swung their metal pipe at the same time. The illusion faded, while the heavy metal crashed against Tel's wrist, forcing the weasel to drop his weapon. The weasel shrieked in pain.

Lucca lost grip of the metal bar as momentum ripped it from his hand. The crude weapon clattered against the stone floor and rolled away, out of reach. The weasel started to turn, wincing in pain but still with his muzzle pulled back in a silent snarl. Lucca didn't hesitate. He brought his knee up hard, striking between the weasel's legs.

Tel howled and swayed. His face passed through several different emotions all at once, before he fell down to his knees with a low grunt. His hands cupped at his crotch as he fell to the side, his tail curled close between his knees. He made no attempt to reach for his sword, instead just whimpering quietly.

Let lowered his guard at the sound of his brother's pain. Russet used that moment of distraction to good effect.

The nightblade lashed out, striking Let across the arm. The weasel yelped and dropped his sword.

Russet struck again. This time with the clenched fist of his right hand.

Let staggered and swayed. Then he fell, dazed, into Tel. The two weasels dropped to the floor together, sprawled out on top of each other, with Let's tail draped over Nyle's torso.

Lucca breathed heavily. He stared for a moment at the three defeated guards. Nyle looked unconscious. Tel groaned.

Russet grabbed hold of Lucca's hand and pulled the lion away. They hurried up the sloping passage before any of the guards were able to recover.

Lucca felt dazed. The lion had never struck anyone in anger before. "Will they be alright?" he asked, a bit of a whimper escaping with his words.

The ferret flicked his ears. "Nyle's gonna have an awful headache. Tel may not have kits, but yeah. They'll be fine."

Lucca breathed a sigh of relief. He couldn't be certain Russet was telling the truth, but the lion had no reason to doubt him. He didn't want to cause any lasting harm to the thieves, despite the aggression and scorn they had shown him.

Russet frisked over the prone thieves, taking their weapons and passing Nyle's sword to Lucca. The blade felt uncomfortable in the lion's hands, but it was a better weapon than an iron bar.

"Help me put them into the cell," Russet said, dragging the groaning Tel towards the open door. With Lucca's help, it wasn't long before the thieves were locked in three of the cells that Russet's nightblade had not damaged, locked with the keys plundered from Nyle's belt. They hurried away before then thieves fully roused, though Tel had already staggered to his paws.

Russet paused at the top of the sloping passageway. The door was closed, and the ferret pressed his ear to the wood. Sounds echoed through the stone walls, coming from almost every direction. Lucca couldn't keep track of how many voices and pawsteps he could hear.

"Ready?" Russet asked, his voice barely audible even to Lucca.

Lucca nodded. He placed his hand on the ferret's shoulder. "*Concordi invisibilis.*"

Both ferret and lion vanished, though Russet remained as a slight shimmer in the air, which Lucca knew only he would be able to see. He also knew he would appear much the same to the ferret. They would be able to see where the other was, but to all others they would be completely invisible.

"Ugh, gives me the creeps," Russet muttered. The shimmer of air moved its hands around as the ferret tested his invisibility.

Lucca kept his mouth closed. He didn't mind the sensation of looking down and finding nothing where his body should have been. More importantly for him though, he didn't trust himself not to let out a concerned whimper. The last thing he wanted to do was step out of the comforting darkness and into the rest of the hideout.

Then Russet pushed open the door and Lucca had no more choice. He had to follow the ferret. Or, more accurately, the shimmer of light that was all he could see of the ferret.

Lucca tried to move as silently as possible. No one could see him, but that didn't mean he couldn't be heard or smelled if he wasn't careful. A pair of musteliads walked past without seeming to notice the two escaped prisoners. Lucca had to hold his hands over his muzzle to quieten the sounds of his breathing. The otter and weasel were both quiet, a frown and a snarl etched onto their muzzles. They paced with haste and purpose towards the main chamber and Sama'Rey's throne.

Only once the corridor was empty again did the shimmer ahead of Lucca start to move again. Russet knew where to go. They moved away from the main chamber.

More voices came from around the corner.

"...his little pet."

Lucca's ears burned and his hand gripped painfully tight around his stolen sword, thinking they were talking about him. A pine marten turned the corner, with a vulpun by his side. Both had mostly shed into their winter coats.

"Musta done something bad," the vulpun replied with a bark of laughter. "Glad someone finally got something over the egg-sucking prick."

They weren't talking about the lion. Lucca could see the shimmer ahead pause for a moment, a soft growl coming from the seemingly empty air. Though the vulpun's ears flicked, neither thief appeared to notice the quiet noise.

"'Bout time too. Gives us something to steal," the pine marten said, pulling back his muzzle to bare his teeth. "Hope the boss has a good punishment for him."

"He better," the vulpun said, matching the marten's expression. They bumped elbows and laughed as the winter fox pushed open one of the side doors. Their voices continued to be heard for a while, but Lucca trained his ears away from them.

Every corridor looked much the same to Lucca. Unchanging stone and flickering torchlight would quickly have left him lost and confused were it not for the shimmering outline of Russet to guide him. The lion's claws occasionally clicked against the stone floor as he struggled to keep them retracted, and his heavy breathing would surely attract attention should another thief come close, but thankfully none did.

Russet moved with absolute silence. If Lucca took his eyes from the ferret's shimmer, then he knew he would quickly lose track of Russet's movements. He needed to keep his eyes open and focused on the ferret, letting his other senses alert him on any approaching thieves.

More voices ahead. They didn't move; instead remaining stationary. Russet's shimmer moved close to a closed door, through which Lucca could hear the voices. One spoke gruffly to at least two others. Lucca didn't recognise the growling tones of Sama'Rey amongst them.

Russet turned away from that door. Instead, he approached the one directly opposite. He gently unhitched the latch and pushed the door open. Immediately, Lucca got a burst of incense filling his nose. Lavender, he thought he could smell. The incense partially masked the ever-present scent of mould that filled the hideout.

Urgent pawsteps pounded against the stone, coming from towards the cells. Lucca hurried after Russet through the door, which was quietly closed behind them with a soft snick of the latch. Another door slammed open and a desperate voice shouted out.

"Russet and the felian, they're gone!"

Lucca could hear the ferret hiss softly. The lion knew why. They had hoped for a little longer before their absence from the cells was detected. It didn't change their plans, but it made them a little bit harder. Now the whole hideout would be on the lookout for them.

Russet lightly tapped on Lucca's arm. Though he couldn't see the ferret at all, Lucca knew what the relic thief wanted. He padded away from the door, finding a soft carpet beneath his paws instead of the usual stone.

They were in a small, square room without any furnishings. Three more doors led off from the room, which was kept lit up by a single sconce hanging from the ceiling. Four incense burners, one in each corner of the room, provided a steady stream of scented smoke that slowly drifted towards the vents at the roughly hewn ceiling.

Two of the doors were unlocked, but the third, directly opposite, had a heavy padlock to keep the door closed. Russet wasted no time in pulling out his nightblade and setting the shadows to the lock. The magical blade appeared as a dark void through Lucca's invisibility spell; an absence of anything rather than an illusion.

The padlock clattered to the floor. The sound was muffled somewhat by the carpet, but Lucca still whipped around to look towards the door behind them, sword wavering as he lifted it. He expected someone to barge it open and confront them, but everything remained mercifully quiet beyond. Pawsteps ran by, but none approached too close.

Lucca backed through the doorway. When he turned around, he couldn't stop the gasp from escaping his muzzle. These had to be the personal chambers of Sama'Rey. Da'Manysque artwork and sculptures lined the walls. Luscious soft carpets and rugs kept warmth inside the room, and a constant infusion of lavender kept the worst of the smells at bay.

Drawers opened up suddenly. Lucca felt a moment of alarm before he saw the shimmer of Russet just in front of the cupboards. The ferret hissed quietly as he rummaged through Sama'Rey's belongings. Each item vanished from view as soon as Russet touched them, before fading back into visibility as the ferret tossed them to the side.

Lucca warily eyed around the room. The back of his neck prickled like he was being watched, but there was no one behind him at all. The room was completely empty but for them.

Russet soon found what he was searching for. Lucca briefly caught sight of a red gem broadcaster the size and shape of a dragon's claw before his magic hid it from view. The gem had to be bigger than Lucca's whole hand, but he knew that dragons could reach incredible sizes. A single red claw was a strong reminder of that.

The ferret's shimmer moved back across the room, close to Lucca. "Ugh, where are you," the ferret whispered. His hand finally found Lucca's shoulder. "That's the first one. Gotta find Palmer and Sama'Rey now."

"Wonderful," Lucca muttered to himself. He was glad Russet would be unable to see him, though the ferret must have felt the shiver of fear that rippled through his body. At least the mask of terror on his face would be hidden.

The ferret's hand slipped away from Lucca's shoulder, and the door to Sama'Rey's chambers opened a moment later. The small room outside was still empty, and Russet hurried through to the outer door, with Lucca trailing right behind. The lion didn't bother closing the door behind him. If the thieves already knew they were loose, then it didn't matter if they knew where they had been. All that mattered was that they didn't know where they were going next.

Activity sounded through the darkened corridors. Doors were being slammed open and the rooms beyond searched, and the sounds of pawsteps reverberated through the stone. Lucca felt almost paralysed by fear as Russet slowly, carefully, closed the door behind them. The lion's grip on his magic almost faltered, and for a brief moment he and the ferret were visible. There were no musteliads at their end of the corridor to see them, but Lucca still squeaked in panic as he struggled to pull the invisibility charm back over them.

Lucca took a deep breath to compose himself, shrouding himself and Russet back in the invisibility spell. Just in time, too. A weasel rounded the curve in the corridor, peering up towards the door with narrowed eyes. She carried a long pike in both hands, the pointed tip held down low. "Nothing," she called out over her shoulder.

An indistinct voice from further down the long corridor called the weasel back. She tapped the butt of the spear against the floor before turning on her toes.

Lucca felt a prickle of magic rippling through the air. He frowned and tensed his hands, struggling to keep hold of his spell again. This time, it wasn't a lack of concentration that had caused him to nearly slip. The thieves were increasing the strength of their magical protections around the hideout, increasing the mental strain on maintaining his illusion. That meant they knew a mage was helping Russet. It also meant Lucca would struggle to keep them both invisible for long. They had to hurry.

The lion moved first, pulling Russet along with him. Though the ferret could not have felt the surge of magic, Russet did seem to understand Lucca's newfound urgency. The ferret quickly moved ahead of Lucca as they warily crept up the long corridor.

Some of the doors had been opened with force. Locks had been splintered and hinges ripped apart. Steel clashed against stone as weapons were jabbed into dark crevasses where a ferret or a lion might be able to hide.

Lucca trusted Russet to know the way, for he was soon lost. The underground hideout was a maze of identical corridors that seemed to stretch out over a large area beneath the city. He couldn't think on what the network may once have been used for. They didn't have the appearance of old sewers. He wondered if they might once have been part of an old fortification system, as the corridors were narrow enough to form regular choke points against invading forces.

Russet's arm pushed against Lucca's chest. The lion only just managed to suppress his yelp of surprise. He was pushed back against the wall as a pair of musteliads walked by, close enough that they almost touched.

The closest of the pair, a marten, wrinkled her nose a couple of paces from Lucca and Russet. She turned to her otter companion. "Do you smell that?"

Lucca's eyes widened. The lavender incense in Sama'Rey's room...

The otter gripped a pair of short daggers in his hands. "They've been in the boss's chambers." He approached the closest door, which had been ripped open. "Must've gone in here."

The marten didn't turn away. "One of them's a mage. They're not in there," she said, drawing her short sword. She spun the blade in her hand, before swinging the sword to the side, sparking the metal against stone just an inch from Lucca's face.

Lucca's nerve failed him. He started to run, no longer caring about how much noise he made. He could hear Russet just beside him, keeping pace despite the lion's longer legs. Behind them both followed the marten, shouting loudly to attract attention. Pawsteps sounded loudly in all directions, with most coming from behind them.

Lucca's chest burned. His focus shredded, the additional pressure of the magical shields made his illusions flicker in and out. He couldn't keep hold of the invisibility charms, leaving Russet and him occasionally visible.

Ahead were the wide double doors that led through to the main chamber of the hideout. No one guarded the doorway, and the doors themselves had been left wide open. They had a clean run through, but Lucca knew that if they were outnumbered in the throne chamber then they would never be able to survive long enough to do what still needed to be done.

He released the faltering magic that kept himself invisible. He had other needs for that magic.

Lucca's courage almost failed him again as he turned around to face his pursuers. He still moved back, retreating backwards until he had passed through the open doors. He extended his hands out. The marten who led the pursuit faltered. She knew he was capable of magic.

Lucca summoned a fireball to his hand. "Who wants it?" he asked, hoping that they weren't about to call his bluff. Throwing a stick would cause more damage than his fireball, but the flames were just a distraction. His magic filtered outwards, reaching into the stonework of the rounded archway in which the heavy oak doors were poorly fitted.

Almost two dozen musteliads gathered just behind the marten. None of them seemed willing to take the next step forward, cautious of the magic Lucca wielded. Against all instinct, he took a step forward. Russet darted in alongside him. Still with one hand holding his lukewarm fire, Lucca pushed one of the doors closed, Russet putting his weight behind the other. They scraped shut, but Lucca knew it would not hold the thieves for long. He extinguished his flames and pressed both hands to the wood.

"*Expunsius*," he barked, pushing his magic into the door. Wood swelled and expanded, growing to the precise mental commands of the lion, who trembled from the effort as the protective shields weighed down on his mind. The door groaned as it wedged itself to the frame, swelling to perfectly fill the space between the walls.

Lucca knew it wouldn't be long before the thieves started to hack through the door. He started to turn, but he had barely moved when he heard a lone person clapping slowly.

Sama'Rey stood on the dais in front of his throne. But for Palmer and Tella, the lion was alone. Russet stood halfway between Lucca and the guildmaster. Palmer waved brightly at Lucca and Russet from his place between Sama'Rey's paws. The second lap-dragon watched with wary eyes, horns fading from bright red to a dull glow.

"My my, Lu'Rahl. I must say, I am impressed. A felian mage? A shame we did not get Mera's warning a little earlier. I might have made extra precautions to keep you safely bound," Sama'Rey said, laughing loudly. He spread his arms wide. "But it is all going to be for nothing, I am afraid."

"You've got what you wanted from us, Sama'Rey," Lucca growled. The lion took a couple of wary steps backwards. "Let us go, and there can be no more trouble."

Sama'Rey smirked at the lion. He reached into one of the many pockets sewn into his leathers. The pridelord pulled out a book and tossed the tome down to Russet's paws. The ferret skipped back a couple of inches to stop the book hitting him.

Lucca recognised his alchemy textbook. He swallowed nervously. The illusion should have lasted much longer than that. His eyes flicked up towards the guildmaster as he struggled to resist the natural urges to kneel before the powerful felian.

Sama'Rey stepped down from the dais. His voice was deep, yet soft. "Give me what I want, and I will consider killing you quickly."

"Doesn't sound like a good deal to me," Lucca said. His hands shook as he lifted his hands up, summoning the useless fireball to his palm again. "Would you care to renegotiate?"

Sama'Rey sneered. "You don't have the high ground here, Lu'Rahl. Give over the book," he demanded, holding his hand out expectantly.

Neither Lucca nor Russet moved. The lion did his best to stare down the guildmaster, but his confidence wavered. He could hear the thieves behind attempting to bash through the swollen door. They didn't have long.

The guildmaster turned his attention to the ferret. "As for you," Sama'Rey snarled, reaching out to roughly pull Russet closer. The ferret darted back quickly. "Someone steal your tongue?"

Russet did not answer. Lucca trembled.

"You will not disrespect me," Sama'Rey snarled. He moved with a speed Lucca had not expected, lashing out with both hands to grab hold of the ferret's shoulders. His hands passed through empty air as the illusion faded. The guildmaster blinked and stared for a moment before he turned to Lucca with a snarl. "You."

Lucca had nowhere to back away to. He was already pressed close to the wall and the doorway, which thumped and thudded against his back and tail as the thieves tried to break through. The only other exit to the chamber was on the far side, and he doubted his ability to outpace the pridelord over any distance.

"Doot!"

Both Sama'Rey and Lucca glanced across to the lap-dragon. Palmer stood on the top step of the dais, a couple of paces above the other lap-dragon. In his hands was the RedClaw broadcaster.

Palmer chirped brightly. "Lowering critical magical defences," he said, grinning from ear to ear as he looked to Sama'Rey. The pewter band around his wrist shone with purple light.

"What?" the pridelord spat. He turned around a little more, his paws sliding over the dusty stone floor. "Undo that, you little scamp. Tella, stop him!"

"Unable to undo that action, Master Sama'Rey" Tella squeaked. His horns flickered red, then faded dun.

While Sama'Rey's attention was held captive by the lap-dragons, Lucca used that opportunity to creep to the side a few paces. He could feel the magical defences lowering, enhancing his own power slightly. More importantly, the hideout could now be seen from scrying. Portals could be opened within the hideout.

"Now, Palmer!" Russet called out, his voice coming from somewhere just behind the throne.

"Doot! Command accepted. Broadcasting location to Archmage Mafren. Would you like to say hi, felian Sama'Rey?"

Sama'Rey roared. A deep, primal bellow shook the chamber and even brought a silence to the musteliads trying to clear the rubble in the doorway. "You will not broadcast that signal," the guildmaster snarled, advancing on Palmer. The lap-dragon stood still, beaming up at the lion without any fear or concern.

"Signal broadcast," the lap-dragon chirped. The dragon's claw grasped in his talons pulsed with crimson light. "Archmage Mafren has received the co-ordinates. He seems angry. He said he'll be here soon."

Russet stepped out of the air, putting himself between Sama'Rey and Palmer. The ferret's arm was raised, the nightblade pointed right at the lion's chest.

Sama'Rey swatted the ferret aside, but his hand passed right through the flickering illusion. A second ferret appeared to the lion's right. A third to his left.

The guildmaster spun on his paws to glare at Lucca, but the lion had already whispered his invisibility charm. "You think you can fool me?" Sama'Rey roared. "You think your tricks can defeat me? I will tear you apart where you stand!"

Palmer scampered away from the throne with Tella, both fleeing towards the shadows around the edge of the room. The lap-dragons slipped out of sight, until only the red glow of Palmer's horns shone from the darkness, continuing to broadcast to the mages. Tella disappeared into the shadows entirely.

Knowing he needed to do something, Lucca quietly padded away from the blocked doorway. Fists hammered against the swollen wood, only with the occasional crack of metal that chipped into the door. Once they got into the main chamber, any lingering advantage Lucca and Russet may have would be quickly eroded away. Somehow, they needed to hold off until the archmage arrived.

Sama'Rey's massive body prowled towards the illusions of Russet. His shoulders hunched forward as he looked, both underplaying his height but adding to the broadness of his chest. His claws had all been sharpened to a wicked point. He carried no weapon, for Lucca knew he needed none.

Illusion after illusion were slashed to ribbons at the pridelord's claws, but they were all just air with nothing tangible to them. Each time the lion failed to rend Russet apart, he snarled and spat that little bit louder.

Once Sama'Rey reached the base of the dais he stopped. A low growl constantly escaped his lips, but he no longer swung wildly at the ferret illusions that approached him. Instead, the lion grabbed the gemstone in his necklace. The purple crystal blazed with magical light and sent a shockwave of energy through the chamber.

Lucca could do nothing to defend himself. The circular pulse of energy stripped away all of his illusions, leaving no defences left. He and Russet stood together, but exposed. The ferret and lion exchanged a quick glance with each other. They both knew what still needed to be done, and there was still no sign of Archmage Mafren and the Mages' Guild. It was still all up to them.

Sama'Rey sneered. He batted one hand against his chest. "Just me against you both now. No illusions. No tricks. No magic." His words dripped with disdain as he flexed his claws. "Not so confident now, Lu'Rahl?"

"*Ignici*," Lucca snarled, cupping his hands together. A lukewarm flame burst into life between his fingers. He thrust his arms out, pushing the fireball towards the pridelord. He knew the flame wouldn't hurt the other lion, but he hoped to provide a distraction while Russet made a move.

Sama'Rey didn't flinch. The fireball struck him square in the chest. He didn't even recoil, but instead started to laugh. "Is that all you've got?" he scoffed. He braced his paws against the floor, ready to charge.

Russet darted to the right. Sama'Rey's eyes followed the ferret.

Lucca tried a different tactic. Instead, he switched to the Winterpaw tongue. Fire magic had the advantage of being showy and dramatic, but Lucca couldn't make it work effectively. He needed ice.

With the guildmaster focused on the ferret's nightblade, Lucca quickly formed and hurled a spear of ice towards the lion. He aimed for the gemstone on Sama'Rey's chest, hoping to overwhelm the defences the crystal provided.

Sama'Rey didn't even recoil as the spear melted. Only a puddle on the floor remained of Lucca's spell. The water pooled around Sama'Rey's paws.

Another idea came to Lucca's mind. He couldn't target the pridelord because of the gemstone he wore, but there were ways around that. Lucca's eyes flicked up for a moment at the sound of splintering wood. The thieves had almost broken through the barrier.

Lucca focused his magic downwards, to the puddle of water around Sama'Rey's paws. The water froze in an instant. The guildmaster didn't slow down, but Lucca lifted his hands to extend the ice upwards, forming a curtain of frozen water around the other lion's legs.

Sama'Rey still tried to take a step forward. His upper body swayed as the ice cracked, but the frozen shield didn't shatter.

Lucca clenched his fingers as he focused his magic. His tail lashed as he struggled to tighten and strengthen the ice as it snaked up Sama'Rey's legs. The ice never made contact with the guildmaster. Whenever the lion's legs touched the frozen barrier, it began to melt, but Lucca was able to keep Sama'Rey occupied, if not contained.

Sama'Rey hammered his fist against the ice. Cracks formed in the expanding barrier as the lion's hand smashed through, but Lucca's magic just about held firm.

Russet sprinted forward. He dodged around Sama'Rey's wild swing and wrapped his arms around the lion's neck. The guildmaster stopped trying to break free of the ice, giving Lucca a chance to reinforce the barrier, almost all the way up to Sama'Rey's hips.

Arms swung as the guildmaster tried to dislodge Russet. Claws snagged against the ferret's leathers.

Before the ferret was able to get a firm grip against Sama'Rey, he was thrown free. The nightblade jabbed up. The shadows of the magical blade snagged against the necklace and severed the chain.

Though Sama'Rey reached for the necklace, the purple gemstone fell from his body and clattered against the floor. Russet quickly rolled as he fell from the lion, piercing the nightblade through the heart of the crystal. The necklace splintered, then shattered with a sudden shockwave of magic.

Lucca's barrier couldn't withstand the blast of magic. The ice cracked and crumbled from the onslaught of magic that radiated from the broken crystal, spilling out the energy it had absorbed for the guildmaster.

Russet was thrown back by the blast, scraping on the floor and rolling to lie still on his belly. Lucca hurried over, not even looking towards Sama'Rey until he was stood over the ferret's body. He held his hands up, ready to summon magic again, but Sama'Rey hadn't approached.

The guildmaster kicked away the last of the ice that had frozen around his legs. He crouched down and picked up the shattered remnants of the amulet. He rubbed the purple shards of crystal between his fingers, before tossing them to the side.

His lip curled up in a snarl as he was joined by a dozen musteliads. The thieves had broken through at last.

Russet struggled up to his paws. His fingers gripped around the nightblade. The ferret stood side by side with Lucca.

"Ready to die yet?" Sama'Rey growled. But for a little dampness on his legs, the lion was completely unhindered from Lucca's magical attempts.

Russet raised the nightblade.

Magic prickled over Lucca's fur.

One portal burst to life. A second followed. Then a third, and a fourth. All within a second of each other.

By the time Archmage Mafren stepped out of his portal, two dozen others had opened up around the chamber.

Thieves began to panic. Several arrows were loosed towards the portals, but the projectiles were swatted aside by the mages who stepped through.

Howls filled the chamber as knives were wrenched from hands and swords turned to molten metal. Those who tried to flee found themselves unable to do so as the entrances were sealed away by smooth stone. They were locked inside with nowhere to run.

Sama'Rey's eyes flicked around the room, then locked on Lucca and Russet. He sneered, a blazing fury behind his eyes as though fuelled by a magic as powerful as that wielded by the archmage. The pridelord charged, shouldering aside any in his way.

Lucca blasted a force of air at Sama'Rey, but the pridelord swatted off the magical attack with ease. Russet darted to the side, slashing up with the nightblade to slice against Sama'Rey's shoulder, but Lucca wasn't so quick.

The lion was thrown backwards from the impacts, feeling all the wind pushed from his lungs. He wheezed as he smashed back against the floor, his head striking the cold stone and sending pain throughout every nerve in his body. For a moment, Lucca couldn't move at all. He could feel nothing but pain, before sensation slowly started to return to his limbs.

Lucca struggled to get up to his knees. A felian paw cracked against his ribs as Sama'Rey kicked him again. The other lion bellowed in rage as a flash of white fur passed in front of Lucca. The nightblade slashed at Sama'Rey's hands, drawing blood from the lion's fingers and palm.

The ferret was swatted aside with a punch from Sama'Rey's offhand. Russet staggered back and was struck by another thief; an otter who tried to evade a badger in mage robes. For a moment, Lucca lost sight of Russet.

A pine marten swept past Lucca and advanced on Sama'Rey. Archmage Mafren snapped his fingers and lifted his palms, and the guildmaster was lifted from his paws. The marten's hands swept to the sides, and Sama'Rey's arms were pulled apart. The lion was held aloft as though by invisible chains, his flailing paws several feet from the floor. Another gesture from the marten silenced Sama'Rey's angered snarls.

Lucca staggered away from the archmage. His eyes found Russet again. He reached out for him, but the ferret was buffeted back across the chamber by a powerful pulse of magic. The ferret rolled several times, the nightblade dislodged from his grip as it skittered away into the shadows in the corner of the chamber.

Mages pushed back against the chaos. Thieves were bound in magical chains, leaving fewer and fewer to fight the losing battle against the magic users. Once more, Russet tried to push his way free from the thieves. Lucca tried to clear a path for the ferret.

The archmage stood in front of Lucca again. The marten's hand raised in the direction of the struggling ferret.

"No!" Lucca cried out, trying to drag back the archmage. An arm wrapped around Lucca's chest and tried to pull him back. "No! Not him!"

No one listened. A familiar voice whispered in his ear. "I've got you, Lucca."

Lucca struggled against Master Roe's grip. "Not him. Not Russet. Bring him back!"

The smell of magic burned Lucca's nose. A portal opened up around him.

"No! You can't take me," Lucca yelled, trying to pull free from the badger, but Master Roe's grip was like iron.

The chamber vanished in a blast of white light.

Lucca was gone. Russet remained.

The lion's heart remained.

Chapter Eighteen

The Thieves' Guild had been shattered. The RedClaw networks were clogged with the news. The guildmaster and dozens of thieves crawling beneath the streets of Cofferknell had been taken into custody. Amongst them, rumour had it, was the notorious relic thief. Justice had finally been brought to the thieves who had dared stand against the might of the mages.

In public, Archmage Mafren had taken all of the credit for the dismantling of the Thieves' Guild.

In private, Archmage Mafren had also taken all of the credit.

Lucca had spoken to the archmage once since his return to Esfyr's Wold. A brief, curt thank you had been exchanged. From Lucca, to the archmage. The pine marten had rescued Lucca from the den of thieves, after all.

The felian had received a pardon for his involvement with the relic thief. Mafren had believed Master Roe when the badger defended Lucca by saying the lion must have been bewitched or hoodwinked by the relic thief. The presence of the pink amulet in Lucca's pocket only helped to confirm this defence, though no tests had ever been made on Lucca to confirm that theory. The lion had been allowed to return to his studies.

In the two weeks since his return to Esfyr's Wold, Lucca hadn't been to a single class. Anger had taken hold of him first. He had blamed the mages for taking Russet away; he had blamed himself for not doing enough to keep Russet safe. The rage had eventually given way to melancholy.

Lucca had spent most of the time under an invisibility spell, ignoring everyone who tried to speak to him. When his quarters had proven too alluring for the likes of Master Roe to visit, Lucca had absconded to the extensive grounds of the chapterhouse. When even that had not been enough to rid himself of unwanted attention, he made his excuses to go to the nearby village.

Unfortunately for Lucca, many mages and students also liked to visit the village that gave the chapterhouse its name. When the noise became too much, he slipped away to the Wolden River. Leaving behind the village and its trappings of civilisation, he traipsed through the forest until he made his way to the bank. Finally, he could enjoy the peaceful tranquillity. He felt secluded, out of direct sight from the chapterhouse and the main road. No one was going to question him and inquire what exactly had happened on the road with the relic thief, nor expect him to return to his classes right away.

The lion had gone over the events in the thieves' hideout through his head so many times. He didn't know what more he could have done to save Russet, but there had to have been something. He dreaded to think where the ferret would be now. All alone in a cell somewhere with no hope of escaping. The ferret must think he abandoned him.

The hum of a thaumaturgical engine buzzed in Lucca's ear. The lion groaned and closed his eyes. The Wolden River serviced Esfyr's Wold, both the village and the chapterhouse, though there was little else further upstream. He hoped the boat passed by quickly to transfer whatever cargo it carried in the village and left him to his isolation. He closed his eyes and curled his ears down, trying to block out the thrumming sound as it grew louder on its approach.

A familiar voice chirped out over the sound of the engine. "Doot! Master Lucca!"

Lucca sat upright so fast he lost his grip on the bank. He rolled and splashed right into the stream with a loud yelp, his hands scrambling to find something to pull himself up with. The water was ice cold and it chilled his body almost instantly. He flailed against the current, struggling to find the right way up until his paws finally struck the stony bed. A strong, webbed hand closed around his and hauled him up from the water.

Spluttering and shivering, Lucca dropped down onto the deck of a familiar narrowboat. He looked up to see Captain Periwinkle looking down at him. "Thanks," the lion gasped. He rose up to his knees, before he did a double take. He looked up to the otter again, then across to the lap-dragon standing by Periwinkle's side. "You're here! Is...?"

Captain Periwinkle shook his head slowly. "Russet was taken prisoner. No way I can get him out."

Lucca blinked and leaned against the side of the boat. "But, Palmer?"

The lap-dragon bounced on his heels. "Nasty felian Sama'Rey got taken away. It was all very exciting!"

"The mages focused on getting the thieves captured, especially Sama'Rey and anyone else they thought was important. That gave Palmer the chance to get to safety," Captain Periwinkle explained. The otter patted the lap-dragon's head, who chirped and looked smug with himself. "Once the mages had finished clearing everyone out, he wandered back to the marina by himself. Took me a while to piece together everything that had happened given how excitable he was. Figured there wasn't a way to get Russet back, but I couldn't think of anyone else to bring Palmer to. I sure can't look after him."

Lucca stared at Palmer. "You... you want me to keep him?"

Captain Periwinkle shrugged. "Is there anyone else who could have him?"

Lucca bit his lip nervously. He wasn't sure how the guildmasters would appreciate the enthusiastic lap-dragon, especially if they knew where he had come from. The lion flicked his tail as he thought things through. He looked up to see the lap-dragon gazing right at him. "What do you say, Palmer? Want to stay with me?"

The lap-dragon squeaked with delight and dived forward, hugging the lion and resting his head against Lucca's chest. "Of course, Master Lucca! Is Master Russet going to be here too?"

Lucca's ears drooped. His gut ached, feeling as though Palmer had physically punched him. "No, he won't."

"Oh," Palmer said simply. He stepped back from the hug and awkwardly twisted his hands together. "I thought you and Master Russet wanted to stay together."

"I do. We did," Lucca whispered. He turned his head to the side in an attempt to hide the tears forming in his eyes from Palmer and Captain Periwinkle. "But he was captured. I don't have any way to free him."

"Don't you?" Captain Periwinkle asked. He turned away for a moment, pushing open the door to his cabin. The otter crouched down and dragged a heavy pack outside. Lucca's pack. On top was Russet's smaller bag. Resting on that was a book, a red silk pouch, and a weapon.

Captain Periwinkle passed the alchemy book, pouch, and knife across to Lucca. The book was his textbook on alchemy, and the shadowy nightblade swallowed all the light around it.

His book and the magical blade he had thought lost to the Thieves' Guild hideout. The pouch he didn't recognise.

"I wanted to return what was yours," the otter captain said. He took Lucca's free hand in both of his own, clasping his webbed digits tight. "I trust you will find a way to return Russet's belongings to him."

"Did you... did you need any scalls for bringing them back?" Lucca asked, unsure if the otter was trying to hint that he still needed to be paid.

The otter shook his head. "No. Russet paid me more than enough for this. Should you need me again, I would expect payment, but this is all covered." Captain Periwinkle squeezed his hands tight around Lucca's, before taking a step back. "Palmer knows how to reach me if you wanted me."

"Thank you, Captain Periwinkle, for everything. For taking us to Cofferknell. For bringing these back for me," Lucca said, holding his hand to his chest. He bowed his head to the otter.

"Just call me Peri," the otter said with a smile. "Would you like to be taken back to the jetty?"

Lucca glanced over the side of the boat. The stream banks weren't far away. "I'll be fine, thank you," he said, judging the gap close enough to jump. The jetty was on the other side of the chapterhouse and meant he would need to walk all the way through the attached school just to get back to his dormitory.

The lion placed on paw on the top of the low side of the boat, ready to push off and leap for solid ground. He took one glance back at Captain Periwinkle, then down to Palmer. "You know where to go," he said to the lap-dragon.

Palmer squealed in delight as he jumped up onto the lion's baggage. With a snap of Lucca's fingers, the pack sprung to life and rose to float a few inches from the deck. Peri took a step back, giving Lucca the space to jump, and the pack room to follow the lion.

Lucca took the jump, but his paws were still damp and they slipped against the railings. He missed the shore entirely and landed with a loud splash, knee-deep in water amongst the reeds. He gasped as the icy water chilled through his robes and fur, before hauling himself up the banks to crawl back onto dry land. Behind him, Palmer floated across the water, perfectly dry as he balanced atop both Lucca's and Russet's bags.

"You jump like a ferret," Peri laughed, holding his webbed hand up in farewell.

"Picked up some tricks from Russet," Lucca replied. He shivered a little from the cold chill as he scrambled up to his paws. He lifted his hand in response to the otter.

The lion watched as Peri started to carefully navigate his boat back down the Wolden River and the expansive network of waterways that snaked their way across the peninsula. The otter turned away long before rounding a corner that obscured the vessel behind the trees that encroached on the far banks, but Lucca didn't go anywhere. The hum of the thaumaturgical engines continued to reach Lucca's ears long after the boat disappeared from view.

"Come on then, this way," Lucca said, gesturing to his pack and the lap-dragon passenger. He slipped Russet's nightblade into his pocket as he made his way back up to the road, keeping the velvet pouch clenched in his fist. The road was still quiet without even a courier travelling between the village and the chapterhouse. Reluctantly, the lion turned away from the quiet isolation of the wilds, not that anything could ever be quiet with a squeaking Palmer squeaking in delight at the colours on the leaves.

They soon made their way back to the chapterhouse, Lucca easily getting in through the gate and having to argue with a security gem that briefly flashed red at the presence of Palmer.

Palmer chirped brightly as he grinned up at the lion, once they had both made it into the expansive grounds. "We're a team again, Master Lucca! Do you have any cool hideouts like Master Russet?"

The lion had to laugh. He shook his head as he looked towards the old stone building. "No. I just have one small dormitory. There'll be enough room for us both."

Palmer clapped his hands together. "And what about when Master Russet gets to come back?"

Lucca rubbed his forehead. "I wish he could come here," the lion said. He nervously crossed the gardens, fingers twitching as he undid the drawstrings on the velvet pouch to sate his curiosity about what Peri had given him. Palmer floated on the luggage by his side. A few young students ran past. One paused to point in excitement at Palmer, but none stopped to bother Lucca. "I think he'd like the village."

"Maybe he'll come back to steal the book again," Palmer said, swinging his legs either side of the baggage.

Lucca opened the pouch and stared inside. A beautiful crystal amulet glistened in the sunlight. He stopped suddenly. The baggage bumped into his legs. "This... The book..." He clapped his hand to his muzzle. "*Ka'heirbek*, I'm a fool. The answer was right there, the whole time!"

"What do you mean, Master Lucca?" Palmer asked, leaning forward on the pack.

Lucca didn't answer the lap-dragon. He closed the pouch and stuffed it into his pocket as he burst into a run. The pack followed just behind him, with Palmer whooping in excitement as the baggage picked up the pace to match the lion's, Lucca's magic like a thread connecting lion to pack.

Lucca hurried into the chapterhouse, focusing his thoughts on his destination so he didn't lose himself in the twisted maze of corridors and halls. There was only one person who could help him. Who could help Russet.

The lion paused outside Master Roe's door, listening quickly to make sure that the old badger wasn't running a class. All was quiet inside, but for the scratch of a lone quill on paper. Lucca almost pushed open the door, but hesitated. Instead, he knocked.

"Come in, Lucca."

Lucca blinked in surprise. He pushed open the door to find Master Roe sat behind his desk, a quill in hand as he scrawled down some notes. The lion cautiously crept inside, keeping the door open behind him long enough for the levitating packs to follow in behind. He held a finger to his lips, warning Palmer to remain quiet as the lap-dragon stared in awe at the never-ending height of the bookshelves around the study walls.

"How did you know it was me?" Lucca asked, surprised that the badger had been able to recognise him just from the knock at the door. "I'm not even wearing any musks."

The badger looked up from his papers. His brow furrowed. "Have you been swimming?" he asked, before his eyes slid past the lion. "Is that a lap-dragon?"

Palmer waved brightly. He didn't say anything as he perched happily atop the floating baggage.

Lucca gestured down to the lap-dragon. "This is Palmer. He belonged to Russet. Captain Periwinkle returned what I'd left with him. There was nowhere else for Palmer to go."

Master Roe put down his quill. He clasped his hands together. "I see."

Leaving Palmer by the closed door, Lucca crossed the badger's office to stand before Master Roe's desk. "I think I know how we can help him."

The badger looked Lucca in the eye. He then looked away and sighed. "We've been over this before, Lucca. There's nothing we can do to help him. I know you developed feelings for Russet, but to everyone else, he is a thief. A criminal."

"Not by choice," Lucca growled. He had told Master Roe the full story already, but he was not sure the badger fully believed him. "Sama'Rey forced him into it. He's the one who deserves to be locked up."

"And he has been," Master Roe said. He adjusted his quill, setting it straight above the blank parchment in the middle of his desk. He clasped his hands together. "But willingly or not, Russet still stole from the guild. He stole a lot. More than we ever realised. He is guilty, and this is too important for Archmage Mafren to even consider letting him go."

"If Russet is guilty, then so am I," Lucca retorted. He sat back on the chair in front of the badger's desk. "I helped him. We stole things, together."

"It's not the same," Master Roe said wearily. "You're a good person."

"And so is Russet," Lucca replied. He placed his hands down on the desk. "Please, Master Roe. I wouldn't ask this of you if I didn't believe in him."

The badger leaned back in his chair. He spread his arms wide. "I know you believe Russet deserves better. I can sympathise that he was given a poor start in life. But that does not excuse what he has done, and I doubt there is anything I can say or do that will convince the archmage that Russet should be released."

A flicker of a smile came to Lucca's muzzle. He took a deep breath. "You don't need to. You just need to make him think Russet isn't the relic thief."

Master Roe tilted his head to the side. His eyes twinkled. "Go on."

"The archmage wants the relic thief. That's all he cares about," Lucca said breathlessly. "He won't look too hard to see who truly fits the description we had of the relic thief. So long as someone takes the fall for it, Mafren won't care. Russet is a good person. He deserves a chance he was never given before. Pin Sama'Rey as the relic thief and Archmage Mafren will never know any different."

Master Roe held his hands to his muzzle, gently tapping his fingers to his cheeks. "An interesting proposition, but you leave out any possible way I can make this happen."

Lucca's eyes flicked to the inscription vault. The gleaming golden doors shone brightly between two bookcases. "The registry."

The badger gasped. "You would have me impersonate the archmage to release Russet? Do you know how many laws that would break?"

Lucca looked down. "How many laws did you break with the love spell?"

"We had to stop Russet quickly, and what other options did we have? Mafren left us with no other choice," the badger said. He slowly rose to his paws.

"And there is no other choice to save Russet," Lucca said, still staring down at his hands. "Please, Master Roe. I know I ask a lot of you, but I have to at least try."

Lucca looked up, expecting to see Master Roe still stood behind his desk, but the badger was not there. Instead, the badger was already stood in front of the inscription vault, his hand resting on the padlock.

"Where would he stay, Lucca?" the badger asked. He did not look back. "What would he do."

"He can stay with me, if Master Alber allows it," Lucca said quickly. His heart pounded. His throat was dry. He licked his lips and swallowed, but that did little to ease the tension that spilled up from his gut. "And he can help around the chapterhouse to begin with, but he told me he always wanted to run his own shop. Maybe he can have a chance in the village."

Master Roe turned away from the inscription vault. "You understand what you're asking of me, don't you? This is the relic thief, the greatest threat the Mages' Guild has ever faced. You would invite him into our chapterhouse."

Lucca shook his head. "Russet was never the threat. That was Sama'Rey. I promise you, if you help me here, the relic thief will never be a problem again. And I can prove it," he said. With a flourish, he extended his hand and revealed the velvet pouch.

The badger furrowed his brow. He reached out to pluck the pouch from Lucca's hands and tipped out the contents onto his desk. He stared. "This... this is. This..."

"The diamond phylactery of guild-founder Neur Auphaven," Lucca said breathlessly. "Russet may not know where all the relics are, but he knows what was stolen and when. Most importantly, he knows how they were stolen. If you welcome him in, I can convince him to help us return what we can and to make sure we're better able to protect the relics."

Master Roe closed his hand around the glittering phylactery. "If there is one thing more important than capturing the relic thief, it is restoring what was stolen."

Lucca nodded. "The archmage will only enhance his victory."

The badger furrowed his brow. "His victory. Yes. Mafren has claimed credit for your work. For my plan."

The lion gripped his fingers against the edge of the table. "To be fair, the plan didn't work. The love charm never did anything. And I was just doing it to help Russet, not because of any loyalty to the archmage."

Master Roe snorted in amusement. "I'll have you know, I think my plan worked better than expected. The Thieves' Guild was dismantled."

"Just as you planned it, Master Roe?" Lucca asked, lifting his brow.

"A few details may have been off," the badger admitted. He grimaced and shook his head. "And yet, no one will ever know, thanks to our noble and humble archmage. All of Lutrea will think the raid on the Thieves' Guild was orchestrated solely by him, rather than a reaction to your clever message."

"I didn't do it for credit," Lucca muttered. His cheeks burned. He had not exactly been eager to accept Master Roe's task, and only the sense of adventure and infatuation with the legends of the relic thief had provided any enthusiasm to the mission. Neither the badger nor the lion could have known what that failed love spell could have caused.

"All the same, the politics of the situation has left a bitter taste in my mouth. It would be amusing to know the archmage's great victory was false, even in some small way." He swept his hand to the side, erasing the padlock from the vault door. He sighed deeply. "For all the things he has done to wrong us, he can help us restore the relics that were stolen. He has helped restore the image of Archmage Mafren and bring down the threat of Sama'Rey. I think I can do this one thing for you. Sama'Rey can be the relic thief, and Russet can be given his second chance."

Lucca's head spun. He almost couldn't believe that Master Roe had agreed to go with his plan. He had fully expected the badger to refuse, cutting off Lucca's last chance to free Russet.

Light bathed the badger as he reached inside the vault for the registry. A moment later, Master Roe returned, the gilded registry held carefully in his hands. He placed the book down on his desk, before settling back in his seat. Using the blank parchment, Master Roe began to transcribe a formal letter to the director of criminal investigations in Cofferknell.

"Have to be careful with the wording," Master Roe explained as he slowly scratched out his letter in his usual spidery handwriting.

"Why is that?" Lucca asked, his voice shaking as he watched the badger work.

"We can't arouse the archmage's suspicions that anything was changed," the badger said, pausing between words to look up at Lucca. "He's a little distracted with so many cases right now, and he hasn't yet interrogated the relic thief. Providing written evidence that Sama'Rey was the relic thief all along will need to be handled sensitively and with great care."

Lucca's tail twitched. "And what will happen to Russet?"

Master Roe looked Lucca in the eyes. The nib of his quill hovered over the parchment. "He will be free to live his life as he pleases. This is a fresh start for him. A full pardon. It is also the only one I will provide him."

Lucca nodded. "He won't squander it, I promise you."

The badger grunted. He returned to the parchment to continue writing the letter. Lucca turned his eyes away, ridding himself of the temptation to keep distracting Master Roe. The lion briefly locked eyes with Palmer, who watched with great interest from the far side of the study.

Once Master Roe was finished with the letter, he opened the registry to the right page, finding Archmage Mafren's personal identifiers. The badger's hands shook as Lucca turned back around, no longer hearing the scratch of quill on parchment.

"I've never done this without the archmage over my shoulder before," Master Roe said.

Lucca quailed back in his seat. "It won't set off any alarms, will it?"

"No. I'm an authorised and trusted user. Archmage Mafren knows I won't do anything stupid with the registry," the badger said. He laughed and shook his head. "Just like this." His hand stopped shaking as he sketched out the elaborate signature of the archmage, adding the marten's official approval to the letter.

The page flared bright for a moment. A weak pulse of magic tickled at Lucca's senses, before quickly fading again.

"It is done," Master Roe said. He rolled up the parchment and sealed it with a stamp of hot wax. He handed the sealed letter to Lucca. "I will open a portal to Cofferknell for you. It's best if you go now."

Lucca stood up as Master Roe also rose to his paws. The lion trembled, before pulling the old badger into a tight hug. Master Roe tensed slightly, before lightly patting his hands on the student's back.

"Thank you, Master Roe," Lucca said quietly. "I owe you so much for this."

"Yes, you do," the badger replied. "You and Russet can repay me by living an ordinary and uninteresting life."

"I don't think Russet can ever be ordinary," Lucca admitted. He smiled nervously. "But I promise you, he will be no threat to the Mages' Guild."

Master Roe gripped Lucca's hand in his own. "That is enough for me. Would you like me to speak to Master Alber while you're away? I can pass on the good news about the miraculous return of the phylactery."

Lucca took a couple of steps back. He glanced across to Palmer and nodded. "Yes, please. If you could look after Palmer until I'm back as well," he said, before crouching down in front of Palmer. "You'll be fine here for a little while?"

Palmer chirped and nodded. "I will, Master Lucca."

Lucca grinned and stood again. By the time he turned around, the badger had already summoned a portal of glowing purple light.

"This portal will take you to the mage's transport centre in Cofferknell. Make sure to remember the identification number above the portal anchor on the other side, as that will bring you back here without having to pay the fee," Master Roe explained. The badger smiled and nodded his head. "Go on, Lucca. I'll make sure everything is ready for your return."

Lucca grinned. "Thank you again, Master. Russet won't let you down." With the letter firmly in his hand, Lucca turned and stepped into the glowing portal.

Everything went white.

The mage's transport centre of Cofferknell was little more than a round room with two dozen slabs of stone leaned against the wall. Each slab had a number engraved at the top. Three had active portals open, while the rest were all blank. Lucca memorised the number above Master Roe's portal, then scampered away before anyone could question his presence.

A couple of mages, resplendent in their pearly robes, looked towards him. One jotted down a few notes on a piece of parchment, eyes flicking between lion and portal.

"Return journey for two?" the second mage asked, this one a rare winter vulpun. Her pale green eyes studied Lucca intensely.

The lion nodded, uneasy beneath her gaze. He couldn't be sure how she knew that information. Portal magic was not something that had come up in his studies, so the intricacies of how they worked eluded him.

Both mages jotted something down on their parchment. "Make sure you're back in less than two hours," the vulpun said. "We will only maintain your portal for that long."

Lucca nodded again. He tore his gaze from the vulpun's green eyes and dusty white fur. He hurried up a flight of stairs, following a sign that showed the way out to the streets of Cofferknell. With his precious letter in hand, Lucca bounded up the stairs two at a time, almost knocking over an otter as she slowly came down the other way.

After blustering out a quick apology, Lucca asked her for directions to the jail. She huffed and replied haughtily, but she told the lion where he needed to go. He didn't have to go far.

Slate grey clouds loomed over Cofferknell. Heavy rain poured through the streets. Lucca reached for his hood, before remembering his student robes didn't have one. He flicked his ears in annoyance. After tucking the letter safely inside his robes, he hurried outside and resigned himself to get wet.

Puddles splashed beneath the lion's paws. The roads were almost completely deserted as the rain shower passed over the city. Even the nearby river looked mostly empty of the usual traffic.

Sweeping the fringe of his growing mane from his eyes, Lucca headed down the hill towards the jail. Now that he knew what to look out for, he recognised the jail. The big, grey building on the bank of the river.

By the time Lucca reached the jail, his mane was plastered close to his head and his paws were caked in mud. Wrinkling his muzzle in distaste, he stepped inside and shook his head to rid his fur of some water.

The interior of the building was as cold and grey as the exterior. The walls were smooth stone with no decorations, with only the windows to break up the monotony. Three desks filled the room, with only one other door behind the three. One desk was attended, with a weasel sat behind it. She waved Lucca over.

"What can I do for you?" she asked.

"I have orders from Archmage Mafren," Lucca replied. He pulled out the sealed letter and handed it over to the weasel.

She cast an appraising eye over Lucca as she took hold of the letter. She checked the seal first, ensuring it was genuine and that the wax had not been tampered with. Confident that nothing was amiss, she sliced the wax open with her claws. She quickly read the letter, and her eyes widened more and more the further down she read.

"Well then," she said quietly. She sprinkled some fine white dust over the parchment. A brief flash of white light illuminated the weasel's desk. She lifted her brow and flicked her eyes up to Lucca, who watched on nervously. She rolled the parchment up and slipped it into a drawer beneath her desk. "I think you'd better come with me."

Lucca's tail flicked. He wasn't sure if that meant something good or not. Either way, he followed after the weasel as she opened the only other door out of the room. She called out to a companion, and another weasel stepped out to take her place behind one of the desks.

The lion was led down a flight of stairs to the dungeon below. They passed by multiple cells; all of which were filled. Musteliads of all species occupied them, all lazily draped back on beds or sat upright on wooden chairs. A few looked curiously towards the weasel and her lion companion, but most kept their eyes down. Purple security gems whirred through the corridors, chirping to each other every now and then and crackling with magical potency.

To Lucca's surprise, he recognised a couple of faces. The twins Tel and Let shared a cell. Neither of them looked up as Lucca passed, and he hurried on to stay with his weasel guide through the cells.

Nyle did notice Lucca. The otter bared his teeth, but he warily eyed the officer who accompanied the lion and said nothing as Lucca walked by.

They went down another level. This one was darker and damper than the first. Fewer cells were filled.

A lion brooded in one cell. Sama'Rey didn't move or react to their presence.

They continued further on.

There was no light at all. The weasel guard took a magical torch from the holster at her hip. She shone the light ahead, illuminating a final cell, in which was a single occupant.

The weasel held out her hand, silently telling Lucca to stay put. The lion held back and watched as she approached Russet.

The ferret didn't look up at all. He kneeled down on the bare stone floor with his head bowed. He didn't move or make a sound, not until the weasel's hands touched him.

With a snick of a lock, the handcuffs fell away from Russet's wrists. The ferret jerked back and blinked as the light fell across his face. He shielded his eyes from the brightness, blinking a few more times. His lips moved, but no sound came out the first time he tried speaking. "How?"

Lucca couldn't hold himself back any longer. He hurried forward and pulled Russet into a tight embrace. Slowly, Russet's arms squeezed back around the lion.

"You're coming with me," Lucca said quietly. He kissed Russet lightly on the cheek.

"I'm... free?"

Lucca flashed a smile. "Full pardon. I'll explain it all when I get you home."

Russet's ears flicked. "Home? Where is home?"

"For now, with me. After that? Anywhere you like."

"Anywhere I like... with you?" Russet asked tentatively.

"Of course, with me," Lucca said. He reluctantly moved out of the embrace, offering his hand to Russet. "Do you think you can walk?"

Russet nodded. He had to lean on Lucca, but he was able to limp out of his cell. The weasel guard said nothing as she closed the cell door once the dark room had been emptied.

"Palmer?" Russet asked quietly, his voice still hoarse like he hadn't spoken much at all in the two weeks of imprisonment.

"He's safe. Peri brought him to me," Lucca replied. He couldn't keep the smile from his face, even as they left behind the dark and damp corner of the prison and walked towards the distant light above.

This time, the imprisoned thieves took notice. While Sama'Rey had remained silent, the thieves on the upper level shouted their abuse at Russet. The weasel guard said nothing to quell their anger, and Russet walked on without a word. The ferret didn't move his eyes, and he looked straight ahead. The lion tried to do the same, but his attention drifted to the cells.

They called Russet many things. Traitor was most common. Cod-choker and egg-sucker were screamed harshly. Some used creative insults Lucca could never have imagined.

Lucca was glad when they reached the stairs. They could put behind all the anger and rage and leave it in the darkness of the jail.

"I don't need anything more from you," the weasel guard said as they returned to her desk. "I'll deal with everything on our end. I don't know what new evidence the archmage found, but it is not my place to question him."

"You have my thanks," Lucca replied. He bowed his head to the weasel.

Barely able to believe what was happening, Lucca helped Russet limp towards the doors. The weasel didn't call them back. No one did. They were free to leave.

Someone waited for them in the rain.

A hooded ferret in dark leathers held her hand out for Russet.

"This way, please."

Lucca had only seen her face for a moment, but he recognised Mera. She gestured away from the transport centre, towards the river.

"We can follow her, it's alright," Russet said quietly.

"Are you sure?"

Russet nuzzled into Lucca's side. "You can trust me. She isn't a threat."

Though Lucca was tempted to flee, he set his jaw and helped the ferret follow after the other thief. Mera didn't look back to make sure they remained close behind.

Russet smiled up at Lucca as they walked. The ferret ran a hand through Lucca's mane. "You're growing it out?"

Lucca shrugged his shoulders. His mane was longer that it had ever been, and the green fringe sometimes got in the way of his eyes. "Couldn't be bothered maintaining it when I got back."

"I like it," Russet said. He reached up to kiss Lucca's cheek.

The lion blushed. His tail swished. He had never liked his mane much, and it had only been laziness that had allowed it to grow out so long. If Russet liked it though, then perhaps he could be tempted to keep it.

On the riverbank, with glorious views of the jail walls, was a picnic table beneath a small shelter. The benches on either side of the table were just about protected from the rain. Mera sat down on one side of the table and gestured for Lucca and Russet to take the bench opposite her.

Mera smirked. "I must thank you both."

That had not been what Lucca had expected. "Thank us?"

"If you had not left me stranded in Willowbanks, I would have been caught up in the mages' raid. I'd have been in those cells right now."

"Oh. Right," Lucca said warily. He flicked an ear. "You're welcome?"

Russet rested his hands on the table. "Why are you here, Mera?"

"To say thank you," Mera replied. She rested her hands on the table. "And to make a deal."

"What deal?" Lucca asked, already feeling defensive. His wrapped his arm around Russet's body.

"On behalf of the Thieves' Guild," Mera said.

Lucca narrowed his eyes. "The Thieves' Guild is dead. We dismantled it."

Both Russet and Mera laughed.

"There will always be a Thieves' Guild, Lucca," Mera said. She smiled brightly.

"You're guildmaster now?" Russet asked. His voice was still cautious, though Lucca noticed there was definitely intrigue there too.

Mera nodded. "I am. I was the first to get back after the raid. I started picking up the pieces right then. Quite a mess you made. Poor Tella hasn't said a word yet."

"I ain't going back," Russet growled firmly.

Mera nodded. "I expected that. The debts you owed to Sama'Rey are not owed to me. Consider them paid. The guild will not come after you. You owe nothing to us, but we owe you for the work you did, and for removing Sama'Rey."

Russet's lip pulled up in a sneer. "How can I trust you?"

Mera held her hand to her chest. "You have my word. From one thief to another."

"I ain't a thief anymore," Russet replied, a pained smile on his muzzle.

Mera nodded her head. "You'll always be a thief to me, Russet. Whatever you choose to do now, you'll have my blessing. I may still sometimes call on you to do some guild work. Paid work."

"You'd have me be a freelance thief?" Russet asked with a laugh. "Not even five minutes outta prison and you're offering me another job? I'll consider it, but I ain't giving you an answer yet."

"The offer will always be there to you," Mera said, bowing her head in Russet's direction. "And you, Lucca. Should you wish it. You have a smart mind, and unlike Sama'Rey, I wouldn't mind a few mages working with us."

"I'll think about it," Lucca said uncertainly. He felt like he had taken the wrong turn in the conversation. His mind felt like it was floundering in deep water and he couldn't see the shore.

Mera rubbed her hands together. "Good. If you're going to be looking after my brother, then I've gotta at least offer you a place in the family business." She looked between them, eyes twinkling. "Who knows, someday I might welcome you to the family proper."

Lucca's mind malfunctioned. He stared at Mera, before he slowly turned to Russet. "She's your sister?"

Russet pinned his ears back. He chuckled nervously. "Did I forget to mention that?"

"Yeah, you did," Lucca said. He stared at the two ferrets, feeling like he had just been let in on a great secret everyone else had already known about.

Mera took hold of Lucca's hand. She then reached out to take Russet into her other hand. "You're both family to me. The Thieves' Guild... the *new* Thieves' Guild, will be at your service. However you may need us, we will wait for your call."

Before Lucca could reply, Mera released his hand and stood up. She waved a hand in farewell, before stepping out into the rain. Her dark leathers seemed to hide her from view quicker than should have been possible. She melted away into the rain.

"That wasn't what I expected," Lucca muttered. He turned to Russet. "And she thinks I should be part of your family?"

Russet grinned nervously. "Maybe someday. Once we're settled down."

Lucca's mind worked slowly. "She's really your sister? From Nesterslip?"

Russet nodded. "Yeah. Ain't no one better to lead the guild now."

Lucca took a deep breath to clear his thoughts. He didn't get very far. He exhaled slowly. "I don't know about you, but dinner and a drink sounds nice right about now."

Russet kissed Lucca's cheek. "I was thinking just the same thing. Know any good places?"

"There's a tavern in Esfyr's Wold that does steaks that are... tolerable," Lucca said. He really needed something to eat. He had reason to celebrate, after all.

The ferret flicked his ears back. "Esfyr's... that ain't somewhere we can reach today."

Lucca grinned. "It is if we've got a portal reserved for us," he said, squeezing his arm a little tighter around Russet's shoulders. "Come on. Let's go home."

"Home?" Russet said. His step faltered slightly. "I like the sound of that."

The lion and ferret kissed once more. Together, they walked into the rain.

It was time to go home.

Acknowledgements

A book is never the work of a single person. Chasing Thieves is no exception to this. Firstly, I have to thank Myles, as this book spawned from a collaborative story that we started working on over a decade ago. There isn't much of that story left, but it provided the spark that would bring Russet and Lucca to life. And Palmer, especially Palmer.

To Faora, a very dedicated beta reader who helped rip apart the earlier drafts and turn it into something more cohesive. His harsh, but always fair, advice has helped turn me into a much better author, and this book is testament to that.

To all the staff at Fenris, who have turned what I thought was a polished book into something even better. To my primary editor, Kiel, who spotted mistakes and plot holes that I had overlooked since the first draft! To my proofreader, Martin, who helped pick out all those nasty little typos that always like to linger. To Izzy, for making the interior look like a proper book instead of a manuscript. To the cover artist, Sleepymuu, for bringing everything to life. And, last, but certainly not least, to Thurston for coordinating all of this and bringing it together.

I would also like to dedicate this to my parents, who fostered in me the desire and passion to read. They also encouraged my desire to write stories of my own.

And to my husband. He has been an absolute rock in my life, and I am so grateful to have his support in all things. Without his encouragement, this book may not have had the chance to flourish.

Finally, to you. The readers! I hope you enjoy Chasing Thieves as much as I have enjoyed working on it. I look forward to hearing what you have to say!

About the Author

J.F.R. Coates was born and raised in picturesque Somerset, England, but she moved to Brisbane, Australia as a teenager. She grew up reading from a young age, starting with Enid Blyton's *The Famous Five* and *Secret Seven*, before finding her calling with J.R.R. Tolkien's *The Hobbit*. Speculative Fiction has gripped her ever since, and now she calls amongst her favourite authors Maggie Furey, Robin Hobb, and Philip Pullman.

She still lives in Brisbane, where she lives with her husband and – as seems ubiquitous for authors –two cats.

For three years, she was the president of the Furry Writers Guild and is also involved in publishing furry books through Transcendent Fiction Publishing.

You can follow her on Bluesky at @jfrcoates.bsky.social.

She also has a Patreon, which allows for sneak-previews of what's to come, as well as additional stories that fit in around her novels. All support is always gratefully received.

https://www.patreon.com/jfrcoates

www.ingramcontent.com/pod-product-compliance
Lightning Source LLC
LaVergne TN
LVHW050926080826
845145LV00001B/225